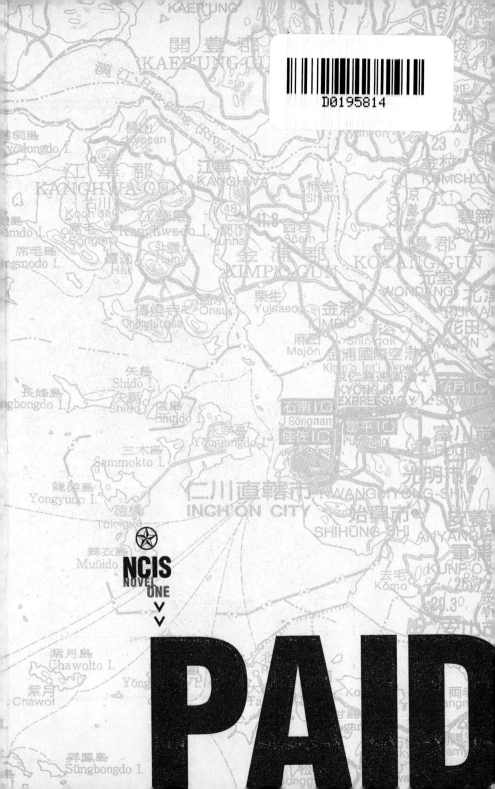

TYNDALE HOUSE PUBLISHERS, INC. >> CAROL STREAM,

Visit Tyndale's exciting Web site at www.tyndale.com

TYNDALE and Tyndale's quill logo are registered trademarks of Tyndale House Publishers, Inc.

Paid in Blood

Library of Congress Cataloging-in-Publication Data
Odom, Mel.
    Paid in blood / Mel Odom.
      p. cm. — (Military NCIS ; #1)
    ISBN-13: 978-1-4143-0306-2 (pbk.)
    ISBN-10: 1-4143-0306-8 (pbk.)
    1. Terrorists—Fiction. 2. United States. Naval Criminal Investigative Service—Fiction. I. Title.
    PS3565.D53P35 2006
    813'.54—dc22   2005035608

Printed in the United States of America
12   11   10   09   08   07   06
 7   6   5   4   3   2   1

✪✪✪✪✪✪✪✪✪✪✪✪✪✪ **DEDICATION** ✪✪✪

A Prayer: God, watch over my children as they grow up and go out into the world. I cannot see them as you can, and I love them with all my heart. Please keep them close to you and safe.

⊛ ⊛ ⊛ ACKNOWLEDGMENTS ⊛ ⊛ ⊛ ⊛ ⊛ ⊛ ⊛ ⊛ ⊛

To Jan Stob, the only editor I know who has shot the Desert Eagle .50 pistol and the Colt .500 Magnum on the same day, and left the target silhouette in tatters with a 12-gauge shotgun!

And to Jeremy Taylor, who went beyond the call of duty to show his support of this novel. Jeremy, it wouldn't have been the same without you!

✯✯✯✯✯✯✯✯✯ **PROLOGUE** ✯✯✯

Intensely alert, the radar operator sat hunched over his equipment in the small cabin of the research ship *Observer.* "The target is holding steady."

"You are certain this is the ship?" Qadir Yaseen stood behind the young man. Yaseen was in his fifties, lean and hard-bodied because he had spent most of his life fighting a jihad against the aggressors of his people. He wore a traditional mogasab over a thobe. The robe's gold trim stood out against the dark cotton. His black smagh framed his face.

"Yes, sir. I have verified the satellite signal you gave me."

"Very well," Yaseen said. "Let us go and get my cargo."

He alerted the ship's crew over the PA system, then strode out of the bridge. Two bodyguards armed with machine pistols went through the hatch first, flaring to either side to take up escort positions.

As Yaseen stepped out onto the deck, the ship came alive around him. Anticipation filled him. Finally, after nearly three years of preparation, bribing, blackmailing, falsifying identities, and careful murder, his plan was coming together.

Yaseen had been born in 1948, a man without a proper country because the Great Satans had given Palestine to the godless Israelis. Since that day, he had fought and shed his lifeblood and the fortunes of his father, pursuing the war to push the Jews from Palestine. But the Americans had constantly shored them up with money and weapons. He had begun his holy war against the Israelis when he was nineteen, serving against the hated Jews in the Six-Day War.

Until 1993 when the Oslo Accords were signed with Israel, Yaseen had faithfully followed Yasser Arafat. Once the agreements had taken place, Yaseen had gone his own way and remained apart. Over the intervening years, he had raised an army to fight against the Israeli occupation of his homeland. For most of his life he had struggled to further Muslim interests in the Middle East. For too long his people had possessed little means to strike back at Israel and the Western world.

Tonight, however, that balance of power would begin to change. He was going to strike back in such a way that others who hated the Americans would attack as well. The Americans, under their warmongering president, had engendered a great feeling of enmity around the world. Everyone would blame them for the chaos that followed.

Yaseen strained his eyes against the dark night that lay heavy on the sea. He could see nothing yet, but he was not dismayed. The ship was out there. So was the deadly cargo it carried.

Observer's engines throbbed to life. The ship shouldered its way through the sea at half speed.

The thirty warriors Yaseen had brought with him by helicopter at sunset took their places across *Observer*'s deck. All of them were young believers in the mission that Yaseen had set for himself. They carried AK-47 rifles and Tokarev pistols. The Russian assault rifles and handguns had been easy to acquire in Odessa, Ukraine. The city was a major Black Sea port and had a large amount of illegal contraband flowing through it. Inhabitants there still referred to the city as Odessa Mama, which had begun life as an underworld trading post.

A pale yellow oval burned a hole in the night. It rose and fell below the dark horizon of the sea.

Yaseen's heart raced. He had spent millions on the weapons he was about to acquire but had not yet seen. Anticipation filled him and made him take a deep breath.

Within minutes, *Observer* overtook the cargo ship. Yaseen could see sailors shifting into defensive positions on deck.

"Sir," the leader of Yaseen's warriors called.

Yaseen nodded.

The leader gestured. Immediately one of the warriors stood and pulled his rifle to his shoulder. The blunted detonation of a round echoed across the deck. In the next instant, a grappling hook arced across the water between the two ships. Loops of rope followed, singing as they spilled from the reservoir beneath the rifle. The hook bounced on the cargo ship's deck for a moment, then caught on the railing.

Instantly sparks exploded into the night as bullets whined from metal surfaces. The cargo ship's crew had opened fire, targeting *Observer*'s prow and deck. The chain around the deck jerked and rattled as bullets struck it.

Yaseen's warriors returned fire, proving their greater skill and precision as their bullets drove back the cargo ship's crew. Yaseen drew his own pistol and fired as well. There was no mercy in him when it came to his enemies. He'd killed his first man, an Israeli soldier, when he was twelve.

"Lights," the commando leader called.

Harsh white illumination strafed the cargo ship's deck. Dead bodies rolled on the heaving surface as the ship fought the water. A few wounded tried to crawl away. One man got too near the deck's edge and tumbled overboard. The black water immediately swallowed him.

One after another, Yaseen's warriors clipped D rings to the cable and slid across the intervening distance. Once aboard the cargo ship, the warriors moved across the upper deck and quickly executed all crewmen they found. Their orders allowed no survivors. Bright muzzle flashes flickered to life, then died.

Clipping his own D ring to the cable, Yaseen followed his men onto the besieged ship. Just putting his feet on the wooden deck empowered him.

Several warriors produced flashlights and stood waiting at the top of the stairs. They went down into the hold at Yaseen's command. Yaseen followed.

The hold stank of fish. A few inches of water sloshed across the floor. Yaseen led the way farther back into the hold. He stopped beside an eight-foot-tall bin packed with ice and fish. "Here."

The arrangement had been simple. Yaseen had paid his money, and his merchandise was to have been hidden within the ship's load. The crew had had no idea what was hidden beneath their feet as they went about their duties on deck. Only the ship's captain was aware of the deadly cargo. Two of Yaseen's men were searching the ship for the captain now. In moments Yaseen would finally take possession of his prize: two nuclear missiles.

At Yaseen's order, two of the warriors laid down their rifles and took shovels from the tool cabinet on the hull. They clambered into the bin and started shoveling ice and fish into the water sloshing across the lower deck. It took several minutes for Yaseen to realize that nothing was buried in the reeking mixture.

A scramble of feet came down the stairs.

Another two warriors brought a fat man down the stairs and dumped him unceremoniously onto the floor. Water splashed across the man's face, and he blubbered in pain and fear. He spoke in a language Yaseen didn't understand but believed to be Greek.

"Do you speak English?" Yaseen peered at the man.

Hiding behind his arms and hands as if they would somehow deflect the bullets from the weapons pointed at him, the man looked up. "I speak English. Yes. Good English."

"Where is the captain?"

"I am the captain."

"Where is my cargo?" Yaseen asked.

The captain shook his head. "What cargo?" He remained huddled on his knees.

Moving as quickly as a striking snake, a warrior backhanded the captain across the face with a pistol, knocking his head back sharply.

"The missiles," Yaseen said calmly. "Where are my missiles?"

Sweat rolled down the man's face. "I have no missiles. Gronsky gave me nothing." He was weeping now. "He said the deal was off. He said you knew."

A black rage possessed Yaseen. He'd hated dealing with Colonel Vladimir Gronsky of the Russian army. The man was greedy and unscrupulous, but he routinely worked in the black-market circles, and Yaseen had needed him to arrange his munitions purchase.

Unable to control the rage that filled him, Yaseen picked up one of the shovels and beat the man to the ground. He didn't stop hitting the captain until he had no energy left. All the years, all the money he'd spent, and he'd been betrayed by another man's greed. Shuddering, Yaseen threw the shovel aside and glared down at the captain's bloody, lifeless body.

Then he took a deep breath. Gronsky was greedy. The missiles still existed, were still within his grasp, as was his vengeance for his family and friends whom the United States had killed and would kill for generations to come. He could still make his plan work.

He turned and walked from the cargo hold. On deck, Yaseen gave orders to place demolition charges. Minutes later, the men returned to the *Observer* the same way they had come. The moment the ship had moved a safe distance away, the munitions blew and the cargo ship broke to pieces.

Yaseen watched the ship and crew settle into their watery grave. Gronsky would be made to pay for his betrayal. He would pay most dearly.

CRIME SCENE ✷ NCIS ✷ CR
NAVAL CRIMINAL INVESTIGATIVE SERVICE

E SCENE ⊛ **NCIS** ⊛ **CRIME SCEN**
NAVAL CRIMINAL INVESTIGATIVE SERVICE

>> WILMINGTON, NORTH CAROLINA
>> THE PRESENT
>> 2053 HOURS

Will Coburn stopped in front of the dead woman lying crumpled on the threadbare carpet. He stared down at her. Violent death still gave him pause even after years of seeing it.

He held his flashlight steady and examined the woman's body. She was in her midtwenties. She'd kept her black hair short and neat, but blood matted it now. More blood streaked her face and made her look of pained surprise even more stark. She wore blue jeans and a dove gray blouse under a nondescript green Windbreaker.

Someone had cut the woman's throat. Crimson streaked the front of her blouse and Windbreaker.

Only a few blood streaks stained the carpet she lay on.

Violence and death no longer shocked Will. Since his transfer to NCIS, the Naval Criminal Investigative Services, three years ago, he had seen every kind of inhumanity one person could show another. But he never got used to seeing it. It was enough, at times, for him to question God, though he knew that God allowed men free will. When men abused their freedom, it was their own fault, not God's. Still, the peace Will had with the Lord was an uneasy thing, made even more uneasy by what was occurring in his own family life these past months.

Will glanced around the apartment, trailing the flashlight beam with his sea green eyes. There was no electrical power to the room. The building super was supposed to be working on that.

Unfurnished and untended, the apartment held the thick smell of must and old sweat. The late March night left the room cloaked in thick shadows. Whirling blue lights from the police car parked in the street outside washed over the spiderwebs clinging to the top part of the window. The lower part of the window was broken. Glass lay inside on the floor, telling Will that the window had been broken from outside.

"Is she one of yours?" The voice was loud and challenging.

Will turned to face the man who had accompanied him into the grim room.

Wilmington police detective Leonard Carpenter stood nearby. He was shorter than Will's six feet one inch and at least twenty pounds above his ideal weight. His sandy hair held streaks of gray and he wore a neat mustache. His pale blue eyes looked permanently bloodshot. His tan suit held wrinkles.

"She's one of ours," Will answered. He ran a hand through his thick shock of black hair, cut within military regulations. Though the room was cool, his khaki Dockers felt like they were clinging to his legs, and he was beginning to feel uncomfortably warm under his blue NCIS jacket. He shrugged the jacket off, revealing the Springfield Extreme Duty .40-caliber pistol he carried in a holster strung across his broad shoulders.

Carpenter flipped through his notes. "Says here that she's Chief Petty Officer Helen Swafford. She was NCIS?"

Will nodded.

Carpenter put his notepad away. "Know what she was doing out here?"

"No."

"If she was working on something, seems like she would have had a partner."

"The rest of the team is accounted for." Will had checked that through Swafford's supervisor.

"Then she was out here on her own hook."

"Looks that way," Will agreed.

"Wilmington's not that far from Camp Lejeune," the homicide detective said, "but she came a fair piece to get herself killed."

"I'm sure getting killed wasn't on her agenda, Detective," a feminine voice stated.

Will glanced up as Maggie Foley entered the apartment. At five feet four inches tall and slender, Maggie didn't look like much of a threat. Her dark brown hair was cropped at the shoulder, and she looked younger than her twenty-seven years. But she had an obsession with the gym and no-holds-barred volleyball that made her tough as nails on a martial-art mat.

Maggie looked as if she'd been at a dinner party when the call had come in. She wore black slacks with razor-edge creases and a charcoal, bias-striped shirt. French cuffs added an understated elegant flair. Her diamond earrings glittered as they caught the light. To Will, Maggie's appearance seemed in stark contrast to her surroundings in this room of death. But then, even in fatigues, Maggie Foley never looked middle class.

The NCIS drafted most of its agents from the civilian sector, including a number of ex-policemen and security guards. Will's unit was different. Because his team handled potentially lethal special assignments, most of his team members had been handpicked from the military. Maggie was the sole civilian. None of the personnel the military had to draw from had the expertise she brought to the team. She'd spent eight weeks in boot camp prior to assignment to the unit, then another month working with Special Ops personnel to bring her up to speed. There were things she was still learning about military ops, but she learned them quickly.

"According to the super, this apartment has been vacant for two months." Maggie shined her beam on piles of empty beer cans and cigarette butts in three corners of the room, and the two stained sleeping bags in the center. "Somebody comes calling while the three bears are out."

"Neighborhood kids," Carpenter replied. "They come up here and party when no one's looking."

"Did one of them make the call to the PD?" Maggie asked.

"Don't know. Caller didn't identify himself."

"According to the phone records of the pay phone outside," Maggie said, "a call was placed to the Wilmington Police Department about an hour and a half ago. That was at 7:17 p.m. Took you a while to call us, didn't it?"

"I wanted to verify the murdered woman's identity before I bothered you," Carpenter said.

Will knew that wasn't exactly the truth. Anytime military personnel were involved in a crime—whether that person was the victim or the criminal—the investigation was turned over to the military. The friction between the local authorities and the military investigators was long-standing.

"How did you make the identification?" Maggie persisted.

"Her ID was on the floor."

"Did you disturb the body?"

Anger stained Carpenter's broad face. "I got better things to do than stand here and answer stupid questions." He started to walk away.

"Detective Carpenter." Will's voice carried command. After twelve years spent aboard ships—six of them commanding one, the aircraft carrier USS *John F. Kennedy*—his voice was a tool, as solid and heavy as a ball-peen hammer. "I can contact your captain. I bet I could free up some time in your schedule."

Carpenter cursed beneath his breath but the sound carried in the small room. "I got fifteen years in on homicide. I know not to mess with evidence. When I checked that ID, this was still my murder scene."

"Now," Maggie said coolly, "it's ours."

Will knew Carpenter wanted to say something. Intent stiffened the man's bulky frame. But he kept silent. A moment later, the homicide detective turned and left the room.

"Well," Maggie said, "I suppose that could have gone better."

"It could have," Will agreed. "It didn't." He turned his attention back to the dead woman.

"He cost us nearly two hours." Maggie pulled on a pair of thin surgical gloves from her purse.

Looking at the dead woman, Will said, "We were already too late."

>> 2139 HOURS

"She wasn't killed here." Maggie moved around the room and shot images with a digital camera from every angle.

"I know," Will replied. He took notes on an iPAQ Pocket PC.

"There's not enough blood and no signs of a struggle." Maggie took another image and moved closer to the body, where small triangular white markers with black numbers on them marked evidence.

"There are bruises on her face and arms," Maggie went on, "and three of her fingernails are broken. She didn't go down without a fight."

Twenty minutes ago, the building super had reconnected the electricity to the room. The bulbs offered a weak yellow incandescence that required an external flash on the camera. But the light relieved the darkness that had filled the room.

"Judging from the blood smears on her clothing, whoever killed her used something to transfer the body." Maggie squatted and took another shot. "I'm guessing a sheet or a piece of carpet from the blotches I'm seeing. Something fabric, not plastic."

Will had already guessed that. When he'd first taken the NCIS assignment, processing a crime scene had seemed beyond his capabilities. There were so many things to know. He'd surprised himself by learning them so quickly. He'd surprised his field training officer as well.

"That transfer material is incriminating," Maggie said. "That's why he or she took it from the scene."

"Maybe we'll get lucky and find it." Luck, Will knew, was part of every criminal investigation. Sometimes it worked for an investigator and sometimes it worked against. But luck was made by effort. They had to start beating the bushes.

>> 2218 HOURS

Dr. Nita Tomlinson was thirty-one years old, a tall, lean redhead with freckles and gray-green eyes. She possessed an easy disposition and could generally be counted on to join the beer-and-pizza crowd after hours. She was also the team's medical officer.

As she stepped from the military Hummer that would carry Chief Petty Officer Helen Swafford's mortal remains back to the medical lab at Camp Lejeune, Nita pulled a lab coat on over the charcoal slacks and green-and-white-striped knit top she wore that enhanced the curves of her body. Her high-heeled boots seemed designed more for clubbing than fieldwork.

"Interrupt something?" Will asked when he went outside to meet her.

Nita brushed her hair back from her face. "What?"

"Nice clothes," Will said. "I thought maybe you got called away from a night out with Joe."

Joe Tomlinson was Nita's husband of five years. They had a four-year-old daughter named Celia. Will knew that with the backlog of work Nita had verifying even routine deaths and checking files on those killed in action, she seldom got home during the evenings these days.

Nita seemed a little disconcerted. "No. I was . . . out. By myself. Just had a couple drinks with girlfriends to clear my head. I wasn't ready to go home and put on my mommy cap. Where's the body?"

"Inside." Will walked beside her as he guided her toward the building. The police had roped off the area with yellow NCIS crime-scene tape and sawhorses.

"Commander Coburn," a young Asian woman called from behind the tape. A press ID hung from the lapel of her jacket. She held a microphone out. "Could you give us a comment?"

"I see the press has learned your name," Nita said.

Will didn't offer a comment, nor did he break stride. He assumed the media people had resourced his picture and made identification. So far the media still didn't have the dead chief petty officer's name.

"Where's the rest of the crew?" Nita asked as they stepped into the building's foyer.

"Frank and Shel are knocking on doors in the neighborhood," Will said. "Estrella is going through the chief petty officer's office files."

"The vic wasn't on assignment?"

"According to her supervisor, nothing she was working would have brought her out to this neighborhood."

Nita frowned. "So it's a mystery."

"So far."

"I hate mysteries."

"When we finish the job," Will said, "there won't be any mysteries left." As he turned toward her, he smelled alcohol on her breath. "Are you in shape to do this?"

Nita shot him a reproachful look. "Yes."

"I smell alcohol."

"At this time of night, you usually would." Nita took a breath mint from her purse and pulled on a pair of surgical gloves. "I'm fine. If I wasn't, I'd call someone else in. I know how to do my job." Her tone was angry and defensive.

Will had heard that in her voice a lot lately. "All right," he said. He'd never known a time when Nita couldn't perform her job. But he was afraid a storm was brewing on the horizon. He'd been a sailor much of his life, and sailors knew storms. Maybe he'd have noticed Nita's situation earlier if he hadn't been dealing with his own.

2

>> WILMINGTON, NORTH CAROLINA
>> 2246 HOURS

The neighborhood was one of the pockets of decay in the city. Wilmington had been a town for a long time, and urban renewal had not yet reached this area. Broken appliances littered the back porches of the small, quiet houses, and many of the tiny front yards featured cars up on blocks.

Shel McHenry glanced at his watch as he stepped up to yet another sagging front stoop. He'd been knocking on doors for an hour and a half, looking for anyone with information about the body in the apartment building down the street. The people he'd spoken to were blue-collar workers, many of them visibly displeased at having been disturbed from their evening routines. None of them had been helpful.

This was one of the most boring jobs he did as an investigator, but time after time it was also the one that turned up the most leads. He'd learned to give the exercise the same loving care that he gave while cleaning his weapons after a trip to the gun range.

He knocked.

"Who is it?" a woman called from inside the house.

The porch light was already on. Moths banged against the naked bulb with audible *plonks*.

Shel stepped back so he could be clearly seen in the light. He held his arms to his sides to show his empty hands. "United States Marine Corps Gunnery Sergeant Shelton McHenry, ma'am. I'm with the Naval Criminal Investigative Service." He tapped the ID case around his neck.

At six feet four inches tall, Shel McHenry looked like he'd been constructed out of railroad timbers. His dark blond hair was cut high and tight, and his eyes were deep, honest blue. His dark skin was from frequent outside activity and the Apache blood he'd gotten from his mother. He knew his appearance didn't immediately inspire confidence in others, despite his official-looking Navy jacket marked with NCIS in yellow letters. That was fine with him. In the two years he'd been with Will Coburn on the NCIS team, he'd learned that an intimidating appearance could be an asset in this kind of work.

"What do you want?" The woman's voice quavered.

"Just have a few questions, ma'am."

"We don't know anything about the murder of that woman."

We? If the husband had been home, he would have probably done the talking. Shel wondered who besides the woman was inside.

"Yes, ma'am. I understand and appreciate that. I promise not to take up much of your time, and I apologize for disturbing you at this late hour."

The peephole grew light for a moment, then darkened again.

"We don't have to talk to you," the woman said.

Shel found the woman's reluctance interesting. Most people were curious by nature. Years of watching crime dramas on tele-

vision and viewing *Court TV* had made most people willing to be
active participants. They might not be thrilled about being disturbed at this time of the evening, but people didn't refuse to
open the door unless they had something to hide.

"No, ma'am," he agreed affably. "It's just that your address
turned up on my sheet, and I need to put down that I interviewed
you."

"I'd like to help," the woman said, sounding as if she would,
"but—"

"It might help you out too, ma'am," Shel interrupted, shifting gears in the interview smoothly. Now that he had her open,
he needed to let her know what she had at stake.

"Me? I don't see how that—"

"When I let my supervisor know that I couldn't talk to you,
he'll probably send someone else around first thing in the morning, ma'am. My boss . . . well, he's kind of a thorough guy. Doesn't
cut me any slack anywhere. If that new investigator my boss sends
can't catch you here, I expect he'll show up at your work to ask his
questions. If we talk tonight, it might save on a lot of gossip wherever you work." He waited. Letting the woman know the NCIS
wasn't going to go away would carry a lot of weight.

A long moment passed.

Shel stood patiently. Prior to his reassignment to NCIS, he had
been a Marine for thirteen years. He could stand post for hours.

"Is that an attack dog?" the woman asked.

Shel glanced down at the black Labrador standing beside
him. "No, ma'am. That's Max. He's my buddy. I go everywhere
with him."

The dog was an impressive one hundred twenty pounds. He
was black as night and had soulful brown eyes that could plead
the last piece of chicken from a bucket of the Colonel's finest
from a glutton.

Max had been military issue from birth. He'd received guard-
dog training as well as search and rescue. In a pinch he could also

serve as a drug dog or even a cadaver dog. He had been with Shel for the last five years, in war-torn battlegrounds as well as on civilian streets. They'd worked long-range reconnaissance and SAR missions together before signing on with NCIS. For his money, Shel figured the dog had better manners than he did.

"I don't allow dogs in my house," the woman said.

"That's fine, ma'am. Max can stay out here and take in the night air. He's been cooped up in the car for a while. He'll appreciate it."

The door opened hesitantly.

"Come in," the woman said. She waved Shel inside.

Shel entered and immediately felt oversized and awkward in the small living room. The furniture was old and showed hard use. The brown carpet was worn but clean.

A large-screen television took up most of one whole wall. An XBox sat on the floor in front of the television. A military video game hung paused, a first-person perspective of a sniper's crosshairs over an alien creature equipped with an impossibly huge sidearm. The alien wouldn't last another heartbeat when the game resumed.

The woman was small and hard used, like her house. Mousy brown hair framed her pinched face. She clutched a cell phone in a thin hand.

"Well?" she asked, folding her arms. "What do you want to know?"

Shel took out a spiral notepad and a pen. "Your name would be a good place to start, ma'am."

"Carla. Carla Teague."

Shel nodded. The name matched what he'd noticed on the mailbox. "Was anyone here in the house between six and eight o'clock tonight, ma'am?"

That was the time frame Will had suggested they work with. Rigor hadn't set up in Helen Swafford's body yet. She hadn't been dead long.

"I was," she answered, "but I didn't see or hear anything."

The cell phone in the woman's hand rang stridently. She glanced at the caller ID screen. "My husband," she said. "Do you mind?"

"Not at all."

The woman turned and walked away. She scratched at the back of her head. "The guy at the door was a police officer," she said to the phone.

Shel didn't bother to correct the woman's mistake.

"He *wouldn't* go away, Bill. He had to come inside and ask questions. . . . Yes. Inside. . . . *Inside* the house." The woman sounded upset. She listened for a moment, then cursed. "You know what, Bill? If you wanted this handled any differently, you should have got off your duff, left your buddies, and hurried home." She closed the phone and turned back around. Pensive lines underscored her eyes. She offered a slight apologetic shrug. "My husband."

"That's what you said," Shel replied.

"Just so you know, Bill will probably be here in a few minutes. He'll have been drinking. Bowling's just an excuse to go out drinking with his buddies." She hesitated. "He could cause a scene."

"I should be gone by that time. Let me get to my questions. You live here with your husband? Just the two of you?"

Hesitating, the woman licked her lips. "I've got a son. He lives here too. He's sixteen."

"Where was he?" Shel kept the phrasing of the question deliberate. A trained investigator asked open-ended questions, not giving an interviewee a chance to respond with a yes-or-no answer.

"Junior was . . . out . . . with some friends." The woman took a crumpled pack of cigarettes from her pants pocket. "Do you mind if I smoke?"

"It's your house, ma'am." Shel watched her hands shake. She had trouble getting the lighter to her cigarette. "Junior's home now, isn't he?"

Out on the porch, Max growled a low warning. Shel had already detected the slight movement in the dark doorway leading off the living room. A trash can filled to overflowing stood in the light. Three beer cans crowned the top of the mess.

"He's still out with his friends," the woman said.

"Ma," a quiet voice called from the doorway, "he knows you're lying. I left the video game on."

"Junior?" Shel asked.

"Yeah." The boy spoke with a sullen voice. When he stepped into the room, Shel saw that his look matched the sound. An unbuttoned plaid shirt with the sleeves rolled up partially covered a black, heavy-metal band T-shirt. Oil and grease stained the blue jeans tucked into motorcycle boots. He had curly brown hair like his mother, but he evidently got his size from his father because he was lanky and almost six feet tall. A small scar pulled at the left corner of his mouth. Earrings dangled from both ears.

"You know what I'm here about?" Shel asked.

Junior looked defiant and smirked. "It's not exactly a secret. There's about a dozen police cars down at the apartment building."

"Yeah." Shel nodded. "Not exactly on stealth mode here."

"No," Junior agreed.

"Where did you and your buddies go while you were out?" Shel asked.

Shrugging again, Junior said, "No place special."

Shel took a picture from inside his jacket and showed it to Junior. Will had printed pictures on the small printer he carried with his crime-scene equipment. "You ever seen this woman around?"

Staring at the picture, Junior swallowed hard. Then he said, "I've never seen her before."

When Junior handed the picture back, Shel gripped it at the edges between his thumb and middle finger. He took an envelope from inside his jacket, then dropped the picture into it and sealed

it. He placed the envelope back inside his jacket without saying a
word.

"Why—?" Junior's voice broke—"why'd you do that?"

"Because I didn't want to ruin the fingerprints," Shel
answered.

"Why are you taking *my* fingerprints?" Junior's voice rose.

"That apartment has a lot of beer cans and bottles. There are
cigarettes over there that match your mother's brand. And empty
beer cans that match the ones I see in the kitchen there."

Mother and son glanced at the overflowing trash can.

"And there are the sleeping bags," Shel went on. "We're a
crime-scene-investigation team. Fingerprints are one of the
things we do best." He paused, focusing on the boy. "If you were
in that room, we'll prove it. And when we do, we're going to
come back with a lot harder questions." He glanced down at
Junior's motorcycle boots. "That looks like blood on the side of
your boot there."

"That's it. You get out of here!" The woman stepped forward and jabbed a finger at the door.

Junior caught her hand. "Stop, Ma."

Looking frightened, the woman said, "Junior, you don't
gotta talk to these people. We should wait till Bill gets here."

"You can hide the boots if you want," Shel said, "while I'm
gone getting a court order to take them and get a DNA sample,
but people are going to know you had those boots. Be awfully
awkward trying to explain why you don't have them anymore."

Junior was silent. His eyes looked troubled and afraid.
"I saw them," he said. "I was around when they came. I saw the
men who dropped that woman's body off."

S ⊛ **CRIME SCENE** ⊛ **NCIS** ⊛ **CRI**

SERVICE

NAVAL CRIMINAL INVESTIGATIVE SERVICE

3

Whistling an old Beatles tune, Chief Warrants Officer Frank Billings walked through the dark alley, following the search grid
he'd laid out with Will.

Walking a search grid wasn't much different from making
the rounds on an aircraft carrier. Frank knew the pattern, knew
what to look for that was there and knew what to look for that
might be missing. He swept the area with his flashlight, which
was long and heavy and required six D batteries. He preferred it
over the Mini Maglite Will and the others chose. Like him, the
flashlight was old and solid. And, in a pinch, it could be used as a
weapon.

The Wilmington PD had offered to send someone with him,
but Frank had declined. He didn't mind being solitary and was
quite comfortable with his own company. Solitude gave him time

to pray, to think about the day and figure out what he should be thankful for.

Mostly, he supposed, he was thankful that his wife still loved him, that his kids were happy and healthy—and grown, thank God, even though he was still helping with Patty's college tuition—and that he had a job that he enjoyed. He had joined NCIS because of Will Coburn. Frank had served under Will on the USS *John F. Kennedy*, and the two men had developed a close friendship. When Will had opted for coast duty, Frank had followed suit. He was glad for the opportunity to continue working with his friend, and he enjoyed being closer to his family. But every day he missed the sea.

He was fifty-five years old, a gray-haired grandfather with a pot gut he just couldn't get rid of these days despite hours of handball and lifting weights and thirty-four years of consecutive service.

After high school, he'd tried working in his father's machine shop in Jacksonville, but that hadn't worked out. He'd wanted to see the world, and he wasn't going to get to do that with the pay his father could afford. So, with his father's blessing and trust in God, he'd signed on with the Navy.

Six years later, he'd met Mildred. She'd been waiting tables in a small café her family owned in Jacksonville. Frank had gone there on leave to have lunch with his father and younger brother. He fell almost instantly in love. Less than two years later, they were married. Even with all the pitfalls of raising five kids while being separated by his career for long stretches at a time, they were still as happy today as they'd been when they married.

Happier, Frank corrected himself. *Much happier.*

A cat exploded out of the darkness, rattling across the top of a stuffed Dumpster.

Frank froze as adrenaline flooded his body. His hand drifted down for the Smith & Wesson .40-caliber pistol he carried at his hip. That was something he didn't have to deal with on an aircraft carrier. He'd seen war conditions before, in both Gulf Wars and several skirmishes around the globe, but he hadn't had to face the threat of sudden violence from an unknown source aboard ship. Guys there generally put on boxing gloves and worked out their differences in the ring. Then they went to the mess hall and got over it together.

During the last three years on the NCIS team, though, Frank had seen a whole different side of civilization that had previously been relegated to the evening news. These years had made those events seem more personal, and he'd had to lean on his faith a little more often these days. He'd been in shoot-outs and violent fights, been shot and stabbed and bitten while bringing men and women in on charges. It wasn't something he'd ever get used to.

He eased his hand off the pistol and walked over to the Dumpster. Something had drawn the cat there. Taking a pair of surgical gloves from his jacket pocket, he widened the flashlight's beam and placed it on the Dumpster's edge. Then he started shifting garbage.

Over thirty years in the Navy, Frank thought in disgust, *and I'm a trained Dumpster diver.*

His phone vibrated against his belt.

Pushing back from the Dumpster, Frank peeled off a glove and took the phone from its holster. A quick check of the caller ID screen gave him the bad news: BARBARA COBURN.

The fact that Will's estranged wife was calling Frank was bad news in itself, but that she was calling this late was an indication that things were even worse.

"Hello."

"Frank?" Barbara sounded tense and nervous, but there was anger in there too. "I apologize for calling so late. But I . . . I needed to call."

Frank felt uncomfortable. He wished Barbara had called Mildred. His wife seemed to handle these things better than he could. Of course, Barbara only called Mildred when she wanted to think things through. Barbara called Frank when she wanted to attack Will.

During the years Frank and Will had spent together aboard the USS *John F. Kennedy*, Will had talked about his wife and kids. Frank had never once doubted that his commander loved his family, but he had sometimes seen the stress Will had been under. Based on previous observations of crewmen and officers, Frank had known the marriage was in trouble.

Will had taken the posting here at Camp Lejeune to forestall those problems. It hadn't worked. For two years the marriage had limped along. A year ago Barbara had asked Will to leave. They hadn't divorced, just separated. Will had taken up quarters at Camp Lejeune, telling himself and Frank that the separation wasn't going to last long.

"Barbara, this isn't the best time," Frank said finally. "We're working a homicide. The first forty-eight hours are critical. Most cases are made or lost in that time."

"I know you don't have time to talk now. I just need to know when Will is going to be in the office tomorrow."

"You could call and ask him," Frank suggested.

"I . . . I don't want to do that. Just give me your best guess, Frank." Desperation strained Barbara's words. "Please. This isn't easy."

Frank sighed. "Tomorrow afternoon," he said. "One way or the other, Will has to be at the office tomorrow afternoon."

"All right." Barbara broke the connection.

For a moment, Frank thought about calling her back. He knew the separation hadn't gone easily for Barbara either. Too many Navy spouses couldn't handle the time they were away from their husband or wife, and then they couldn't handle the times those spouses came back into their lives. It was a series of constant adjustment and disappointing expectations for many of them.

Calling Barbara wasn't the answer, he knew. If she had

wanted him to know what was on her mind, she'd have told him. Better yet, she'd have told Will.

Frank holstered the phone and pulled another surgical glove on. When he shifted the flashlight this time, fluttering caught his attention.

He picked up the flashlight and directed the beam into the far right corner of the Dumpster. A group of insects huddled on a crimson-stained carpet. It took Frank only a second to realize the insects were feeding on blood.

>> CAMP LEJEUNE, NORTH CAROLINA
>> NCIS HEADQUARTERS
>> 2338 HOURS

"Petty Officer Third Class Montoya?"

Estrella looked up from the computer screen at the mention of her name. "I'm Special Agent Montoya." She still carried her Navy ranking, but while in NCIS capacity she used the special agent designation.

A fortyish woman with dishwater blonde hair stood in front of the desk. Tears streaked her face. She wore a tan janitorial uniform. A pushcart with a mop, a broom, and a collection of cleaning solvents sat in the middle of the big room.

"Is it true?" the woman asked. She was thin and slumped from years of hard work and worry. "Is Helen—" the woman's voice broke—"is Special Agent Swafford . . . dead?" Tears rolled down her thin cheeks.

The murdered NCIS agent's name still hadn't been released to the media, Estrella knew, but the military had a grapevine like no other. "What's your name?"

"Annie." The janitor wiped her eyes. "Annie Hernandez."

No way is this woman Hispanic, Estrella thought. Her own

Latino heritage showed in her dark bronze hair, her warm brown
eyes, and her olive complexion. She kept her hair pulled back in a
ponytail and wore jeans, a red fleece shirt, and a black hoodie.
She'd been at the park with her son, Nicky, when the call came
in. Making arrangements for a sitter on short notice was something she often did, but it left little time for changing clothes.

Will had assigned Estrella to invade Helen Swafford's personal files in the hopes of finding out what had taken the agent to
Wilmington.

Estrella kept her voice easy and relaxed. That was a skill
she'd developed as a single mother of a rambunctious five-year-
old boy. "How do you know Helen?"

"Oh no. It's true, isn't it?" Annie put a trembling hand to her
mouth.

Standing, Estrella quickly crossed to the woman and helped
her into one of the seats from another desk. Then she pulled up
her own chair and sat beside the woman, deliberately aligning
herself with Annie Hernandez. "You know Helen Swafford?"

Annie nodded. "I clean her area—this area." She looked
around. "Helen works late a lot. She's very dedicated. But
friendly, you know? Not like some that work here. They say her
body—" she had to stop for a moment—"that she was found in
Wilmington."

"Yes."

Annie covered her face with her hands.

Grief was a powerful thing. Estrella knew that firsthand.
Sometimes it lasted for years. Sometimes the feeling of loss never
went away.

While Annie composed herself, Estrella glanced around the
cubicle. Helen Swafford's professional area was neat and tidy.
Pictures of pets and people that Estrella had identified as family
filled the cubicle walls. Swafford hadn't been married, but she'd
been engaged. In cases of murder, husbands, wives, and lovers
were always investigated first. Clearing them meant widening

the circle of suspects. Swafford's fiancé had been at a poker game
with his friends at the time of the murder.

"Do you know what Helen was doing in Wilmington?"
Estrella asked after a bit.

"No." Annie wiped her eyes with her shaking hands and
tried to pull herself together. "Earlier this evening, she was supposed to be over in Jacksonville."

"Why?"

Annie hesitated. "I asked her to do a favor for me."

"What kind of favor?"

"I got a stepson," Annie said. "His name's Rudy. Rudolpho.
Rudolpho Hernandez. He's my husband's son by his first marriage." She looked at Estrella. "He's a mixed-up kid. Got a lot of
problems. His father, Emilio—my husband—is serving time at
Catawba Correctional Center. I promised him I'd raise Rudy.
I have." She calmed a little, seeking understanding. "But it's been
hard. Raising a boy by yourself is always hard."

Thinking of Nicky, Estrella silently agreed.

"I love Emilio," Annie said. "As much now as ever. Maybe
more. He'll be out soon. He went away for drugs. He was caught
holding. For his brother. His name is Carlos—Carlos
Hernandez."

Estrella took no notes, but she filed everything mentally. She
had a good mind and didn't easily forget things. "You asked
Helen for a favor."

Annie nodded. "Lately, Rudy has been hanging around with
some bad kids. Kids I knew he shouldn't be hanging around
with. I found pot in his room, in a hiding place he doesn't think
I know about. I wanted to go to the police, you know? Let them
know something was going on. But I didn't know how much
trouble Rudy was in." She held back her tears with visible effort.
"Rudy's nineteen. He's already been in some trouble. Juvie stuff.
Trespassing. Drinking. Fighting. But nothing since he turned
eighteen. He knows he doesn't want to get into trouble as an

adult." She shook her head and swallowed. "I'm afraid for him. He gets caught in anything serious, he's going away. I can't let that happen to Emilio's boy."

Estrella took the other woman's hands, willing her to trust and give up the whole story. "What did you ask Helen to do?"

For a moment, Annie couldn't keep control of herself. Then, gradually, she quieted. "Just to look into it, you know? Maybe follow Rudy. See where he went. Who he went with. Like that. Helen—she said once we knew more, we'd know what to tell the police. Maybe we could keep Rudy clear somehow."

"What was Rudy into?" Estrella asked.

Annie pulled her hands free of Estrella's grasp and wrapped her arms around her stomach and looked like she was going to be sick. "Last week—" she took a deep, shuddering breath—"last week I heard Rudy talking to one of his friends. He said he knew where his friend could buy a gun."

Estrella waited patiently.

"I went into his room," Annie said. "I was mad. He knows what happened to his father. He knows that the police will put him away because he's an adult. He knows." Emotions swept through Annie so strongly she shook. "I asked him what gun he was talking about. He just looked at me for a second like I'd gone out of my mind, and he told me he was talking about a new video gun for an XBox."

"But you didn't believe him."

Annie shook her head. "No. Not for a second. If something . . . something bad happens to Rudy, I don't think my husband will make it out of prison. While he's been in, Emilio has changed. He's learning welding, construction work. When he gets out, there's a man in Jacksonville supposed to give him work."

"That's good news," Estrella said.

"I just didn't want anything to happen to Rudy. Our family . . . we need some good luck, you know? I just asked Helen to take a look. Just let me know how bad it was." Annie took a deep breath. "I didn't mean to get her killed."

Estrella took Annie's hands again and held them tightly for a moment. "What you did, what Helen Swafford did—those things were done through a mother's love. That didn't get Helen killed tonight. Something else did. I give you my word that we will find out what it was."

The woman collapsed into tears.

Guarding her own emotions, knowing she had to be clear-headed, Estrella took the woman into her arms for a moment and offered what comfort she could. Then, when the worst of it was over for the moment, Estrella got up to call Will.

S ⊗ CRIME SCENE ⊗ NCIS ⊗ CRI
NAVAL CRIMINAL INVESTIGATIVE SERVICE

E SCENE ⊗ **NCIS** ⊗ CRIME SCEN

NAVAL CRIMINAL INVESTIGATIVE SERVICE

>> CAMP LEJEUNE, NORTH CAROLINA
>> NCIS MEDICAL LAB
>> 0041 HOURS

"This is the body of a young woman in her late twenties," Dr. Nita Tomlinson said, speaking in the clear, distinct voice she used for the autopsy room.

She wore a wireless lapel microphone with new batteries that recorded her observations directly onto the hard drive of the notebook computer she used as well as the lab's computer.

"She's approximately five feet six inches tall. One hundred thirty-five pounds. Relative good health." She lifted the corpse's arm, then let it gently back down to the examination table. "Even hours after the recovery of the body, signs of rigor are only now beginning to settle in. Death came apparently from the slashed throat."

Using a micrometer, she measured the length and breadth of

the slash. "Bruising under her chin and jaw suggests that her head was held when she was killed. The slash measures 23.82 centimeters across." She inserted a metal ruler. "The depth of the wound varies from 3.12 centimeters to 6.68 centimeters. There are no hesitation cuts."

Cutting the throat of another human being was messy, scary work. Nita had spent years in medical school learning how to cut open corpses. She had never had any desire to work as a surgeon cutting open living people.

With confidence, skill, and experience, she moved quickly and cleanly from the outside to the inside. Nita had been doing autopsies for years. There were no wasted moves. She cut the victim's clothes away and bagged them. Her field of expertise was the body. Will and the others would process the clothing.

Taking a scalpel from the tray, Nita pressed the edge against the dead woman's chest, took a breath through her surgical mask, and sank the blade. In years past, autopsies on men and women had differed. Men's bodies had been opened with a Y incision while women's bodies had been opened with an X incision. These days, all autopsies were performed with Y incisions.

During the procedure, while Nita slowly talked her way through the various steps, her cell phone rang.

She cursed silently, then spoke in a flat monotone voice. "Go to sleep." On the nearby stainless-steel table, her notebook computer's screen froze. The command had shut down the recording function.

Irritated, she ripped off the bloody surgical gloves and dropped them in the biohazardous container near the table. She walked away from the corpse but didn't take her eyes off of it. Her work still drew her into it.

She answered the phone on the third ring. "Hello."

"Hey," her husband said in a polite voice.

That was Joe Tomlinson: always polite, always soft-spoken. A man of few words and the first to pitch in and help a friend. It was strange, Nita sometimes thought, how those things about him had first attracted her to him and yet now they drove her away.

He was a beautiful man, too. Not quite six feet tall, he was broad shouldered and had a wolf's hips. His sun-kissed blond hair made a halo around his head, long enough to barely touch his tan and freckled shoulders. His work building and repairing boats kept him lean and hard and nut brown. Light hazel eyes held a child's innocence but he was nobody's fool. Usually he wore cutoff jeans and went bare-chested and barefooted.

"I've got a body on the table." Nita deliberately didn't soften the announcement even though she knew Joe didn't want to know much about her work. "Is anything wrong?"

"No," Joe replied. "We're okay here. Celia's asleep in my lap. She tried to stay up and wait for you."

Guilt ate at Nita. She pushed it away, and it instantly turned into anger at Joe. "You shouldn't let her do that. You know I don't know when I'm going to get home."

"Tonight's Tuesday," Joe said quietly. "You told Celia last week that you'd be home by seven tonight."

The play! The guilt came back at Nita again, stinging fiercely. She'd forgotten. Joe had enrolled Celia in a community theater. Tonight was her daughter's first onstage performance.

And she'd missed it.

Resolutely Nita pushed the guilt away again. *I'm not perfect. If anyone in the world knows that, it's Joe and Celia. They can't expect me to be perfect. They have no right.*

"A Navy investigator was killed tonight," Nita said. "I got called in." But Will's call had come through at the bar where she'd gone. By the time she'd received it, she could have seen her daughter's play.

"Must be harsh," Joe said. "She have any family?"

"I don't know yet. I stay away from information like that." Nita closed her eyes. She wanted a drink. She wanted to be back in that club where she'd been before Will had called. But then she'd have gone home maybe a little tipsy and seen Joe sitting on the couch with Celia in his lap. They would have been the very picture of guilt.

That would have been too much.

"You okay?" Joe asked.

"Tired," Nita said. "Just really tired." At some point in the past few minutes a headache had flared to life behind her eyes. She stared at the corpse, noticing something on the left eyelid. When the body had been brought in, both eyes had been fully open. Now with the gases building up in the flesh, no longer scrubbed clean by the lungs and exhaled, the body was starting to bloat a little.

"I really wish you'd think about taking some time off," Joe said. "We had a good summer at the boat shop. I've got some extra money put back that will take care of Christmas and a vacation for you."

"Is that what you want to do, Joe?" she asked, letting a little anger into her voice. "Take a vacation? I thought you were help-ing your brother with his house."

"I am."

That was one of Joe's problems, Nita reminded herself. He was always helping other people. Especially his family.

"Tate would understand," Joe went on. "He's in a good place with the house right now."

If he'd admitted that he couldn't leave yet, Nita was fully prepared to point out to Joe that it was his fault. She decided on another tack, one that had never failed her in their arguments. "I don't have that kind of job, Joe. I've also got a dead woman on my table right now, and I don't want to let her murderer escape."

Joe was quiet for a moment. "Maybe this isn't a good time."

"It's not," Nita accused. The headache throbbed against her temples. "When I'm working, it's not a good time."

"If you need anything," Joe said, "let me know. Remember that I love you."

"I'll be home when I can," she told him, then broke the connection. She stood for a moment, breathing hard and trying to recover. She hated the guilt that came with her relationships with her husband and daughter.

Memories of her own childhood stirred inside the wall of pain the headache erected. Her mother had been single, chasing man after man to make her happy. Was that what she was turning into? Her mother?

For a moment Nita felt sick. *You're not your mother,* she told herself. *Your mother never graduated high school. Your mother got pregnant at sixteen. You have a career that will take you anywhere you want to go.*

Before she'd met Joe, Nita had had her whole life planned out. She was going to be single and never rely on a man. She was never going to have children.

Then she'd ended up pregnant.

Taking a deep breath, Nita let go of the negative thinking, the guilt, and all emotions. She pushed her mind back into her work.

At the table, she pulled on another set of surgical gloves. Carefully, she pulled down the dead woman's eyelid. There, captured in some type of black grease, was a fingerprint.

Someone had touched the woman.

Centered now, excited about the find, Nita stopped thinking about the problems at home and prepared to lift the fingerprint from the dead flesh.

>> **WILMINGTON, NORTH CAROLINA**
>> **0113 HOURS**

Will sat behind the wheel of his metallic blue Chevrolet Avalanche Z71. He felt the weight of the long day and the stress of keeping his emotions walled off. He'd finally gotten ahold of Swafford's parents. They'd been on vacation in Las Vegas when he'd informed them of their daughter's death. He hated delivering news like that over the phone. It was cold and impersonal. But, in this case, there'd been no choice.

The pickup's crew cab afforded enough room for six grown people. At the moment, it held only three. Shel lounged in the backseat and sixteen-year-old Junior occupied the passenger seat. Flashing lights from the military vehicles securing the crime scene continued to strobe the night, striping the boy's face.

Shel had quickly reiterated how he'd found the boy and the fact that Junior had seen the men who had probably dumped Helen Swafford's body in the apartment.

"How many men?" Will asked. He took notes on the iPAQ, scribing them on the screen with the stylus in longhand where they were immediately converted to type.

"Three. Like I said."

"Ever see any of those men before?" Will asked.

"No."

Looking at the boy and thinking of Steven and how frightened his own son would be in similar circumstances, Will smiled to reassure the boy. "Can you identify the vehicle they used?"

"It was a van. A Ford, I think."

"What color was it?"

Concentration pinched Junior's face. "White. Gray, maybe. Not green or blue or red. It wasn't bright."

"Old or new?"

"Maybe a few years old. It wasn't new, but it wasn't falling apart either."

"Notice anything about it?" Will asked. "Dents? Scrapes? Maybe a sign or telephone number written on it?" Service vehicles tended to be invisible in neighborhoods, but a lot of them were white and gray in this area.

Eyes widening, Junior said, "It was a work van! There was writing on the side!"

Will smiled. "That's good, Junior. You're doing fine. What kind of work van?"

The boy shook his head. "I don't know. I didn't read it. All I remember is that it was out of Jacksonville."

"Tell me about the men," Will suggested.

"They were all dark. Hispanic." Junior nodded to himself. "Old guys."

"How old?"

Junior looked at Will. "About your age. You know, old guys."

In the rearview mirror, Shel grinned, out of sight of the boy.

"All right." Will wrote down *thirties*. "Tell me what happened."

Junior proceeded to explain how the three Hispanic men had taken a roll of carpet out of the van. They'd gone inside the apartment building and reappeared a few minutes later. Junior had just assumed that the men were going to change one of the room carpets. They'd carried a carpet back out a few minutes later, but he'd supposed that was to be expected. The boy didn't know how long the men were inside the apartment building.

Junior and his friends had been gathering in the apartment for the last month. Once the men were gone, Junior had gone into the apartment through a broken window in the back to wait for his buddies. That's when he found Helen Swafford.

"I've got to ask you this question," Will said, staring the boy in the eye, "and you've got to give me an honest answer."

"I will."

"Did you touch the dead woman's body?"

"No. Cross my heart." Dragging a dirt-stained finger over his chest, Junior crossed his heart. "I ain't ever touched nobody that was dead. I just wouldn't do it."

"Okay," Will said. "Why don't you stay in the truck a minute."

Junior nodded.

Will opened the door and stepped out. Shel joined him.

"Finding that boy was good work, Shel," Will said.

"I got lucky." Shel gazed at him quizzically. "What are you holding that you haven't told me?"

"Estrella called a few minutes before you got here. It appears that Special Agent Swafford was conducting an investigation off the books for a friend. Swafford was tailing the son of a janitor at NCIS headquarters. The son's name is Rudolpho Hernandez."

A grin split Shel's rugged face. "Sounds Hispanic."

"That it does," Will said. "Rudolpho has an uncle who works at a paint-and-body shop in Jacksonville."

"Be interesting to know if he has a commercial van."

"I was thinking that same thing." Will checked his notes on the iPAQ. "The uncle, Carlos Hernandez, has a history of trafficking in stolen merchandise and drugs. He's been put away a couple times, but it's always been for a short sentence—a few months here and there."

"He on probation?"

Will shook his head. "Hernandez did the full bit."

"Too bad," Shel said. "No probation, no probation officer. No probation officer, we have to have a reason to go open his business this time of night and take a look around. Still, we have enough circumstantial evidence to go to Jacksonville for a peek at things."

"The carpet Frank found is spattered in several different colors of paint and oil, as well as blood," Will said. "If it's automobile paint, there could be a link to Carlos Hernandez's shop, but we won't know that until we process it at the lab."

Shel took in a breath and let it out. "Maybe knowing what kind of paint it was would put a bow on everything, but I don't like giving Hernandez more time to think about how intelligent running would be."

"I don't either."

"We could go up, take a look around on the QT. It would be better to know more sooner. Maybe we can't go inside, but we can peek through the windows."

Will silently agreed. His iPAQ rang. The screen showed the phone function and caller ID brought up Estrella Montoya's picture. He touched the screen and answered.

"Nita found friction ridges on Swafford's body," Estrella said. She explained about the dead woman's eyelid. "I ran the fingerprint and got a match. Those friction ridges belong to Rudolpho Hernandez."

"The janitor's son?" Will asked.

"Yeah." Estrella paused. "I haven't told her."

Will immediately felt sorry for the mother. Murder always made for hard business with families. In most cases, no one understood why violence reached that level, not even the families of the murderer. "Does his mother know where her son is?"

"At his uncle's. He's been there a couple days."

"Do you have addresses for Carlos Hernandez?"

"Already e-mailed them to you, Commander."

"Good. We'll need warrants for both of those addresses to start with."

"I'm processing them now. It'll take me about twenty or thirty more minutes. I'll have them in hand and be at Jacksonville before you get there."

Camp Lejeune was only minutes from Jacksonville. Wilmington was an hour, at the posted speeds. Will intended to cut that time significantly.

CRIME SCENE NCIS CRI
NAVAL CRIMINAL INVESTIGATIVE SERVICE

E SCENE ✶ NCIS ✶ CRIME SCEN
NAVAL CRIMINAL INVESTIGATIVE SERVICE

>> **JACKSONVILLE, NORTH CAROLINA**
>> **0156 HOURS**

Pulling to a halt down the street from the paint-and-body shop Carlos Hernandez owned, Will walked to the rear of his pickup. He took black nylon equipment bags from the lockbox in the bed.

Shel and Max got out the other side.

Will strapped on a bulletproof vest first, snugging the Velcro closures so the Kevlar covered him front and back. Heavy padding shielded his elbows and knees to take the sting out of bruising impacts. Then he added the ear/throat headset and shrugged into his NCIS jacket once more.

"This is Steadfast Leader," he said over the headset. "Confirm copy." He shoved extra magazines for his Springfield XD-40 into his pants pockets and changed out the batteries in his Mini Maglite. A pair of leather gloves covered his hands, and clear shooter's glasses with wraparound lenses protected his eyes.

"Steadfast Three," Shel said, talking on the other side of the pickup bed and sounding twice in Will's hearing. "Ready."

"Steadfast Two," Frank said. He'd driven up with Maggie Foley, complaining about lodging his solid bulk in her little sports car. "Reading you five by five, Leader."

"Steadfast Four copies," Maggie said.

"Steadfast Five reporting." Estrella had driven up from Camp Lejeune and had arrived only eight minutes prior to Will and the rest of the team. She was currently parked on the east side, covering the alley beside the paint-and-body shop. Frank and Maggie guarded the back door.

"Wolf Leader," Will called.

"Wolf Leader is standing by, Steadfast." The Marine captain's reply was tight and reassuring. The contingent of Marines provided a loose perimeter around the area. They were in place in case anything went awry.

Will went forward, following the high, metal hurricane fence surrounding the shop.

The main building was a single-story structure with four bay doors, all of them closed. The outside walls were white, and in the mercury security lights Will could make out the airbrush design of a Corvette painted with flames and dragons on it. Huge letters proclaimed ROLLING FANTASIES BODYWORK.

"Up and over." Will leaped up, caught hold of the edge of the fence, and hauled himself over. He landed in front of an SUV with four flat tires and drew his pistol. Sweat beaded under the Kevlar armor, and he knew it wasn't all due to the humidity.

God, Will prayed as he scanned the inside landscape of the business, *I know I ask you this a lot and it's a familiar prayer, but could you keep an eye out for my team and me?*

"Clear," he called to Shel.

"Coming."

Hunkered down behind the SUV, Will saw Max at the top of the fence and knew that Shel had heaved the dog up. Nimble and adroit, Max touched the fence for an instant, then landed on the gravel. The dog never made a sound.

Shel followed, dropping into position beside Will. "Dog's putting on weight." He slid the M4A1 off his shoulder.

"Maybe you're just getting weaker." Will smiled.

Together they moved forward. Shel commanded Max to guard, and the dog stayed close. As they got closer to the building, they heard power tools operating inside.

"Kinda late to be working," Shel observed quietly.

"It shows dedication," Will replied. "But I keep remembering we haven't found Swafford's car yet."

In seconds they were at the front door to the office area. Four cars, all of them lowriders with immaculate paint jobs, occupied berths in front of the shop entrance. Will avoided them in case they had security alarms.

Will tried the doorknob. "Locked." He tapped the transmit button on the headset. "Two, what do you see?"

"No activity outside the building." Frank's voice was quiet and controlled.

Will relaxed a little. With Frank watching his back, he always felt safer. "We're going—"

At the front of the yard, the remote-controlled gates suddenly shrilled to life and rolled back.

Will dropped into a squatting position and duckwalked behind the corner of the building. Shel and Max joined him in the shadows pooled there.

Lights from a late-model silver Honda Civic flared out on the street. Rubber burned as the driver cut the wheel and pulled into the yard. Gravel popped and shot out from under the tires. Halfway to the building, the driver cut the lights and honked twice.

The first bay door on the end rose, clacking through the grooved tracks. Light inside the building cut a long rectangle out over the yard. Once the car pulled into the bay, the door slid back down.

"Open for business," Shel said.

"Seems so." Will looked around the corner.

"Must be that dedication you were referring to."

In motion now, Will went toward the shop door. He nodded toward the lock. In less than two minutes, Shel had the lock picked and the knob easily turned in Will's hand.

The shop was dark, empty. Latino rock and roll blasted from the shop area, warring with the sound of power tools.

Tense, sweating profusely under the Kevlar, Will made his way through the small customer waiting area to the door. He peeked through the Plexiglas viewing rectangle and could see the main shop area.

Crews worked on three vehicles. Cutting torches sprayed flaming bits of metal. Air drivers whined like deep-throated bees. Saws threw sparks in fountains. Electrical cables hung from the ceiling like octopus tentacles, providing power for all the tools.

Eight men worked on the cars. All of them wore shop coveralls. At the far end, the driver got out of the Honda Civic. He was lean and lanky, black and young. A do-rag wrapped his head. Even though it was night, he wore smoke-colored sunglasses. He slapped hands with one of the short Hispanic men. They talked for a moment; then the mechanic directed the driver to the rear of the shop.

Carlos Hernandez stood in the back with two other men. One of them was Rudolpho, the nephew. Even from across the shop, Will could tell that one of the younger man's eyes was swollen shut. He wondered if Helen Swafford had gotten in a few licks before she'd been murdered. He hoped so.

Hernandez and the other man wore casual street clothes with Windbreakers. Both of them looked tense.

"Wolf Leader," Will said.

"Go, Steadfast."

"I count twelve on-scene. Two of them are our targets."

"Understood, Steadfast. Confirm two targets and ten extras."

"I want them alive, if possible, and in one piece."

"Yes sir."

"On my go."

"Yes sir."

Taking in air through his nose, Will blew it out. Then he stood and opened the door.

The noise and heat of the main shop area slammed into him as he stepped over the threshold. The smell of marijuana mixed with the burning odors and paint fumes.

Will walked, unhurried, with the pistol hidden beside his thigh. Holding his badge case and ID in his left hand, he approached the first shop mechanic.

The guy was working a saw, cutting the front end of the car away, getting it ready to be stripped of parts. Smoking on a reefer and bobbing his head in time to the music, the man didn't know Will was behind him.

Will shoved his pistol barrel into the back of the guy's neck.

The man froze.

"Naval Criminal Investigative Service," Will shouted into the man's ear. "You're under arrest."

For a moment, the situation seemed to be in hand. Then the mechanic yelled, "*Policia!*" and spun around with the saw going full blast. He tried to bring the blade up into Will's face.

Will stepped back to avoid the saw. At the same moment Shel reached in almost lazily and clipped the man's jaw with the M4A1's butt.

Unconscious before he hit the cement floor, the man released the saw. The blade cut into the floor, changing the pitch of the whine and drawing as much attention as the man's yells. Then it powered off and lay still.

By then, the other mechanics had taken up the fallen man's cry. "*Policia! Policia!*" They abandoned their tasks and started fleeing the shop.

Carlos Hernandez took cover behind a tall shop chest on

wheels. As soon as he was in place, he pulled a pistol from inside his jacket.

"Gun!" Shel shouted, taking cover behind the car.

Will dropped into a crouch and made his way to the end of the vehicle.

Hernandez unloaded at once, popping shots at Will and Shel. Two of the rounds exploded through the car's windows. The rest—at least seven or eight by Will's count—struck the car. Pressed against the fender, he felt the vibration of the impacts.

"Wolf Leader," Will called over the headset.

"Go, Steadfast," the Marine captain replied.

Shel popped up long enough to squeeze off two three-round bursts. All the bullets hit the toolbox where Hernandez hid. The unit shivered.

Max streaked off, circling around to the right, angling for the gunner the way he had been trained.

"Contain it," Will ordered the Marine captain. "Shut it down. No one gets out."

"Affirmative, Steadfast. We're on our way."

Rolling back into cover, Shel joined Will at the rear of the car. "I ever tell you how much I love the Marines?" He had to shout to be heard.

"Every day, gunney," Will replied.

"Well," Shel said, grinning, "I just don't tell you enough."

The lanky black man ran for the Honda Civic he'd driven in. Throwing himself through the door, he slid behind the wheel.

"Nobody leaves," Will said.

Giving a short nod, Shel stood briefly and aimed at the Honda. He ripped through the rest of his 25-round magazine and took out three of the Honda's tires as the driver got the vehicle into motion.

Unprepared for the blown tires, the driver lost control of the car. The vehicle slammed into the support pole beside the bay opening and stalled out. Immediately the driver came up firing, holding a pistol in each hand as he bolted out of the car. Bullets chopped into the car and screamed over Will's head.

Shifting, Will took up the XD-40 in a two-handed Weaver stance. He centered the sights in the middle of the man's body. Law enforcement and military trained shooters to put targets down, not try for disabling shots. Even trained snipers were taught to shoot for the center of the ten-ring.

Will squeezed off a double tap, two shots close together, then aimed again and fired another double tap.

The bullets crashed into the driver and sent him stumbling backward into the bay door. The pistols fell from his hands as he toppled to the floor.

Some of the mechanics came up with weapons as well. One man had a .12-gauge shotgun that blew out the back glass of the car Will had taken cover behind. Fragments of safety glass rained down on him. As the man racked the slide, Shel spun out into the open and dropped the man with a burst angling from the guy's right hip to his left shoulder.

Moving together, Will and Shel flanked the building's interior and raced toward the rear. Another mechanic wheeled out from behind a car. Even as Will lifted his pistol, Max lunged out of hiding and seized the man's gun wrist in his powerful jaws.

Squalling in fear and pain, the mechanic went down. He dropped his pistol and spoke in rapid, frightened Spanish, pleading with the dog. Moving automatically, Max released the man's wrist and clamped his jaws around the man's throat. The mechanic tried to push the big Labrador away, but failed.

"Stop fighting or he'll tear your throat out," Shel advised from cover. He spoke again, this time in Spanish.

The man lay still, crying and begging. Will didn't understand what the mechanic was saying, but he could guess. Having an animal as large as Max clamped to his throat would be a definite wake-up call to mortality.

Holstering his sidearm, Will approached the man. He took a

pair of plastic disposable handcuffs from his vest, then grabbed the mechanic's elbow. "Good dog," Will whispered to Max, patting the dog on the shoulder. "Release."

Max opened his jaws and left the man, already moving to rejoin Shel.

Will rolled the man over, snapped on the cuffs, and pulled them tight. Then, taking his weapon out again, he went forward. No one was firing now, he realized. There had been a brief skirmish outside, but that was quiet now.

Will stopped beside the hollow-core door that said OFFICE in black letters. Shel and Max took up a position on the other side of the door.

"Steadfast Five," Will called.

"Five reads you, Leader," Estrella answered immediately.

"I'm looking at an office at the back of the building," Will said. He listened intently, trusting that the Marines had sealed the area.

"Yes, sir," Estrella responded. "The blueprints I looked at showed a small office space."

"Points of egress?"

"Small window at the back. Four and I are on our way there now."

"Roger that. I'll give you a count of five to get into position, then we're going in."

Maggie and Estrella radioed back and let him know they would be there.

Shel pulled a tear-gas canister from his Kevlar vest. "Party favor," he suggested.

Will nodded. He held up his free hand and flipped fingers and thumb out as he counted down. When he reached five, he swung out and slammed his foot into the door beside the knob.

The lock gave with a nail-biting screech, and the door flew inward.

In the harsh fluorescent light Will had a brief impression of a desk cluttered with a computer, monitor, and stacks of automobile books and magazines. Carlos Hernandez was squirming through the window at the back of the office, standing on a car fender to get out. The young man, Rudolpho, stood behind the desk with a large revolver clutched desperately in his shaking hands.

All that passed in the space of a heartbeat before Will stepped back out of the line of fire. He touched two fingers to the bridge of his nose, signaling Shel that two men were inside; then gunfire boomed and bullets slammed through the Sheetrock walls.

Shel crouched and twisted his body, hurling the gas grenade inside the office as chunks of Sheetrock sprayed out over him. The gas grenade exploded with a distinct *bamf!* almost immediately.

Keying the headset radio, Will said, "Carlos Hernandez is going out the back."

"Affirmative," Maggie replied.

Taking a gas mask out of his chest pack, Will pulled it on and stayed hunkered down as the white tear gas boiled up and filled the room.

The gunfire stopped punching holes in the wall. Hollow clicks of the hammer falling on empty cylinders punctuated the silence that followed.

A moment later, hacking coughs erupted from the room. Will continued to wait outside the office, watching Shel flattened against the wall with Max close to his side.

Rudolpho Hernandez stumbled out of the office with a hand over his face. Tears streamed from his burning eyes, and mucus ran from his nose. The pepper-laced tear gas was a juggernaut of pain and discomfort. He carried the massive pistol in his right hand.

"Gun," Will shouted. He heard his own voice distorted by the mask. Then he was moving, twisting and jerking his right leg out to sweep the young man's legs from beneath him.

Rudolpho Hernandez fell forward as his feet shot backward. Only his hand over his face kept him from losing teeth. His nose broke with a sickening crunch.

But he's alive, Will thought as he fell on top of the boy and kicked the revolver away. The young man didn't have any fight left in him. He didn't move when Shel shoved the M4A1's muzzle into the back of his neck.

"Stay," Shel growled.

Rudolpho stayed, but he cried like a child as Will swept his hands behind his back and cuffed him.

Will stood and looked at Shel. "You got this?"

"You bet," the big Marine rumbled.

Will entered the office. The gas was still a thick fog that made the interior of the room indistinct.

The window was open. Carlos Hernandez was gone.

Holding his sidearm at the ready, Will stepped onto the fender and shoved himself through the window. After the bright intensity of the lights in the garage, the darkness waiting outside seemed impenetrable. He used his peripheral vision to scan the immediate vicinity. Peripheral vision was always the first to return, and the first to pick up movement. That was a predator's skill, and the military reinforced the use of it.

Carlos Hernandez hadn't escaped. In fact, he hadn't gone far. Less than twenty feet away, Maggie knelt atop the man's unconscious body and cuffed his hands behind his back. Estrella stood with her pistol aimed at the man, bent elbows tucked in at her sides, forming a shooter's triangle.

"He's down," Maggie said.

"I see that." Will glanced around, spotting the Marines farther out where they'd established their perimeter. "Any problems?"

"He never saw us coming," Estrella said. "Maggie took him out from behind. I think he's going to have to wake up to learn he's been taken into custody."

Will withdrew back into the office. Now that the arrests had been made, the investigation could begin. With luck, all the action hadn't destroyed the crime scene.

6

SCENE ✹ **NCIS** ✹ **CRIME SCEN**
NAVAL CRIMINAL INVESTIGATIVE SERVICE

>> JACKSONVILLE, NORTH CAROLINA
>> 0914 HOURS

"They murdered her in here," Shel said.

Will stood in the office doorway and surveyed the scene. They'd been at it all night, and he felt like he was running on dregs. But there had been no choice. The motto on crime-scene investigation was to get it all, get it right, and get it the first time. There were no do-overs in evidence collecting, and a high-travel crime scene was a red flag to a defense attorney looking to attack the chain of custody concerning recovered evidence.

The room still smelled like tear gas. But that was better than the metallic blood smell that clouded the paint and gasoline fumes in the garage area.

"Show me," Will invited.

Moving carefully through the markers he'd set up, Shel spoke succinctly. "You saw the rug was missing."

Will nodded. After the tear gas had cleared, that had been the first thing he noticed. When working crime scenes, the first thing a trained investigator looked for was anything that had been brought to the scene or taken away.

Locard's Principle, one of the prime directives any investigator adhered to, stated that a perpetrator could not commit a crime without leaving some trace of physical evidence at the scene or taking something away. Sometimes, though not always, those pieces of evidence were objects that were used in the commission of the crime.

The rug Frank had found in the Dumpster near the apartment where Special Agent Helen Swafford's body had been discovered would no doubt match exactly the dimensions of the discolored section of the office floor. Years of grime and dirt colored the floor outside the rug area. Trace evidence would connect that grime and the paint samples to the stains on Swafford's shoes as well as to the residue on the rug.

"The rug we found fits the dimensions," Will said. "If we get a match—and by that I mean *when* we get a match—that means her body was wrapped with the rug taken from this room. Doesn't mean she was killed here."

"Uh-huh." Shel knelt and pointed up under the desk. "Arterial spray is hard to control."

Kneeling beside the Marine, Will looked under the desk. Brownish splotches coated its underside. The vanity screen and the sides of the desk didn't have any splotches.

"They cleaned up," Will said.

"Tried to." Shel nodded. He reached into the black evidence case he'd carried into the room and took out a pair of ultraviolet enhancing goggles. He passed the goggles to Will, then got out another pair for himself. "Hey, Maggie, kill the lights, will you?"

Looking up, Will saw Maggie standing in the doorway.

"When you get a minute," she told Will as she switched off the lights, "I've got something for you to look at."

"Sure." Will turned his attention to what Shel was showing him.

The Marine switched on an ultraviolet blue lamp and played the beam over the vanity screen and the sides of the desk. Bright, elongated splotches of light marred the surfaces.

"Velocity splatters," Shel said. "When they cut her, her heart was pumping."

Images of what Special Agent Swafford's last few minutes must have been like swarmed through Will's mind. She would have been terrified, fighting for her life, not wanting to die. The blood had exploded out of her and coated the underside of the desk.

"Okay," Will said. "We have the murder scene. What did you use to expose the blood spatter?"

"Merbromin. I didn't want to destroy the genetic markers if we needed them."

Luminol had become the popular choice for revealing hidden bloodstains, thanks to several television shows and movies. However, the chemical was harsh and had a tendency to destroy the genetic markers. It was one thing to prove that a lot of blood had been spilled in an area, but it was another to be able to prove exactly *whose* blood it was. Merbromin was gentle and effective, and it left the genetic markers in place.

"I also found a broken fingernail." Shel held up a small plastic evidence bag with a half-moon of fingernail inside. "I didn't see Swafford's hands—"

"She has broken nails," Will said, remembering the dead woman's bloody fingers.

Shel shined the light at the desk, showing scratches in the thick black paint. "We'll need to have her nails checked for paint particles. I found the fingernail under the desk. We can match it up to one of her fingers."

"She fought." Will looked at the scratches and the dried blood. Staying distant from this case was hard. "So we'll check Hernandez and nephew for scratches."

Shel nodded. "I'll finish this up. I know I'll find more, but we have the murder scene."

"Good work." Will stood. Finding the murder scene was important. The location where the crime took place usually turned up the most evidence tying the perpetrator and the victim together. "I'll see what Maggie has."

❀ ❀ ❀

>> 0931 HOURS

Maggie led Will through a maze of demolished and disassembled vehicles outside the shop. In addition to the specialty paint business, Carlos Hernandez operated a junkyard. Deep ruts and dead and dying weeds filled the red-dirt path.

"The junkyard serves as a cover for the chop-shop operation Hernandez has going," Maggie said. She stopped at the remnants of a red late-model Mercury Cougar.

The car had been taken apart by a wrecking crew. It lay in three sections, all of them looking shiny and new. The windshield was broken out. A Georgia license plate hung on the rear bumper.

"Swafford drove a Cougar," Will said.

"Yes she did," Maggie confirmed.

"That's a Georgia plate."

"The plate belongs to a twelve-year-old Dodge van." Maggie indicated the dashboard, pointing to a row of vehicle identification numbers. "The VIN, however, belongs to the Cougar Special Agent Swafford owned."

Will walked to the back of the car and knelt, studying the brake lights. The right light had a diamond-shaped chunk with curved ends broken out of it. He shifted, studying the ground.

"What are you looking for?" Maggie asked.

Will pointed to the broken taillight. "A piece of the puzzle."

"That taillight could have been broken before last night." Maggie knelt and began searching as well.

"Check with the provost marshal's office back at Camp Lejeune," Will suggested. "See if one of the gate guards reported Swafford's broken taillight."

The broken taillight was a traffic violation. The gate sentries logged damaged vehicles and sometimes even left notes for the owners.

Will took his iPAQ from his pocket and keyed up the phone function, then punched Frank Billings's picture. The phone rang and was answered almost immediately.

Frank was currently walking a grid outside the paint-and-body-shop premises. They'd made the early assumption that Hernandez had discovered Swafford on one of the streets or alleys outside the junkyard. Frank had initially been searching for the woman's car.

"We found the car," Will said.

"Inside the yard?"

"It's been cut up. But I don't think she drove it in." Will looked at Maggie and mouthed, *Fingerprints on the steering wheel. Seat adjustment.* Both of those avenues could provide more evidence.

Maggie nodded and rummaged through her evidence kit.

"What I want you to look for," Will said, "is a taillight section. A piece of red plastic. I'm going to send you a picture. Maybe we'll get lucky."

"Yes, sir."

Will broke the connection, then opened the camera option on the iPAQ and took a picture of the missing taillight section. When he was satisfied with the picture, he sent it to Frank's phone.

"Carlos Hernandez has a floor safe," Estrella reported. She waved a hand at an accumulation of things on a metal desk in the garage's second bay.

Will surveyed the items, taking in the bundles of cash, glassine packets of white powder, and sheaves of contracts and legal records. There were also seven pistols, two semiautomatic and five revolvers, and a Nikon SLR digital camera with a telescopic lens.

"What about the pistols?" Will asked.

"I'm running the serial numbers now. We'll see if they're in the system. The camera belonged to Special Agent Swafford. She had the serial numbers of all the equipment assigned to her on one of her computer files. She was very thorough. This camera was listed there."

"Were there any pictures on the flash card?"

Estrella shook her head. "It was completely empty. It's possible that Agent Swafford didn't get the opportunity to take any pictures."

"Possible. But I don't think Swafford would have missed the opportunity." Will called Shel and told him to look for a flash card in the office. If Swafford had lost it during the struggle, the card could have ended up in there.

It was another missing piece Will wanted to find.

>> 1142 HOURS

A glimmer of red at the side of the road caught Frank Billings's attention. He didn't get excited. For the last hour he had found a number of pieces of broken taillights, juice bottles, and marbles. That didn't include foil, glass, and sundry other items.

Still, without getting his hopes up, Frank walked to the red glimmer. It was in an alley behind a small neighborhood grocery with various faded advertisements hung in windows.

An Asian man with a stained butcher's apron over his white shirt and slacks stood in the alley glaring at a big dented Dumpster in front of the store's rear door. He looked up as Frank approached.

Frank knew the man's attention was mostly on the two Marines who flanked him. "Good morning," Frank called, waving a hand.

The Asian man studied Frank suspiciously. He had lines around his eyes. His age could have been anywhere from thirties to fifties. "Good morning." He took a step back, wary. "Can I help you?"

Frank knelt and examined the piece of red plastic nearly buried in the dirt and gravel. Even though he couldn't see the whole piece, it looked like it could be what he was looking for. He carefully brushed away the dirt, revealing the entire piece, then took out his phone and pulled up the picture Will had sent him to make sure.

The piece matched perfectly.

Dusting his knees off, Frank said, "I think you can. I'm Frank Billings." He offered his hand.

The man wiped his hand on his apron and shook Frank's. "I am Mr. Cho."

Frank looked up at the supermarket sign: Cho's Groceries. "Do you own this place?"

"I do. For the last seventeen years."

The supermarket had a second level. Houseplants filled the second-story windows. Apparently the Chos lived above their business.

One of the curtains moved. Dimly outlined behind the curtain, a small Asian woman stood watching them.

"Were you here last night, Mr. Cho?"

"Yes. What is this about?"

Frank ignored the question. People often answered questions more freely and with less worry when they didn't know for sure they were talking to an investigator. Too many of the younger officers, detectives, and investigators were badge heavy. They couldn't wait to flash their ID and pull rank. Frank didn't work that way. People got along better when they didn't feel threatened.

"Did you notice anything out here last night?" Frank asked.

Cho narrowed his eyes. "What would there be to notice?"

"I don't know," Frank said blandly. "Maybe you could tell me. Anything at all."

Police investigation had been new to Frank a few years ago, but he'd learned a lot of the rudiments while chasing down reports aboard the aircraft carrier. One of the first tenets was to keep what he knew and what he didn't know concealed. And act wise. That way people who were interviewed just assumed he knew everything they did.

Angrily, Cho gestured to the Dumpster. "Someone drove into my trash last night. Very stupid. Probably drunk."

"Somebody running into your Dumpster, that must have made quite a racket. Did you hear anything else?"

"No."

"Did your wife?"

Cho hesitated.

"If you're not certain, maybe we could ask her," Frank suggested.

"She heard," Cho admitted reluctantly. "She called to me. I was working in the front."

"Was she standing at the window?" Frank asked, looking up. "Like she is now?"

Self-consciously, Cho gazed up at his wife. She stepped back out of view.

"No," Cho answered. "She was in the kitchen. Preparing our meal."

"But she must have gone to the window to look after she heard the noise, right? Did she see the car?"

Cho glanced at the Marines standing behind Frank. "Yes," he admitted finally. "She saw the car that ran into the Dumpster."

"Maybe I could talk to her." That was when Frank brought out his ID.

"I do not wish to be involved. I do not wish my wife involved either."

"I appreciate that, Mr. Cho. Really I do. But I have to get some answers. That piece of plastic there?" Frank pointed at the red plastic still in the dirt. "That's part of a broken taillight on a car I have to ask questions about. That makes this a crime scene."

"No crime was committed here," Cho insisted.

Frank ignored the statement. "Now I have to mark off crime scenes. How big I make them depends on me. My judgment. What I think I need to secure the area. I mean, if I knew what happened here last night, I could just rope off this alley. But—" he shrugged—"if I have no idea what happened here or how that piece of plastic got here, I'm going to have to rope off the whole building. That could cost you business today. Maybe tomorrow and the next day too. So how do you want to do this?"

Cho called his wife down. She entered the alley hesitantly. She was small and bird thin, dressed in a traditional cheongsam.

"Just have her tell me what she saw when she came to the window," Frank suggested.

Cho spoke with his wife in Chinese and told Frank what she said. "She came to the window when she heard the crash. When she looked down, she saw a red car." He took a moment to confer with his wife. "She doesn't know what kind of red car. All she knows is it was red."

"Who was driving?" Frank asked.

The couple talked briefly. Then the husband said, "A young woman. She had black hair. A man was hanging on to the car door. He was yelling at the woman. She was acting very scared, trying to get away. He took a camera from her."

"Did your wife get a good look at the man?"

After a brief conference, Cho shook his head. "Not so good. There is no light back here after it gets dark."

That would explain why Swafford was back here, Frank thought. "Then what happened?"

"The woman scooted over in the car," Cho said. "The man got behind the steering wheel and drove away."

"Where did the car go?"

Cho asked and listened to his wife's answer. He pointed to the street. "There. That's all she knows. It turned north."

Frank looked at the street. North led to the junkyard, but the area wasn't visible from where Mrs. Cho would have been standing. He thanked the couple, then set the Marines to marking off the crime-scene site.

Now they had the location where Hernandez or one of his men had found Special Agent Swafford. It was all coming together.

7

>> CAMP LEJEUNE, NORTH CAROLINA
>> NCIS HEADQUARTERS, INTERVIEW ROOM A
>> 1509 HOURS

Will entered the interview room and let the door slam shut behind him. He carried a thick folder and a tall cup of black coffee.

Clad in an orange jumpsuit and handcuffed hand and foot, Carlos Hernandez looked up at him. "You the man I got to deal with?"

"Commander Will Coburn, Naval Criminal Investigative Services," Will stated flatly. "I *am* the man you're going to have to deal with."

"Why am I on a military base?" Hernandez demanded. "Why ain't I in Jacksonville?"

"Because you committed a crime against the United States military, Mr. Hernandez." Will kept his voice clear and distinct, a military man's voice and not a cop's. He wanted Hernandez to feel the difference every minute he was in their custody. Will also wore his khaki Navy uniform instead of street clothes; it tended to make an impression on prisoners.

Hernandez cursed. "I ain't done no crimes against the military!" He cursed again.

Will sat down on the other side of the table and carefully arranged the thick folder. "Your men shot at me and my team last night."

"Hey, you got nothin' on me! I didn't tell them to start shootin'! An' that was your fault anyway! You come in there, didn't tell nobody you was comin'!"

"You run a chop shop, Mr. Hernandez."

Hernandez shrugged. "That's between me an' the local police, man. Got nothing to do with the Navy."

"Did you know Special Agent Helen Swafford?" Will asked.

"Man, I don't know nobody by that name! You got the wrong guy!"

Like a blackjack dealer turning cards, Will reached inside the folder and took out a five-by-seven photograph of Swafford as she'd been in the apartment building. Hernandez might not recognize her in a regular photo.

Will placed the photo on the table between them. "This is Special Agent Helen Swafford."

Hernandez stared at the photo. A flicker of fear passed through his eyes; then it was gone. "Never seen her." His eyes met Will's.

Will pulled out another photo, this one of the scratches on Hernandez's face. "I think you do."

"These?" Hernandez shrugged. "I work in a body shop, man. Sometimes I don't look where I'm going."

"We took tissue from under Agent Swafford's fingernails." Will took out an official-looking report concerning a different DNA test. The ones for this case weren't back yet, but Hernandez didn't know that. And inside the interview room in pursuit of testimony, an investigator was allowed to embellish and fabricate. "The tissue under her fingernails matches your DNA."

Hernandez slumped back in his chair. "I think I'm done talkin' to you."

Showing the man a cold smile, Will said, "No. We're just getting started."

"You need to get out of here. I don't want to look at you no more."

Will locked eyes with the man. "Do you know where I'm going next?"

Hernandez refused to respond to the bait.

"I'm going to go talk to Rudolpho," Will said. "He's nineteen. He's scared. He's never been in this kind of trouble before. I'm going to offer him a deal. I'm going to tell Rudolpho that I can keep him from the death sentence, maybe even give him a second chance on a reduced plea. If he names you as Agent Swafford's killer."

"Man, he ain't gonna do that," Hernandez replied fiercely. "We're blood. Ain't nothin' stronger than that."

"I suppose," Will said, "that we're about to find out." He gathered up the photos, the file, and his coffee.

"Hey," Hernandez said, "I want my lawyer. I *get* a lawyer. I know my rights."

"You haven't been arrested yet, Mr. Hernandez. Only detained. I'll get someone in here to read you your rights—in case you don't remember them from last time—and then we'll get you arrested. Sometime after that you'll have an attorney." Will stared at the man. "Then I'm going to nail you for the murder of Agent Swafford. I give you my word on that. And I never break my word."

>> INTERVIEW ROOM D
>> 1549 HOURS

"Are you listening to me, Rudy?" Will kept his voice calm and understanding.

"I'm listening." Despite his grown-up features, Rudolpho

Hernandez wept uncontrollably. He'd been up all night in Navy custody, confronted by violent death, and was going through withdrawal from whatever drug of choice he'd given himself to.

"I'm trying to help you," Will said. He sat on the same side of the table as the young man. Where he had been confrontational with the uncle, Will now showed empathy to the nephew. Some people had to be forced into admission; others had to be guided.

"I know you're tryin' to help me," Rudolpho croaked. "I just want to talk to my mom."

"Your mom can't help you, Rudy," Will said patiently.

"I can."

The young man tucked his chin into his chest. Tears cascaded down his face. His mouth quivered and his hands shook. He wore the orange jumpsuit but he didn't wear the chains. Will had taken them off himself. The handcuffs and chains lay in a pile in the corner of the room, out of sight but never out of mind.

"I don't want to be here," Rudolpho whispered.

"A woman is dead," Will said. "She had parents. I had to tell them that she wasn't coming home today. Just like I had to tell your mom that you weren't coming home."

Rudolpho put a hand over his mouth. He shook his head, then looked at Will. "Is my mom—is she okay?"

Will looked earnestly at the boy. "She's not happy. She's worried about you."

"Can I see her?"

"I'm afraid not. See, we have to figure out what we're going to do."

"We?"

"Yes." Will put a hand on the boy's shoulder. *God, give me strength to do this.* Even though he knew what he was doing had to be done, not just to get justice for Helen Swafford's family but to allow Rudolpho to make amends as well, winning the young man over felt like betrayal. "We're in this together. I promised

Helen Swafford's family that the man who killed their daughter would be punished."

"But I didn't do it! I swear! I didn't kill her!"

Gazing into the young man's frightened eyes, Will wondered if now was the time to strike. He was good at doing interviews. One of the best. Maggie had told him he had a gift for it.

"Rudy," Will said solemnly, "that's not how your uncle is telling it."

>> **CRIME LAB 2**
>> **1601 HOURS**

Dressed in jeans, boots, and an olive green Marine T-shirt with the sleeves hacked off, Shel worked on the three sections of Helen Swafford's red Cougar in one of the NCIS evidence garages. Carefully and methodically, he'd taken the car apart while searching for more evidence that would help the team build a case against Carlos Hernandez and his people. The pieces lay scattered across the shop floor, all carefully labeled.

They'd found prints on the steering wheel, the seat adjustment lever, the rearview and side mirrors, and the radio. Evidently the guy who'd intercepted Swafford behind Cho's Grocery hadn't been able to kidnap without a sound track to the action.

The prints had matched one of the dead men in the garage.

The working hypothesis at the moment was that one of Hernandez's goons had spotted Swafford in her observation post while picking up munchies at the grocery store. Until they knew for sure what had happened, Shel figured the scenario worked.

The radio in the corner blared '80s rock, and Shel worked to the driving beat. Max lay curled up in the corner, patiently awaiting the moment Shel would take him out for a run again. When he saw Shel looking at him, the dog wagged his tail hopefully.

Shel had discovered over the years they were together that having a dog for a partner meant having to plan in regular playtimes to keep the muscles toned and the attention sharp. Max benefited from the diversions. But just now wasn't the time.

"How's it coming?"

Glancing up, Shel saw Frank standing at the side of the car. He hadn't heard the older man come in. Gripping the carpet, Shel ripped it free of the chassis.

"Good enough," Shel said. He told Frank about the prints.

"If you can tie one of Hernandez's guys to the car," Frank asked, "what more do you need?"

"Nothing," Shel said. "But I like to see a job through to the end. Will wanted this car tore down the whole way. I intend to see it done."

Frank rubbed his chin and observed the three pieces of the car. "I don't see that it's going to get torn down much more."

"Estrella's going through Hernandez's computer," Shel said. "Maggie's assisting Will with the interviews."

"Sounds to me like you could catch up on your sleep," Frank said.

Shel looked at him and grinned. "Like you are?"

"I'm an old warhorse, son. I don't know any other way. I'm not leaving till Will closes down the circus." Frank bent down and looked at the driver's side door. "Does this panel look like it's been taken out before?"

Examining the panel, Shel had to agree that it showed signs of frequent removal. The screwheads showed wear, and the panel wasn't quite flush with the door.

"Maybe she had trouble with the window," Shel suggested.

"Maybe," Frank agreed. "And maybe not." He used the battery-powered screwdriver to remove the panel.

A small notebook and a memory flash card occupied the hollow space inside the door.

Frank hunkered down and looked at the flash card.

"Swafford knew she was caught that night," he said quietly. "That's why there weren't any pictures in that camera Estrella found. Swafford dumped the memory card inside the door so she wouldn't get caught with any pictures of Hernandez or his operations. Probably thought she'd get it later." He plucked the card up. "If you're through deconstructing the car, maybe you'd like to come up with me and have a look at this."

>> INTERVIEW ROOM D
>> 1604 HOURS

"What do you mean?" Rudolpho asked. "What's my uncle saying?"

Will looked into the young man's frightened eyes and said, "Your uncle says it was an accident."

"An accident?" Rudolpho wiped his face. He looked confused. "He said it was an accident?"

Nodding, Will said, "Your uncle insists that you didn't mean to kill her, that it just happened."

Rudolpho looked perplexed. "I didn't kill her."

"It's okay," Will said. "Carlos explained. It was an accident. I just need to hear you say it."

"I didn't kill her."

Will reached into the folder and brought out the picture of Helen Swafford. He knew Rudolpho wasn't used to looking at death and that the photo would shake the young man's resolve. Seeing death like that, with the after tones of violence still fresh and clear, left an impact. That was why prosecutors used photos of victims and crime scenes in court, and why they were now using full-color images.

"We found her dead in the empty apartment where she was left." Will placed the photo on the table between them.

Rudolpho leaned back from the photograph as if trying to deny its existence.

"We matched the carpet she was wrapped in to the one that was in your uncle's office," Will went on in a soft voice, closing in on Rudolpho, taking away all hope of escaping the fallout from the murder. The young man had been there when it happened; Will was certain of that. "So we know where she was killed."

"It wasn't me."

Will pressed on relentlessly. He hated seeing the young man fall apart. It was hard on him, but he felt better about the closure he would be able to bring Helen Swafford's parents. And, truth to tell, the closure he could bring to himself. Not every investigation he worked on ended with the guilty party in jail.

"We know that Miguel Torres found Special Agent Swafford behind Cho's Grocery," Will said. "His fingerprints matched the ones we recovered from her steering wheel, seat-adjustment lever, mirrors, and radio."

Rudolpho rocked helplessly in his chair.

"We know that Torres took Agent Swafford prisoner and brought her to the paint-and-body shop," Will went on in that calm monotone. "But Torres is dead. He won't be tried and convicted for Agent Swafford's murder."

Photos of Miguel Torres, dead at the scene, and fingerprints on Swafford's car hit the table.

"All we need is an admission from you," Will finished. "I'm sure the court will be lenient." He paused. "Of course, you'll be tried in a military court, not a state court, so there's a chance you could get the death sentence."

Rudolpho broke down. He wept for a long time. Then he looked up at Will through his tears. "I can't believe Uncle Carlos would say that."

Will shrugged. "Carlos left your dad holding the bag on that drug deal." Estrella had given him that detail from the information she'd gotten from Rudolpho's mother. "I guess Carlos doesn't care who goes down as long as it's not him."

"It was Carlos," Rudolpho whispered. "Carlos killed her. Miguel found the woman behind Cho's Grocery, like you said. When Miguel brought her to the shop, Carlos lost it. He knew she had been taking pictures. But there weren't any pictures in the camera. She wouldn't tell him anything. She said she was just waiting for a friend. But you knew she was lying, man. She wasn't very good at it. Then—" the young man took a deep breath— "then Carlos went crazy. He pulled a long knife and went at her. She fought him off, scratched his face with her fingernails."

Will waited patiently as Rudolpho provided the testimony that would put his uncle away. The video cameras mounted in the room recorded everything.

CRIME SCENE **NCIS** **CR**
NAVAL CRIMINAL INVESTIGATIVE SERVICE

8

>> CAMP LEJEUNE, NORTH CAROLINA
>> NCIS HEADQUARTERS, INTERVIEW ROOM D
>> 1617 HOURS

"Where did the guns come from?" Will asked Rudolpho.

Rudolpho sat drained and empty in his seat. He shrugged. "Uncle Carlos knew this guy. Said he could get them. 'Military-grade weapons,' he said."

They were, Will admitted to himself. Estrella's background check on the weapons had revealed they were part of a United States military stockpile that had gone missing in Germany. The theft was still under investigation.

"What guy?" Will asked.

Rudolpho shrugged. It was the nonvocal expression of a child. "Don't know. He didn't say."

"When was the last time you saw the guy?" Will asked.

"Yesterday afternoon."

"Was Agent Swafford in the office when this guy came by?"

"No. Miguel found her after."

Will ran the timetable through his head. It was possible that Agent Swafford had been there during the exchange. But what had she seen that had gotten her killed? He tried another tack. "Where did the cocaine come from?"

"Uncle Carlos," Rudolpho said. "He's got a supplier. He . . . he trades the coke for the guns."

"Can you tell me anything about the guy who brought the guns?" Will asked.

"Told you all I know." Rudolpho squinted for just a moment. He looked at Will. "Wait. I heard a name. Uncle Carlos called the guy Ben."

"Ben."

Nodding, Rudolpho said, "Yeah. Ben."

"Describe him to me."

"About as tall as you. Skinny, though. Younger than you. Brown hair, brown eyes."

Will didn't hold out much hope on the description. They needed a break.

>> NCIS COMPUTER LAB
>> 1620 HOURS

Estrella took the flash card that Frank gave her and fed it into an adapter that she connected to her tower with a USB cord. Using her wireless optical mouse, Estrella opened a window to reveal the contents of the drive. Several columns and rows popped up on the monitor. "Photographs."

"Right." Frank hooked a chair with his foot and pulled it over. "The question is, what photographs?"

Estrella clicked on the first file. A prompt box flared to life and demanded a password.

"Is that going to be a problem?" Frank asked.

Estrella almost smiled at the question. Frank was old school when it came to regular computer technology. He was whizbang with weapons systems and mechanics, but he lacked finesse and experience when it came to programming.

"It could be," Estrella said. "I could run one of my snoop programs on it and come up with the password. Or I could try a crack utility and see if I can bypass the password altogether." She tapped the keyboard quickly, bringing up the files she'd copied from Helen Swafford's hard drive. "Otherwise, I can look up Agent Swafford's pass-code index and find out what she was using for her photo flash cards."

"Show-off," Frank commented dryly.

Shel, standing on Estrella's other side, grinned.

"We all have our fields of expertise, Chief," Estrella said.

The first photo on the flash card opened, showing a view of Carlos Hernandez's paint-and-body shop and the junkyard. In quick order, Estrella flipped through the images. Most of the shots centered on Carlos and Rudolpho Hernandez. Other images showed the garage crew.

"She was close when she took these," Estrella commented quietly.

"Yeah," Frank agreed, "but look at how she framed the shots. Always catching a piece of the hurricane fence to show that she was on the outside looking in."

Estrella knew that was important. If Agent Swafford had taken the photos while trespassing, they wouldn't be allowed in court. "She was good."

"She was," Frank said.

But she took one chance too many last night, Estrella thought. She kept moving through the images.

"Stop there," Shel said.

Estrella paused on the picture. It showed Carlos Hernandez talking to a Caucasian in front of the garage. The new arrival stood in front of a late-model, pearl white Mazda RX-8. He was tall and thin, too thin maybe, with brown hair and wraparound sunglasses and in his late thirties or early forties. He wore khaki pants and a turquoise pullover.

Shel lounged behind them, leaning against the next desk. Max curled at his feet and chewed on a dog bone. "Can you enlarge that guy?"

Estrella dragged a rectangle over the Caucasian, then moved the section over to a new file. Once there, she quickly enlarged the image.

Shel leaned in. "I know that guy. His name is Cooper. Had a run-in with him a year or so ago. He was operating a loan-shark business just outside Camp Lejeune."

Loan-shark businesses thrived around military bases, Estrella knew. Young guys couldn't wait to get their next paycheck, and families sometimes ended up on hard times. Instead of going to the military for help, they tried to fix things themselves and often ended up in debt to the wrong people.

"This guy Cooper," Shel said, "used a couple leg breakers who put a private in intensive care. After the private made the ID, the commander and I got warrants for their arrest and went after them."

Estrella continued cycling through the images. A few files later, they watched as Cooper took a black bag from the Mazda's trunk. "You recovered a black bag from the crime scene, right?" she asked.

"We did," Frank agreed. "There was gun oil all over the interior." He leaned forward, looking closely at the image. "If that's not the bag, then it's the bag's twin."

"Okay," Shel said, "we really need to find this Cooper guy. Those guns were swiped from a U.S. base in Germany. How did an ex-loan shark come by military hardware?"

Estrella flipped back through the images till she located one that showed the Mazda's license plate. She focused on that part of the image and blew it up in size. Once she had the plate number, she put on her phone headset and called a friendly contact in the North Carolina Department of Motor Vehicles. In seconds she had the name the car was registered to: Benjamin Cooper.

Estrella logged on to the North Carolina court records site, entered her ID, typed in Cooper's name, and pressed Enter. She had time to take a sip of water before the computer database at the other end chugged to life and spit out information.

Cooper, Benjamin Taylor, had a half dozen aliases. Each one had a list of prior convictions and open investigations attached to it.

"Wow," Shel said. "Magic."

I love my job, Estrella thought with a smile. "Do you want an address for him?"

"Does he have a current one?"

Estrella scanned the list and found what she was looking for. "We'll call his parole officer and find out. In the meantime, let's see if Rudolpho Hernandez can ID Cooper. If so, we can get a warrant."

Estrella copied the picture of Cooper and used the building's Wi-Fi network to e-mail the image to Will's iPAQ.

>> INTERVIEW ROOM D
>> 1631 HOURS

Can you ID this guy?

Will read Estrella's message on his iPAQ. He opened the attachment and looked at the man in the image. The junkyard was recognizable in the background.

Turning to Rudolpho Hernandez, Will held the iPAQ out so the young man could see the screen. "Tell me who this is."

Rudolpho studied the image for just a moment. Without hesitation he said, "That's Ben."

"The guy who sold Carlos Hernandez the guns for the cocaine?" Will kept his questions direct and clear so the audio-capturing devices wouldn't have trouble recording them and so there would be no mistaking his intent or what he had asked at a later date.

"Right," Rudolpho said. "That's the guy."

Will used his stylus to close the image on the small screen, then wrote a quick e-mail to Estrella: *ID confirmed. Get a warrant. Have Shel and Frank bring him in.* He sent the e-mail and turned his attention back to Rudolpho. "Okay, Rudy, I'm going to need you to write out a statement about what happened, okay?"

"A statement?"

Reaching into the folder, Will took out a yellow legal pad. He took a pen from his pocket, uncapped it, and laid it on the pad. "Just write down what happened last night."

Hesitant, Rudolpho picked up the pen. "I got spelling problems, man."

"That's okay," Will said. "We'll work through them together. The main thing is to get it written. Do you want something to drink?"

Rudolpho shrugged and smiled hopefully. "Sure. Can I get a soda?"

Will tried not to feel guilty about what he was doing. Even with all the cooperation Rudolpho was giving, it didn't mean the courts were going to be lenient with him. In all likelihood, given the severity of the crime and the fact that Rudolpho Hernandez was on hand when Helen Swafford had been murdered, Rudolpho would no longer be a young man by the time he got out of prison.

"Sure," Will answered. "You can have a soda."

❋ ❋ ❋

>> JACKSONVILLE, NORTH CAROLINA
>> 1703 HOURS

Shel drove through the parking lot on the south side of the Shoreside Apartments in Jacksonville. Benjamin Cooper's parole officer had verified the address.

"There." Frank pointed to the pearl white Mazda RX-8 in the parking slot for number 122.

As he pulled toward the sports car, Shel glanced at the license plate. The number matched the one Estrella had turned up in her search.

"And there's our boy." Frank reached under his Windbreaker and loosened his pistol in his shoulder holster.

Dressed in brown slacks and a green coat, Cooper trotted down the stairs. He popped a key ring in his free hand, tossing them up in the air and catching them while he held a cell phone in the other hand, talking fast as he walked.

"Going somewhere in a hurry," Shel commented as he made his way toward the Mazda. "Does he have a day job?"

"Clerks at a video-rental store."

"Think he's carrying?"

"Don't know." Frank watched Cooper closely.

Shel parked his Jeep behind the Mazda, blocking it.

Hand on the door now, Cooper continued talking on the phone and tossed Shel a glance filled with irritation.

Shel opened his door and got out, Max leaping out after him. Frank got out the other side. Putting an affable grin on his face, trusting his cowboy hat and jeans would confuse Cooper just long enough, Shel said, "That's a nice ride."

"Thanks," Cooper said uncertainly. "Can I help you with something?"

Shel stopped at the rear of the Mazda. "I wanted to apologize and give you my insurance number. I didn't see your car until it was too late. I hit the back end. Just got back from the office. I was trying to find out who owned this car. And here you are."

Dark anger filled Cooper's face. "You hit my car?" He closed the phone and came around to the vehicle's rear.

When the man looked at the bumper, Shel moved, grabbing Cooper's right wrist, pulling it back and slipping it up between Cooper's shoulder blades. Shel put his left hand behind Cooper's head and shoved forward, bending the man over the car.

Cooper jackknifed and lay facedown on the car's abbreviated trunk. He tried to fight but couldn't gain leverage against Shel. Frank clipped the handcuffs over Cooper's left wrist, folded his arm behind his back, and secured the right wrist as well.

"Owwwww!" Cooper cursed, drawing the attention of a handful of teenagers, an older couple walking a dog, and a young mother with three small kids in tow.

Shel grabbed the back of Cooper's head and slammed him into the trunk hard enough to get his attention. "Watch the language. You got kids around."

"You're kidding, right?" Cooper glared at Shel in disbelief. "You jump me and handcuff me and I don't even know you."

Grinning, Shel touched his hat in a two-fingered salute. "That's easy enough. I'm one of the good guys. I wear a white hat." He grabbed Cooper's elbow and pulled him away from the car. "You're one of the bad guys, and you're busted."

>> CAMP LEJEUNE, NORTH CAROLINA
>> NCIS HEADQUARTERS
>> 1712 HOURS

"Are you Will Coburn?"

Caught off guard, deep into his own reports and running on

empty from exhaustion and lack of sleep, Will glanced up at the man standing in his office doorway. The answer should have been obvious. Pictures of Will at different postings he'd had during his career shared space on the walls with framed commendations and certificates involving different facets of criminal investigation with Will's name on them.

"I'm Coburn," Will answered.

The man was big and blocky, probably in his early forties. Scars under his eyes and his crooked nose spoke of a history of violence. Despite that, though, he didn't have a military man's carriage.

Crossing the room, the man laid a manila envelope on the desktop to one side of Will's monitor. "You've been served. Have a good day." Without another word, the man turned and left.

Served? Cold dread wormed through Will's stomach as he stared at the manila envelope.

Maggie knocked at the door. "I just got off the phone with Frank. He and Shel have Cooper in custody."

"Good." Will was surprised at how thick his voice sounded. He opened the envelope and pulled out the papers inside. The cold, impersonal print centered on the top page told the story. Three words stood out among the rest of the legalese: *PETITION FOR DIVORCE.*

"Will?" Maggie said.

Divorce. In spite of all his efforts.

"Will?" Maggie said again.

Will looked up at Maggie and had to force himself to respond. "What?"

"Are you all right?"

No, Will thought, but he said, "I'm just tired. Let's get Cooper processed and see where we end up."

Maggie nodded and left, but the concerned look in her eyes told him she didn't fully believe him.

Will took in a deep breath, held it for a moment, then tried to figure out what he was going to do. *Where are you, God? Isn't this something you're supposed to be taking care of? Haven't I asked you enough? Haven't I prayed enough?*

There was no answer.

9

E SCENE ✳ **NCIS** ✳ **CRIME SCEN**
NAVAL CRIMINAL INVESTIGATIVE SERVICE

>> CAMP LEJEUNE, NORTH CAROLINA
>> NCIS HEADQUARTERS, INTERVIEW ROOM B
>> 1823 HOURS

Maggie Foley opened the door to the interview room and strode
in with Shel at her side. The big Marine was the obvious intimi-
dation factor, but Maggie fully intended to become even more
threatening.

Benjamin Cooper occupied the chair on the other side of the
table. His semirelaxed behavior even under the circumstances
spoke of his long and intimate history with the wrong side of the
law. He gave a sullen glance at Shel, then stared with open hostil-
ity at Maggie. "Who are you?" he demanded.

"Special Agent Foley." Maggie dropped her folders onto the
table.

"I thought maybe you were my attorney," Cooper said.

"He's coming." Maggie sat down.

"You're not supposed to ask me any questions until my attorney gets here," Cooper said.

"I won't." Maggie arranged the pictures neatly, knowing that Cooper couldn't help looking. She continued sorting through the papers the investigation had so far netted. She deliberately put a picture of Special Agent Swafford's mutilated body on the table so Cooper could see it.

"Who's that?" Cooper asked.

Maggie surveyed the man's face, his eye movement, and his body language. He was sitting open and forthright, no hint of subterfuge. If he didn't recognize the picture of Swafford, that meant he'd been gone by the time Carlos Hernandez had killed her.

"Someone Carlos Hernandez murdered," Maggie replied.

Cooper waved at the pictures and the folders. "What does all of this have to do with me?"

"Don't you want to wait on your attorney?" Maggie asked, looking up at him.

"You're not asking me any questions," Cooper pointed out.

"You're going to be charged for trafficking in stolen military weapons and for accessory to murder."

Cooper suddenly looked more concerned. "I don't know what you're talking about."

Maggie took out a stack of pictures she'd prepared for this segment of the interview. She laid them out. "Here's you meeting with Carlos Hernandez."

"I knew the guy. Big deal. He slapped the paint on my car, did some vanity work. Every now and again I'd score him some tickets to a Tar Heels game."

Unperturbed, Maggie continued. "Here's you getting a black bag out of the back of your car. You again, this time handing the bag to Hernandez. A picture of the bag." She took out a sheet of paper. "And the report that stipulates the gun-oil residue in the black bag, with your fingerprints on it, matches the gun-oil residue left on guns in Hernandez's possession that were stolen from a U.S. military base in Germany."

With that revelation, Cooper was quiet for a moment, having trouble holding Maggie's gaze. "That doesn't mean I had anything to do with the murder of that woman."

Maggie locked eyes with Cooper. "Agent Swafford was investigating those weapons. That means you were part of the reason Agent Swafford was there. Which means you were part of the reason Carlos Hernandez murdered her."

"I wasn't there."

"Won't matter," Maggie stated. "Agent Swafford's death came as a result of a felony. Everyone connected to that felony is held accountable." She paused. "That means you."

Cooper squirmed in his chair. "So what are we working here? Some kind of deal?"

"What we want is the person who gave you these guns. We want Agent Swafford's death to count for more than taking down a chop shop and a two-bit hustler."

"That wasn't friendly," Cooper whined.

"I'm not your friend," Maggie assured him. "But I'm the closest thing you're going to have to one in this room."

"Then what do I get out of this? What's my handle?" Cooper leaned forward, obviously worried.

The door to the interview room suddenly opened, and a lean young Marine second lieutenant in full uniform stepped into the room.

Shel got up and stood at attention.

"At ease, gunney," the second lieutenant said.

"Thank you, sir." Shel stood at parade rest. Even though he was in the NCIS and was technically out from under the military chain of command, Shel chose to remain a soldier first and a crime-scene technician second.

Cooper looked at the new arrival. "I get a soldier for a lawyer?"

"Military court," Maggie said. "Military representation."

"Do I get a choice?"

"If you can afford a civilian attorney trained in military courts, sure," Maggie said.

The second lieutenant put his hat on the conference table and went around to sit by Cooper. "I'm Second Lieutenant Dwight Richmond." He popped the briefcase locks. "I'll be representing you in this matter, Mr. Cooper."

Cooper looked at the younger man. "Are you shaving yet?"

Richmond grimaced. "Mr. Cooper, I assure you that I'm fully qualified to handle your defense."

"That's terrific," Cooper growled. He swiveled his gaze to Maggie. "That's the deal then? I give you the name of my supplier?"

"That's it," Maggie said. "You won't even have to testify."

"Wait a minute," Richmond protested, looking reproachfully at Maggie. "You were not supposed to be questioning Mr. Cooper until I got here."

"I didn't," Maggie said. "Not even one question."

"Just chill, junior," Cooper said, waving the protest down with his bound hands. "Let the grown-ups talk." He kept his eyes on Maggie. "I want the murder one dropped. I wasn't there when that woman was killed. You got the guy who did her. Let me walk on that. I'll take the fall for the guns."

"Done," Maggie said. She handed Cooper a legal pad and a pen. "Write it down. The sooner I get the details, the sooner I can fix the charges so you can get an arraignment and get bail set."

>> **WILL COBURN'S OFFICE**
>> **1847 HOURS**

Standing at the window looking out over Camp Lejeune at the line of trees in the distance behind the family units, Will punched in his wife's phone number. *My phone number,* he thought bitterly. *It used to be mine, too.* But that had changed a year ago when she'd asked him to leave the house.

As he listened to the phone ring, he couldn't stop himself from glancing at the fistful of papers that was going to make that change permanent.

He was scared. And hurt. He freely admitted those things to himself. For the last year—longer than that really—divorce was what he'd been afraid of. Fear of divorce and losing Barbara and the kids and such a big part of his life had gnawed at him constantly for the last three years. He'd been hoping that things could change, that he and Barbara would once more find what they'd had.

One of the pictures on his desk was of his wedding. In it he was younger, more certain of his life. Barbara was slender and athletic. Her chestnut hair tumbled across her shoulders under the bridal veil. Her blue eyes sparkled as she hung on to his arm.

But those people didn't seem to exist anymore.

The answering machine picked up. Will listened to Wren's voice, his daughter explaining that they couldn't come to the phone now and that a message could be left.

Will didn't leave a message. He hung up and called again.

Where are you in all this, God? Why aren't you making this go away?

This time Barbara answered the phone. "Hello, Will."

"I've been trying to call," Will said.

"I know. I haven't been answering the phone."

Will felt as if a yawning pit had opened beneath him. "Why?"

"My attorney told me not to. He said it wouldn't do any good."

"Your attorney?" Will's hurt and frustration grew.

"Yes." Barbara sounded angry.

"We need to talk," he said.

"No, we don't. There's nothing to talk about."

"I don't want a divorce."

"I do."

Will's throat was so tight he thought his voice might crack if he tried to speak. He had to pause for a moment. "Barbara, we can work this out."

"A divorce *is* working it out, Will," she told him. "Whatever we had, whatever brought us together, it's over. It was over a long time ago. I want to get on with my life."

Will didn't know what to say to that. Part of him wanted to explode, to vent his anger and jealousy. But that wouldn't have done any good. He didn't trust himself to speak.

"The only reason I answered the phone this time is so you will stop calling," Barbara said. "I don't want to listen to the phone ring, and I don't want to keep avoiding your calls. You need to accept this. It's over. *We're* over."

Stay calm, Will told himself. *Take it one step at a time.* "I just want to talk."

"I'm all talked out, Will, and there's nothing left to say. Just get a lawyer and sign the papers. You'll feel better, too, once this is over."

The phone clicked dead in Will's ear. He held it in his hand, surprised it didn't shatter from the tight grip he had on it.

God, you're going to have to help me here, because I don't know what to do.

Will looked out the window, seeing kids playing in the distance and young Marines on the go carrying out their assignments. He felt hollow.

A knock sounded at the door.

Walling the emotions away, Will turned to face his desk. He cradled the phone and did not look at the wedding picture or the pictures of his son and daughter. It didn't matter; he had the images engraved in his head.

Maggie stood at the door.

"Are you finished with Cooper?" Will asked.

"Yes. He agreed to the terms. He gave me a name."

"Does the name look good?"

"United States Marine Corps Lance Corporal Virgil Kent Hester. He's had a few skirmishes with the law of late. Nothing serious."

"Where is Hester now?" Will asked.

"Chinhae."

"South Korea?" That surprised Will. "How did Cooper get to know Hester?"

"Cooper spent some time here at Lejeune on temporary duty just over a year ago."

"Who initiated contact?"

"Hester. They met at a bar in Jacksonville. According to Cooper, Hester was looking to score some cash by selling guns."

"All right," Will said. "Let's run it by Director Larkin and see what he thinks."

>> NCIS CONFERENCE ROOM 1
>> 1932 HOURS

Before he'd accepted the role as Director of NCIS, Michael Larkin had been a New York City homicide detective. He'd never been in the military, but he'd recognized early on that a contingent well versed in the military was needed in his department. Will's team had been created at Larkin's discretion.

The director was in his early fifties, a slim, immaculate man with dark brown hair and thick eyebrows that hugged the ridges of his deep-set dark gray eyes. He had a heavy cleft chin, and even though it was evening in Washington, D. C., he was freshly shaved. His dark blue pin-striped suit wasn't off the rack, but it wasn't flashy either. He knew how to dress.

He also, Will discovered once again, knew how to listen.

Larkin's image filled the teleconference screen in the center of the table. He was an advocate of technology and liked to be hands-on with his team.

"To reiterate," Larkin said, "we have Special Agent Swafford's murderer in lockup."

"Yes, sir," Maggie said. "With enough forensic evidence and three witness testimonies to put him away."

"The gun angle is something new," Larkin said.

"Special Agent Swafford was investigating the weapons," Will said.

Larkin reviewed his notes. "You say the weapons were stolen from an arsenal in Germany?"

"You'll find the reports in the documents I sent you, sir," Estrella said.

Flipping through the printed pages, Larkin rubbed his chin. "Hester transported the weapons through Navy support ships?"

Support ships were often civilian units contracted by the military.

"That's what Cooper said," Maggie replied.

Larkin sighed tiredly. "Not hard to believe. We all know that's done much more frequently than any of us would like to admit. Has Hester been to Germany?"

"He has been, sir," Estrella answered. "But he wasn't there at the time the weapons went missing from the arsenal or since."

"Meaning he got them from someone else?"

"That's correct," Will said.

"You say he's at Chinhae? in South Korea?"

"Chinhae's a submarine base," Frank said. "We keep a pen there and the ROK does too."

The current situation in the Republic of Korea remained tense. There wasn't a day that went by that Will didn't see or hear a story about a mysterious bird flu or possible biological-weapons testing or the threat of nuclear war. The Navy had ships constantly in the area, including subs equipped with long-range missiles.

Larkin was quiet for a moment. "We could hand this situation over to the NCIS offices at Chinhae. They could pick Hester up and follow up on this."

Silently, Will hoped that was exactly what would happen. He didn't know how he could keep his mind on the investigation with everything coming to a head between Barbara and him.

"Or I could send your team in there, Commander Coburn," Larkin went on. "You'll have fresh eyes. If Hester has been operating under their noses there, they might not see what we're looking for. Also, given that Hester has been there for a while, he could see them coming." He sipped from the coffee cup at his elbow. "How is your schedule?"

Will answered honestly. It was all he'd ever known to do. "There's nothing pressing, sir." But he wanted more than anything to stay at Lejeune and wait for Barbara to realize what she was doing. He was convinced that if he could just talk to her, he could persuade her to wait a little longer.

"Very well. Get your team together. I want you in Chinhae as soon as possible. Has Cooper's name been given to the media in connection with Special Agent Swafford's death?"

"No, sir."

"Let's keep it that way. If we get the chance, maybe we can blindside Hester and catch him before he has any idea we're onto him. If someone is using Navy vessels to move contraband around, I want to put them out of business."

"Yes sir," Will said.

"Good hunting, people. Will, let me know if there's anything you need." Larkin leaned forward and tapped a button. The monitor went blank.

Will stood and looked around the room. "All right, we're on. Grab your gear. Estrella, see how soon we can catch a flight out of here."

Estrella opened her notebook computer and started tapping keys.

Will led the way out of the conference room.

Frank was at his side. "You doing okay?" he asked quietly.

Taking a deep breath, Will stepped into another hallway, stopped, and said, "No, Chief, I'm not."

"Want to talk about it?"

Will looked at Frank suspiciously. "Do you know what happened today?"

Frank shook his head.

"Barbara had me served with divorce papers." Unable to remain still, Will paced a few feet away, then returned. "I don't understand how my marriage has come to this. Everything I did, all the career moves I've made, I've made for the good of my family."

"I know."

"But it's like that doesn't count for anything," Will said. "Not in Barbara's eyes and not in God's eyes."

"You're wrong about that, Will."

Unable to stop himself, Will glared at his friend. "Am I, Chief? Do you really think that?" He shook his head, denying the possibility. "Here I am, facing a divorce, praying for help every chance I get, and I have to ask myself, where is God?"

Frank put a hand on Will's shoulder. "He's right beside you where he always is. He won't leave you. You've got to believe that."

Irritably but unable to be truly angry with Frank, Will shook the chief's arm off his shoulder. "I don't."

"Will—"

Not wanting to listen any further, Will held up a hand, turned, and walked away. "Get your duffel, Chief. We've got a plane to catch."

He knew he shouldn't have left Frank like that, shouldn't have left the weight between them, but he couldn't help himself. Nothing seemed to be making sense anymore, and that scared him.

SCENE **NCIS** ⊛ **CRIME SCEN**
NAVAL CRIMINAL INVESTIGATIVE SERVICE

```
>> CHINHAE, REPUBLIC OF KOREA
>> OUTSIDE BLUE ORCHID BAR
>> 2008 HOURS
```

Seated behind the wheel of the small midnight blue Daewoo Kalos sedan, Will kept surveillance through the car's side mirror as the bicyclist pedaled up the small grade from the coast. Will tried to shrug off the feeling of jet lag, but failed. He hadn't slept well since receiving the divorce papers.

Farther down the hill, lights glimmered on the decks of military ships lying at anchor in the Port of Chinhae, warring against the indigo night that had settled over the port city.

The U.S. Navy's Commander of Fleet Activities monitored the continuing volatile political and military situations existing between North and South Korea and also kept an eye on China just across the Yellow Sea. Tucked away at the southern end of the peninsula, Chinhae possessed a number of natural geographic protections from North Korea as well as from China to the west and Japan to the east. That was the reason the Republic of Korea kept its navy located in the same place.

Protected by the dark, moonless night, Will was certain he was hidden from the bicyclist's view. He watched the figure grow closer.

The bicyclist wore civilian clothes—jeans and a faded gray New York Giants sweatshirt against the chill sweeping up from the Korea Strait. According to his military jacket, USMC Lance Corporal Virgil Hester had served six years with no real distinction. On the surface, Hester looked like a guy just biding his time, not choosing the military as a career, but not going away either.

Hester pulled the bicycle over to the curb in front of the Blue Orchid Bar. The tavern was one of the many watering holes favored by the American and South Korean sailors and servicemen, as well as the crews of cargo ships that sailed into the port on business.

Neon lights glimmered in the hazy, spitting rain that had begun hours ago and seemed determined to linger. The neon gleams reflected on the black surface of the narrow street. The bar was sandwiched between an electronics store and a small café that was currently closed. A large plywood sign illustrated with Korean characters hung over the door.

Hester left the bicycle sitting at the curb. Without hesitation, he strode toward the front door of the bar. The blue neon light from inside the structure spilled over Hester's face, revealing that he had sandy hair and an unblemished face that looked years younger than twenty-seven, the age listed on his jacket.

"Steadfast Leader, this is Steadfast Three." Shel's deep voice rumbled through the ear-throat transceiver Will wore. "Do you have visual?"

"Affirmative, Three," Will responded. "Leader has visual."

Shel drove smoothly past Will's position, his large frame

crammed behind the wheel of a nondescript Daewoo subcompact. "Good hunting, Leader. Stay frosty." The big Marine kept
going, moving up the winding street to a preselected location a
few blocks away.

With the handoff completed, Will stepped out of the sedan,
waited for a truck to barrel past, then crossed the street. The
black shell jacket he wore against the chill sweeping in from the
ocean covered the pistol snugged into the pancake holster at the
small of his back.

Lance Corporal Hester vanished into the building.

Will's heart rate elevated a little. "Steadfast Two," he stated
calmly as he jammed his hands into his jacket pockets, "do you
have visual?"

"Affirmative," Frank Billings replied from inside the bar.
"Confirm visual."

So far, everything was proceeding just as they had planned.
When they had arrived in Chinhae two hours ago, a quick
check with the duty sergeant revealed that Hester was currently
on a two-day leave. He hadn't been in barracks, so Will had his
team start cruising the hot spots. Shel had located Hester two
bars ago.

Rather than pick Hester up immediately, Will had decided to
let the man run for a couple hours. The team maintained surveillance, logging contacts and taking pictures. Hester hadn't stolen
the guns from the German arsenal himself, so it meant he wasn't
working alone. Will wanted to know who Hester was working
with. The more knowledge he had when he went into the interview room with the man, the better his position would be.

Fatigue chafed at Will, but he kept moving through sheer
determination. During the long hours of the flight to Korea, his
thoughts had centered constantly on Barbara, the divorce
papers, and his children. He'd tried twice more to call, once
before leaving and once after landing. Neither call had been
answered.

Leave it, Will told himself. *Concentrate on what you have in front of you.*

Hester was the target, and the target was moving in dangerous waters. The black market remained a thriving business wherever a port was, and the presence of a foreign navy—in this case, the United States Navy—elevated the profits . . . and the danger.

"Steadfast Four and Five," Will said, finishing the comm circuit, "are you in the loop?"

"Four confirms loop," Maggie replied.

"Five reads you five by five, Leader," Estrella answered. "Standing by. We have full electronic."

Will took a fold of South Korean–won bills from his shirt pocket and paid the cover charge to enter the bar. He had his hand stamped with ultraviolet ink and stepped into the crashing thunder of the industrial music flooding the Blue Orchid.

>> NCIS SURVEILLANCE VAN
>> 2011 HOURS

Estrella stared at the six computer monitors built into the wall of the undercover van parked on the street behind and two blocks down from the Blue Orchid. On the screens she watched Will enter the target site while at the same time she kept up with Lance Corporal Hester's progress through the bar through another vid view.

When Shel had monitored Hester two bars back, he'd overheard Hester say he had "something working" at the Blue Orchid. Will had assigned Frank, Maggie, and Estrella to the surveillance setup at the bar. Whomever Hester met with, talked to in passing, or seemed interested in would be captured by the video-and-audio recording equipment Estrella managed.

Thanks to Frank's advance recon of the target environment,

video currently pumped from four different sites inside the bar. With a size befitting the name, the button cams pasted easily to most surfaces through an adhesive backing. The greatest difficulty lay in hiding the finger-sized battery packs that kept the button cams going.

On one of the screens Estrella saw Will enter the main barroom. The commander flicked his eyes over the room, then went to join Frank at the small table the chief held down at the back.

The monitors cycled through eight different points of view. Four of the views came from the cameras Frank had hidden inside the bar. The other four showed the exterior of the building from cameras in Will's rental car as well as in the van Estrella occupied. She could even access the camera Shel carried with him if she found that necessary.

A reflection took shape in the monitor screen. Someone had stepped into position behind Estrella and she had to calm herself, realizing it was only Maggie. Estrella stripped the earphones from her head and looked back.

"How's it going?" Maggie asked.

"We're good," Estrella replied. "For the moment, we have good reception."

"Noisy, though."

"The programs I'm using can handle it. We can filter and sort later."

Maggie crossed her arms above the twin Beretta 9 mms she carried in a double shoulder holster. "I'll feel better once we take Hester in."

Estrella tapped the mouse, designating Hester as the focal point for the vid. In response, the young Marine was highlighted in a yellow oval on the screens.

On another screen, Will sat with Frank Billings at the small table where they could see most of the bar's interior as well as the entrance and the alley exit.

Working the keyboard and mouse, Estrella downloaded

data and saved off video and audio feeds. On surveillance, she never knew what would be needed, so—like the crime-scene investigations she worked—it was best to get it all the first time.

>> **BLUE ORCHID BAR**
>> **2014 HOURS**

Will kept his attention centered on Lance Corporal Hester, who had made his way to the phones in the back and was dialing. The number was a local one. Hester didn't punch enough numbers to make an international call.

Hester leaned over the phone, hugging into it as he looked around the bar. His eyes looked sharp, and his gaze held the hunger of a predatory animal.

Tapping the ear-throat communicator, Will said, "Steadfast Five."

"Five reads you, Leader."

"Can we get a connect on the landline?" Hester wasn't using a cell phone. If he had been, his conversation would have been easier to intercept.

"Trying."

Hester continued to talk on the phone. His demeanor grew tense. Whomever he was conversing with, the conversation wasn't a pleasant one.

A young hostess dressed in a revealing strapless red dress approached Will and Frank's table. Despite her bright smile, her eyes held fatigue. She had to talk loudly over the crash of the industrial rock. "What you have to drink?"

"Coffee," Frank said. He held up two fingers. "Two coffees. Black and hot."

The waitress nodded and walked away.

When the waitress returned with their coffees, Will paid her out of his shirt pocket. The habit was one his father had taught him. "A poor man's ways," his father had said. Money Will intended to spend at a bar always went into a shirt pocket so he didn't have to take his wallet out. The habit made even more sense on an operation like this one. The last thing he wanted to do on assignment was wave around a wallet containing his badge and NCIS identification.

He blew on the coffee, then sipped it. The coffee was weak, watered down to the point that he suspected the bag had been run through twice.

Hester hung up the phone. Rolling his wrist over, he checked the time on his watch.

Will tapped his transmitter again, double tapping it so the comm stayed open. "Five, did you get access to that landline?"

"Negative," Estrella replied. "Landlines are spaghetti here."

"We're going places," Frank said, nodding at Hester, who was making for the front door of the bar.

"I see," Will replied. "Copy, Three?"

"Five by five," Shel responded laconically.

Hester stepped through the entrance.

Conscious of the weight of the pistol holstered at the small of his back, Will pursued his quarry. "Confirm visual, Three."

>> OUTSIDE BLUE ORCHID BAR
>> 2021 HOURS

Shel eased the subcompact down the street in front of the bar. He spotted Hester coming through the door, framed in the blue neon light that filled the entrance.

"Confirm visual," Shel said. "Three has the ball."

Hester paused to light a cigarette, then headed for the street corner away from Shel.

A black Toyota Supra rolled out of a nearby alley, turning its lights on as it reached the street.

Shel tapped the brakes, slowing to allow the sports car to cut in front of him. The Supra pulled to a stop beside Hester, brake lights flaring crimson. The door opened but the interior stayed dark except for the glow of the instrument panel. Shel could make out the silhouettes of three figures in the car, but nothing more. That was interesting, he thought. Apparently someone had removed the dome light so no one could easily see inside the vehicle.

Hester talked briefly, took a final drag on his cigarette, and tossed it away before sliding inside the Supra. The car was underway before Hester had the door closed.

Automatically, Shel read the car's license plate, slipped a notepad from his jacket pocket, and recorded it. "Five, did you get visual?" He shifted his foot from the brake to the accelerator pedal and started after the Supra, allowing one car to get between them before cutting off the next.

Horns blared in Shel's wake, but the sound wasn't unique at this time of night in the city.

"Five confirms visual ID," Estrella said. "I'm running the plates now."

"*Bueno, mi amiga,*" Shel said. Even though Estrella hailed from Chicago and he got his Spanish by way of West Texas, they shared a language.

"*Tener cuidado, vaquero.*"

"*Si, senorita. Gracias.*" Shel grinned. He'd be careful, all right. But he lived for the hunt, thrilled for the chase. It was in his blood.

Max whined in the passenger seat next to Shel. At one hundred twenty pounds, the black Labrador was as tight a fit for the space as Shel.

"Three, stay with the subject," Will said. "We'll be up and online in a minute. Ready to take a handoff if you need to make one."

"Affirmative." Shel drove confidently, easily meshing with the nighttime traffic of Chinhae.

S ✸ **CRIME SCENE** **NCIS** ✸ **CRI**

SCENE ⊗ **NCIS** ⊗ CRIME SCEN
NAVAL CRIMINAL INVESTIGATIVE SERVICE

>> DIMASHQ ASH-SHAM, SYRIA
>> SOUK AS-SILAH
>> 1426 HOURS

In years long past, Souk as-Silah had been a weapons market. Masters of the sword from the East and the West, from England and France and China and Japan, had met to sell their wares, their skills and willingness to kill, and to tell stories of past conquests. They had mocked each other and fought each other. Some had walked away with horrible scars or another notch on their sword hilt. Others, not so lucky or skilled, ended up buried in unmarked graves outside the city.

Qadir Yaseen went there because the Americans could not reach him there. The Syrian leader didn't allow the forces of the Great Satan inside his country, although he didn't publicly admit to supporting Palestinian freedom fighters either. Several terrorist groups had found refuge inside Syria's borders. They had made bases of operation and trained troops.

Dimashq ash-Sham, also known as Damascus, had become known for its steel and as a haven for refugees driven into hiding by the United States. It was also a place where Yaseen felt at home. He walked the streets dressed in his robe, his weapons hidden from sight, and hated Colonel Vladimir Gronsky. For the last few days, the Russian military leader had ignored every message Yaseen had sent him.

But he would not ignore the one Yaseen was sending today.

Yaseen tracked his quarry easily through the crowded marketplace. These days, the shops containing swords and knives—and eventually pistols and rifles—had given way to purveyors of gold and jewelry. Weapons and money still changed hands in the alleys, but no longer in the open.

A half dozen of Yaseen's warriors flanked him, easing through the shoppers and tourists. All of the warriors remained intent.

Unconcerned and unaware, the woman walked north through the marketplace toward the Umayyad Mosque. She was tall and beautiful, golden-haired and blue-eyed. Despite her Russian heritage, she wore American jeans and a pullover. Her name was Natasha Ormanov. She was there to sell yet more of the Russian munitions Gronsky had managed to "lose" while in command of weapons transportation.

Yaseen hated Ormanov more for her Western ways than for the fact that she was Gronsky's lover. Today Gronsky would learn that Yaseen thoroughly researched every one of the people he chose to do business with. They all had their weaknesses.

The woman stopped in front of a shopwindow. Lifting a hand, she shaded her eyes and peered inside.

Without pause, Yaseen stepped in behind the woman. He took a small pistol from a sleeve holster and pressed the barrel into her back.

Ormanov started to turn.

Yaseen hammered her forward with his forearm, keeping the pistol glued to her back. "If you move or scream, Captain Ormanov," he whispered, "I am going to empty this pistol into your back. If you are not immediately dead, you will be dead before anyone can help you. Do you understand?"

She looked at his reflection in the shopwindow and nodded.

"Good." Yaseen locked eyes with her in their combined reflection. "Do you have a phone?"

"Yes."

"Call Colonel Gronsky."

"Now?"

"Yes."

"My phone is in my purse."

"Get it," Yaseen cautioned her, "gently."

Moving slowly, Ormanov removed her phone. "He might not be there."

Yaseen leaned forward, intimidating her with his presence and the gun at her back. He whispered, and his voice came out like drawn steel. "You are his lover, Captain. One of them. If he does not answer your phone call, you will die. Do you understand."

Despite her best efforts, fear touched Ormanov's face. "Yes."

"I speak Russian," he said in that language, "so do not think you can fool me."

Ormanov dialed. After three rings, an answering machine picked up. She started to panic. "Vladimir! It is Natasha! You must pick up!"

The automated message started to spin, replaying the colonel's deep-voiced greeting.

"Vladimir!" The woman's voice sounded more strained. She stared in wide-eyed horror at Yaseen.

Gronsky picked up, breaking the automated message, and spoke in an angry voice. "Natasha, what is it? I told you never to call this number unless it was an emergency."

Yaseen plucked the phone from the woman's hand. "Ah, Colonel Gronsky," he said, "you and I need to talk."

Gronsky was silent for a moment. "I could not ship the missiles as we agreed. The Americans—their Central Intelligence Agency—their agents were very close to—"

"I don't want to listen to your excuses," Yaseen said. "I want what I paid for."

"You'll get it," Gronsky said. "I swear. We have a deal. But there have been extenuating circumstances that have necessitated—"

"We are going to talk, you and I," Yaseen said. "If you do not meet with me, I will kill this woman. From what I am told, you care about her."

Ormanov's eyes grew wider. She started to speak, but Yaseen jabbed her with the pistol, slamming her face into the glass.

"I do care for her," Gronsky said after a pause.

Yaseen didn't believe it for a moment. The Russian colonel didn't care for much outside his own skin, though he was protective of his possessions. Ormanov was one of those possessions.

"We will talk, then," Yaseen said.

"Of course, but I will need to renegotiate the price for the delivery of the missiles. There have been unfortunate changes that I've had no control over. You must understand."

"I do," Yaseen said. "We will meet in Seoul. I will make the arrangements." Meeting there suited his purposes. Once he had his hands on the nuclear weapons, things would have to happen very quickly.

"What about Natasha?" Gronsky asked.

"I will take care of her till then," Yaseen said. "After we meet, you may have her back. As well as the money she has negotiated from your latest bargain. I will call you with the particulars of the meeting soon."

"All right."

"Do not avoid my calls," Yaseen warned, "or I will send the

woman back to you in pieces." He folded the cell phone and handed it back to the woman.

"Thank you," Ormanov said automatically. She started to put the phone away.

Signaling his warriors, Yaseen lifted the silenced pistol and placed the barrel against the back of the woman's head. Two of the warriors closed in with a large rug, walking behind Yaseen and the woman to block the view from the street.

Yaseen fired the pistol twice. The silencer reduced the noise to quiet coughs. The .22-caliber rounds cored through the back of the woman's head, then bounced around inside her skull, too depleted to escape. They razored her brain, killing her instantly.

As the dead woman fell, Yaseen caught her and guided her into the folds of the rug. Moving quickly, the warriors wrapped the corpse in the rug and lifted it over their shoulders. A truck drove up and they tossed the rug and body inside.

Yaseen felt some of the anger leave him. In a few days, he would have the operation running smoothly once more. Gronsky's betrayal had slowed the outcome but not negated it.

He walked toward the mosque, intending to spend some time praying to Allah for the guidance and divine help he would need. He would spend his time in prayer, remembering all of the brave Palestinians who had fallen while trying to reclaim their homes from the hated Israelis. And he would ask for intervention on behalf of his plan to rid the Jews of their American benefactors.

His cell phone rang before he reached the mosque. He stopped outside the entrance, watching in disgust as Western women donned traditional clothing so they might enter. The mosque was sacred, but it had been turned into a tourist attraction.

"Hello," he said.

"Fortune be with you, my master."

"And you, Ahmed," Yaseen said.

Ahmed Achmed was one of Yaseen's warriors. Achmed's

parents were killed during the Israeli invasion of Lebanon in
1982, and Yaseen had taken Achmed and his brothers into his
home. But then Achmed's brothers and Yaseen's two sons had
died on October 1, 1985, during Operation Wooden Leg when
the Israeli Air Force had dropped bombs from F-15s supplied by
the Americans. Through the anguish and rage of that day, Yaseen
had realized that the Americans would have to be negated in
some way before the Israelis could be routed.

"There is a problem," Achmed said.

>> **CHINHAE, REPUBLIC OF KOREA**
>> **DOWNTOWN**
>> **2029 HOURS**

Shel watched the car carrying Hester and the three unidentified
South Korean males pull into an alley. He patted Max on the
head as he drove by the alley and saw the car's brake lights flare.

"I think we're gonna see some action tonight, big guy," Shel
said softly. "What do you think?"

Seated in the passenger seat, Max loosed an eager whine.
The Labrador's shoulder muscles jerked in anticipation.

Shel tapped his ear-throat transmitter. "Subject has pulled
into an alley, Five. Do you have him?"

"Affirmative," Estrella called back immediately.

"I've driven past him. How do you want to handle it,
Leader?"

"I want ID on the people the subject's meeting with," Will
replied. "If we get a positive on the ID, something we can work
with, I want to shake our guy down."

Shel smiled happily. Military work wasn't a spectator sport.
Not the way he was used to handling it.

"Five, can you acquire clear video?"

"Negative, Leader. I can keep track of the subject, the vehi-cle, and the people, but I can't get clear vid for ID."

"If we're going to push this, Leader," Shel said, "we're going to have to have clear video." Anticipating what was about to come, he pulled over into an alley three blocks from where the car containing Hester had pulled over. "I've got a digicam relay."

Will hesitated only a moment. "Okay. Do it, Three. We'll take up support positions."

Shel levered himself out of the small car. Max held back, awaiting orders, but the animal whined plaintively. Shel slapped his thigh. Instantly, Max erupted from the car and took his posi-tion at Shel's side. The dog's thick nails scraped slightly against the concrete.

Moving to the rear of the car, Shel popped the hatchback, opened the equipment bag there, and took out the digicam head-set. The setup was a skeletal affair, a headband with Velcro fas-teners accompanied by another strap that went over the top of his head. Two lightweight lenses ran along his head and pointed forward, capturing everything he looked at. He ran the wire down inside his shirt and clipped the small battery unit to his belt.

"Five, do you have connect?" he asked.

"Confirm connect," Estrella said.

"Tracking?" Shel moved his head around.

"Confirm tracking."

Reaching into the bag again, Shel took out a matte black Mark 23 Mod 0 SOCOM .45-caliber semiautomatic pistol that matched the one already leathered under his left arm. In the field, Shel habitually carried two of the pistols. That was one of the reasons he liked Maggie Foley even though she wasn't military. She understood firepower. He dropped extra magazines into his jacket pockets.

"Preparing for war, Three?" Estrella asked.

"I always prepare for war," Shel responded.

"We want to keep this on the QT," Will said.

"Understood." Shel closed the hatchback. "I just want to make sure I can make it back if this turns ugly."

Shel loped toward the back of the alley, Max was a silent shadow at his side.

>> **DIMASHQ ASH-SHAM, SYRIA**
>> **1430 HOURS**

"What problem?" Yaseen demanded.

On the cell phone from Chinhae, Ahmed Achmed reported, "Virgil Hester has drawn the attention of the Naval Criminal Investigative Service. A team from the U.S. is here in Chinhae. They are following him now."

Yaseen thought furiously. Virgil Hester had been an important part of his operation in South Korea at one time. That importance, however, was over. Yaseen had hated dealing with the man. Though he wasn't a Westerner, he was Western in his thinking.

"Why are they following him?" Yaseen asked.

"I do not know. I have made arrangements with one of the local South Korean gangs to take Hester to a point where I can . . . eliminate the problem if you wish."

Yaseen thought only for a moment. "I do not want Hester to talk to the investigative team. He will not be able to maintain our secrets. Wait to see if you have a chance to take care of it in a less public manner. But if you do not, take him out. But you must not be apprehended."

"What about the Navy team?"

"If they get in your way, kill them."

"I understand, master."

"Thank you, Achmed. You have always been loyal to our cause. I will pray for you."

"Thank you, master."

Yaseen folded his phone and put it away. Then he went into the mosque to pray for the deaths of his enemies and anyone who would betray him.

>> CHINHAE, REPUBLIC OF KOREA
>> NCIS SURVEILLANCE VAN
>> 2034 HOURS

Estrella kept surveillance through the sat link. The ambient light in the alley was just enough to disallow night-vision and thermographic display. She was stuck with a grainy transmission that looked only a little superior to a black-and-white vid.

Shel's digicam, on the other hand, showed clear video of the area. Except that Shel was on the move and constantly swung his head around to view his surroundings.

Despite years of maintaining watch over a digicam feed, Estrella still teetered on the brink of nausea when she watched the movement. She'd gotten the same feeling from some of the old flat-screen console games she'd played with Julian throughout high school and during the early years of their marriage.

Thinking about Julian, about how things had been, brought up a lot of pain. It had been five years since his death and the betrayal still hurt.

Stay away from the past, Estrella told herself. *There's nothing for you there.* She concentrated on her task, but the St. Christopher medallion she wore around her neck lay heavy against her chest. It was a constant reminder that Julian was gone. She only hoped that the day she gave it to Nicky some of that weight would be gone.

❀ ❀ ❀

Ahmed Achmed put away his cell phone and knelt at the window. He looked out at the alley below where the South Korean gang members had pulled in with Hester moments before, as planned. Achmed had never trusted Hester and had sometimes monitored his activities. However, he hadn't been able to watch the man's every move.

Something had happened to draw the attention of the NCIS.

Strong anticipation filled Achmed. He owed his life to Qadir Yaseen. In 1985, his master had pulled him from the burning rubble of a building that had been bombed by the Israelis. His master's two sons had been killed in those blasts. Neither of them was over ten years old. Achmed's own brothers had died that day as well.

Since that time, his master had taken a strong interest in Achmed, training and guiding him, and praying personally with and for him. Achmed would have gladly laid down his life for his master.

He knew his master trusted him. Achmed was the primary contact Yaseen kept in Chinhae. Burning with a desire for vengeance that he was certain was eclipsed only by that of his master, Achmed hated everything the Western world stood for, and, most of all, he hated the way they supported the Israelis.

Soon, though, the Great Satans would be too wrapped up in their own problems to help the Israelis. Israel would fall then, because the Arab states would finally unite, knowing they had nothing to fear from the Americans. The rest of the world would support the Arab states. They would have to. The Middle East had most of the oil in the world, and the usage was outpacing production these days. Oil-driven countries could do nothing but curry favor with a united Arab world.

And they would. All they needed was an excuse to take a stand against the United States so they would be first in line to accept oil shipments.

Achmed adjusted the handkerchief he wore on the wound on his left hand. The old woman had surprised him. She'd had more fight in her than the old man.

Glancing over his shoulder, he looked at the dead bodies of the old man and woman lying on the bloodstained sheets. He'd felt no particular animosity against them, but they had stood between him and his divinely given goal. He'd had to kill them. It hadn't been personal.

Still, after the old woman had wounded him, he'd been only too glad to kill her.

He shouldered the heavy Barrett sniper rifle again. Even before he'd infiltrated the ranks of the Great Satan's Navy, Achmed had been familiar with the rifle. The weapon was one of the best Achmed had ever used.

Peering through the sniperscope, he searched for Hester. Deliberately, he settled the crosshairs over Hester's head.

>> **2036 HOURS**

Will took point once he and Frank left the car on the street a block and a half from the alley where Hester and his group had turned in. Will's impulse was to draw his sidearm and keep it ready. He couldn't do that, though. The team was already operating on Republic of Korea territory without sanction. The Rules of Engagement regarding criminal activity on the mainland outside of areas designated as sovereign by the U.S. Navy stated that they weren't supposed to do anything without consulting their military police counterpart in the ROK.

Will was worried now. He'd planned on following Hester and engaging him back on the ship, making the arrest clearly the domain of the U.S. Navy without involvement from local law enforcement.

Frank stayed behind him, both of them hugging the building wall as they neared the mouth of the alley. Will stopped at the corner. He strained his ears, listening to angry voices.

"Didn't know the subject knew so much Korean," Frank whispered.

"Four," Will said, "do you have audio?"

"Yes," Maggie replied. She knew seven different languages. Korean was one of them. "They're warning the subject, telling him if he continues interfering with the business they've set up, they're going to kill him."

Will they kill Hester now, or kill him later? Will wondered. His stomach knotted.

"I'm in position," Shel called over the radio. "Five, you should have video lock on target."

"Five has video lock."

"Can you ID any of the others?" Will asked.

>> 2039 HOURS

Estrella dialed in the focus of the digicam Shel wore. She tapped the keyboard, saving off image after image that she captured. Another tap of the keyboard sent the saved images winging toward the U.S. Navy's intelligence database. Shel's gaze kept roving, checking out the men as well as the alley.

"Three," Estrella said, "I need focused shots. Keep your head still." Fear writhed within her too, because at the moment she was the extra eyes that Shel, Will, and Frank needed. She had to watch over them all.

"Copy," Shel replied. The camera locked into position.

All three of the men with Lance Corporal Hester looked Korean. They wore dark clothing, looking almost like

American gangbangers with bright red do-rags, piercings, and tattoos.

She adjusted the digicam's magnification, tightening on Hester. The Marine was back up against the alley wall. One of the Koreans had a big pistol shoved into his face. Obviously in fear for his life, Hester pleaded, his voice coming in a rapid rush of Korean.

"They're gonna kill him," Shel said. "If we want him alive, we have to move."

"They're not going to kill him," Maggie said. "They're only threatening him."

Without warning, Lance Corporal Hester's head exploded.

12

>> CHINHAE, REPUBLIC OF KOREA
>> DOWNTOWN
>> 2040 HOURS

"They shot him!" Shel said. He cursed. Although he was certain he'd never have liked a guy like Lance Corporal Virgil Hester if they had gotten the chance to meet, he liked the idea of idly standing by while a fellow Marine was gunned down in cold blood—even if he was a disgrace to the Corps—even less.

Almost decapitated, Hester's body slumped back against the alley wall, then slid bonelessly to the ground.

Shel reached into his jacket and under his arm for the Mark 23s, pulling both pistols free. He flicked the safeties off with his thumbs.

"He's down!" Shel said, taking advantage of the cover provided at the corner of the alley. "He's dead, Leader! How do you want to handle this?"

Max braced at Shel's knee, already on alert, his ears pricked and his attention divided between his fellow warrior and the alley.

"Shut them down," Will said.

Shel took a deep breath, reminded himself he wasn't wearing Kevlar, and lifted the pistols to his shoulders. He rolled the hammers back with his thumbs.

"They're loading into their car," Maggie said.

The sound of the engine turning over filled the alley, followed almost immediately by the thunder of the exhaust.

"Stay," Shel ordered Max, knowing the dog would be at risk when facing a speeding car. He dropped the pistols forward, taking aim at the center of the car's grill.

The car burned rubber as it accelerated toward Shel.

Grinning slightly, remembering the Old West gunfight stories his daddy used to tell him while they worked the cattle on their ranch, Shel squeezed off rounds with methodical deliberation.

The bullets punched through the grill, shredding metal and throwing sparks.

>> 2041 HOURS

Heart hammering in her temples, Estrella tapped the keyboard. Four of the monitors carried Shel's point of view, and she saw the car fishtailing to a halt in the alley. Shadows on the inside of the windshield glass jerked into action. The driver slammed the transmission into reverse and sped back toward the alley exit at the other end.

Maggie stood behind her. "Did you get the shooting on tape?" she inquired urgently.

"Yes, everything's being recorded."

"Play it back a minute."

Estrella hit a button, and one of the monitors scrolled backward through the digital recording of the shooting. Estrella made herself watch as Lance Corporal Hester's head flew back together and he stared once more at the Korean man who held him at gunpoint. "What did you see?" she asked Maggie.

"I don't know. Maybe nothing. Just play it forward, half speed."

Not knowing exactly what she was looking for, Estrella allowed the recording to proceed again in slow motion. She watched as Hester stared at his captor. Then his head jerked violently to the left and down, toward the camera and Shel, tilting down hard as if jerked by a string.

Abruptly she saw what Maggie had seen.

She played the segment back again. Hester's head jerked to the side and down again. *To the side!* If he'd been shot from in front, his head would have jerked backward.

"Did you see that?" she asked.

"Yeah," Maggie said, staring at the monitor. "And there's something else. That pistol the guy is holding in front of Hester's face is a 9 mm. It's not big enough to do that kind of damage."

Someone else had fired the bullet that had killed the Marine. And the person who had pulled the trigger hadn't been in the alley.

Where had the shooter been?

>> **2042 HOURS**

"They're retreating!" Shel yelled in warning. Gray-white smoke roiled from the car's hood; he'd holed the radiator. He adjusted his aim and sighted on the tires, hoping to take them out.

The car sped backward, weaving from side to side and slamming against trash cans and Dumpsters. Shel's bullets left a pattern of sparks just inches from where the tires had been.

The man in the passenger seat leaned out and opened fire with an assault rifle. Bullets sprayed the alley wall, chopping close to Shel.

"They didn't kill Hester," Estrella said. "You've got a sniper!"

Shel looked across the street and spotted the tall buildings there, then dodged back behind the corner of the building just as the line of bullets from the assault rifle pumped through the space where he'd been standing. He pressed the magazine releases on both his pistols, dropped the empty magazines, then shoved full ones into place. Tripping the slide releases to strip the first rounds off the new magazines and ready the weapons, he peered around the corner.

A large-caliber bullet splintered brick only a few inches above his head. Definitely not one of the 5.56 mm rounds from the AK-47 the man in the car had opened up with.

Ducking back, Shel said, "Three confirms the sniper. Where is he?"

>> 2042 HOURS

Will stepped out into the alley in a modified Weaver's stance and took aim on the speeding car's rear tires. He fired steadily, listening as Estrella and Shel informed them that a sniper was on the scene.

Shadows bobbed on the other side of the car's back windshield. The man in the rear seat shoved his pistol out the window and started squeezing off rounds as fast as he could.

The right rear tire blew. Hunks of rubber sheared off and went spinning across the alley. Instantly, the car became even harder to control. It slammed into the alley wall, threw up a cloud of sparks, and grated along the brick.

As the car bore down on Will, he set himself to leap out of its path. Just as he was about to move, something hit him a glancing blow in the left side and knocked the wind from his lungs. He stared at the car as it bore down on him, knowing he couldn't escape getting run over.

✮ ✮ ✮

>> 2042 HOURS

Maggie jumped out of the rear of the van and looked hard across the street. She thought she spotted a brief bit of color that winked into existence for just a second on the third floor of an apartment building. Then she saw it again. If she hadn't been looking for it, knowing that it had to exist, she probably wouldn't have noticed it.

Flash hider, she thought. The special device concealed a sniper weapon's muzzle flash from enemy soldiers. An instant later she was in motion. The loud *blam!* of the sniper rifle rolled out over the street.

"I've spotted the sniper's position," Maggie called over the headset. "The building due south of the alley. Three stories tall. Sniper's in the fourth window from the left on the third floor."

She waited till a car passed, saw enough of a gap before the next one, and sprinted across. She drew her twin Berettas and held them at her sides, tucked in close to her thighs so they wouldn't immediately be seen. Part of her mind was already dealing with the problems facing the team.

The ROK authorities wouldn't be happy with the fact that an NCIS team was operating unsanctioned on their turf. The director wouldn't be happy that they'd gone ballistic on what should have been an easy case. And none of them were safe at the moment. Was there only one sniper? Or were there more?

"Will's hit!" Estrella yelled.

Blood freezing in her veins, Maggie halted on the other side of the street and peered toward the alley where Will and Frank were. As she watched in helpless horror, Will tried in vain to move from the path of the speeding car.

✷ ✷ ✷

>> **2042 HOURS**

With the car bearing down on him fast, Will was hit from the side again. The breath left his lungs in a rush, and he was knocked from his feet.

Had the car hit him?

Then he realized Frank had thrown his arms around him and driven them both clear of the alley. The chief landed on top of him on the other side of the alley.

Will's head struck the pavement, and for an instant he saw stars. His breath remained locked tight in his lungs. Searing pain filled his left side and warm blood trickled down his skin.

He rolled over onto his side as the car rocketed out into traffic and collided with two other cars. The bumpers locked, and for a moment Will thought the car might be stuck. He lifted his Springfield XD-40, actually surprised he'd maintained his grip on the pistol.

The car fought free of the other vehicles and shot forward. Without warning, the driver suddenly lurched to the side. The car went out of control and ran up onto the sidewalk, coming to a sudden stop against a building wall.

The sniper, Will realized.

Three men, including the wounded driver, pushed the car doors open and fled. One of them managed four steps before he was hammered to the street by the sniper's unerring aim. Another went down in the space of a drawn breath as he tried to duck into the nearby alley.

The remaining man ran, weaving between vehicles that had come to a halt behind the wrecked car. Blocked by the stalled traffic, the man leaped to the top of a car, then jerked violently sideways as a bullet caught him and knocked him to the ground. He disappeared in the traffic, but Will was certain the man wouldn't be getting up again.

Aware that the sniper could pick any second to complete the job he'd started on him, Will pushed himself to his feet. He glanced down at his side and saw that blood had soaked through his shirt. Dizziness spun through his head and his knees almost turned to water.

"You're hit," Frank said, getting to his feet. A scrape on his chin bled.

"Get to cover," Will said, staring over Frank's shoulder at the building where the sniper was staging the attack. He backed up, feeling behind him with his left hand, keeping the XD-40 raised before him. He squinted and struggled to cling to his fading senses. He was going into shock.

Frank took off his own loud-colored shirt. "I'm going to make a compress."

Will hardly noticed the chief's ministrations. His eyes roved the building across the street. He knew Maggie was already on her way there.

Frank knelt and pressed his balled-up shirt against Will's side.

A wave of throbbing, insistent pain tore through his side. Blackness ate at the edges of his vision. His head swam, and for a moment, he thought he was going to fall.

"Through and through," Frank said. "Doesn't look like the bullet hit anything vital. You're lucky."

Will didn't feel lucky.

"If that .50-cal round had hit your pelvis, you'd be dead or crippled." Frank shifted the pressure.

Stuttering sirens sounded across town.

"Five, have you notified the locals we're on the scene?"

"Affirmative, Leader. They're not happy about it."

Thinking that the sniper was getting away or turning his attentions to Maggie or Shel, Will pushed out of the shadows and tried to disengage from Frank's ministrations. "Come on."

"You're bleeding too badly to go anywhere," Frank

growled. "If I don't slow this down, you could bleed out here in the next few minutes."

"It's not that bad. I can still move." Will didn't want his team moving into danger without him.

"It's bad enough." Stubbornly, Frank kept the compress in place.

Will didn't have the strength to fight him.

>> 2049 HOURS

Maggie surveyed the three-story apartment building in front of her. It was old and showed signs of disrepair. There was only one door on this side of the building.

"Five," Maggie said in a steady voice as she adjusted the micro digicam on her shoulder, "do you have video?"

"Confirm video," Estrella answered. "The ROK military police have asked us to stand down."

Maggie leathered one of her Berettas and took out a small Mini Maglite. Holding the flashlight so it pointed down from the bottom of her fist, she crossed her wrists, placing her gun hand on top. She kept the light switched off.

"What's their ETA?" Maggie asked.

"They didn't say."

Too long, Maggie thought. *That's for sure.* "The sniper might get away. I'm going in."

Maggie abruptly opened the door and stepped through it into a dimly lit hallway. A handful of the inside doors were open. Fearful faces peered out.

"Go back inside your homes," Maggie said in Korean. Most of the doors closed, but a few remained open a crack. She kept moving forward, then spotted the stairs to her right.

"Four," Shel called over the headset.

"Copy," Maggie said.

"I'm at the west end of the building. Opposite you. Coming through the door."

"Come ahead." Maggie kept the pistol braced. "Any other ways out?"

"None that I saw."

Between Shel and her, they had the apartment building boxed.

At the other end of the hallway, Shel eased the door open and let Max inside. The Lab entered cautiously and quickly scouted the territory. Then the big Marine stepped inside with pistols in both fists. "I've got stairs here."

"Me too," Maggie said.

Shel gave Max the command to go up. The dog took to the steps immediately with the man one step behind.

Heart pounding, her breath short and her nostrils filled with the scents of close-packed humanity—sweat and urine and cooking—Maggie went up the stairs on her side of the building. She and Shel stayed in contact as they moved onto opposite ends of the second floor.

On the third floor, a skinny old Korean man in a sleeveless T-shirt and black pants stepped into the hallway. He pointed at the door across the hall. "There," he whispered in English. "There. Big man. Big gun." He retreated back inside his apartment and closed the door.

Maggie put her ear to the door the old man had pointed to and listened. There was no sound.

Shel drove a foot into the door, knocking it off its hinges. Max started in. Something thudded to the floor inside the room.

Moving quickly, Shel yelled, "Max, come!" and threw himself at Maggie, catching her, shielding her with his body, and propelling them both down the hallway.

The Labrador skidded on his haunches and ran out of the room.

A tremendous explosion drowned out Shel's explanation. Fire and smoke belched out of the room.

Instantly Shel was on his feet, pistols pointed before him. Max was at his side. Rolling to her feet, trying to get back the breath Shel's unexpected lunge had ripped from her, Maggie followed.

"Are you all right?" Shel called back.

"I'm okay," Maggie said. "What was that?"

"Sniper booby-trapped the door."

Maggie followed Shel into the room. The grenade's explosion had reduced the disparate living-room furnishings to kindling. Charring scored the walls. Chunks of plaster had fallen from the ceiling, leaving beams exposed. Stepping to Shel's right to get her own field of fire, she directed her flashlight around the room. The acrid scent of the explosion filled her nose and wrenched a cough from her throat.

Shel went to the side and covered the doorway. "Kitchen. Clear."

Maggie stepped to the doorway on her right and shone her light inside. The beam touched porcelain and a mirror. Her finger slid over the pistol trigger and she almost shot her own image.

"Bathroom," she croaked. "Clear."

Shel took the next door. "Bedroom." He paused for a moment as Maggie stepped in behind him. They were all out of rooms. "Clear." He cursed. "Got away from us."

An old man and woman lay in the small bed in the center of the room. Blood stained the sheets. The old man had a look of surprise on his face. The old woman had her arms wrapped around her head. Judging from the wounds on the old woman's arms, whoever killed her had shot through her arms.

It hurt Maggie to look at the old man and woman, their lives apparently taken with almost casual ease.

"The sniper killed them so he could set up in here," Shel said. "Let's hope he left something we can use."

Holstering her weapon, Maggie said, "We've got to make sure the ROK military police secure the bodies of those men who picked Hester up. We'll cross-reference them with everything we find in this room."

Shel looked at her, understanding then. "One of them was working with the sniper. That's the only way this guy could have known Hester was going to be in that alley." He shook his head. "And if one of them was working with him, the sniper sure didn't believe in team loyalty. He killed the Koreans who picked Hester up, too."

Maggie nodded. But it didn't make sense. Why would someone murder two innocent people just to kill a small-time, black-market operator? And why did the sniper kill whoever he'd been working with?

13

SCENE ⋆ NCIS ⋆ CRIME SCENE

NAVAL CRIMINAL INVESTIGATIVE SERVICE

>> CHINHAE, REPUBLIC OF KOREA
>> DOWNTOWN
>> 2116 HOURS

Whirling blue lights slashed across the ROK military police captain's face as he disembarked from his cruiser. His khaki uniform showed care and attention and sharp creases. His black boots looked freshly polished. He was about forty, Will guessed, but he had tired eyes, worn and weary from having seen too much.

As he surveyed the crime scene, the captain frowned.

"Not a happy guy," Maggie said.

"No," Will agreed. He didn't blame the man. He wouldn't have been happy either. His knees buckled a little and he caught himself, leaning against one of the military jeeps that had arrived to back up the NCIS team. Commander Greg Yardley, commander of the American naval base in Chinhae, had wasted no time in responding to Will's call for help.

Maggie eyed Will. "You need to get to the hospital."

"Once I see how we're going to handle the crime scene."

After a few minutes, the ROK captain took a slimline PDA from his shirt pocket and consulted it briefly. Then he looked in Will's direction. "Commander Coburn."

Gathering his strength, Will stepped forward.

"I am Captain Minjin Pak."

"I'd like permission to work the crime scene."

The captain regarded Will with flat black eyes. He pursed his lips and folded his hands behind him. "You are wounded, Commander Coburn."

"My team will work the crime scene," Will amended.

"Your people are not the only ones who know how to investigate a murder," Pak said.

"The Marine who was killed was an American."

"And I have five dead Koreans, Commander." Pak looked at the corpse slumped in the alley. "You should have gone through my office, Commander Coburn. Not once did you follow chain of command."

"You're right, and I apologize for that, but I didn't plan on trying to take our man down in the city," Will said. "We originally wanted to make the arrest aboard ship after we gathered enough evidence."

"Someone executed him," Pak said. "And someone betrayed him. Otherwise the sniper across the street would never have known where to set up."

"That's our assessment as well." Will respected how quickly the ROK captain's mind worked.

"Do you know which of the three men was driving?"

"No."

"Pity."

"Why do you say that?"

"Their boss requires utmost loyalty. It would be interesting to know who betrayed him."

"Let us work this scene," Will said. "We can tell you who was behind the wheel of that car. If that can gain you leverage you can use, I can guarantee it will be in your hands."

Turning, Pak glanced at the three bodies still sprawled in the street. "Their boss has been a thorn in my side for a long time. Knowing who betrayed him might prove beneficial." He looked back at Will. "Chain of command on this investigation will be followed from this point on."

"Absolutely," Will answered.

"Then your team may handle the investigation. Who is your second?"

"Special Agent Maggie Foley." Will waved her over and quickly made introductions.

Maggie stuck out her hand and Pak shook it.

Pak turned to Will. "You will return to base and have that wound tended."

Will nodded. He felt light-headed and spots swam in his vision. With Maggie's help, Will pulled himself into the passenger seat of the jeep. As the driver wheeled the vehicle around, the whirling blue lights of the ROK police cars splintered against the jeep's windshield.

Will closed his eyes.

>> DOWNTOWN CHINHAE
>> ALLEY CRIME SCENE
>> 2153 HOURS

"You are young, Ms. Foley."

Maggie glanced at the ROK captain. "But I'm good at my job, Captain Pak. Otherwise the Navy wouldn't have stationed me here."

Pak nodded. "I meant no disrespect. It was only an observation that the job you have chosen is filled with terrible things. I prefer not to deal with violence."

"So do I." Maggie pointed to the dead men in the street. "You told the commander you knew these men's boss. Can you identify them?"

"Certainly." Pak led the way to the three dead men. Without moving them, he identified each in turn.

Maggie used a digicam to capture images of the dead men. The digital pictures would add to the footage Estrella had captured on her surveillance cameras before the attack. "Who do they work for?" she asked.

"Sunghee Han," Pak told her. "He is a bad man, Ms. Foley. A killer."

"Do you think he's behind this?"

"No. When Han kills someone, he does not do it so publicly. Whoever did this was sending a message."

Maggie surveyed the bodies, her gaze stopping on Lance Corporal Hester's body in the alley. "A message to Han?"

"Possibly. Or else a message to whomever the lance corporal was working for."

Maggie knew the man was fishing for answers, wanting to know if the additional wrinkle was something that came from Chinhae or if it was a problem that came from outside his jurisdiction. "As far as we know, Hester was working alone."

"You may have to rethink that," Pak said. "From the looks of the wounds in these three men, and in Hester, they were killed by a large-caliber rifle. From the size of the wounds and the damage, my estimation is that the rifle was at least a .50-caliber weapon."

Maggie looked at the ROK captain. "What are you saying?"

"The only .50-caliber sniper rifles I've seen in Chinhae, Ms. Foley, belong to the American military," Pak said quietly. "I don't think the answer to this problem is going to be found within my city. More than likely, it is to be found inside the American naval base."

❀ ❀ ❀

>> CHINHAE AMERICAN NAVAL BASE HOSPITAL
>> 2215 HOURS

"You're a lucky man, Commander Coburn."

Lying on the emergency-room bed, Will didn't feel like a lucky man. Thankfully the local anesthetic the doctor had injected was starting to take hold. The pain was slowly ebbing away.

The doctor, a young man with a military haircut and an ingratiating smile, tapped a button on the X-ray unit beside the bed. Instantly, a skeletal representation of Coburn, Commander William Travis sprang to life on the wall.

"The round missed the pelvic girdle, the intestines, and the kidneys. Someone was watching over you." The doctor smiled. "You should say an extra prayer before you go to bed tonight."

Will said nothing. In his recent experience, praying didn't help with much. The divorce papers lying on his desk back at Lejeune were proof of that.

"You're going to be sore," the young man went on, "but a few days of rest and some rehab to get the stomach muscles back in shape and you're going to be fine."

"Thanks," Will mumbled.

"I'm going to have to staple that wound together, though," the doctor continued. "It's going to take a while. If you want, I can put you out."

"No. My team is out in the field. I want to be alert if they need me."

"All right then." The doctor switched the X-ray unit off. "Give me a couple minutes and we'll get to it."

"Sure."

The doctor left the room.

Will tried to think about what his team must be doing, how the investigation must be progressing at the crime scene. But his thoughts kept drifting to his family, to the divorce papers waiting for him back home. He needed something to numb his mind.

>> DOWNTOWN CHINHAE
>> ALLEY CRIME SCENE
>> 2218 HOURS

A medical examiner from the Chinhae American Naval Base arrived at 10:18 p.m., looked at Lance Corporal Virgil Hester's headless body, and declared him legally dead one second later. Until such a declaration was officially made, Maggie hadn't allowed anyone to enter the crime-scene area.

As always in an investigation, the ME's office took possession of the murder victim. The scene itself was left to the CSIs.

Two Naval paramedics bundled the dead man into a body bag and carried him from the alley.

Captain Pak started to follow Maggie and Frank onto the crime scene.

Maggie turned on the ROK police captain abruptly, drawing him up short. Still, he was as graceful as a dancer and stopped himself easily.

"Sorry, Captain," Maggie said. "I don't mean to offend you, but I need you to stay back."

Pak lifted an inquisitive eyebrow.

"Ever hear of Locard's Exchange Principle?" Maggie asked him.

"No."

"Basically, it states that anyone who enters a crime scene leaves something at the scene and takes something away. Because it is a public place for humans as well as animals, processing this scene will be difficult enough without adding to it."

"But the murder is simple," Pak said. "A sniper shot these men from across the street. What can you hope to find here?"

"I don't *hope* to find anything," Maggie replied. "I'm going to look for what there is."

"I would have thought you would begin in the apartment building across the street. That would seem to offer the best chance of identifying the sniper."

"That's why I sent Gunney McHenry and Petty Officer Montoya there. They'll process that scene."

Pak nodded. "Very well. You will let me know what you find out."

"Yes." Maggie pulled on a pair of disposable surgical gloves from her back pocket, then picked up the equipment bag and looked at Frank. "Ready?"

"Yeah." Worry showed in Frank's eyes.

Maggie had to curb her own anxiety over Will's condition. "He's going to be all right."

"I know," Frank said. "It's just . . . he's going through a lot right now."

"I know." Maggie hesitated. "I didn't mean to, but I saw the divorce papers on Will's desk. He left them out."

"Don't talk to him about it," Frank suggested. "If he wants to talk, he will."

Maggie nodded, then looked at the blood-smeared alley wall. "Let's do this, Frank. This crime scene is talking. We just have to listen." She led the way into the alley.

>> DOWNTOWN CHINHAE
>> APARTMENT BUILDING CRIME SCENE
>> 2220 HOURS

In the quiet darkness of the apartment, Estrella regarded the dead couple lying on the twisted bloody sheets. The scene-investigation kit she held in one hand felt like the only thing anchoring her to the ground.

She had trouble distancing herself from the deaths. The men on the street, even Lance Corporal Hester, had been bad, but those deaths didn't get past her defenses. This old couple did. The apartment building and the quiet, scared people living here reminded Estrella too much of the Chicago neighborhood where she'd grown up and returned to after Julian had . . . died. She'd never intended to raise Dominic there. It hadn't been her plan or Julian's. They'd wanted out, had sacrificed everything to get out.

Shel placed the bigger bag on the floor just outside the door of the apartment. He told Max to guard, and the Labrador obediently sat and surveyed the hallway. Several local residents stood in the hall or peeked out doors. Captain Pak's men kept them away from the door.

"You okay?" the big Marine asked softly. His broad face held concern.

Estrella took a deep breath through her open mouth. When she was working around the dead, she tried not to breathe in through her nose. Too much of the scent of blood and death seemed to clog in her nostrils. "Yes," she replied. "It's just sad."

"Yeah, well, let's do what we're good at and catch the creep who did this."

Estrella lowered her kit to the floor and took out a sample case.

"Lotta blood," Shel commented. He tore open a package of surgical gloves as he gazed around the bedroom.

Estrella nodded. "Do we know when these people were last seen?"

"I don't speak Korean. If anyone out in the hall can say anything except 'Go home, American dog,' I don't know about it."

Estrella smiled a little. "Maybe they were talking to Max."

Shel shook his head. "You know, *chica,* I really didn't get that impression."

Without another word, they set to work.

 SCENE ✶ **NCIS** ✶ **CRIME SCEN**
NAVAL CRIMINAL INVESTIGATIVE SERVICE

>> CHINHAE, REPUBLIC OF KOREA
>> ALLEY CRIME SCENE
>> 0154 HOURS

Maggie returned to the equipment pack on the other side of the military-police barricade, satisfied that she'd canvassed the alley as well as she could.

Pak was waiting for her. "You told me you could identify the driver," he reminded her.

"Sure. Come with me." Maggie walked to the wrecked car sticking out of the building front. She pointed to a hole in the top of the car; it was almost disguised by the wrinkled mess caused by the accident. "The sniper's bullet went through there and hit the driver, causing the car to go out of control." She indicated the blood on the steering wheel, the air bag, and the instrument panel. "The bullet didn't kill the driver. He was able to get out and run."

"How can you be sure?" Pak asked.

"Because one of the bodies has two bullets in it."

"I see," Pak said. "That makes identification of the driver much easier."

"Yes," Maggie agreed. "He was the only guy shot twice." She approached the body closest to the wrecked car.

Pak gestured toward the blood inside the car. "I'd thought the blood was from the wreck," he said.

"Impact spatter would be thicker. The blood on the air bag came from an expirated wound—blood blown out through the nose or mouth, or forced into motion by air." Maggie knelt by the covered body at her feet and pulled back the sheet to reveal the gash on the side of the young man's face. "The bullet missed him, but the flying metal blasted free from the roof slashed his cheek." She hooked a gloved finger inside the dead man's mouth and tugged a little to show that the wound went all the way through. "What you have here is a communicating wound. One that goes all the way through an organ or tissue mass." She took her finger from the dead man's mouth. "This man was driving. He was hit by the flying metal or bullet fragments, then breathed blood out onto the air bag during the impact." She pulled the sheet back over the body. "Do you know who he is?"

"Yes. His name is Junwan Mok."

"He works for Sunghee Han?"

"Yes."

"I want to talk to Han."

Pak hesitated. "You must realize that Sunghee Han is a dangerous man, Ms. Foley. In addition to operating a large black market here in Chinhae and Pusan, he has connections in China and Japan and many other interests. Clubs. Gambling. Prostitution. Some say he traffics in white slavery. These three men may tie Han to this investigation, but they don't give me any leverage over him. If we meet him, it will have to be on his terms."

Maggie folded her hands. "I want to talk to him," she stated. "Tonight if possible."

Pak showed her a thin smile. "You are a very determined young woman." He sighed. "Let me make a phone call."

>> DOWNTOWN CHINHAE
>> APARTMENT BUILDING CRIME SCENE
>> 0201 HOURS

"We caught a break," Shel said. "Take a look at this."

Estrella reached into her kit and took out a new pair of surgical gloves.

"The sniper cut himself," Shel continued. "We have a chance at DNA."

Interest flickered in Estrella's gaze. DNA was a major case breaker. "Where?" she asked, coming nearer.

"Turn out the light." Shel switched off the lamp beside the old couple in the bed.

Estrella turned out the bright shop light they'd brought in with them. The apartment building didn't come with many light fixtures, and the additional light was necessary.

"Here," Shel said, walking over to the windowsill. He'd covered the glass with black felt to block out the ambient light coming from the military-police lights brightening the street below. Gradually, their eyes adjusted to the cottony dark.

Shel handed Estrella a vapor mask and pulled one on himself. Both added luminescence-enhancing goggles. Then Shel picked up a spray bottle filled with a merbromin mixture and misted the windowsill. In seconds, pale bluish green smears appeared where the merbromin interacted with blood cells. Two smears marred the sill. Six fluorescent spatters about the size of elongated dimes tracked the wall, sending spidery shoots legging down toward the floor.

"It might not be the sniper's blood," Estrella said. "Maybe he got blood on his hands when he killed the old couple."

"The blood is the sniper's."

"What makes you so sure?"

Shel knew that as a trained crime-scene investigator, Estrella was versed in merbromin applications. She was also the team's cybernetic and communications whiz. But she wasn't trained in blood spatter. That was one of his chosen fields and the linchpin that had gotten him moved to Will's team.

"Do you see the spatters on the wall?" he asked.

"Yes."

"Fluid dynamics. The blood dripped from the shooter's hand or arm. I'm betting it was his hand." Shel squatted at the window, positioning himself like he believed the sniper had. Taking a small flashlight from his pocket, he switched it on.

Pale blue light, not bright enough to eradicate the chemical signature of the merbromin, played over the wall.

Shel pointed. "Each of these splatters is about the same size. Not a declining amount or significantly different." He shifted himself so that his right knee touched the floor and his left was braced against the wall. He held his hands up as if he were cradling a rifle. "The sniper held his hand here, getting ready for the shot, supporting the weight of the rifle. He probably didn't even notice he was bleeding at first."

Estrella moved closer to Shel. "If he's right-handed, the blood came from his left hand."

"He's right-handed," Shel stated.

"How do you know?"

Taking up the spray bottle, he misted the section of wall adjacent to the six elongated spatters. Immediately, a patch the size of his palm lit up. "The sniper had blood on his left knee. Either from the two people in that bed or from his bleeding hand. My guess is that he nicked a finger and blood ran down the edge of his palm."

Dropping down into a squat beside him, Estrella nodded. "Okay. I'll go along with that so far."

"If it was a .50-cal rifle like Pak thinks it was, then we're talking about a Barrett M82A1 or A2. That would make it a U.S. weapon, one of ours. Though packing a thirty-two-pound sniper rifle up and down these stairs would be no picnic. I'd choose a lighter weapon. But maybe our shooter wanted to make an impression. He also shot through an automobile, so maybe he wanted the penetration. A .308 cartridge would have done the trick, though."

"We'll need to show the witness pictures of rifles. Maybe we can get identification on the weapon."

Shel nodded. "If it was a .762 millimeter, then it could be U.S. or Russian, or one of the knockoff Chinese versions used in Korea. If it was U.S., I'd say it was an M25, which is the Navy designation for the Army XM25 that was developed for the Persian Gulf War. If it was Russian, my guess is that it was an SV-98."

"Why one of those weapons?"

"All of those rifles come with ten-round magazines. The Barrett is semiauto. Both the lighter weapons are bolt-action, but an expert could have gotten off the rounds as quickly as we were shot at as long as he didn't have to swap magazines or hand-feed rounds."

"So?"

"So the sniper fired seven times. Rapidly. He killed Hester. Chased me to cover. Shot Will. Hit the getaway-car driver twice. Then killed the other two men with one shot apiece. That's impressive. There was also no time to work reloads, either per round or popping shots from a five-round box."

Estrella wrapped her arms around herself and shuddered.

"What's wrong?"

"Nothing." She hesitated. "I just hadn't seen a man die like that before. Not while I was watching."

Shel felt guilty. He hadn't remembered that Estrella had served her time aboard ship in a tactical-support role. She wasn't used to being shot at. Or watching a man's head blow up from a sniper round.

"What I'm trying to say," he went on in a softer voice, "is that the guy we're looking for has got specialized skills. This isn't someone who just showed up for the job."

"And he might be an American serviceman."

Shel sighed. "If it's a .50-cal, then, yeah, I'd have to say he's wearing one of our uniforms or is connected to the Navy base in some fashion. You're not just gonna get a Barrett sniper rifle through ROK customs like it was a box of chocolates. The guy we're looking for is used to handling weapons. And he has access to them."

"The blood spatters," she reminded.

"Right. The uniform size of the spatters indicates a flow of blood, not just a few drops of someone else's. And see how they're smeared? Our sniper noticed he was bleeding pretty quickly. He wiped at the drops. If the blood had stayed on the wall long enough, the lines would have become smooth. He wiped them before they had a chance to start dripping."

"And that's significant because . . . ?"

"Because the guy caught his mistake almost at once and tried to wipe away the blood. He knew it was his. Not his victims'." Shel stood. "And if he was bleeding here at the window, I have to ask myself where he started bleeding."

>> **CHINHAE AMERICAN NAVAL BASE**
>> **0208 HOURS**

Achmed dialed the number for Yaseen's cell phone. His own phone was set not to retain dialed numbers in its memory. Such simple yet important details would avoid any trace of evidence pointing to Yaseen should this phone fall into the wrong hands.

Placing this call from a cell phone instead of one of the base phones meant that no record of it would exist in any base computer.

He heard only a single ring tone in his ear, and then his master was on the line.

"It is done," Achmed told him. "Hester is dead. But there is a complication."

"Tell me," Yaseen said.

"I was unable to take out the NCIS team following Hester. I hit only one of them before they discovered my location and I had to flee. And I was unable to recover Hester's body."

Silence. Then, "You understand the seriousness of this situation. An autopsy must not be performed on Hester. Where is the body now?"

Achmed glanced at his laptop, still connected to a secure page on the base's intranet. As always, he had accessed the intranet through multiple buffers; no one would ever know he had been there. "Base reports indicate that the body is here at the hospital morgue."

"Then do what you must."

"I understand." Achmed broke the connection. His night's work was not yet finished.

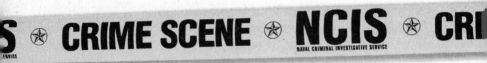

>> CHINHAE, REPUBLIC OF KOREA
>> APARTMENT BUILDING CRIME SCENE
>> 0211 HOURS

Shel circled the bed, distancing himself emotionally from the bloody sheets and the two dead bodies. But it was hard to forget that only hours ago they had been an old man and woman still getting through life together.

On the other side of the bed, Estrella kept her arms folded around her as she studied the couple. "The sniper forced his way into the room, then shot them both."

Shel nodded. They'd found the picklock marks that he'd missed earlier during the mad rush into the room. "First the old man. The sniper figures if he's going to get a fight from any quarter, it's going to be the man. So he puts two into the man's chest and one into his head. He probably died before he knew what hit him."

Estrella looked pale. "All right. So he's got the woman left. Only she's not still sleeping."

Shel nodded, never taking his eyes from the dead woman as he reconstructed the deaths in his mind. Crime-scene investigation centered around formulating a working hypothesis from the empirical evidence that could be gathered. He misted the wall over the bed with the merbromin solution. Bright dots proved that the spots clinging to the wall were blood.

"The old woman comes up out of bed and surprises the sniper." Shel directed the light over a group of waist-high, bluish green patterns that looked like mist on the wall beside the bed. "That's high-velocity blood spatter. Only goes a couple feet. She was close to the wall when she was hit. He shot her when she was out of bed." Tracking the angle of the mist, he found a bullet hole in the wall. He took an adhesive marker from his belt kit and tagged it to the wall.

"She got to her feet?" Estrella asked.

Studying the pattern of fluorescent droplets, Shel nodded. "She must have. That's the only way that blood and that bullet got there."

"Why does she get out of bed?"

"Because she's seen the sniper. Maybe she thinks she can still save her husband." Shel shined the light on the wall and used the spray again. A second mist pattern indicating a high-velocity blood spatter showed on the wall. This time it lay in the opposite direction. "The sniper shot her again. Here."

"What could she have been hoping to accomplish?" Estrella asked.

Shel leaned back over the old woman's corpse. "She couldn't shout for help. She was shot in the throat. Maybe that was one of the first shots. We'll find out when they do the autopsy and match the bullet in the wall. There could be tissue residue." He watched the old woman in his mind, moving quickly even though she was already choking on her own blood.

"Where was she trying to go? You can't get out of the bed-room that way."

Shel silently agreed. A chest of drawers and a mirror covered with photographs nearly filled one wall of the tiny room. "She was after a weapon." He noted the overturned sewing kit on the floor. He knelt and sorted through the thread, patterns, needles, thimbles, and bobbins. Satisfied, he sat back on his heels. "My granny did a lot of sewing when I was growing up. Quilts. Shirts. Pillowcases. Anybody in your family sew, amiga?"

"My mother," Estrella answered. "One of my older sisters. They tried to teach me, but I didn't have the knack. Both of them have made clothes for Dominic."

"See anything missing here?"

Estrella looked. Her understanding brought a slight sad smile to her face. "Scissors."

"Yeah. My granny used to say she'd take on a grizzly bear with her scissors because they were so sharp."

"When I was very young, my oldest sister showed very poor choice in men. She always liked the *cholos*."

"Bad boys, eh?" Shel grinned.

"Yeah. My sister was running around with this *cholo* and my mother got tired of it. She would come home tired from the packing house where she worked, all worried and frustrated about the job and about the home, and she would find this *cholo* lazing on her furniture, eating the food that she and my father worked hard to buy. One day, she had had enough. This man, he was supposed to be a bad man. But my mother took her scissors from her sewing basket beside her chair and chased the guy from our home. She cut his shirt to pieces before he made it through the door. He never came back."

A brief smile slighted Estrella's face, and Shel was glad to see it. Even there in the little room with death, they had to remember that they were human and that they had lives outside of the job.

If they didn't, the constant barrage of murder and violent cruelty they saw on a regular basis would destroy them.

Estrella's smile quickly faded. "The woman came at her killer with scissors. He probably held a hand out, moving on pure instinct. She cut him—his hand or his fingers."

Nodding, Shel said, "He shot her again." He played the blue light over the second patch of misted bluish green and found a second bullet hole. He marked the hole. "Only now he's upset. By this time he has to know he's hit her in the throat. But that's not going to stop him. He pushes her back onto the bed, then—while she covers up her head with her arms, knowing she's about to die—he empties the pistol into her."

"Shooting through her arms," Estrella whispered as she looked at the dead woman.

"Yeah." Carefully, Shel sorted through the bedding, moving it slowly, unable to avoid the blood that had soaked into the sheets.

Estrella joined him. She was the one who found the bloody scissors. She took her flashlight from her jacket pocket and played the beam over the scissors. When she opened them, she found a small piece of skin stuck in the drying blood.

Shel took an evidence bag from his vest pocket. With a pair of tweezers, he removed the piece of skin, dropped it into an envelope. Anything with fluid in it was stored in paper till it was dry. He wrote out the collection data and put the envelope in his kit.

Estrella put the scissors in an evidence bag, then into a large manila envelope and wrote out the information.

"Okay," Shel said, "Let's finish up. You want to run the vacuum cleaner to look for fibers or recover the bullets?"

"I'll vacuum," Estrella said.

E SCENE ✳ **NCIS** ✳ **CRIME SCEN**
NAVAL CRIMINAL INVESTIGATIVE SERVICE

>> CHINHAE, REPUBLIC OF KOREA
>> CHINHAE AMERICAN NAVAL BASE HOSPITAL
>> 0311 HOURS

Will came to in the darkness. He looked around, careful to move only his head and eyes. Any other movement set off a fresh wave of pain in his side. IV bags hung overhead, and a tube led to an IV shunt in the back of his hand. The surgical tape pulled at the skin around the needle. Machines against the nearby wall monitored his vital signs through sensors attached to his chest.

"Are you okay?" Frank's voice came unexpectedly. Will's friend stood and approached the bed. In the darkness, he was a big, shambling, bearlike shadow.

"I'll live." Even to his own ears, Will's response sounded disconnected and dry. "I told the doctor not to put me under."

"He didn't. You passed out."

"Why are you here? You should be at the crime scene."

"We finished up. Maggie sent me to check on you."

"Where's Maggie?"

"With Captain Pak."

"Pak?" Some of the details of the night had come loose in Will's head, and he couldn't quite place the name.

"The ROK captain working law enforcement here in Chinhae."

Will remembered. "What's she doing with Pak?"

"Following up on the three South Korean men who picked up Hester."

"Do we know who they are?"

"Pak does. He knows who they work for too. That's where Maggie went. To talk to the boss."

"She went by herself?"

"She went with Pak."

"You should have gone with her. She doesn't have the same experience with foreign countries that you do."

"I tried," Frank said. "She wouldn't have me. Pak wouldn't either. Seemed to think that an American male military figure, even one not in uniform, would be a problem with the guy they were going to see. Probably has authority issues." He paused. "I think Maggie knew I wanted to come check on you."

"I'm fine, Chief."

"Do you need anything?"

"No."

"Feel up to hearing what we've found?"

"Tell me," Will said.

"Mind if I turn on the light?"

"All right."

Frank turned on the bedside lamp, then put the tablet PC he'd brought in with him on the table. "We'll start in the alley."

✸ ✸ ✸

>> DOWNTOWN CHINHAE BAR
>> 0313 HOURS

A cloud of cigarette and reefer smoke filled the interior of the small bar and stung Maggie's eyes. The sour scents of beer and urine and human sweat seemed ingrained in the walls. Loud techno music slammed against her ears. A damp miasma hung in the air, clinging to her skin.

She made her way through the scattering of tables and chairs in the center of the bar. Booths lined two of the walls. Above the booths, television screens showed international news, sports, and porno movies. If the bar had a name, Maggie had missed it.

Scantily dressed young women entertained men in several of the booths. In the center of the room, gyrating to the booming music, a slim-hipped young woman danced suggestively, drawing catcalls from American and ROK servicemen and civilians.

"This is not a nice place for a young woman," Pak said.

"I gathered that," Maggie said. "I'm a trained observer, remember?"

Pak smiled slightly. "You may regret your wish to come here." He gestured toward a circular booth at the back of the bar. "There is Han."

The gang leader was in his late twenties. Despite the darkness in the bar, he wore sunglasses with smoky red lenses. Spiked hair, dyed blond and black and tipped with blue, stood up in wild disarray. He was lanky and slim, and his clothing fit him well. His jacket was cut to conceal the pistol Maggie was certain was lodged under his left armpit. A thin mustache colored his upper lip. His mouth seemed skewed into a permanent pout. He sat between beautiful women, one Korean dressed in shimmering green and an American blonde in red satin.

As Pak and Maggie approached, three husky bodyguards

dressed in dark suits that didn't have the loving touch of Han's tailor stood and formed a living wall before their master. The ROK captain came to a halt and waited.

Grinning like a spoiled child, Han motioned to his men and told them to let Pak through. "Ah, Captain Pak," the gang leader said in Korean. "Come, come. I will buy you a drink."

Pak stood his ground. "I'm here on official business," he stated in English.

Maggie knew that the captain wasn't aware that she spoke Korean. She decided to keep that little fact to herself for the time being.

Han switched to flawless English. "Will I need legal representation, Captain Pak?"

"I think perhaps tonight we can exchange favors."

Han smiled engagingly. "Then you must sit." He waved to the women, chasing them from their seats. They shot territorial warnings to Maggie with their eyes, but they got up and walked away.

Han looked at Maggie for the first time, and she saw her own reflection in the smoky red lenses. "Ms. Foley. How nice to make your acquaintance."

"You know who I am?" Maggie wasn't truly surprised.

"Of course I do," Han said. "I wouldn't be a very good criminal if I didn't, now would I?" On the table in front of Han was a small notebook computer. Han opened it and tapped the keyboard. Then he turned it so Maggie could see the monitor. Images of Maggie filled the screen. Some were of her working the crime scene in the alley and in the street. But others were from Navy bases and file copies. Evidently Han had a clever computer hacker on his payroll.

"I'm impressed," Maggie said.

"You should be." Han closed the notebook and sat back with a smile.

Pak stepped back and allowed Maggie to seat herself first.

She slid across the cloth seat halfway to Han. Pak sat on the end across from the younger man.

"What would you like to drink?" Han asked in English.

"Nothing," Maggie replied. "I came here to investigate the deaths of three of your men."

Han shrugged and smiled. "I don't think we've come to the conclusion that those men worked for me."

"Captain Pak," Maggie prompted, without looking at the ROK captain.

"Those men worked for Han."

Maggie smiled. "Conclusion."

"Okay," Han said. "They worked for me."

"I want to know who killed them."

"From the reports I hear, it was an American military man. The weapon was a .50-caliber sniper rifle."

Again Maggie was impressed with the man's information. His intelligence source must be very good indeed. "The reports could be wrong," she said. "And maybe someone else has acquired a .50-caliber sniper rifle. Someone, say, who makes his profits from the black market."

Han grinned. He reached under his jacket and took out a pack of cigarettes. He offered one to her, but she shook her head. He lit up and blew smoke over his shoulder. "If I had trafficked in such a rifle—or even knew someone who did—I think I would be the first to wish to speak to that person. After all, the weapon cost me three of my men tonight."

"Did it take the life of a competitor as well?" Maggie asked. "Or a connection?"

Shaking his head, Han laughed. "You have a very suspicious mind."

Maggie waited.

"Don't you think I would have done something if I knew who had killed three of my men?" A dark look crossed Han's face.

"I'm also investigating Lance Corporal Hester's ties to the black market here in Chinhae," Maggie said. "I have two investigations. Both have different resolutions."

"Are you asking me to implicate myself?"

"You're a known black-market trafficker." Maggie kept constant eye contact with the sunglasses. "No implication is necessary. Were you dealing with Hester?"

"What would the American military do to me if I admitted such a thing?"

"Recommend that you be tried for your crimes. Ensure that you're kept away from American holdings in Chinhae."

"I would listen to such a recommendation," Pak said, "but unless you were to come forward and testify against yourself, I doubt much would be done."

Han stubbed his cigarette out in a glass, mermaid-shaped ashtray the color of marmalade. "I was not dealing with your lance corporal. He was cutting into my business."

Maggie kept her face expressionless, not allowing the satisfaction she felt at Han's admission to show. "Was Hester working for someone else?"

"Not as far as I know. He worked for himself."

"Why did you send your men after him tonight?"

"He wanted to make a deal. Open up a larger operation." Han shrugged. "The prospect amused me. And Hester was very savvy in what he was doing. He had quite an operation established. He was moving drugs and weapons. Nothing large, but he trafficked in enough to keep himself busy."

Maggie thought about that. There was nothing in Hester's background to suggest that he was even conversant in black marketing. "What were you going to do to Hester?" Maggie asked.

"Threaten him. Tell him that I would kill him if he didn't desist."

"Would you have?"

Han said nothing. The man was arrogant but smart, Maggie

noted. He wasn't saying anything that she or Captain Pak could later use against him.

"It only takes one man to open a floodgate," Han said after a moment in a quiet, steely voice. "Whether you approve of what I do or not, I have worked hard to get what I have. I won't let someone take it away from me."

"Your men could just as easily have threatened Hester in the bar. Why did you give them orders to take Hester to that alley?"

"I didn't."

So her suspicion that one of Han's men had betrayed him was correct. Maggie decided to explore that. "Then why did they take him to the alley?"

The black-market dealer turned a hand over and shrugged. "I don't know."

"The sniper was set up across the street," Maggie said. "He knew they were going to stop in that alley. So if you didn't arrange it, one of your men did."

"Which one?"

"I thought maybe you could tell me."

Han showed her a thin smile. "No."

Maggie considered that. There was no conclusive proof that the driver had set up the execution of Lance Corporal Hester, but someone had chosen the alley. The fingerprints on the steering wheel proved that Junwan Mok had driven the car all night. It was also registered to him.

"I want the man who did this," Maggie said.

"Look fast." Han grinned. "Whoever did this will not have many places he can hide from me. The killer made a huge mistake by attacking me."

"He killed whoever helped set up Hester's execution," Maggie pointed out. "I'd say he's covering his tracks pretty well." She looked at Pak. "I'm ready to go."

The ROK captain eased out of the booth and made room for her.

Maggie got out, then looked at Han. "I'm going to clear this case. I'm going to prove that Hester was involved in black marketing, and I'm going to find his killer. If his killer *disappears,* and he's an American sailor or Marine, I'm going to nail you for it. Are we clear on that?"

Han lit another cigarette and regarded her thoughtfully.

As Maggie stood there, a big Korean man wandered over from the bar, obviously drunk. He stood at Han's table, swaying slightly. He was young, dressed in American jeans and a Gap T-shirt under a New York Yankees jacket.

"Mr. Han," the young man said in Korean, "I offer you my respects. And I wish to know if you would sell me this woman."

Han smiled and spoke in Korean. "Do you really want her? She is skinny and round eyed."

The man hiccupped and covered his mouth with his hand. "I want her."

"Then you may have her," Han said. "For five won. Because I am feeling generous today."

Grinning, the man turned around and reached for Maggie. She knew Pak was already in motion, trying to step in front of the big man.

Setting herself, Maggie grabbed the man's right wrist with her left and punched him in the throat with her right fist. He *hurked* as his air was temporarily shut off, and he stumbled. Pulling on his right arm, stepping forward and swinging with his center of gravity, Maggie whirled around and slammed the man into the middle of Han's table. The man's eyes rolled back in his head as he lost his tenacious hold on consciousness. By the time Han's bodyguards had realized what was happening, she'd drawn a Beretta in her right hand and had it pointed into the center of Han's face.

"If they pull their weapons," Maggie said in Korean in a tightly controlled voice, "I'm going to kill you."

Han held up his hand and told his men to leave their guns alone. He smiled at her. "You speak Korean."

"And I don't miss what I shoot at," Maggie promised.

"I'm more impressed," Han said. "I believe you."

"Good," Maggie said. "Then you can also believe me when I say that you're under arrest."

Han's smile faded. His face darkened. "Arrest for what?"

"Unauthorized sale of United States property," Maggie said.

Han looked at Pak. "She's crazy. She can't do this."

Pak reached behind him on his belt and brought out a pair of handcuffs. "I believe she just did. As a law enforcement officer in a military city that is friendly to the United States, it is my duty to support her."

"You're both crazy."

Pak dangled the handcuffs.

"You can walk out of here," Maggie said, "or I can drag you out of here. Either way, you're coming with me." The charge wouldn't stick, but she could at least throw Han in jail for a day or so. That would give her and the team a little more time to find the killer before Han did.

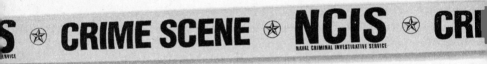

SCENE ✴ **NCIS** ✴ CRIME SCEN
NAVAL CRIMINAL INVESTIGATIVE SERVICE

>> CHINHAE, REPUBLIC OF KOREA
>> CHINHAE AMERICAN NAVAL BASE HOSPITAL
>> 0343 HOURS

"We've got DNA on the sniper?" Will moved his finger over the wireless touch pad for the tablet PC. On-screen, the view inside the small apartment where the unidentified man had killed the old couple and set up to execute Hester and the three Chinhae criminals rotated, allowing him to peer around the room.

"The blood Shel found on the wall below the window doesn't match either of the victims." Frank stood at the foot of Will's bed with the small notebook he habitually carried. "The spatter also supports Shel's premise that the sniper was wounded by the woman."

Will glanced at his watch and saw that it was a quarter to four in the morning. "What do we have on Hester?"

"Nothing at this point. We're still digging. Shel went to Hester's apartment to see if he could turn anything up there."

Frustration chafed at Will. His head swam, and exhaustion and pain threatened to overwhelm him as the events of the past few days came over him in a rush. Helen Swafford's death, the takedown at Carlos Hernandez's shop, the long flight to Korea, Hester's brutal murder, being shot himself. And on top of it all, looming over everything else like a black curtain, Barbara's request for a divorce. All at once he felt close to tears.

Frank regarded him for a moment, then said, "Your team needs you focused, Will. Whatever's going on over here, it's big and it's complicated and you need your head in the game."

Will knew his friend was right, but he couldn't pull himself out of the spiral of despair. He lay back on the bed and gazed at the ceiling. "Barbara wants a divorce, Frank. Do you know what that's going to do to my family?"

"Yes, I do. I've seen it a number of times. So have you. But do you know what you need to work on first?"

"Making sure the kids are okay."

"No. The kids *are* okay. Maybe Barbara doesn't want to be a wife right now—*your* wife—but she's still a mother. Steven and Wren are fed and cared for. They're not your first concern right now."

Will had to force himself to breathe. He felt dizzy from the hurt and confusion.

"Your first concern is *you*," Frank went on in a quieter voice. "Your family needs you healthy and whole, and I'm not just talking about physically. They need the guy who throws footballs to Steven. The guy who talks about how great Wren's artwork is. They need that guy. They don't need a guy who's feeling sorry for himself."

Silence stretched between them for a while.

"Frank," Will whispered, unable to look his friend in the eye, "I'm scared."

"I know. And that's okay."

"This last year . . . it's been hard. I sit in my quarters . . . and all I do is miss Barbara and Steven and Wren."

"I know. I've seen it in you."

"It was bad enough when I thought there was still a chance we'd get back together. But this—" Will shook his head— "there's nothing left after this."

"You're thinking wrongheaded," Frank said. "There's plenty left. Steven and Wren still need their father. I still need a friend. NCIS still needs a team leader who can figure out who killed Lance Corporal Hester. A divorce doesn't negate all that."

"I just . . . feel . . . so lost."

"You're not lost."

"The worst thing is that I don't understand why Barbara asked me to leave a year ago. Or why she plans on divorcing me now."

"Do you think that would really help?"

Will let out his breath. "I don't know. I thought things would be different after I joined NCIS. After I moved off the aircraft carriers like Barbara wanted. I thought maybe I'd have more time at home. I did after all those years at sea, but it just didn't seem to matter. *I* didn't seem to matter. Barbara was never happy again the way she'd been when we were first married."

"Marriage is a series of changes," Frank said. "Truthfully, I think Barbara is dealing with those changes worse than you are."

Frank had always been a good friend, a good source of advice. Will tried to rely on it now. "What am I supposed to do?"

"Let go."

"Of my marriage? Of my family? I can't do that."

"You need to let go and let God sort things out."

Will shook his head. "Judging from the divorce papers on my desk, God isn't handling this very well."

"You don't know what's in his plans."

"My divorce is?"

Frank was silent for a moment. "If it comes to that, then yes, I believe he did make a plan for it."

"He didn't ask me, did he?"

"That's not how it works. Barbara has her own free will too."

"I prayed, Frank. Every day, I prayed. All I got in return were those divorce papers."

"You have to let go and trust."

"I . . . just don't believe with the kind of strength you do. I don't have that kind of confidence."

"It's not confidence, Will," Frank stated. "It's faith. You can't base faith on fact or figures or past experiences. You can't base it on training or understanding. It comes out of acceptance. It boils down to trusting God."

"I've never had to trust like this before, Frank. I don't know if I can."

Frank looked at him for a moment, silent. Then he said, "When I was a kid, I loved to sail. I went out every chance I got. When I was twelve, I sailed out of sight of land for the first time.

"When I first headed out to sea, I wasn't even thinking about leaving land behind. Mainly it was a thrill because I wasn't supposed to be out so far. My dad would have chopped my sailboat up for kindling if he'd known. But I was excited. I couldn't wait to get out there. After all, I had my compass, and it wasn't like I was going to miss the coast when I turned back.

"But after a while, when I turned around and couldn't see land anymore, things suddenly felt different. I wasn't excited anymore; I was scared. I got stuck for a time. Couldn't catch the wind right. Instead of sailing back toward land, I kept getting pulled farther and farther out to sea."

Almost in spite of himself, Will was interested. "So what did you do?" he asked.

"I just kept trying to get back. I couldn't tell if I was getting anywhere, because I didn't have any landmarks to guide me. But because I had a compass, I knew I was going in the right direction. And, in time, I saw land again.

"That's what this part of your life is about, Will. Getting through it. Planning and doing what you can, but relying on faith to get you through the hard times. Believing. Let God be your compass. Your life is out there. Happiness is out there. You've just got to let him direct you to those things. God will give you what you need, Will. He always does. Most people just don't realize that."

"You think he's going to make this all go away?"

"I don't claim to know how God does his work."

"Oh, yeah," Will said bitterly. "Mysterious ways. I forgot about that."

"God *does* work in mysterious ways," Frank said.

Will closed his eyes and laid his head back on the bed. He felt hollow and empty. "You know what, Chief? I'm tired. I'm going to abdicate on this conversation. If you want to believe in God and his mysterious ways, you're welcome to him."

Frank was quiet for a moment. Then he said, "Have you ever seen true Evil, Will?"

Taken aback, Will just looked at his friend.

"I'm not just talking about crime," Frank continued. "I'm talking about true Evil. The kind of Evil that wants only to oppose God and his work in the world. The kind that desires nothing more than the simple pursuit of Evil for its own sake. I've seen it. Not everywhere, and not often, but I've seen it enough times to know what it is."

"Chief—"

"Most people don't think much about evil," Frank continued. "Sure, they think about sin. About the effects and repercussions sin will demand on their lives. But they get so busy looking for the bad things in themselves when they get lost that they forget that true Evil is out there waiting for them. True Evil is hungry, Will. I've seen it. I've run for my life when I've encountered it."

"Frank, I don't—"

"Listen," Frank interrupted. "The job we're doing is more than just solving crimes. We're in a battle against forces that we can't see or understand. If we're going to have any hope of succeeding, we've got to put our trust in God. He's the only one who can give us victory. He's the way, Will. Maybe you can't see that now, but he's the way. What you need now more than anything is to ask for his help."

Will ignored his friend's advice and handed the tablet PC back to Frank. "I'm going to sack out for a while, Chief. Why don't you check on Hester's body? See if it's here at the lab."

After a brief hesitation, Frank nodded. "All right. I'll see you later this morning. We can talk again." He left the room.

Talk all you want, Will thought bitterly. *It's not going to change a thing. God and I just aren't on the same page at this point in my life.*

18

>> CHINHAE, REPUBLIC OF KOREA
>> CHINHAE AMERICAN NAVAL BASE HOSPITAL
>> 0418 HOURS

"It's just going to take some time for Will to come around, honey," Mildred, Frank's wife, told him over the phone. "He's been through a lot."

As Frank walked down the stairwell leading to the medical center's basement, he listened to his wife's calm voice over the cell phone. In fact, at the moment, he cherished her belief.

"I know he's been through a lot," Frank said. "And he's got a lot more to go through. I don't think I'm helping."

"But you're trying, Frank," Mildred said. "All any of us can do is try. After that, you simply have to—"

"Acknowledge that it's in God's hands." Frank sighed. "I know that. God's taught me that lesson a few times."

"Maybe he's reminding you of that now."

Frank stopped at the bottom of the stairs. He leaned against the wall beside the door to the morgue. "You're right. I know you're right." He peered at the weak light overhead. "It's just that Will is one of the best friends I've ever had. I hate to watch him go through this."

"I know. What about the investigation there? the soldier who was killed?"

"Looks like he was caught in a cross fire between rival gangs. I mean, why would anyone single out a guy who's dealing in small-time, black-market stuff? It doesn't make any sense. But it shouldn't take us long to figure out."

Mildred's voice became playful. "So how long do you think it's going to be before you're home, sailor?"

Despite the seriousness of their earlier conversation, Frank couldn't help but respond to her good-natured taunting. He loved his wife and her irrepressible spontaneity. Even at the worst of times, he could always count on her to find something to laugh about or that would make him laugh.

"Not soon enough, baby," he told her. "I love you. Don't know if I tell you enough, but I've always loved you." Without warning, his cell phone went dead. He pulled it from his face and tried the number again.

Nothing.

>> **CHINHAE AMERICAN NAVAL BASE MORGUE**
>> **0424 HOURS**

Achmed worked quickly to secure Virgil Hester's cold, stiff corpse to the gurney. So far his body-snatching operation had gone off without a hitch. The two technicians he'd encountered upon entering the morgue had not provided any resistance, and now he was moments from exiting the building with his prize and completing his night's mission.

Virgil Hester's body must be removed at all costs. His flesh held far too many secrets.

Achmed heard footsteps scuff outside the door of the morgue. Was he about to be interrupted? He turned away from the corpse and drew the silenced Beretta 9 mm from his waistband. He looked up at the security monitor showing the view outside the door. Yes, someone was there.

Achmed smiled grimly as he heard the hand fall on the doorknob. Soon there would be a third body joining the two already littering the morgue's floor.

The man entered the room and glanced at the body on the gurney. "I'm Chief Warrants Officer Billings. With NCIS. I'm here to check on—" His eyes widened as he saw the bleeding bodies of the two scrub techs lying on the floor in pools of blood. A shocked expression filled the NCIS agent's face. He clawed for the weapon he carried under his jacket.

Letting go of the corpse, Achmed squeezed the 9 mm's trigger and stepped forward, walking right at the man. He kept his aim centered at the man's heart. The subsonic rounds allowed the silencer to work, keeping the noise to a minimum.

Dark blood spread across the front of the man's shirt. He stumbled backward, driven by the bullets. The weapon he'd managed to free from its holster tumbled free of his nerveless fingers.

Achmed kept moving forward. He fired three more times as the man fell backward, jerking, quivering, dying.

>> CHINHAE AMERICAN NAVAL BASE HOSPITAL
>> 0619 HOURS

Frank's dead!

Will struggled to get his thoughts wrapped around that. The sedative the nurse had given him a short time ago still muddled his brain.

Frank can't be dead.

Maggie stood at the foot of his bed. She looked more shaken than Will had ever seen her. "An orderly making her rounds found Frank's body in the morgue." She spoke clearly, in a controlled manner, but Will could see the tear tracks on her face.

Fighting the drowsiness and spinning light-headedness that jerked inside his skull, Will sat up. "Where are Shel and Estrella?"

"Shel's at Hester's apartment building. Estrella is organizing our file in the hotel. What are you doing?"

Will ignored her as he ripped the sensors of his chest and head and sent the machines into a frenzy. "Get them here. *Now.*" He untaped his hand and eased the IV shunt from the vein. A drop of bright blood oozed from his flesh. He used the tape to bind the tiny puncture and put pressure on it. His side was another matter—it felt like a shark was chewing on it. But there was no time to worry about that now.

"If you move around, you're going to rip your stitches loose."

"Maggie, get the rest of our team here. That's an order. If you disobey it, I'm going to pull rank on the first sailor I see and give him or her your duties. Now get moving."

Maggie looked at him fiercely as she dug her cell phone out of a pocket. "Fine."

"Good." Unsteadily, Will stumbled to the small chest of drawers against the wall. His personal effects—ID, badge case, wallet, change, and keys—were in the top drawer. His clothes were nowhere to be found.

A nurse ran to the door, then looked shocked to see Will up and around.

"Where are my clothes?" Will demanded. Then he remembered that the techs in the OR had cut them off him because of all the blood. He was scared because he couldn't seem to get his mind to work properly. And right now he needed to be able to think straight. "Get me some scrubs."

"Commander, you shouldn't even be out of bed."

"I *am* out of bed," Will growled, "and if I don't get some clothes in the next thirty seconds, I'm going to be parading through the hospital nearly naked."

Maggie turned to the nurse. "Get him some scrubs."

A wave of dizziness almost sent Will's senses plunging into blackness. He leaned against the wall and concentrated on staying conscious.

"Are you all right?" Maggie asked.

"No. I'm not all right. Somebody killed Frank while I was lying in that bed." *Right after I threw him out.* "Have you . . . have you seen the site yet?"

"Yes." She hesitated. "It's hard. Not easy to look at. We've got it contained."

Tears were running down Will's cheeks before he knew it. He felt them hot and rapid against his cool flesh. He turned from Maggie and acted like he had to rest his side.

How am I going to tell Mildred that you're dead, Frank?

>> **CHINHAE AMERICAN NAVAL BASE MORGUE**
>> **0626 HOURS**

Minutes later, clad in green hospital scrubs and thin-soled disposable hospital slippers, Will stepped out of the elevator and followed the hallway to the murder scene. Dizziness whirled sickeningly inside his head. Maggie, Estrella, Shel, and Max trailed behind him.

The way was easy to find. Navy MPs and Command brass were everywhere.

Commander Greg Yardley, the base commander, stood outside the morgue. He was in his early fifties, ramrod straight, and hailed from the Los Angeles area. His khaki uniform was pressed and neat.

"Commander Yardley," Will greeted as he limped over.

"Commander," Yardley replied. "Shouldn't you be in bed?"

"No. One of my men was killed."

A sour look framed Yardley's face. "Two of mine were."

Will looked at Maggie. She hadn't mentioned that. Or maybe he hadn't given her time to mention that.

"Two surgery techs were on duty last night," she said. "They were killed first."

"Have you kept the crime scene clear?" Will asked.

The base commander looked uncomfortable. "When the bodies were first discovered, the scrub tech on rounds went in and checked them. To make sure they were all beyond help."

Will nodded, thinking, *One person. One person's no problem. One person can't have hurt the scene much. We can work around that. Let there be something there. Bread crumbs. I'm willing to work for them. Just give me Frank's killer.*

Two MPs with M4A1s guarded the door.

"If you'll get these people out of here," Will said, "we'll get to work."

"I've got my own team handling this."

Will took a step closer to the commander, feeling the anger and hurt well up in him and almost slip past his control. "That is one of my men lying in that room. This is *my* crime scene."

"No, it's not," Yardley said. "NCIS Director Larkin asked me to keep your team out of this."

Will couldn't believe it. He felt like the floor had just been pulled out from under him. Larkin had no right to shut him out of the investigation. Not this investigation.

19

>> CHINHAE, REPUBLIC OF KOREA
>> CHINHAE AMERICAN NAVAL BASE HOSPITAL
>> 0903 HOURS

"Sir," Will said, staring into the computer monitor that connected him to Director Larkin's office back in Washington, D. C.,
"with all due respect, you can't pull us off this case."

"I *can* pull you off this investigation, Commander Coburn,"
Larkin said, "and I have."

Will struggled to get control of himself. He looked away
from the monitor for a moment. He'd borrowed an office down
the hallway from where the crime-scene investigation was taking
place. Through the window, he saw Maggie, Shel, and Estrella in
the small visitors' waiting area. Maggie and Estrella worked on
Tablet PCs and Pocket PCs, getting their investigation notes
together. Grim and solid, Shel leaned against the wall with arms

folded. Max slept at his feet. Although the big Marine looked the
most relaxed, Will knew that Shel seethed inside.

"Mr. Larkin," Will said, deliberately using the civilian title
to remind Larkin that, although he worked for the Navy now, he
wasn't a Navy officer and he was still an outsider when it came to
the military, "Frank was my friend."

"I understand that," Larkin said. "Why do you think
I pulled you off the investigation? You're too close to it."

"Frank was my friend," Will said again. "You can't ask me
to just step away from this."

"I'm not asking you to stay away, Commander," Larkin said
in a hard, authoritative voice. "I'm *telling* you to stay away.
Yardley's team will handle it."

"Why are you doing this?" Will asked. "Let us do our jobs.
That's all any of us wants to do."

Larkin took a deep breath. "Seventeen years ago, when I was
working homicide in New York, I had a partner who was found
dead in his personal vehicle. He was off duty. Alone. In a place he
shouldn't have been.

"On the surface, it looked like he had committed suicide,"
Larkin said. "The evidence showed that he sat there in that car,
put his service weapon in his mouth, and pulled the trigger." He
paused, his voice getting tight. "I didn't want to believe he'd
killed himself. I couldn't accept it. I wanted to be primary on the
investigation. I felt certain he'd been set up. I wanted to find out
who had done it."

Will waited for the other shoe to drop. Larkin seldom told
personal stories, and never without a reason.

"I was sure one of his snitches had set him up to look like a
suicide," Larkin said. "I was ready to knock doors and knock
heads, to do whatever it took to find out who had staged my
partner's suicide.

"My captain kept me off the case, and it was a good thing,
because I would have been wrong. After a few days, the detec-

tives handling the case turned up a witness, a prostitute who had seen the muzzle flash of my partner's pistol as he pulled the trigger. She said it lit up his face inside his car. And he was alone. He shot himself. She didn't want to come forward because this was the death of a cop. She knew no one would believe her." Larkin shook his head. "I wouldn't have. I didn't want to believe it even after we found out he owed a gambling debt that was crushing him. I didn't know about that either."

"This isn't like that," Will said. "Frank didn't know anybody here. None of us do."

"I know, Commander. What I'm trying to get across is that you and your team are too close to the situation to see things clearly. What's needed here is distance. You don't have that."

"We're professionals, sir."

"Then be professional, and accept what I'm telling you. Give Yardley's men some time. Let them do their jobs. I'll instruct Yardley to see to it you and the team get copies of everything they discover."

Will nodded. It was a small compensation, but one he was willing to accept. "Thank you, sir."

"I notified Mrs. Billings," Larkin went on. "Telling her Frank was . . . was gone was a hard thing to do."

Emotion clogged Will's throat. "Is Mildred all right?"

"As well as can be expected. I hated telling her over the phone, but I would have hated her finding out from an impersonal visitor or the media even more."

Some of the anger left Will and he felt drained. "I didn't know how I was going to do it."

"Mrs. Billings made one request. She wants you to bring Frank's body home, Commander. She asked me to allow you to do that."

"Sir, the investigation—"

"—is in good hands. I'm going to honor Mrs. Billings's request. You and the team need time to regroup. That's an order, Commander."

"Yes, sir," Will said before he broke the connection. Leaning back in the chair, he tried to focus and couldn't. He was hurting too badly, both from Frank's death and the pain in his side. All he could think about was how someone else was doing the job that he should be doing. About how he hadn't done his job well enough to keep Frank safe.

>> CHINHAE AMERICAN NAVAL BASE
>> 1024 HOURS

Will was asleep at his desk when he heard someone approaching and roused groggily. He opened his eyes and saw Maggie standing there. She still looked immaculate for someone who hadn't slept in over thirty-six hours, but red lines as delicate as spun sugar gleamed in her eyes.

"Whoever killed Frank," she said, "took Lance Corporal Hester's corpse. It's missing."

Will thought about that, having trouble concentrating on the strangeness of the concept. "Were any other bodies missing?"

"No."

Will tried to find a comfortable position in the swivel chair and couldn't. "Was anything else taken last night?"

"No. But Estrella said the security system had been cracked."

"How did she find that out?"

"She cracked the system herself and took an electronic peek over the shoulders of the computer techs chasing through the system. Whoever breached the computer security on the base came from inside."

Will waited for elaboration.

"Estrella said that there were no 'footprints' in any of the usual places where the base connects up the Internet."

"Can she find a trail?"

"She's trying, but these guys are good."

"What about Hester's clothing and personal effects?" Will asked. "Did whoever took his body take those as well?"

"No. We've got the clothes and personal effects. Or rather, Yardley's men have them."

"Why weren't they taken?"

"Evidently because whoever killed Frank was only after Hester's body."

Will pried at that piece of the puzzle. Crime-scene investigators worked with what they had, not what they wished for. "Not something Hester carried. Not something he had on him. So what does that leave us?"

"Possibly something inside the body?"

"Like what?" Will asked. "Is it possible Hester was acting as a mule?"

"Carrying drugs inside his body? I suppose it's possible, though he doesn't fit the profile for most drug mules. The autopsy wasn't scheduled till this morning, but X-rays were taken of Hester as well as an ultrasound. I'll see if I can get them."

Will shifted again. "When are they going to release the chief's body?"

"A few more hours. There's no need for an autopsy. The cause of death is apparent."

For a moment, Will couldn't speak. "We're taking him home, Maggie. Get the team squared away. As soon as we can get a flight, we're leaving."

"All right."

"But we're not backing off the Hester investigation." Will turned to face Maggie. "Maybe the director can keep us from working this crime scene, but Lance Corporal Hester is the key to Frank's death. Whatever Hester was involved in got Frank killed. I want to know what it was."

⊛ ⊛ ⊛

>> **OFF THE COAST OF CHINHAE**
>> **KOREA STRAIT**
>> **1051 HOURS**

Achmed stood in the wheelhouse of the small fishing boat and looked out over the rolling hills of brown water in the Korea Strait. He had to move quickly. It was almost 11 a.m., almost time for fishing ships to call an end to their day and head back to shore to clean their catch. What he was about to do must be witnessed by no one.

He wore the clothes of a fisherman. Cheap cotton pants that had long ago given up being white, a stained cotton shirt, and a patched peacoat blunted the wind. The clothes had come with the boat.

It had now been over six hours since Achmed had retreated from the medical center and gotten Hester's corpse out of the naval base in a garbage truck. He'd driven to the docks and picked a boat at random. He'd planned to kill anyone aboard, but the boat had been empty. It had taken only minutes to load Hester's body into the hold and start the engines.

Achmed cut the engines. The boat settled into the rocking rhythm of the sea. Nothing moved out on the water.

Here, midway between the South Korean coastline and the Tsushima Islands, the sea was at its deepest. The bottom lay almost three hundred feet down.

Achmed went down into the stinking hold, tied a rope to Hester's corpse, and climbed back out, hauling the dead man up after him. He chained the boat's steel-and-concrete anchor to Hester's feet, then threw it and the dead man overboard. The anchor plummeted immediately, dragging the body deep into the brine.

20

>> ARLINGTON, VIRGINIA
>> ARLINGTON NATIONAL CEMETERY
>> 1028 HOURS

Three days later, Chief Warrants Officer Frank Thomas Billings was laid to rest in Arlington National Cemetery with full honors.

Dressed in his Navy whites, Will stood a short distance from Mildred Billings as they said good-bye together. Will blinked tears from his eyes and refused to let them fall. He was surprised there were any left.

Standing there in the bright spring sunshine, Will couldn't help thinking that his world was falling apart. In just a few more minutes, Frank would be gone forever, just another gravestone in a field of perfectly placed markers, and his team would never be the same.

The preacher finished the graveside service. He was an older man with a strong voice that boomed over the crowd. When he asked that everyone join him in prayer, Will stared at the ground. Mildred stood between two of her grown sons, her hands clasped tightly in theirs.

Maggie stood beside Will. She wore a simple black dress and little makeup. Shel, wearing his Marine dress uniform, stood on his other side. Also in a black dress, Estrella stood at the end with the medical examiner, Nita Tomlinson.

Once the prayer was finished, the honor guard delivered the twenty-one-gun salute. The harsh rifle cracks echoed over the cemetery, splitting the morning air. Shel and Will went forward and folded the flag spread out over Frank's coffin.

Presenting the flag to Mildred was one of the hardest things Will had ever done in his life. His hands shook and his chest felt so tight that he could hardly breathe.

Tiny and demure, her frosted hair neatly in place, Mildred accepted the flag, pulling it close against her bosom. She looked older and more frail than Will had ever seen her. Before he could step away, she caught his arm and pulled him to her.

Will steeled himself and spoke even though it felt like his throat was being crushed. "I'll miss him, Millie."

"I know," she said, holding him fiercely. "He loved you, Will. Don't you ever forget that."

Unable to speak, Will nodded. When Mildred released him, he walked back to join the team only a few feet away.

Director Larkin had given the whole team a week of leave. Maggie had plans to fly home to Boston immediately after the service. Shel and Estrella also had made arrangements to return to their homes. Will had no such plans. He had called Barbara from his quarters at Camp Lejeune but had failed to reach her. No one had picked up after three tries, so he had left a message. Will didn't know how to feel about Barbara's missing the funeral.

After the preacher had dismissed the service with a final prayer, Will heard a familiar voice from behind him. "Daddy!"

Surprised, he turned around to see Wren running toward him. Will knelt to scoop his daughter from the ground, but the wound in his side suddenly felt as if a red-hot poker had been shoved inside. He settled for a hug.

At six years old, Wren had gotten to be a handful. She had waist-long black hair that matched his in color, an elfin face, and a pug nose. Two of her upper front teeth had fallen out only a couple weeks before and left her with a gap-toothed smile. She wore a black dress and a small black hat.

"What are you doing here?" Will asked.

"Mommy brought me." Wren's face grew pensive and sad. "She told me Uncle Frank died."

Will brushed a curl of hair from the corner of his daughter's mouth. "He did, honey."

"Mommy said you were sad."

"I am," Will said in a strained voice.

Her small hands played with the medals pinned to his uniform. "Steven said some bad people, some terrorists, killed Uncle Frank."

"He shouldn't have told you that."

"He didn't tell me." Her hands stayed busy with the medals. Wren was never one to sit quietly. "I heard him talking about it on the phone."

"Oh." Will looked back through the crowd. "Where's your mom?"

"She's at the back." Wren pointed. "With Jesse."

"Jesse?"

Wren nodded. "He's from our church." Leaning close, cupping her hands the way she did when she shared secrets, she whispered loudly, "I think he's Mommy's boyfriend."

Pain—sharp, bright, and hard—stabbed through Will's heart. Even during their separation, he'd never imagined a time when Barbara would be with anyone else. Then he saw Barbara. Steven stood on one side of her and a man who looked vaguely familiar stood on her other side. If Barbara saw him, she gave no indication.

At thirty-four, his wife was a slim five foot six. Her chestnut hair hung to her chin. Dark glasses hid her blue eyes. She looked beautiful in her black dress.

Steven, at fourteen, was already taller than his mother by a couple inches. He was starting to fill out, his shoulders broadening and his chest deepening. His hair was dark brown and currently cut so he could spike it. He looked almost grown-up in his black suit.

Will stood and took Wren's hand. "Let's go say hi to Mom."

Barbara stiffened as he approached. "Hello, Will," she said.

"I must have missed your call," Will said. "Things have been—"

"I didn't call," Barbara said, glancing at the man beside her as she did.

Will felt angry and hurt at the same time. Adding the weight of his failing marriage to the loss of Frank was almost more than he could bear. He held tight to Wren's hand and let her be his anchor.

"Were you with Uncle Frank when he . . . when he died?" Steven asked. He stared at Will, tight eyed and almost challenging.

"No," Will said hoarsely. "No, I wasn't."

"Did you get the guys who did it?"

"No." Returning his son's straightforward gaze, Will felt guilty.

"Are you going to?"

"I don't know. We don't know who they were."

Steven's face crumpled a little then. Tears bled down his face. He'd been friends with Frank too.

With no thought to the tension that had been between them, Will went over to embrace his son.

"No!" Steven pushed Will back. "I'm all right. Just leave me alone."

Conscious that some of the people in the crowd had seen the exchange, Will breathed out to control himself. He told himself that Steven's lack of respect was the result of the strain that had been placed on the family.

"You're an investigator," Steven accused. "You're supposed to catch people who do stuff like this. You're supposed to catch whoever . . . hurt Uncle Frank."

Will didn't know what to say.

Barbara put an arm around her son, but he shrugged it off and walked away. She looked at Will, and though her voice was neutral, he knew she blamed him. "He doesn't mean what he said. He's just . . . angry. He'll get over it. He'll be fine."

"Maybe I could talk to him," Will suggested. "He could stay a couple days with me."

"Oh, Daddy," Wren squealed, jumping up and down and holding up a hand. "I will! I will!"

"I don't think that's a good idea," the man beside Barbara said. He was tall and wore his brown hair in a shag cut. His tan was ultraviolet perfect. Will figured him for thirty-five or forty.

Will squared off with the man unconsciously. "Who are you?"

Obviously aware of the strong feelings that hammered at Will's temples, Barbara stepped forward so she was partially between the two men. "Will, this is Jesse Harlan. Jesse, Commander Will Coburn."

Not "My husband, Will." The introduction stung, and Will tried to bottle his feelings before they got away.

"Jesse goes to my church," Barbara said. "He's a friend."

Will didn't look away from Jesse's face. "A friend who feels like he can tell me how to handle my kids."

Harlan's face hardened. He was on the verge of making a retort of some kind when Barbara said, "We're not going to do this." She looked at Harlan as well. "This is a funeral." She looked back at Will. "You don't want to do this to Mildred."

Will made himself breathe out. He was a naval commander. He was used to being in control of himself. He could do this, no matter how badly he didn't want to. "I just think Steven could use some time with me," he said.

"I'll ask him," Barbara promised. "If he wants to visit you for a few days, that's fine. But if he doesn't, Will, he's not coming."

Will didn't like the answer, but he knew he couldn't fight it. "All right."

"I want to stay with Daddy," Wren said excitedly. "I want to stay."

Barbara looked at her daughter and smiled. Then she looked at Will with some of the old softness. "Are you sure you're ready for her? After this?"

Will didn't know if Barbara was referring to losing Frank or finding out his wife had a new man in her life. But he told her that it would be fine. For that moment, it felt good to be the father of the happiest kid in the world.

>> **CAMP LEJEUNE, NORTH CAROLINA**
>> **BARRACKS**
>> **0851 HOURS**

Showering with his side bandaged up wasn't easy, but Will did the best he could. Most of the puffy redness was gone from the wound, but the bruising and soreness would last another week or two at least.

The last two days with Wren had been great, a bright spot in the middle of a dark week (more like a dark year, Will sometimes thought). She'd certainly kept Will on the go. They'd visited the rec center and the playground, gone to the theater, and eaten out. They'd also shopped, and she had new clothing and toys to take back home with her. All the activity had given Will the perfect excuse not to think about Frank, God, the divorce, or anything else except the joy of having his daughter with him.

As he gazed in the steam-covered mirror in his small bathroom and looked at the misty outline of the saucer-sized bandage, he knew the doctor was right when he'd said Will had been lucky. If the .50-cal bullet had been only an inch or so higher and hit a rib, it would have torn his rib cage out, disemboweled him, and probably sent bone splinters into his heart.

He would have been dead.

Wouldn't have met Jesse two days ago, Will thought sardonically. *Wouldn't have had to deal with that. Wouldn't have had to bury Frank. Wouldn't have had to deal with Steven not wanting anything to do with me.*

Maybe dead would be better.

He looked at his face in the mirror and couldn't really see himself for all the steam. It seemed more comfortable that way. He couldn't remember when he'd last looked in the mirror and known exactly what he wanted to do with his life.

He knew he was supposed to go to God for that.

Lately God had been in his thoughts a lot. He couldn't think about Frank without thinking about church and missed opportunities. Will knew that if Frank were here now, the chief would tell him that God was laying a message on his heart. Mildred hadn't helped when she'd insisted that Will take the Bible that Frank had wanted him to have. It lay on his desk, another reminder that God was waiting for him somewhere out there.

Wren pounded on the bathroom door with a six-year-old's excitement. "Daddy! Daddy! A man's here to see you!"

Will pulled the door open and stepped into the hallway dressed only in gym shorts.

"Commander Coburn." NCIS Director Michael Larkin stood in the center of the living room, looking somewhat uncomfortable. He wore a suit. "I didn't mean to intrude, but

I thought maybe I could drop in for a casual visit. Away from the office."

"Sure," Will said.

"I wouldn't have come in unannounced," Larkin apologized. He smiled at Wren. "Your daughter didn't give me much choice."

"Unexpected company seems to be a by-product of having kids," Will said.

"I know. My boys used to do that to me all the time when they were teenagers."

Will was surprised. He didn't know Larkin had children. The director kept his family life out of the office. "Give me a minute." He waved Larkin to the mismatched chair and couch.

Will felt embarrassed about his base apartment. It was cramped and small, an enlisted man's digs, filled with whatever the thrift store had that was in reasonably good shape and at a fair price. Still, it was just like a ship: there was a place for everything and everything was in its place.

Turning around, Will almost ran over Wren.

Her eyes widened and she put her hand to her mouth as she stared at his bandaged side. "Ooooooh, Daddy. How did *that* happen?" she asked in a soft voice.

"I hurt myself at work," Will said vaguely. He didn't want his daughter thinking about a world where people tried to kill each other. She was too young for that.

"Are you all right?" Wren touched the bandage tenderly.

"Yes," Will answered. "I will be. I went to the doctor and he took good care of me." He tousled her hair and went to the bedroom to dress.

After a moment he heard his daughter's voice through the open door. "Hi," she said to Director Larkin.

"Hi." His reply was warm and genuine. He was obviously relaxed around kids.

"Do you want to watch cartoons?" Wren asked.

"I love cartoons," Larkin said.

"I like Scooby-Doo. Maybe he's on."

Will dressed quickly but with some trepidation. He didn't know what had brought Larkin here, but he wasn't expecting good news.

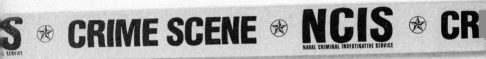

21

>> CAMP LEJEUNE, NORTH CAROLINA

>> BARRACKS

>> 0913 HOURS

"You've got a great kid in there," Larkin said.

"Yeah," Will said, "I do." He placed the coffeepot on the small plastic patio table off the living room. He was on the second floor and had a terrific view of the next apartment building.

Rock music blared outside. Young Marines with shaved heads and wearing USMC T-shirts and shorts played Frisbee between the buildings. At the next building down, another young Marine hung out his laundry, and Will knew the guy was trying to save a few bucks by taking advantage of the warm weather. Camp Lejeune was primarily a Marine base but housed some Navy personnel as well, along with the NCIS office of the Carolinas.

"You're an officer," Larkin said. "Couldn't Housing find you a better place to live?"

"After my wife and I separated last year, I wasn't too choosy about where I lived. I took the first billet Housing had open. With the workload we've been carrying, I haven't seen the point in taking a larger apartment that I don't need."

Larkin nodded. "When I was living in New York, before I married, I roomed with a guy who was doing his internship at one of the hospitals. Friends used to ask me how we both lived in such a small apartment. The trick was neither of us was home much."

An uncomfortable silence stretched between them for a little while. Finally Will said, "I can't help but be blunt, sir. What are you doing here?"

"Partly I'm here just to check on you. Make sure you're all right. You've had a lot on your plate."

"I'm fine," Will said.

"And the rest of the team? How are they holding up?"

"Fine, as far as I know. They're all home on leave." Will couldn't stop an accusatory tone from slipping into his response. Larkin was the reason the team wasn't back in Chinhae investigating Frank's murder.

"I put you and Frank together for a reason, you know," Larkin said. "You two were the experienced leaders of a relatively new team."

"Shel isn't green," Will said.

"Shel is a Marine," Larkin said. "A Special Forces commando. He's a one-man army when necessary. But he doesn't have your experience or the way with people that Frank had. Both you and Frank understand military structure, thinking, and life more than I do even after all the years I've been involved with NCIS. Your team has been taking the hard catches—the ones that matter most, the ones that go deep and hurt bad if they're mishandled. I've depended on you guys for that. That's why I put you together."

Will broke eye contact and sipped his coffee. "So what now?"

"You're a man down," Larkin said. "I've got someone I'd like you to train. For your team or maybe another. He's a Navy man, too. A SEAL."

"SEALs are hard to control," Will said immediately. The ones he'd known seemed to thrive on adrenaline and pushing themselves to the point of destruction. There were several SEALs that were extremely competent men, but the great ones were restless and creative and independent minded no matter who the CO was. Most of them believed they were indestructible. They had to believe that in order to face what they had to face, and to do the things they did. "Is he any good?"

"He's seen action in the Persian Gulf, China, South America, and Kenya. Full-on battles as well as covert work. His name is Remy Gautreau. He's a petty officer with medical training as well as the diving, parachuting, and explosives background. He should complement your team."

"Why does he want a transfer to NCIS?"

"He doesn't want one. His CO wants one for him."

"Why?"

"Apparently he's exhibited some self-destructive tendencies of late. He's always pushed his luck, but lately he's been going over the top with it. The last action they saw in Iraq, the SEAL team commander said he went into a firefight by himself against seven opponents. He was on rehab for that and is coming back into rotation and into the field."

"What if Gautreau doesn't want to go to NCIS?"

"Then he's up for a psych eval and probably an honorable discharge."

"That sounds harsh."

"It's better than him ending up dead. That's how his commanding officer feels like it's going to end. I want you and your team to train Gautreau. He'll be here in another week. I want the team back together by then."

Will nodded. He knew part of the reason Larkin was saddling him with the addition to the team was to keep him busy. Part of him wanted to resent the director's concern, but he knew that in the director's shoes he would have made the same call.

>> 1819 HOURS

Sitting on the patio that evening, Will watched Wren laughing at cartoons while curled up in a ball on the thrift-store couch. The sound touched his heart. It was so pure and innocent. Despite the changes going on in her life, Wren remained stable, open, and giving.

Restless, he went to his computer in the corner of the living room. He called up the files he'd had sent from Chinhae, the X-rays and ultrasound of USMC Lance Corporal Virgil Hester.

Close examination of those records indicated nothing hidden inside the body. The skull fragments had even been pieced together and examined. There were no drugs. No computer chip containing state secrets or corporate espionage. Just the bedrock of one very dead person.

"Do you like looking at skeletons, Daddy?" Wren asked in a quiet voice.

Her presence at Will's side startled him. He'd never even heard her get up from the couch. The laugh track on the cartoons continued.

"Sometimes," he told her. He switched the monitor off and picked her up. He loved holding her, but knew there wouldn't be many years of that left.

"Why?" Wren snuggled against him, something she always did when she was tired.

"Because you can learn a lot from a person's skeleton."

"Like what?"

"Like how old the person was. Whether the person was a boy or a girl. Where that person has been during his or her life."

"How can you tell where somebody's been?"

"Sometimes by the minerals that are in the person's bones. Sometimes by the minerals that are missing from the bones."

"If you looked at my bones, I hope you couldn't tell where I've been."

"Why?"

"Because last week I went over to Mr. Potter's house to feed his dog, and Mommy told me not to go over there unless she knew. Boy, would she be mad if she found out."

Will smiled. "Why didn't you just tell Mommy?"

"Mommy and Jesse went shopping."

Will took a deep breath and pushed away the sudden surge of emotions. He wasn't going to deal with that now. He was going to concentrate on his daughter.

"I told Steven that Wrinkles needed feeding, but he told me to stop being a brat and leave him alone. He was talking to some *girl* on the phone." Wren managed to make *girl* sound like the worst disease in the world.

Will remembered Mr. Potter's basset hound. The name Wrinkles certainly fit the dog. "I think you need to listen to your mom and not go over there unless she tells you that you can."

"I know. But Wrinkles needs to eat more. That's why he has wrinkles. He's getting too skinny, and his skin doesn't fit him anymore."

"Wrinkles has been skinny for a long time. I wouldn't worry about him."

Wren was quiet for a moment. "Is Uncle Frank going to turn into a skeleton?"

Will felt like he'd been broadsided. Children had the most amazing, most flexible minds in the world.

"I know it makes you sad," she went on, "but I wanted to know 'cause I like Uncle Frank and I don't want to be scared of him."

"Why would you be scared of him?"

"When Jesus calls Uncle Frank up from his grave, I just

wanted to know what he would look like. So I could recognize him. If he was all bones, he wouldn't look the same."

"I see." Will didn't know what else to say.

"Pastor Bob says we'll all get new bodies when Jesus comes," Wren announced. "Is that true?"

Will took a deep breath. It really wasn't his day for hard questions. "If Pastor Bob says that's true, then it must be true."

"If we're all going to get new bodies, why don't we get buried with name tags?"

"Name tags?"

Wren nodded in serious contemplation. "Like they give out at church for the new people. The ones that say, 'Hello. *My name is* ____.' And then you write your name in. That way we would know each other in heaven."

"I think that's a good idea."

"I'm going to pray to God about it tonight," Wren said. "I'll tell him."

>> **2111 HOURS**

A little while later, Will put Wren to bed in his bedroom. He planned to sack out on the couch. When Wren got down on her knees beside the bed to pray, she asked Will to pray beside her.

Feeling awkward and too big, Will knelt and listened to his daughter say her prayers in a quick, singsong voice. As he knelt beside his daughter in such a simple practice, holding on to the belief in her voice, he was surprised at the peace and calm that seemed to touch him. Then it was gone.

As she finished, Wren added a quick note to let God know that he should consider giving everybody name tags when he gave them new bodies.

She was asleep almost as soon as her head hit the pillow.

On the couch, Will tuned in FOX News and left the volume

low. Over the past few months he'd learned that he couldn't sleep well if there was no noise in the house.

The phone rang.

"Coburn," he said, glancing at the clock and seeing that it was 10:14 p.m.

"Mr. Coburn . . . ," a man's voice said tentatively.

"Yes." Carefully, feeling the protest in his side, Will swung his feet around and dropped them to the floor. He didn't recognize the voice.

"My name is Ben Hester. I got your number from the phone book."

Will recognized the name. He was USMC Lance Corporal Virgil Hester's father. He'd called and left messages at the NCIS offices every day since his son's death.

"What can I do for you, Mr. Hester?"

"I don't believe what you people are saying about my son. He was a good boy. He wasn't involved in any kind of black-market dealing or drugs or any other criminal thing."

"Sir," Will said gently but firmly, "we've got written testimony that says he was."

"Well, it's wrong," Hester said in a more forceful voice. "That testimony, and whoever gave it, is terribly wrong. Virgil wasn't any criminal mastermind. He never did anything illegal in his life."

Will was tired and beaten up. He didn't want another argument on his hands that he couldn't win. "Sir, I can't—"

"They also told me that they'd lost my son's body."

"His body was stolen," Will said.

"Who stole it?"

"We don't know, sir."

"Why was it stolen?"

"We don't know."

"Well, there has to be a reason," Hester protested.

Silently, Will agreed. And whatever the reason was, it was also the reason that Frank was dead.

"He was our only child. His mother and I aren't even going to be able to grieve properly until his body is found and returned home so we can bury him."

"People are searching for him, Mr. Hester."

"Are *you* searching? It said in the news that you were the superior officer in the investigation."

"I was shot," Will said. "One of my men was killed."

Hester was silent for a while. "That's right. I'd forgotten you were shot. I hope you get to feeling better. It's just—" his voice broke again—"it's just that if it was your boy out there who'd been killed and had his body stolen, wouldn't you want to know what happened? Wouldn't you want to know?"

Will held on to the phone, saying nothing. He knew whatever lame consolation he could offer would mean nothing to the grieving father.

When Hester regained his composure and hung up, Will lay back on the couch and tried to relax. He reached for sleep, hoping it would take him away. Instead, Ben Hester's voice and questions haunted him all night.

22

>> JACKSONVILLE, NORTH CAROLINA
>> 1748 HOURS

Will parked his pickup in the street in front of the house where he used to live. Looking at it was strange, like a half-remembered memory.

Wren unbuckled her seat belt, pushed the door open, and ran to the front door. As much as she'd said she'd wanted to stay with her daddy, she'd missed her mommy, too.

Instead of the old minivan that Barbara had driven for so many years, a bright yellow Volkswagen Beetle sat in the driveway. Behind it was a sleek, baby blue Mercedes coupe.

Barbara has company.

The realization gave Will pause; then he took a deep breath and hefted the box of things he'd bought Wren on their multiple shopping trips. Yesterday they'd added a couple computer games for the system that Steven liked to play. Will had also picked up two baseball hats from Steven's favorite teams.

Will wasn't trying to buy his son's love, but he was willing to admit that he was trying to buy Steven's attention. He got out of his truck dressed in jeans, a dark blue Navy T-shirt with yellow letters, and a matching Navy ball cap.

Carrying the box, Will walked up to the front door and rang the bell.

The neighborhood was small, compact. People who lived here kept their yards mowed and worked on flower gardens. Kids played touch football and Rollerblade hockey in the streets. Sprinklers watered lawns on a regular basis so everything stayed green even during the hottest part of the year. At this time of the day, several people were grilling and the air was filled with the scent of charcoal and cooking meat. He missed the comfort of that familiarity.

No one came to the door.

Then Wren poked her head around the side of the house. "Back here, Daddy." She smiled broadly. "Everybody's back here." She waved.

Will followed his daughter around the side of the house to the deck he and Steven had built four years ago. He'd laid the brick grill himself, working from a design he'd found in *Popular Mechanics*.

Barbara flipped burgers with a long-handled spatula. Behind her, dressed in khaki shorts and a golf shirt, Jesse showed Steven how to use a putter. He tapped a white ball gently and sent it speeding toward an overturned cup.

"I'm sorry, Will," Barbara said. "I was busy turning the burgers, and Jesse and Steven are really wrapped up in golf. Steven's gotten interested in the sport."

Will choked back a bitter reply. He'd always stuck to football, basketball, and baseball with Steven. His son had never shown the slightest interest in golf. *Guess it makes a difference when you've got someone to play with, though.*

"I just brought a few things," Will said, lifting the box. "Wren and I went shopping."

"Just put them down there." Barbara pointed at the small potting table at the back of the house.

Will put the box down and watched as Wren ran to the swings he'd first put up for Steven right after they'd bought the house.

Jesse looked up but didn't acknowledge him. He kept talking to Steven, working on his stroke and the positioning of his feet.

"So how serious is this . . . thing getting to be?" Will asked. The question was out of his mouth before he could stop himself.

Barbara gave him an arch look. "You," she said in a distinctly cold voice, "have no right to ask that."

Maybe he didn't, but that didn't keep Will from feeling upset and frustrated.

Jesse left Steven practicing and came over. His manner was possessive. "Is everything all right here?"

An instinctive urge to assert himself filled Will. This was *his* backyard. He'd mowed it—whenever he was in town—for ten years. He'd built the swings, the deck, and the grill. And he felt certain that even wounded he could take Jesse Harlan apart. The man had never stepped foot inside Will's working world.

"Everything is fine, Jesse," Barbara said. "Will was just leaving."

Jesse kept his eyes fixed on Will. "Maybe I could walk him out."

"No," Barbara said. "Will knows the way."

Without a word, Will turned to go. He reached his truck before he heard Barbara call his name. She came after him and stood in the driveway behind the Mercedes.

Pausing, Will pulled his Navy cap a little lower. "What?"

Barbara folded her arms and looked pensive. "I'm sorry, Will, but things have changed."

He gave her a short nod. "I guess so." Sliding behind the wheel, he started his pickup and drove away. He tried not to look back, but he couldn't help himself.

Barbara remained in the driveway, looking after him till he turned the corner and she vanished from sight.

❋ ❋ ❋

>> KINSTON, NORTH CAROLINA
>> 2037 HOURS

Will heard a sharp tone and glanced down at the gas-tank indicator on the pickup's dash. The tank was almost empty.

Will's talk with Barbara had left him in no mood to face his empty apartment, so instead of heading home after dropping Wren off, he had driven around aimlessly, mulling over his phone conversation with Hester's father.

Will looked around to get his bearings. He knew he was in Kinston, maybe fifty miles north of Camp Lejeune, but beyond that he didn't know exactly where he was. He remembered passing a gas station recently, so he hung a quick U-turn and headed back.

Pulling up to one of the pumps, Will got out of the truck. Across the street was a neon-lit bar with more than a dozen cars and pickups in the small parking lot. A shabby-looking sign over the entrance proclaimed Dewdrop Inn.

Will swiped his credit card and started the gas pumping. He engaged the autopump device and let go of the handle, leaning against the side of the truck. Thoughts of Barbara flashed across his mind and evoked a heavy sigh from him. He closed his eyes for a moment, resting them against his fatigue.

A voice from the bar across the street cut into his reverie.

"Get in the car, Darlene!" The harsh voice was a male's.

"No, Earl! I'm not going with you! I told you it was over!" The woman sounded scared and angry, and all bets were off as to which way the scales were going to tip.

Will glanced over, trying to be surreptitious. *Don't get*

involved, he told himself. *This is none of your business.* A domestic dispute at a bar was one of the worst situations for a law-enforcement officer to handle. *You stop a fight tonight, they just start it up again somewhere else later.*

"You don't have a choice!" the man shouted.

"It's over!" Darlene shouted back. "I told you that! Your mother told you that! The judge told you that!"

Suddenly, the meaty smack of flesh meeting flesh split the shadows covering the parking area. The woman cried out in pain.

Will stepped away from the pickup, trying to remain in the shadows near the street but still get a better view of the dispute.

Darlene was a thin peroxide blonde in her early twenties. She wore jeans and a revealing shirt, making it evident that she'd come to party at the bar. She was sprawled on the ground, one hand to her face. Blood tricked from her nose.

Earl was a steroid monster, broad and beefy and surely no older than twenty-five. His eyes were too close set, his mouth weak and pink lipped. His head was shaved, leaving only a smear of hair color behind. Dressed in jeans and a T-shirt featuring a vampire clown in chains and waving a meat cleaver, he looked distinctly threatening. Piercings through one eyebrow and his nose glinted in the moonlight and neon glare from the bar window.

Without a word, Will approached.

Two other men got out of the fire-engine red Camaro Iroc behind Earl.

"Company," one of the men said. He was young and thin, and his long hair fell into his face. He carried a beer bottle in one hand.

The third man was a bruiser like Earl. He wore a goatee colored bright pink.

"Don't you come over here, man," Earl warned, turning slightly to face Will. "You make the mistake of comin' over here, I'm gonna bust you up."

Darlene looked up with fear etching her face. Bruises were already forming under her tears. "Help! He'll kill me, mister!"

Earl kicked her viciously.

Will knew calling the police wasn't an option. Earl and his buddies would be gone before the police responded. Maybe they would take the young woman with them. Will couldn't allow that.

Earl reached to his hip and brought out a hunting knife. He pointed it at Will and grinned. "Takin' part in this is the worst thing you could do, pops."

The other two men came around the car to flank Earl. The one with the beer bottle smashed it against the car's bumper, leaving a jagged shard with deadly edges gleaming from his hand. The third man held a length of chain.

Will stopped a short distance away. "Let her go."

Weakly, hiccupping in pain and fear, Darlene tried to crawl away.

Earl stomped on one of her outstretched hands. One of her fingers snapped.

Will moved without thinking, going straight at Earl.

Grinning, Earl stabbed at Will with the knife.

Will blocked the effort away with the back of his left wrist, set with his left foot forward, and brought a straight jab up from his hip, twisting at the waist to get everything he had behind the blow.

Earl's head snapped back. His nose broke and blood gushed. He stumbled backward and sprawled over the Camaro's hood. Cursing and howling, he wiped at his face, smearing blood down his chin.

Burning pain shot through Will's side, and he hoped the wound wouldn't tear open again. The fluid movement he was accustomed to didn't come without a price despite the rehab he'd been doing.

The man with the broken bottle hesitated just a moment before attacking. He lunged at Will, but Will sidestepped, caught the man's arm in his hands, then pulled his opponent forward and drove a knee into the man's side. He collapsed in a mewling heap, the breath driven from his lungs.

When the guy with the chain attacked, Will knew it was going to hurt. A chain was fluid pain and destruction in the hands of someone who knew how to use it. The third man did.

He whipped the chain toward Will's face, then flicked the other end around Will's forward leg and yanked. Will came off his feet and fell heavily on his back. The fall hammered the breath from him, but he scrambled to his feet, pushing up with his hands.

Earl threw himself away from the car. "Leave him, Tommy! He's mine!"

Tommy backed away with obvious reluctance. The man with the broken bottle got to his feet with ragged, wet gasps.

Trying to block the burning agony from his side, Will stood in an L stance, left foot forward, and raised both his hands in front of him.

"Pops." Earl grinned evilly through a crimson mask. "You're gonna regret hornin' in here tonight. I guarantee that." He feinted with the knife, driving Will back.

Darlene attempted to get away again, actually getting to her feet this time. Distracted, Earl turned to the thin man. "Get her, Keith!"

Keith ran forward and caught Darlene. The young woman squealed in fear.

Earl swiveled his attention back to Will. "The best thing you could do for yourself, pops, is to get out of here." He wiped at his bloody face. "I'm willin' to overlook this. Cuttin' you a deal here."

"I'll cut you one," Will said. "Let the girl go, and I won't hurt you."

Earl said, "All right," and acted liked he was going to walk away.

Will wasn't fooled for a moment. Too many men he'd taken down had tried the same tactic, yet each one thought he was clever. Earl had the advantage of the big hunting knife to bolster his courage.

Earl turned and swung the knife like a sword, aiming at Will's head. Will ducked to the left and brought his right hand up under Earl's elbow, then performed a reverse spin, hammering his left fist down on Earl's wrist. The knife flew from his lax grip.

Still on the move, Will drove forward and slammed his elbow into the front of his opponent's right shoulder joint. The brachial nerve plexus clustered there caused excruciating pain and temporary paralysis. Will swept a leg behind Earl's right knee, dropping the man to the ground.

Tommy whirled his chain and tried the feint again. This time Will was ready. Instead of ducking back out of the way, he stepped into the arc of the chain's path and grasped the chain at its midpoint. The chain's momentum whipped its free end around Will's hand, and he pulled back on it sharply, taking the man by surprise. The chain dropped from Tommy's hand. Now Will was the one with the weapon. Reaching forward, he cracked his chain-reinforced fist against Tommy's skull, taking care not to hit him too hard.

Tommy dropped without a sound.

Turning to the last man, Will said, "Let her go."

"You stay away," the man said, holding the broken bottle at Darlene's throat. "You stay away or I'll cut her."

Will kept his voice low and calm. The guy wasn't drugged out. He'd been drinking, but he could still be reasoned with. "Hurt her and I'll make you wish you hadn't."

The man held on to the woman for just a moment longer. Then he lost his nerve and fled, leaving his friends and the car behind.

Will's side felt like someone had shoved a red-hot branding iron against it. He walked over to the young woman.

She came into his arms. "I thought he was going to kill me," she said, shivering.

"No," Will said. "That's not going to happen." He held her, offering all the comfort he could as people came out of the bar.

She shook in his arms as they waited in the neon-drenched shadows. Sirens swelled in the distance. The police were on their way.

S ⊛ CRIME SCENE ⊛ NCIS ⊛ CR

23

>> CAMP LEJEUNE, NORTH CAROLINA
>> NCIS HEADQUARTERS
>> 2306 HOURS

Will had given his statement to the Kinston police officers who had arrived on the scene soon after the fight. His NCIS identification had expedited the process, and a quick check on the two men in custody revealed that both were in trouble with the law frequently and that Earl had violated a restraining order filed by Darlene. The girl, along with several other witnesses from the bar, had corroborated Will's version of the conflict, and he was allowed to go.

As he drove toward his apartment, Will's thoughts had returned to Barbara. But he had also realized that being who he was without Barbara was important too. Tonight he had saved Darlene—at least for now. That part of himself that he had given to the NCIS, that part of him responsible for saving lives and bringing the guilty to justice, was important. In his capacity as a naval investigator, he could help people and right a lot of wrongs.

Will thought of all the questions that Lance Corporal Hester's father had asked, and the fact that he'd had no answers to give the grieving man. That wasn't right. That man needed answers. Will needed them too. For Frank. So he could explain to Frank's wife why her husband had been murdered.

Somehow Frank's and Hester's murders were connected, and Hester's missing body was the key. No criminal got away without leaving a trail. It was time to pick this one up. So instead of going home, Will had headed toward the office.

He began running video footage of the crime scenes sent to him by the Chinhae forensics unit.

Why had the lance corporal's body been taken?

The question remained unanswered and was hammering at Will's mind. Something had to be there. No crime scene was pristine. A clue, a lead—*something*—was always left behind.

He looked at the tool markings reports from Frank's murder. All the bullets were fired from the same weapon. Nine had struck Frank's chest. All were of consistent caliber and rifling impressions. All possessed similar land-and-groove striations.

The land-and-groove marks were caused by the barrel rifling as the bullet passed through. Rifling patterns were as unique as fingerprints. Unfortunately, the only weapon recovered at the scene had been Frank's.

The General Rifling Characteristics had been calculated on the spent rounds. The GRCs consistently revealed that the bullets were fired from a weapon with a 6/right-rifled barrel, a land width of .054, and a groove width of .125. The GRCs indicated that the bullets had been fired from a Beretta 92F—the standard sidearm of the United States military. So both the .50-caliber rifle used by the sniper and the 9 mm used to kill Frank insisted on tracking back to American forces most easily.

Will turned away from the crime scene video. *I'm not doing
anybody any good here,* he thought bitterly. *If there was anything to be found, it would have been found already.*

Abandoning that avenue of investigation, Will turned his
attention to Lance Corporal Hester's private files. He pulled up
the X-rays that had been taken of Hester's body at the base hospital before the corpse had been stolen.

Will compared what he saw to Lance Corporal Hester's service record. He read through it for several minutes, unable to
shake the feeling that there was something he was missing, something he'd read that had caught the attention of his subconscious
mind.

Flipping through the papers again, Will spotted the report of
how Hester had broken two fingers on his left hand while on
assignment in Okinawa, Japan. Will glanced back up at Hester's
X-rays.

None of the fingers on the man's left hand revealed fractures—old or new.

>> **CAMP LEJEUNE**
>> **BARRACKS**
>> **0734 HOURS**

Morning turned the sky pink in the east. Will sat on his patio and
watched dawn break. He hadn't slept all night. His mind was
consumed by the enigma that had been and currently was USMC
Lance Corporal Virgil Hester.

Unable to wait any longer, Will dialed Ben Hester's number.
Hester answered on the first ring.

"Mr. Hester," Will said, "this is Commander Coburn of the
NCIS here in North Carolina. I was wondering if I could ask a
favor of you."

"What favor?"

"I'd like to visit you," Will said. "Talk to you about your son. Something has come up."

"What?"

"I'd rather talk to you in person."

Hester hesitated for a long time. "We can't live like this, Commander Coburn. His momma needs some peace. And quite frankly, so do I. We've been praying to God that somehow this mess sorts itself all out. Family means everything to us."

Another pause.

"When can you be here?" Hester asked.

"I can be there by midafternoon today," Will said.

Hester's resignation resonated in his voice. "Come ahead. But I'm going to have some questions."

We both will, Will thought as he cradled the phone.

>> **CLYDE, OHIO**
>> **THE HESTER RESIDENCE**
>> **1518 HOURS**

Ben and Gabriella Hester lived in a small two-bedroom home in an older community of Clyde, Ohio. Clyde was a small metropolis that boasted of being the largest washing-machine manufacturer in the world.

Will parked his rental sedan at the curb. The yard was immaculate and showed off a small flower garden. A flagpole flew Old Glory over the neighborhood.

Ben Hester rose from the Adirondack chair on the small front porch. He was tall and lean, dressed in brown slacks and a pearl-gray shirt that didn't strike Will as everyday wear. His hair was sandy blond but a band of white started at his temples and went around his head.

Will identified himself, showing the man his NCIS identification.

Hester shook Will's hand, then ushered Will into the house.

"My wife's not here," Hester explained. "I didn't know how she'd handle this."

The house was small and neat, like the yard outside. The furniture was old but well cared for. A painting of Jesus with a lamb tucked under his arm and surrounded by children adorned the mantelpiece.

"That's fine," Will said, taking a seat on the couch.

Hester excused himself and went into another room. He returned a moment later carrying a large photo album and several DVDs. "His momma put this together," the man said as he put the materials down on the coffee table in front of Will. "She was always . . ." His voice broke. He wiped his reddened eyes with a palm but didn't cry. "She was always taking that boy's picture."

"I appreciate you having me here, Mr. Hester." Will opened the photo album and began leafing through the pages.

The album started with baby pictures and moved into the toddler years. Virgil Hester had been a healthy, happy kid. His mother had included pictures of him with missing teeth, chicken pox, his first tricycle, first puppy, and first stitches. There were sport pictures, too: baseball, soccer, football, and wrestling.

The picture that caught Will's attention was one of Virgil Hester at a junior high dance with a young girl about his age.

"That's Darla Timmons," Hester said. "Virgil had it bad for that one for a long time. Got his first stitches trying to impress her with his skateboarding."

Will touched the picture. "When did your son break his leg?"

In the photo, young Virgil Hester stood smiling with one arm around Darla Timmons. The white cast on the boy's left leg matched his date's white dress.

"Football," Hester answered immediately. "His eighth-grade year."

"How bad was the break?" Will asked.

"A bad one. Broke the thigh and the shin. For a while, the doctor didn't know if Virgil's leg was going to grow the way it was supposed to. But we prayed a lot, and Virgil just kept at his rehab. He was starting at wide receiver again by the next season."

Taking out his Pocket PC, Will said, "I need you to tell me about Virgil's other injuries."

S ✦ CRIME SCENE ✦ NCIS ✦ CR

NAVAL CRIMINAL INVESTIGATIVE SERVICE

24

SCENE **NCIS** ✪ **CRIME SCENE**
NAVAL CRIMINAL INVESTIGATIVE SERVICE

```
>> CAMP LEJEUNE, NORTH CAROLINA
>> NCIS MEDICAL LAB
>> 0132 HOURS
```

Will looked up from his notes from the Hester interview as Nita Tomlinson arrived.

The medical examiner's red hair hung to her shoulders with carefully orchestrated abandon. She wore white cargo pants and a dove gray sweater. Her makeup was flawless.

"Sorry," Will apologized. "I didn't intend to pull you away from anything." Actually, at one-thirty in the morning, he'd felt certain he'd be getting her out of bed. Instead, Nita looked like she'd just walked out of a club. Her husband and little girl had been in bed when Will had called the house. He'd called her cell phone next.

"I thought the team was down for a break," Nita said.

In the enclosed room, Will smelled alcohol on her breath. It mingled with the delicate perfume she wore. Her jade earrings caught the light and gleamed.

"We are," Will said.

Nita folded her arms and arched a brow. "Pet project?"

"No," Will said. "The investigation we were on in Chinhae."

"The one where the body was stolen?" Interest flickered in Nita's gray-green eyes.

"The one where Frank was killed," Will said, putting the weight of the matter squarely where it belonged.

"You don't have a body to work with," Nita said. "I don't know why you called me in."

"We don't have a body," Will said, "but we do have X-rays and an ultrasound." He held up his iPAQ. "We've also got some new information. I wanted a second opinion on some things."

"All right."

Will quickly put the X-rays of the dead man on the wall scanners. "I have a list of injuries here. Injuries suffered by Lance Corporal Hester as he grew up. Injuries documented by these." He tapped his iPAQ and brought up digital images of the pictures Ben Hester had shown him.

"Okay," Nita replied, "you've got me interested."

"In eighth grade, Hester broke his left leg in two places."

Nita grinned. "He should have stayed out of those places, shouldn't he?"

Smiling a little himself, anticipating what Nita was going to discover, Will pointed at the X-rays and said, "Show me where."

Nonchalantly, Nita glanced at the negatives. Then her arms dropped to her sides, and she studied them more earnestly. "The left leg has never been fractured."

"During his sophomore year, Hester suffered three broken fingers and a broken thumb on his right hand when he fell from the top of a water tower while painting *Virgil Loves Darla*. He also suffered a skull fracture."

The skeleton's head was a spiderweb of fracture lines. They looked gray against the white of the bone.

"Plenty of skull fractures here, but no broken fingers."

"We don't know about the skull fractures," Will admitted. "Forensics reassembled the victim's head after a .50-caliber bullet blew it apart."

Nita looked at him. "You called this 'the victim.' Not Hester."

" 'Not Hester' is how I've started thinking about him." Will returned to his list. "Two front teeth knocked out during hockey his freshman year of college. Had implant replacements."

Nita examined the negatives. "No implants. Do your notes say anything about these cracked ribs?"

"No."

"Or the right kneecap replacement, which is not supposed to be allowed in the military?"

"No."

"The dislocated shoulder?"

"There is a dislocated shoulder, but it was the left shoulder, not the right."

Totally curious now, Nita turned to Will. "Are you sure these files are Hester's?"

Will nodded. "We took control of the body on-site. The medical examiner at the base there ran the X-rays and ultrasounds. I called his office. These are those." He held up the iPAQ. "And these are copies of Hester's photographs."

"You want a professional opinion?" Nita asked.

"That's what I asked you here for."

"That," Nita said, pointing at the negatives, "is not USMC Lance Corporal Virgil Hester."

"Somehow," Will replied, "I knew you were going to say that."

⊛ ⊛ ⊛

"Have you had any sleep?"

Will sat at his desk in the Camp Lejeune NCIS office. The divorce papers were filed in a drawer out of sight. "Some. Not much."

Bright morning sunlight filtered in through the polarized window behind him. What little sleep he'd gotten had been in the chair in between processing files and writing up his report for the director.

On the monitor broadcasting on a scrambled frequency from his Washington, D.C., office, Larkin looked thoughtful. "Could be a clerical error." He referred to the Hester's incongruent findings. "Maybe the wrong X-rays and ultrasounds were sent to you from Chinhae."

"I followed the chain of custody," Will said. "The medical examiner's office in the naval base guarantees the handle. These are copies of Hester's files taken right after the shooting."

"Maybe it wasn't Hester in the alley that night."

Will tapped a key on the keyboard in front of him. Immediately a window containing video footage opened up on both his and the director's monitors. The digital footage showed Hester, then showed the ruin left by the .50-cal bullet.

"Looked like Hester to me," Will said. "But I didn't rest on that. I cross-checked DNA from the body with what the Marine Corps has on file. The body we recovered was, according to the match, Virgil Hester. Interestingly enough, the DNA recovered from that body matches neither of Hester's biological parents. I took samples from both of them while I was in Clyde, Ohio."

"Hester could have been adopted," Larkin suggested.

"His father says no. Of course, that leaves you with the possibility of babies accidentally getting switched at the hospital. Want to know what the chances of that happening are? I checked. If we hit on that, we're going to Vegas."

Larkin leaned back in his chair. "Doesn't make sense."

"Here's something else for you," Will said. He punched another button. "Hester's military medical records. They match the X-rays we have of our victim, except for the reconstructed right knee, which should have kept him out of military service. Especially the Marines."

Sighing, Larkin pushed back in his chair. "So the Marine in Chinhae was not the Virgil Hester that was raised in Ohio."

"No."

Larkin picked up a pencil and tapped it against the desk. It was at times like this that Will really respected the man. When it came to pure skull work, Larkin was one of the best around.

"Was Hester in contact with his parents?" Larkin asked.

"E-mail on a semiregular basis. A few phone calls. I've got e-mail samples."

Larkin nodded. "Notice any changes? Word choice? Length of message? Forgetting to tell stories about friends aboard ship? That kind of thing?"

The questions made connections inside Will's mind. He pulled up the e-mails and flipped through them. "All of those things." He hadn't even noticed that until Larkin had asked.

"The father didn't mention them?"

"I didn't think to ask him that. He said he noticed that Virgil had seemed more tense, more forgetful, and more preoccupied. He wrote it off as Virgil serving on a new base, getting used to the people and the operations there."

Larkin leaned forward and tapped keys. "I'm looking through Hester's military jacket. When did Hester change posts?"

"He was transferred from Japan to South Korea in July of last year."

"What was the reason for the transfer?"

"Requested change of MOS. He was a rifleman in Japan. Shifted his Military Occupational Specialty to mechanics. Claimed that he always had an interest in that field."

"Save that for now. Let's find out if anyone transferred with him. It's difficult to set up a black-market operation—even a small one—without help."

Will brought up the files regarding transfers between the two bases.

"If Hester was working the black market," Larkin said, "he had to have a partner."

"No one from Japan," Will said. "He was alone unless he met someone there he went into business with."

"Look at the other end, then. Did anyone transfer to Chinhae at the same time Hester did?"

"Two other Marines arrived at the base in the mechanics pool within a three-week window of Hester's arrival."

"What do we have on them?" Larkin asked.

Scanning the information on the two sailors, Will said, "Looks like they're clean. No reprimands. No warnings. Both of them have been in the service for a while. Five years and eight years respectively."

"They're vanilla. All the same, I think we should talk to them." Larkin made a note. "Did your team do a workup on the Marines and sailors Hester hung with?"

"We've got a short list. Nothing promising."

"It'll have to be worked. Hester couldn't have made all the connections himself. There had to be a network in place that he tapped. And there's another thing."

Will waited.

"Hester's body was stolen. Someone didn't want you to find this out."

"And that same person killed Frank to protect the secret," Will added.

Larkin sighed. "Call your team back, Commander. Let me see if I can arrange transport for you."

Will was surprised that Larkin had so readily offered what he was prepared to fight for. "Back to Chinhae?"

"Yes. That's where this thing began to unravel. We'll start there. I want to know why this man chose to impersonate a Marine, and I want to know how he did it."

"When do we leave?"

"As soon as you can get your team together."

>> **0839 HOURS**

After Larkin broke the connection, Will sat back restlessly in his chair. He felt uncomfortable and edgy, as if he would explode if he moved the wrong way.

The mystery surrounding Hester—or whoever the man ultimately turned out to be—was a step in the right direction. He felt that in his bones.

He glanced through the door at the desk where Frank had always sat. The loss descended upon Will like a heavy blanket.

Even if he solved the puzzle—*when,* he told himself, not *if*—Frank would still be dead. The realization was sobering.

Then he saw Frank's Bible lying on his desk. Frank's words filled his mind again, imploring him to turn to God during his time of need.

Slowly, almost in awe, Will took Frank's Bible in his hands. He knelt there on the floor of his office and bowed his head in prayer.

"God, I know you know the kind of man I've been," Will said in a hoarse whisper. "I know I can't hide anything from you. Not even my doubts and fears." He hesitated, uncertain about how to go on. But the words seemed to keep coming to him. "I'm away from my wife and children, God, and I need you to help me be strong while I sort that out. In the meantime, I can feel that I'm at a crossroads in my life. Help me make the right choices. Lead me in the direction you would have me go."

He remained on his knees, trembling and afraid.

Then a quiet strength filled him, nourishing him and lifting his pain and his worries. Relief flooded over him, and Will turned loose his fears. They would return, he knew, but he would be better prepared to deal with them when they did.

"Thank you, God," he whispered as tears fell down his cheeks. "Thank you for remembering me."

CRIME SCENE ✸ NCIS ✸ CRI
NAVAL CRIMINAL INVESTIGATIVE SERVICE

25

E SCENE ⊛ **NCIS** ⊛ **CRIME SCEN**
NAVAL CRIMINAL INVESTIGATIVE SERVICE

>> SEOUL, REPUBLIC OF KOREA
>> DOWNTOWN
>> 2044 HOURS

Qadir Yaseen peered through the darkened window of the armored SUV at the crowded streets of Seoul, South Korea. The sturdy vehicle prowled like a great cat through the Myeongdong District of shops and entertainment. Scarlet light and neon glows from dozens of nightclubs and bars called forth the young and the daring and the predatory every evening. The tall vertical signs were in Korean, but Yaseen didn't need to be able to read them to understand what they said.

Yaseen despised the downtown nightlife. Dark dreams, twisted fantasies, and evil that didn't dare show during the light of day found homes in the night. The confusion and lust that the scene conjured up were prime examples of the cancer the Western world was spreading. Nightlife had been a favorite pastime of society since the first red lantern had been invented, but only the influence of the West could have turned it into such a pervasive sickness.

The American Satans had spread their poison to the rest of the world, gaining power and popularity so they could invade the Middle East and support the hated Jews.

The SUV passed the Korea Theater and the Midopa Department Store, two of the best-known sites in the downtown area. The driver took a right turn into one of the numerous alleys and glided to a stop at an awning-covered private entrance.

A doorman in a red jacket opened the SUV's door.

Yaseen unfolded himself and stood, shaking out his robe, instantly putting the three security men watching over the door on full alert.

A maitre d' approached. "Your party awaits you in the private salon, sir," he said. "Please come this way."

The private salon was lavish. Crimson curtains covered large windows filled with bulletproof glass. White-noise generators strategically placed throughout the room guaranteed that no one would peek into the room electronically.

An ornate table set for three filled the center of the room. Full wineglasses stood next to decorated plates. A man sat at the table. He was small and compact, with long blond hair and a bold beard. He was in his early thirties and had light gray eyes that caught the light from the candles burning in the center of the table. His name was Isidor Kuzlow. He was the head of a Russian *Mafiya* family that operated in Moscow and Eastern Europe.

At Yaseen's approach, the Russian dropped a hand into his lap. Yaseen had no doubt the man kept a pistol of some kind there.

"I am Qadir Yaseen, Mr. Kuzlow."

"It's very good to finally meet you, sir," Kuzlow replied.

"I trust you had a pleasant flight?" Yaseen took a seat at the head of the table.

"It was uneventful," Kuzlow said.

"The cocaine was satisfactory?"

"More than satisfactory," Kuzlow said. "I expect to make a healthy profit." Russians had an appetite for the drug, but the supply was extremely limited. In return for the services received from Kuzlow, Yaseen had provided the Russian with the connections he needed to funnel the deadly white powder into the country.

"I'm sure you will," Yaseen said.

Servers replenished Kuzlow's vodka. A few moments later, the maitre d' entered the room again. "Your second guest has arrived, sir," he announced in flawless Russian as Vladimir Gronsky came through the doorway.

The new arrival was a man of huge girth. He had gray hair and bright blue eyes. He wore an expensive suit and freshly shined shoes.

He stopped, obviously surprised to see Kuzlow at the table. "You!"

Kuzlow stared back at him without reacting.

Yaseen smiled calmly. "I see you two know each other. How nice." He gestured to the remaining chair. "Please sit," he directed.

Reluctantly, Gronsky sat. "What is the meaning of this?" he demanded.

"Since we appear to have some problems with transferring the missiles I have purchased," Yaseen said to Gronsky, "I thought the three of us should meet. You are the supplier; I am the consumer. Kuzlow is the delivery agent. But there has been no delivery. How do you think we should address this problem?"

Gronsky waved the question away. "I told you. It's not a problem—just a delay."

"A delay," Yaseen mused. "And yet I had to persuade one of your colleagues to call you so I could even talk to you."

Kuzlow watched in silent interest.

"I would have been in touch," Gronsky said. "As soon as I figured out how to handle the CIA."

"CIA?" Kuzlow asked.

"Colonel Gronsky intimated that the CIA was tracking you," Yaseen said.

Kuzlow was quiet for a moment. "I never saw any sign of anyone following me. After we took the missiles, we've not seen anyone."

"That's because you don't know what you're looking for," Gronsky said. "Your experience in these matters is limited."

Kuzlow started to object.

Yaseen smiled and spoke first. "I defer to your judgment in this, Colonel."

"Good. You should," Gronksy blustered but looked somewhat relieved.

"I want those missiles," Yaseen said.

"I have been willing to deliver them," Kuzlow said. "But the colonel told me you weren't ready."

Gronsky looked uncomfortable again.

"Because of the CIA involvement, no doubt," Yaseen said. He spoke to Kuzlow but continued to stare at Gronsky. "That's why I thought it would be better if we coordinated the transfer together from now on. Instead of working through Colonel Gronsky."

Gronsky didn't look happy. Sweat beaded on his massive forehead. He grabbed the wineglass on the table in front of him and took a long swallow. His eyes flitted back and forth between Yaseen and Kuzlow. "We will make the transfer," Gronsky said, his voice almost pleading. "You didn't have to go to all this trouble."

"It was no trouble," Yaseen assured him. "In fact, it was my pleasure."

"We just need to make a few more payoffs," Gronsky said. "The CIA is not incorruptible."

"Greed," Yaseen agreed, "is the downfall of so many."

Gronsky pulled at his collar as if it were too tight. He took another swallow and tried to clear his throat. His face turned beet red. "Something is wrong," he gasped hoarsely.

Kuzlow looked at Yaseen.

Yaseen smiled.

Frantic, unable to breathe, Gronsky slapped the table. He made piggy, whining noises.

Kuzlow stood and aimed his pistol at Yaseen.

"No," Yaseen's voice thundered. "Had I wanted you dead, Mr. Kuzlow, I would have killed you long before Gronsky showed up."

The Russian colonel choked and wheezed at the end of the table. He shook feebly, like an arthritic old man.

Yaseen stared into the small, pleading eyes in the center of the fat face. "Avarice, Colonel, is one of the deadliest sins. You should have taken what I paid you and been thankful for having it. Instead, your greed has cost you your life."

Moments later, Gronsky toppled from his chair and stopped moving.

"I would not advise you to drink from Gronsky's wineglass," Yaseen said brightly.

Kuzlow looked at him. He held his pistol in his hands, acting like he didn't know where to point it.

"Please," Yaseen said, "sit. I want you alive, Mr. Kuzlow. We still have things to do. I still require the missiles I paid for."

Kuzlow sat and put his weapon away.

"Why did you want me here?" Kuzlow asked.

"I want those missiles delivered," Yaseen said. "With Gronsky out of the way, there should be no further holdups. And I will not tolerate further failure. Do you understand?"

"Yes," Kuzlow said. "Perfectly." But his eyes were on the prone figure on the floor.

E SCENE ⊛ **NCIS** ⊛ CRIME SCEN
NAVAL CRIMINAL INVESTIGATIVE SERVICE

>> JACKSONVILLE, NORTH CAROLINA
>> ALBERT J. ELLIS AIRPORT
>> 0948 HOURS

Dressed in civilian clothes—khaki Dockers, a red golf shirt, and a North Carolina Tar Heels baseball cap—Will stood on the other side of the security area in Jacksonville's Albert J. Ellis Airport and awaited his team's newest member.

Six feet three inches tall and slender, barely packing a hundred and eighty pounds, Remy Gautreau didn't look like the poster image for a U.S. Navy SEAL at first glance. His skin held the deep luster of dark chocolate. His head was shaved. His face was a hard mixture of angles, a strong jaw, and pronounced cheekbones from his Creole heritage. A thin mustache shaded his upper lip.

He wore a sleeveless green-mesh basketball jersey, knee-length white basketball shorts, and Nike high-tops. Wraparound sunglasses hid his eyes. A slim gold chain and cross hung around his neck.

He carried two magazines and chatted easily with a young flight attendant in uniform, who was obviously enjoying his company. Remy said something and the young woman laughed.

Will stepped out from the wall. "Petty Officer Gautreau."

Remy's head swiveled at once. The boyish, shy, and flirting smile dropped from his face. The orange metallic lenses caught the light as they focused on Will.

"Who are you?" Remy said in an unexpectedly soft voice.

"Commander Will Coburn, NCIS."

Coming to attention smoothly, Remy saluted.

Will returned the salute. "At ease, sailor."

"Petty Officer?" the attendant repeated.

"U.S. Navy," Remy explained to her shortly, continuing to look at Will. "I thought I had a couple days off before I reported to duty, sir."

"Not anymore," Will said. "We're scrambling. New assignment."

Remy turned to the woman. "*Chéri*, guess I gotta take a rain check on dinner."

The woman took a final look at Remy and smiled a little bigger. "Don't wait too long to call."

Remy just smiled.

The attendant walked away and glanced once over her shoulder to make sure Remy was watching. Remy waved.

"You make friends quick," Will commented.

"I try to live in a friendly world," Remy said. He looked at Will. "But I guess that's not where we're headed."

"Not even," Will agreed. "Let's get your bags."

>> ALBERT J. ELLIS AIRPORT PARKING LOT
>> 1033 HOURS

"Your team," Remy said in his musical accent as he tossed his bags into the back of Will's pickup, "how deep did they go into this man Hester's network?"

During the wait for the luggage, Will had given Remy the highlights of the investigation. "We never had the chance to dig." Will slid in behind the steering wheel.

Remy got in on the passenger side. "Because this guy Billings got killed?"

Will kept his eyes straight ahead. "Frank Billings wasn't just a team member. He was one of my closest friends."

Remy trained the orange-tinted sunglasses on Will. "So this thing we're doing, it's personal?"

Will didn't respond. He pulled out of the parking lot.

When Will said nothing, Remy continued, "I'm surprised the director allowed you to work on this after your *podna* was killed."

"We're not doing this because Frank was our friend." Will swallowed some of the pain that still echoed within him. "We're working the case because we're good at what we do."

"That's another thing I don't understand. If your team is gonna up an' jump right away, why did they bring me in on this now?"

"Because the director told me that was how it was going to be."

"Doesn't make any sense. Your team's gonna need trained people. People trained in crime investigation. That isn't me."

"We can train you to do everything you need to."

"Just like that?"

"Your CO says you're smart and you learn quick."

Tapping his chin, Remy studied the countryside. "Did he also tell you I didn't put in for this change of MOS?"

"Yeah."

"Me, I was happy where I was at."

"Getting shot at on a regular basis?"

Remy grinned but the effort lacked true humor.

"I was told that you like to take risks," Will said.

"Ah." Remy nodded and smiled again. "And is that what you're lookin' for, Commander? A man who likes to take risks?"

"No." Will didn't say anything further. He let the silence push against the noise of the pickup's tires humming over the highway.

"Why didn't you decline the transfer?"

"I wasn't given a choice," Will stated.

Grinning, Remy said, "You don't hold back, do you?"

"If I'd lied, you'd have known it."

"True. I got a nephew who says detecting lies is my mutant ability." The smile on Remy's face thinned.

Will studied the man briefly, wondering if he'd just seen pain on the petty officer's face. "Your nephew likes superheroes?"

Now it was Remy who didn't respond. He merely continued looking out the window.

Will felt the cold distance that lay between them and knew he was treading on private ground. "My son liked them when he was younger. Now he's fourteen and it's all about sports. My daughter prefers Scooby-Doo."

"Family's nice," Remy said. "Sometimes you don't appreciate them till they ain't around no more, though." A thin note of sadness sounded in his words.

Will couldn't help thinking about Barbara and the kids. Suddenly, he didn't much feel like further conversation either. "True." He turned his attention back to his driving.

NCIS **CRIME SCEN**

E SCENE

NAVAL CRIMINAL INVESTIGATIVE SERVICE

>> OUTSIDE BOSTON, MASSACHUSETTS
>> THE FOLEY RESIDENCE
>> 1114 HOURS

"You're leaving?"

Maggie Foley despised the guilt that flooded her when she heard the reproach in the commanding voice. She put her carry-on suitcase down on the hardwood floor of the large living room and turned to face her father.

Harrison Talbot Foley III stood halfway up the curving stairs on the right side of the room, one hand on the wrought-iron railing and the other folded behind him as if he were a ship's captain standing in the stern.

Maggie's father looked a full decade younger than his nearly sixty years. He kept himself fit and trim through harsh self-discipline and the assistance of personal trainers. He had his hair professionally colored. His black Italian suit fit him like a glove. His eyes were cold, ice blue.

"Yes," Maggie said in answer to his question. "I'm leaving."

"So soon?" Those two words, spoken in a soft voice, held the physical impact of a sharp backhand.

"Commander Coburn called. Something has opened up on an investigation. He called the team back in."

"The same investigation that got one of Commander Coburn's team killed?" her father asked. He never acknowledged that she was one of the team—only that she spent time there that he felt would be put to better use elsewhere.

"Yes." Maggie's father was skilled at using her words against her when he could, so she didn't mince words with him.

"You weren't going to tell me?"

"You were on a conference call."

"Then this decision was made only this morning."

"Yes."

"What is it that could be so important?"

"I don't know." Maggie didn't like being grilled, but she had no choice. Not if she wanted to continue seeing her mother. And she did want that. No matter how much it pained her. If she made her father angry, he would remove her from the visitor's list.

"You know I don't approve of your career choice, Margaret," her father said.

"I think that you've made that clear." Maggie knew that her words came out angry the instant she saw sparks ignite in her father's eyes.

"Don't take that tone with me," her father ordered.

Remember Mother, Maggie told herself. *You want to see her.* She calmed.

Over the years of her mother's exile—and there was no way it was anything but that—to the mental-health facility where she had lived for the last fourteen years, her father had taken Maggie off the visitor's list for periods of time as punishment. Unable to see her mother, not knowing if she was being properly cared for, hurt Maggie. She knew that after her mother passed, her father would no longer have a hold over her. But she also didn't want that day to come.

"I apologize," Maggie said. "The call came as a surprise to me."

"You should tell Director Larkin to send someone else," her father said. "They've already proven their ineptitude by letting one of their own get murdered. You're fortunate that you weren't killed as well."

"I was there, too," Maggie said, wanting to shift the blame from the others.

"Yes," her father said, "I suppose you also let that poor man get killed. I can only imagine how you must feel."

The butler, a new man who doubled as a bodyguard, stepped into the room. He wore black and looked sleek and deadly. "Pardon me, Mr. Foley," he said. "Miss Foley, your car has been brought around."

"Thank you," Maggie said.

Quietly, after a brief nod from her father, the butler left the room.

Maggie picked up her carry-on. "I really have to go. My flight leaves soon."

"I didn't get to see much of you this time, Margaret," her father said. It was more guilt, of course, and inferred that the missed opportunity was entirely her fault.

"You were busy."

"Next visit, then."

"All right," Maggie replied, knowing that the next visit wouldn't be any better.

"Did you get to see your mother?"

Maggie inhaled through her nose slowly and counted to three. "Yes." She glanced at her watch. "My flight."

"Of course." Her father waved his dismissal, turned, and

walked away. "Stay safe, Margaret. You've chosen to travel in parts of the world beyond my protection."

And beyond your control, Maggie added to herself as she walked through the door.

The Alfa Spider parked in the circular driveway was new. Her father always bought her a new car every time she left. She never knew what make or model it would be, but it was always a sports car, always a convertible, and always red. The cars were her father's version of Post-it notes, constant reminders of all that she was choosing to walk away from.

But the cars were nothing more than pretty and powerful shackles.

Maggie tossed the carry-on into the passenger seat and slid behind the wheel. She didn't look back when she put the Spider in gear and blasted forward. The road to her father's mansion led through acres of landscaped grounds patrolled by security guards and cutting-edge technology.

The guards at the entrance barely got the huge iron gates rolled back in time for her to pass with inches to spare. Then she was on the highway headed back toward Boston. She rolled the top back and let the wind pull through her hair.

Maggie felt a tremendous weight lift from her shoulders as she left her father's house. Like she'd escaped.

Again.

E SCENE ⊛ NCIS ⊛ CRIME SCEN
NAVAL CRIMINAL INVESTIGATIVE SERVICE

>> **WEST TEXAS**
>> **PERMIAN BASIN**
>> **1034 HOURS**

The hot West Texas sun blazed down, branding Shel in the saddle. Mounted on an American Paint horse, he trailed after the cattle he was helping move through the Permian Basin country. Three other men rode horses ahead of him: Peter Turnbill; Peter's son, Bobby; and Shel's father, Tyrell McHenry.

Shel rode drag, at the end of the herd. Red dust boiled up from the ground all around him, fogging his sunglasses and coating the bandanna he wore over his nose and mouth. Sweat trickled under his chambray shirt, jeans, and leather gloves. More dust covered his white cavalry hat.

Only Max seemed undeterred by the heat and the long miles of slow-moving cows. The Labrador kept alert to his surroundings and gave chase to the occasional jackrabbit.

Shel wiped sweat from his brow with the back of his sleeve and stared through the constant wave of dust at the two riders to the right of the herd. He tried to block out the anger that twisted sickeningly inside him. *Coming along for this was a mistake,* he told himself again.

The bigger rider's body language showed that he was constantly berating the smaller rider. Shel couldn't hear the exchange now, but he'd heard plenty of it earlier. He was sick to death with it and had volunteered to ride drag just to be away from it.

After the military, where he'd found his true passion and calling, Shel's first love was ranch work. All of it—from fencing to herding to mucking out the barn—appealed to him. The work was clean and honest, done with two hands and a strong back, done outdoors and in wide-open places. Of course, it was also done from sunup to sundown, during the rain, and sometimes in the middle of the night. A working ranch didn't afford many days off. When a man did miss a day because of sickness or other obligations, he knew he'd just have to hit it harder the next day to catch up.

And if a man got caught up, he helped his neighbors with the full expectation that he would some day need to call on them for help. That was what had brought Shel out to the Broken Y Ranch.

Pete Turnbill owned the Broken Y. Shel's father, Tyrel McHenry, owned the Rafter M, which occupied the land to the south.

Back in high school at Fort Davis, the nearest city to the ranch, Shel had played on football teams and baseball teams with Pete. Shel hadn't liked Pete as a boy, and he found that he disliked him even more now as a man.

Pete had inherited the Broken Y from his father, who had been a hard-drinking man. Pete had evidently inherited that trait from his daddy.

Pete's boy, Bobby, was twelve. He looked like his father. Shel knew that by ranching standards the boy was practically grown, although he hadn't yet reached a man's size. He was still slender and only a few inches over five feet tall. Still, he was old enough to work full-time as a ranch hand, which Pete had him doing. Unfortunately, the boy wasn't keeping pace with the riding and herding, and Pete had been berating his son for that inability all day.

An hour later, they reached the lowlands at the foot of the Davis Mountains. Shel was ready to cut and run, unwilling to be around Pete and his son anymore. He stepped down from the saddle, though, while his father spoke with Pete.

"I appreciate everything you did, Tyrel," Pete said.

Hearing Pete address his father by his given name and not as Mr. McHenry was strange to Shel.

"Tweren't nothin'," Tyrel said. Years of hard work had stripped the excess flesh from him, and he looked tough as rawhide. His straw hat curled up on the sides, and his silver-and-turquoise hatband glinted in the sun. He wore a Colt .45 on his hip for snakes and varmints. He was sixty-two, hard eyed, and taciturn. "That's what neighbors are for."

Pete was as tall and broad as Shel remembered, but he'd gotten beefy and sloppy with the drinking. Still, ranching was hard on a man. Underneath the excess weight, he was strong as an ox. His black hair hung long and shaggy and he wore a gunfighter's mustache. He wore jeans, cowboy boots, and a denim shirt with the sleeves hacked off.

Max circled the cattle and waded into the slow-moving stream that lived and died by the amount of rainfall or the lack of. The dog swam lazily and barked at the cows.

"Should have already had this done," Pete said. "Bobby an' a couple of his friends hired on to do it, but they didn't get it done. Never saw hide nor hair of 'em."

Pain and frustration shot across the boy's face.

"But you know these kids today," Pete said, sounding just like his daddy had all those years ago when Shel had listened to Morgan Turnbill complain about his own son. Pete had been known for shirking work. "Ain't none of 'em worth the powder it would take to blow 'em up."

Tyrel didn't say anything for a minute. "This place you got here, it should be good enough for them cattle for a while."

Pete nodded. "I'll leave 'em be for a couple weeks, then see if Bobby an' his no-account friends can get up from them video games long enough to help out."

"You didn't pay them," Bobby snarled.

Anger tightened Pete's face as he turned to his son. "You better shut your mouth, boy."

But Bobby's anger wouldn't be held back. For the last two days, his daddy had done nothing but find fault with him and his friends. Shel didn't know how Bobby had gone for as long as he had without blowing up.

"The reason my friends didn't show up when you asked them to," Bobby said, "was because you didn't pay them last time! And you didn't pay them the time before that! They're not no-accounts! They're my friends! But they're not gonna work for free! And you don't do nothin' but gripe at 'em and cuss 'em out while they're around you!"

Quick as a snake, Pete lashed out at his son. Bobby stumbled a few steps back, then sat down with a bloody mouth.

Max bolted from the water, racing for the big man. The dog attacked as he was trained, without a sound.

Without thinking, Shel called Max off and stepped forward.

Then Tyrel's hand dropped over his arm with a grip of iron. "Don't you be buyin' into this," Shel's father said in cool voice. "This here's between a father and his son."

Pete cursed foully and yanked at his belt, freeing it through the loops. "I'm gonna teach you to sass me, boy." With the leather looped in his fist, he approached Bobby.

Shel looked at his father and felt the old distance swim between them again. Tyrel had always kept to himself. He didn't step out of his chosen world much, and he didn't interfere in the affairs of others. He'd turned a blind eye to things other men had done to their families.

By the time Shel shook Tyrel's hand off, Pete was already hammering Bobby with the heavy belt, striping Bobby's hands as he tried in vain to protect his face.

Shel grabbed Pete by the arm and spun him around. "Enough," Shel said.

Pete didn't hesitate. He fired off a short right that exploded along the left side of Shel's face. Staggered, Shel took a step back as his hat fell and his broken sunglasses dropped to the ground. Blood trickled down his face.

"Don't know what them Marines taught you," Pete roared, "but around here you don't interfere with a man whippin' his boy for disrespect!" He came on, throwing punches.

Shel held his ground, keeping his hands tucked beside his head as he used his forearms to block the blows. Then he threw two quick jabs that rocked Pete's head back. Blood spewed from Pete's broken nose, but he bawled curses louder and started flailing harder. He tried to kick Shel. Catching the leg and trapping it with his left hand, Shel drove a hard right into Pete's face and knocked him flat.

Cursing and spitting, his hair in wild disarray, Pete pulled the thick-bladed bowie knife from his boot and stood up.

Shel set himself, knowing he couldn't hold back anymore. By Marine standards, Pete was an unskilled fighter, but the knife could open Shel up like a split watermelon.

Max barked in warning, poising to leap into action.

A gunshot rang through the air.

"All right now," Tyrel said in his raspy voice. "That'll be just about enough of that foolishness." He held his smoking .45 in his right hand, still pointing toward the sky.

"No!" Pete shouted. "Shel had no right puttin' his hands on me! I ain't about to take a whippin' from no man because of that lazy son of mine!"

"Pete," Tyrel said, stepping forward, "you put that knife on down, or I'm gonna shoot you just as sure as we're standin' here. You know I'll do it."

Pete looked at Tyrel wildly.

"You come at him with that knife," Tyrel said, "Shel's likely to kill you. He don't play at fightin' the way you do. I'll shoot you an' cripple you up before I let him kill you an' go to prison for it. Now are you hearin' me?"

After a moment, Pete let the knife drop to the ground. "You get off my land. Both of you."

Tyrel nodded. "We're going. We're ready to be shut of this place anyway." He raised his voice. "Bobby, you fetch up your horse. You're ridin' back with us."

"Bobby," Pete shouted, "you stay here!"

Tyrel shook his head. "No, sir. We ain't gonna do it that way. We're gonna do it like I said. Bobby'll be staying with us a few days till you cool off. An' don't you be takin' it into your head to come around after him. If I see you lurkin' around my land, I'll beat the hair offa you."

Bobby brought his horse over. He was shaking so badly that Shel had to help him into the saddle. Bobby was crying.

Pete cursed them all as they rode away.

Shel looked at his father, amazed at the man's cool calm. Tyrel McHenry wasn't a man given to violence, but when it took him up, he gave back everything he had. The threat he'd given Pete wasn't talk. All of them knew it. ·

>> THE RAFTER M RANCH
>> 1228 HOURS

Back in the ranch house at the Rafter M, Shel found his father in the kitchen, nursing a cup of coffee. Shel had settled Bobby in the room he'd once shared with his brother.

"He's sleeping," Shel said. He'd left Max curled up on the bed with the boy, and Bobby had taken solace in the dog's presence.

"Boy gonna need stitches or a dentist?" Tyrel asked.

"No. He's got a few cuts on his lip. I got him to gargle with salt water. Should keep infection away and start him healing faster."

"Coffee's fresh." Tyrel waved to the camp pot on the stove. He didn't like electric coffeemakers.

Shel took a cup down from the cabinet and filled it, then sat at the long table across from his daddy.

"You didn't do that boy no favors steppin' into it with Pete," Tyrel said.

The old confusion over his father and his solitary, aloof ways twisted inside Shel. He'd never understood why his daddy had insisted on living his life apart from others.

"Pete was beating him," Shel said.

"Some," Tyrel admitted. He looked at his son. "Do you even realize what it is you done?"

"I stopped him from beating that boy."

"This time," Tyrel acknowledged. "But you ain't gonna be here forever, Shel. You're gonna leave again, an' Bobby's gonna be here with his daddy. Only instead of dealin' with just his daddy's anger, he's gonna be dealin' with his daddy's pride too. Over the fact that you whipped him or that I kept him from tryin' to carve you up like a Christmas turkey an' gettin' killed or whupped good for his trouble. That's gonna take Pete Turnbill longer to get around than just bein' mad at his kid."

"What would you have done?" Shel asked.

"Left it alone."

"And let him beat the boy?"

"Ain't none of it your business. Or mine." Tyrel sipped his coffee.

"No kid should have the kind of life Pete's giving Bobby. He can't protect himself. I'll call the sheriff's office. The Department of Human Services can help out."

Tyrel shook his head. "They can come out and keep Bobby from gettin' beat up as much, but can they give him a proper daddy?"

Shel couldn't answer that.

Another voice said, "No they can't, but something else can be done."

Shel looked up to see his brother, Don, standing in the doorway. Don looked a lot like him, but he was three years younger, several inches shorter, and had a wiry build. His hair was longer, and he wore a Western-cut suit and round-lensed glasses.

"Pete beat Bobby again?" Don asked wearily.

"Yeah," Shel said.

"Where's Bobby now?" Don asked.

"In our room."

"How is he?"

"He'll be all right."

"God help him," Don said.

And it wasn't just mentioned in passing, Shel knew. Don was a preacher. The way Don could put his complete faith in God without reservation unnerved Shel somewhat. Their mother had read stories to them from the Good Book. Shel had preferred the Old Testament's tales of the warriors and battles, but Don had embraced the teachings of Jesus.

"I tried to explain to Shel that he made a mistake," Tyrel said, sounding mildly disgusted. "Went an' upped the ante for Pete Turnbill. Ain't no goin' back for that boy now."

"I've got a few more days of leave coming," Shel said. "I'll see if I can straighten this out."

"You don't have more days," Don broke in. "That's why I came out here. You got a call from Commander Coburn this morning. If you check the answering service, you'll find his message. He called my office, too. In case you were out and I had a way of reaching you."

Cell phones didn't work out in the Davis Mountains and much of the basin area.

"Did the commander say why he called?" Curiosity thrummed within Shel.

"He said they're going back to Korea," Don answered. "Some new evidence has turned up. He wants you on the first flight you can get to Camp Smedley D. Butler in Okinawa."

"Why?"

"Didn't say."

Shel knew that Marine Corps base. He'd served temporary duty there a number of times.

Tyrel picked up his coffee cup, threw the remains in the sink, and put his hat on. "Good thing Bobby isn't countin' on you to hang around," he said. Then he walked through the back door.

Shel pushed away the sudden hurt he felt. He didn't think his daddy meant what he'd said in a mean way. It was just a fact. But it still hurt.

"Don't worry about Bobby," Don said. He'd always refereed the arguments and tensions that occurred between Shel and his daddy. "I can take care of him."

"I appreciate that." Shel stared through the kitchen window, watching his father walk to the corral. Two Paint ponies and a Morgan came over to him. Tyrel handed them apples from the barrel behind the house. "I didn't intend to create a mess, then just up and leave it."

"You haven't," Don said. "Pete Turnbill was already a mess. Now maybe we can do something about it." He paused. "And don't worry about Daddy either. What he said . . . that's just how he is."

"I know. Doesn't make it any easier." Shel looked at his brother. "You've lived around here longer than I have. Haven't you ever found someone who knows why Daddy's the way he is?"

Don shook his head as he gazed through the window. "No.

But I pray for him every night." He turned his attention back to Shel. "I pray for you too."

Shel didn't say anything, but he didn't think any amount of prayer would help his dad and him understand each other. Then he turned his thoughts to Will, wondering what had broken loose on the black-market investigation.

CRIME SCENE ⊛ NCIS ⊛ CRI
NAVAL CRIMINAL INVESTIGATIVE SERVICE

E SCENE ⊛ NCIS ⊛ CRIME SCEN

NAVAL CRIMINAL INVESTIGATIVE SERVICE

>> CHICAGO, ILLINOIS
>> THE MONTOYA HOME
>> 1425 HOURS

"One more day, Mommy. Please?"

Estrella Montoya's heart nearly shattered as she looked at her son. Dominic was on both knees, his hands clasped before him like a medieval peasant pleading for leniency from a cruel lord. Dominic even blubbered convincingly.

Estrella couldn't believe how fast her son was growing up. He was almost as tall as her waist now, well proportioned and more graceful every day. A thick shock of black hair hung down into his brown eyes, and in that he looked so much like his father that it ached.

Oh, Julian, if you had only lived to see your son.

A thousand wished-for memories flooded her mind. She didn't have any pictures of her husband holding their son. He'd

died only months before Nicky had been born. But sometimes
she couldn't help painting images in her mind of what it might
have been like.

"Please, Mommy," Nicky went on. "Just stay one more day.
Please?"

"I can't, baby," Estrella whispered. "I have to go to work.
I'm sorry."

"But you said three more days," Nicky wailed.

"I know. I know I did."

Nicky folded his arms and pouted. "You lied."

"No, I didn't." Estrella kept her voice firm. It was hard when
she always had to be in control. As a single parent, she always
ended up being the "bad parent" and couldn't share that burden
with anyone else. "I got called in. You know it happens."

"I know." Nicky's wrath crumbled as he reached up for her.

Quietly, holding her tears back, Estrella lifted her son into
her embrace. They stood out on the small patio behind her parents' house. She rubbed Nicky's back and comforted him as best
she could. Somehow, no matter what she did, it never seemed like
she did enough. And in moments like this, she didn't know how
she was going to stand the consistent series of disappointments.

The patio door opened.

Estrella quicky wiped away her tears. They felt cool against
her skin. She didn't want her son or whoever had stepped
through that door to see them. She was past that. She didn't cry
like that anymore.

"Estrella." It was her mother.

"Yes, Mama."

"Papa and I have been thinking." Dulcinea Montoya walked
to her daughter's side. She took Estrella's arm and patted it.

"Yes, Mama."

"Since you have been called away, we were thinking maybe
we could keep Nicky here with us for a few days. Till you can
come back for him." Dulcinea ruffled the boy's thick hair.

The years had been kind to Estrella's mother. Perhaps she was heavier than her wedding pictures, and she wore glasses now, and gray crowned her head and gradually crept down into her long hair, but she remained strong and vital. She wore a bright blue dress she'd made herself. Being frugal was a way of life for her.

"I have a sitter for him," Estrella said. "She's one of the mothers on base. She adores Nicky."

Dulcinea smiled. "And who could not adore my grandson, eh?" She paused. "But a sitter is not family. Let us keep Nicky for you. Till you return. Papa and I don't get to see this little one often enough."

More guilt tightened around Estrella's heart. "I visit when I can, Mama. It is just so expensive." Sometimes her mother and father had helped her pay for the trips. She knew they weren't much better off financially than she was, but they helped when they could.

Dulcinea leaned into the boy. "Would you like to stay with Nana, little one?"

"Can we go to the park?" Nicky asked.

"Of course," Dulcinea said. "Every day if you like."

Nicky looked up at Estrella. His emotions changed so quickly she could scarcely keep up with them. "Can I, Mama? Can I stay with Nana?"

Estrella knew she couldn't refuse him. She looked at her mother. "Are you sure this is all right with Papa?"

Dulcinea waved the question away. "Of course. Nicky will have a good time here."

"Thank you, Mama. But like I told you this morning, I don't know how long I will be gone. It could be days."

"Good," Dulcinea declared. "Then I will have a better chance to spoil my grandson."

"I'm going to go tell Papa I'm staying," Nicky chirped.

"All right." Estrella put her son down and watched him run

back into the house screaming happily at the top of his lungs. Only seconds later she heard her father's voice and the laughter that followed. Her father was a gentle man, quiet and strong.

"He grows so quickly," Dulcinea said.

"I know," Estrella whispered. Tears threatened her eyes again. "Mama, I feel like I miss so much time with him."

"Then you should quit the Navy and move back here with Papa and me. As I have told you before."

Estrella shook her head. "I can't do that."

Dulcinea hugged Estrella. "I know." She framed Estrella's face with her hands. "There is only one thing I wish for you. Do you know what that is?"

Estrella dreaded what her mother would say. From time to time, Dulcinea had broached the subject of marriage. Estrella hated the awkwardness of those occasions.

"I only wish that you knew God as Papa and I know him," Dulcinea said. "I wish you could accept that he loves you and that he has a plan for you that he has yet to unveil."

Tears spilled down Estrella's cheeks. "I try, Mama. Truly, I do."

"You can't let yourself be hard-hearted against him for what happened to your Julian," Dulcinea said.

Then whom should I be hard-hearted against, Mama? Who else is supposed to look out for Nicky and me in this world? Estrella wanted to demand. But she didn't.

"I'm trying, Mama," Estrella whispered.

SCENE **NCIS** ✶ **CRIME SCEN**

NAVAL CRIMINAL INVESTIGATIVE SERVICE

```
>> EN ROUTE TO CHINHAE, REPUBLIC OF KOREA
>> U.S. NAVY CARGO PLANE
>> 2319 HOURS
```

"Shel." Will stared at the monitor. The camera mounted atop it carried his image to Shel's notebook PC.

"Copy," Shel replied. Static crackled over the communication, making it hard to hear over the constant droning of the engines of the cargo plane. The team was bound for South Korea.

Will, Maggie, Estrella, and Remy occupied a berth in a specially prepped office area between the pilots and the cargo area. The plane had satellite reception while in flight, which was what Will was using to connect with Shel.

Estrella managed the encrypted communication at the computer array. Maggie sat across the small conference table bolted to the plane's metal floor. She looked distracted and tired. Remy sat at one end with a neutral expression, arms crossed over his chest and his legs stuck out before him.

Shel was currently over the Pacific Ocean in a USAF transport jet and nine and a half hours ahead of their schedule. Transportation to Okinawa had been arranged through Laughlin Air Force Base in Val Verde County close to the Mexican border. Laughlin had more flights in and out in a day than any other base in the United States. Shel had caught a cargo supply run to Okinawa at Edwards Air Force Base in California that would see him in Japan in a matter of hours.

"I've got you cleared through the base commander at Camp Smedley D. Butler," Will said. "Once you're on the ground there, you've got free movement through the provost marshal's office. They're going to assist with whatever you need."

"Lance Corporal Hester was assigned to Okinawa before getting moved to Chinhae," Shel said. "You want me to background him?"

"Exactly. I want you to talk to his friends. Anybody who knew him. Somewhere between there and Chinhae, the real Hester was replaced with the imposter. I want to know what happened to make that possible."

Will's earlier briefing had brought the team up to date regarding the DNA evidence. Knowing *what* had happened would give them the *who* and the *how*. But that was only a small part of an investigation. A case would never go to court until an investigator could pin down the actual physical events with recovered evidence.

"How deep did the fingerprint exchange on the imposter go?" Shel asked.

"The exchanges were made throughout federal and state levels," Maggie answered. "If Will hadn't thought to lift prints from Hester's room in his hometown, we wouldn't have his true prints."

"Replacing prints at federal and state levels isn't easy or

cheap," Shel said. "Doesn't figure that this guy managed the switches just to get himself a Marine job."

"The proud," Remy said quietly. "The few." He smiled.

Shel's lips twitched and he might have smiled. "New guy?"

"New guy," Will confirmed, and he made the introductions.

"I think the first question to ask is *why* this imposter was put in place," Remy said in his soft voice.

"Because he looked enough like Hester that the required plastic surgery would fool the right people," Maggie suggested.

"Or maybe they made the match from the other end," Estrella suggested. "Found a guy who would do whatever they needed him to do, then tried to find someone in the military who looked like him."

Remy shrugged. "What was this imposter selling through his black-market operation?"

"Drugs and weapons," Maggie said.

Looking at her, Remy asked, "Did you find those things?"

"No. Frank was . . . we had to leave before we could follow up on that."

"You didn't find a stash at the base?" Remy seemed puzzled.

"No."

"No place else?"

"No," Will said. "The Navy investigators at Chinhae have followed up on all the leads they had."

"And nobody found anything?"

"Nothing," Will answered.

"Then how do you know that the imposter sold them?"

"I had an interview with Sunghee Han," Maggie replied.

"He's a South Korean gangster?"

Maggie nodded. "We had to consider the possibility that whoever killed the imposter and Han's men might have been after Han's operation."

"But since the Hester imposter was shot, has Han had any more dogs set loose on him?"

Will looked at the laconic petty officer with renewed interest. "We don't know."

"Knowing that might be important," Remy said. "If the imposter was taken out by someone just out to even the table, he might have stepped crossways with a connection at either end."

"What do you mean?" Maggie asked.

"At first you thought maybe this Sunghee Han had the imposter killed. Then you thought one of Han's enemies killed the imposter, since Han's men were killed too."

Maggie nodded.

"Okay. But what you got to look at is that the imposter— if he was a target for someone—had become a danger to somebody. The imposter, he was one man. Maybe he could get a little of Sunghee Han's business. But Han was after something else when he had the imposter confronted."

"What?" Will asked.

"A connection ain't got but two ways it can go: where it's goin' an' where it's been."

"We don't know how many drugs and weapons the imposter was moving," Will said as understanding dawned on him.

Remy smiled slowly. "Now that would be interesting to know, wouldn't it? If the imposter was just nickel an' dimin' Han's organization, I don't see how Han would be interested in the imposter. A guy like that, he'd just shoot him and drop him in the water. Send out a message to whoever was helping him. But Han wanted to *talk* to the imposter."

"To get to the supplier?" Will asked.

"Or else the people the imposter was selling to," Remy agreed. He held up two fingers. "A connection has two ends. If the imposter was bringing a lot of stuff in, he had to be shipping it out, too. Otherwise, there would be a warehouse full of it somewhere."

"The imposter was killed to protect the operation," Will said.

"That's what I'm thinking. And Han was sniffing along the trail. Maybe whoever killed the imposter found out you people were there, but I'm willing to bet the imposter was already marked to be taken out of the play."

"Why would his partners want to kill him?"

"Because he'd been skimming off the top. Taking a little of what he was passing along. I think that's where those guns Special Agent Swafford was investigating came from."

"That's good, Remy," Will said. His mind was busy, already altering the plans he'd made for the team once they touched down in Chinhae.

"If I'm right," Remy said softly, "there could be people looking for us, ready to settle our hash, once we get there."

"He's got a point," Maggie said.

Will sighed and straightened up. Although his side was healing nicely, the pain was a grim reminder of how bad things could be. The fact that Remy, not Frank, was sitting among them was even more of a reminder. He massaged the back of his neck. *Lord,* he prayed silently, *I need you to help me through this.*

Remy said, "We'll need to be careful. But maybe we're not just looking for the imposter's identity. Maybe we're looking for something bigger."

"The operation," Will said.

"Right. And if that's the way of it, there's gonna be people there ready to stop us."

Will looked at his team. "Hostile environment," he said. "I think Remy's got a point. If anybody wants out, I can give you a pass on this one."

"I'm going," Maggie said.

"So am I," Shel agreed over the monitor. "We draw the line in the sand on this one, Will."

Remy smiled easily. "I got to admit I'm curious. My grand-mère always told me that some itches weren't meant to be scratched. But I always scratch. I'll ride in with you."

"I'm in," Estrella said.

"All right," Will said. "We start with the imposter. Since Remy has brought the matter up, I want to work on the imposter's black-market network." He glanced at the computer monitor, knowing his face was being broadcast to Shel. "Shel, find out what you can in Okinawa. We need to know what the lance corporal was doing that made him vulnerable there. Maggie, you and I will take the black-market connection through Sunghee Han. Estrella and Remy, I want the base covered. Estrella, work up the electronic records, e-mail, Internet, every public communication the imposter had. Let's see if we can turn up something there."

For the first time in months, Will felt his thoughts turning toward something other than his family problems. He felt excitement about the work ahead. He felt alive. But he knew Remy was right. They were playing for very high stakes.

31

>> OKINAWA, JAPAN
>> CAMP SMEDLEY D. BUTLER
>> 1604 HOURS

Shel dressed in the gym. He had arrived at Camp Smedley D. Butler late in the afternoon, bone tired and stiff from the long flight. He'd gone to the gym partly to work out the jet lag and kinks—and give Max a chance to do the same—but also because he wanted to stay off the radar until the camp slid into evening mode.

If he started hitting the bricks during daylight hours, news of his arrival and what he wanted would spread like wildfire through the camp grapevine. In the evening, the men he was looking for would be more relaxed and willing to talk. If his luck broke right, maybe he'd have some answers by morning.

He knew what he was looking for. Only two things made a guy change his view on life or led him to destruction: new friends and girlfriends. Shel wanted to know who Lance Corporal Hester had gotten to know at camp.

A young private met Shel at the entrance to the motor pool. "Gunney McHenry," the private stated in a strong voice.

"Yes."

"Gunney Tarlton asked me to give you the keys to the jeep waiting outside." The private opened his hand to reveal the keys.

"Walk with me," Shel said. He shouldered his field duffel and signaled for Max to follow.

The private fell into step beside him on the other side of the Labrador.

Shel slipped his iPAQ out and punched up the information he'd gotten from Estrella and the base commander's office. "Do you know where I can find Lance Corporal Mike Branscom?"

The private nodded. "This time of night, you'll find Branscom at the range. He gives lessons to men who want to finish up their sharpshooter quals and newbies still struggling to figure out which end of the weapon is which. Do you need directions to the range?"

Shel pulled himself up into the driver's seat in the jeep. Max leaped onto the rear deck and threw his nose into the air. Then he yawned and laid his big head on his front paws.

Shel keyed the ignition and the engine turned over smoothly. "I remember the way. Thanks." Shoving the gearshift into reverse, he backed into the street and turned west.

>> CAMP SMEDLEY D. BUTLER
>> FIRING RANGE
>> 1626 HOURS

Lance Corporal Mike Branscom was a Marine's Marine. His accent was Southern—Shel guessed Mississippi or Alabama. His skin was black, so black that the gray mortar scars standing out on the left side of his face looked white. He wore his hair cut short, tight against his skull. His fatigues had started out the day pressed and clean, but he had the sleeves rolled up now and sweat darkened his collar and made a cross on his back.

"You're fightin' the weapon, newbie," Branscom growled in a deep voice. "Just point it at the target an' let it do its job."

The smooth-faced private beside Branscom was dwarfed by the instructor's bulk. He stood at the firing line with an M4A1 assault rifle pulled tightly against his shoulder.

The outdoor target range was swathed in shadows except for cool fluorescent lights at the security post. Branscom manipulated the control panel to one side of the alley, bringing up targets in swift succession and at various ranges.

The private rushed his shots despite Branscom's calm voice. Dirt kicked up within inches of the targets and grew steadily closer. By the time the private finished the 25-round magazine, he was scoring hits.

"Better," Branscom said.

"Yeah," the private agreed.

Branscom cut his gaze to Shel, letting him know he'd seen him there. "Take five, kid. Load up an' we'll go again. I'm gonna make a Marine outta you yet."

The private nodded and walked away.

"Somethin' I can help you with?" Branscom demanded.

"I hope so," Shel said. He reached into his breast pocket and brought out his NCIS ID, then took out his iPAQ and thumbed up Lance Corporal Hester's picture.

Branscom accepted the device for a minute, regarded the photo, then passed it back. "Hester. Private Virgil Hester when I knew him. Got himself killed over in South Korea." The dark eyes narrowed. "Heard somethin' about the NCIS bein' involved in that."

"We're trying to find his murderer," Shel said. "We have reason to believe that the person or persons who killed him followed him out of this camp."

"Come inside," Branscom suggested. "I'll buy you a cup of coffee."

Shel followed the man into the command building. They got paper cups of coffee and sat at a small table in a break room. No one else was there. At this time of night, only serious shooters were out and about.

Branscom drummed his fingers on the table. "So, tell me what you're looking for."

"In Chinhae, Hester got crossways with a local gang."

"Doing what?"

"Black market."

Branscom shook his head. "No way. That boy was straight as an arrow. He wrote his daddy every week. Did whatever the corps asked of him. Drugs and stolen goods—he'd never have touched any of that."

"Something happened here," Shel said. "By the time Hester reached Chinhae, he'd learned to wheel and deal."

Scowling, Branscom ran a big hand over his lower face. "Before Hester left, he got involved with a woman."

Shel's interest pricked up. The file on Hester hadn't mentioned that wrinkle. "What woman?"

"A dancer from one of the bars in Okinawa City."

Shel took out his PDA. "Tell me about her."

"Not much to tell," Branscom responded. "Hester was gonna marry her. Then he wasn't."

"What happened?"

Branscom shrugged. "It's the military, gunney. If you don't have a woman who is ready to marry you *and* the corps, it ain't gonna work. The marriage fell through. Probably a good thing."

"Do you know her name?"

"No."

"Where did she dance?"

"Place called the Jade Flower." An unpleasant look filled Branscom's broad face. "It's a dive—a place any decent man ought to stay away from."

⊛ ⊛ ⊛

Ignoring the fatigue that draped him like a heavy cloak, Will surveyed the basement offices assigned to his team in Chinhae. The HQ was fully equipped, including computer access where they could bring up information gathered in the databases. Workstations and lab equipment filled the room.

He turned to Maggie, who was slotting removable hard drives filled with the encrypted information they'd brought with them into the workstations. Working online against whoever they were after would have left them vulnerable to spying or attack.

"I didn't get the name and address of the bar where you met Sunghee Han," Will said.

"The Happy Pagoda."

Will looked at her. "The Happy Pagoda?"

Maggie nodded. A brief smile touched her lips. "Presents a nice image, doesn't it?"

Will agreed.

"It's a hole-in-the-wall," Maggie said. "Probably changes names every so often, depending on how many code violations they're in trouble for. As a result, it's probably listed as something else right now." She paused. "Are you thinking about going to see Han?"

"I am."

"Then I'm going with you. I've got prior experience with the man."

"You also initiated a situation that may make simple conversation untenable," Will said. "You threw a pistol in his face and had him arrested in front of his men. He's not going to ignore that."

"Do you think he's going to ignore the fact that we both work for NCIS?"

"No."

"Then I'm coming with you. I didn't come all this way to sit on my hands."

Will started to object, then realized that he would have to issue an order to get Maggie to stay. He didn't want to pull rank over something like this. And arguing with her would simply be a waste of breath. In the end, he would have to take her or arrest her.

"All right," he said.

>> **CHINHAE NAVAL BASE**
>> **2005 HOURS**

Achmed watched the man and the woman—Coburn and Foley, he reminded himself—exit from the building where the NCIS team had been stationed. Sitting in the passenger seat of the Ford cargo van, he adjusted the night-vision binocs and focused on the pair as they got into a small Daewoo sedan.

He'd been surprised when he'd seen on the base's secure intranet that the NCIS team was returning to Chinhae. He'd thought they were out of the picture for good. On the other hand, maybe their return was a blessing. Now he'd have the chance to finish what he had started.

The sedan started up and the lights slashed into the darkness of the night. The woman drove. She'd won the keys after a brief exchange.

Achmed let them go. It didn't matter where they were going. And he had things to do while they were gone.

32

>> OKINAWA, JAPAN
>> DOWNTOWN
>> 2107 HOURS

Driving in Okinawa was backward from driving in the United States: traffic stayed to the left instead of the right. Shel's borrowed jeep maintained the usual configuration with the steering wheel on the left since the corps didn't want to have to retrain Marines with handling equipment.

Shel had spent an accumulated three years and seven months on this island during his military career. Since his USFJ-4A U.S. Forces Japan operator's permit was still valid, he was allowed to drive himself instead of having to be accompanied by a qualified driver. Only a few minutes after leaving the base, reflexes took over and he no longer had to think about driving. The skills came back.

The Jade Flower was in Matsuyama, the red-light district. Buildings lined the thoroughfare and traffic—cars as well as motorcycles, scooters, bicycles, and pedestrians—choked progress down to a crawl. Neon lit the night and barkers called out in a dozen different languages, all extolling the virtues of whatever vice they pandered.

Over the years of United States' presence in Okinawa, the cities had loosely split into military friendly or closed Okinawan communities. Several bars and shops were listed as *nonGaijin*, where American GIs weren't welcome. But other establishments welcomed the extra revenue that American soldiers brought. The Jade Flower was one of these.

Shel looked for a parking area, then paid an exorbitant fee to leave the jeep. Max stood and stretched.

"Stay," Shel ordered.

The dog whined and barked his displeasure, then hunkered down with his head on his forepaws.

Two hard-faced security men, both Japanese, stood watch over the door.

"GI?" one asked.

"Yeah," Shel said. When the cover price was paid, he submitted to a quick wand search. He'd left the pistols with the jeep, locked up tight in the rear-deck compartment. He passed through, walked to the elevator, and went up. The Jade Flower was located on the third floor.

He heard the throbbing beat of rock music even before the elevator doors opened. Lights and music whirled around the club. Disco lights glittered and sparked.

Young GIs whooped and laughed, calling out to the women dancing on the stage and to each other. Stateside, most of them wouldn't have been as out of control, but here in Okinawa anything went.

Shel talked to six servicemen before he found one who had known Hester. His name was Gary Rice.

Rice sat in the back of the club. He was in his midtwenties, and had black hair, blue eyes, and deep dimples. His grin was infectious, and he didn't look like a guy who took anything seriously.

"Lance Corporal Gary Rice," Shel said as he stopped in front of the table.

Rice glanced up and some of his good humor evaporated. His eyes flicked past Shel, then back. "Who are you?"

"Gunnery Sergeant Shelton McHenry. NCIS." Shel displayed his ID.

"Why is the NCIS interested in me?"

"Mind if I sit?" Shel asked.

Rice shrugged.

Shel sat. "You were friends with Lance Corporal Virgil Hester."

"I was."

"Tell me about him."

"We were friends in the States in boot camp, then hooked up again here. A while back, Virgil took reassignment to Chinhae and left. There's really not much else to tell."

"Did you stay in contact with Hester while he was in Chinhae?"

"Some. Virgil grew kind of distant. He seemed to be busy a lot."

"Why?"

Rice shrugged. "I didn't ask. In the service you learn to leave friendships when you don't have face time, then pick them right up again when you're on temporary duty together somewhere, or if you go through training or get reassigned together."

"What was he like?"

"Nice guy," Rice said without hesitation.

"Did he ever do drugs?"

Rice shook his head. "You ever pulled duty here?"

"Yeah."

Waving a hand around, Rice said, "Then you know there's plenty of access to drugs around here if that's what you want to do. Virgil didn't."

"Would it surprise you to learn that Hester was involved in a black-market ring in Chinhae?"

Rice leaned in. "Yeah, it would surprise me. It doesn't jibe with the Virgil I knew."

Switching tactics, Shel said, "What was Hester involved in here? After hours. Personal time."

"Nothing out of the ordinary," Rice said. "Mostly we just club hopped. You know they call Okinawa The Rock, right?"

Shel nodded.

"The reason they call it that is because there's really no place to go. Once you've done all the sight-seeing trips, gone out on the boats, looked at the museums, and eaten at all the restaurants that allow *Gaijins*, there's not much else to do with free time."

"Someone told me Hester was getting married to one of the girls who used to dance here."

"They were talking about it," Rice said. "Or, I guess I should say *Virgil* was talking about it. Viv, she was just listening. For a while. I think she liked the attention. Then when Virgil started trying to set a date, she shut him down."

"Viv?"

"That's what everybody called her." Rice stopped himself. "No, actually everybody called her Sunset. That was her stage name. Her real name is Vivian Layton. She's British."

"Does she still dance here?"

"No."

Shel found that interesting. "When did she quit?"

Rice shrugged. "She quit working here about the same time Virgil got his transfer approved."

"What ended the relationship between Hester and Vivian?"

"I don't know. I never asked. Sometimes you ask, you get to borrow the pain and baggage too. I can be a friend without going through the mud with somebody."

"How did Hester take it?"

"Bummed him out. Just—really bummed him out. He wasn't

quite the same afterward. But everybody understood. He stopped coming around as much. A few weeks later, his transfer to Chinhae came through. During that time, it was almost like he was another guy."

Shel figured that was probably true. If Hester hadn't been another guy before leaving Okinawa, he was when he arrived in Chinhae. "Where is Vivian Layton now?"

"Around. I still see her at the clubs every now and again."

"She's not dancing?"

"No."

Suspicion deepened inside Shel. Dancers made good money in some places, maybe even in the Jade Flower. But they also spent everything they earned. "Is she working anywhere?"

"Don't know."

"Would anyone here know where I can find her?"

Rice nodded toward the bartender. "He might know. His name's Flynn. Irish, or something. He's got an accent like a machine gun."

Flynn looked almost as wide as he was tall. His thick neck and heavy shoulders advertised the time he'd spent in the gym years ago. Since then, though, he'd developed a pot belly. His thick black hair hung down to his shoulders in wild disarray.

Shel laid a twenty-dollar bill on the table. "I'll buy you the next couple rounds. Take your time and show up at camp sober."

Rice covered the twenty with a hand and made it disappear. He smiled. "Thanks, gunney."

Putting out money never hurt. If nothing else, the money increased the likelihood of a favorable response from anyone else in the camp Shel needed to talk to. Gary Rice would spread the word.

Crossing the crowded floor, Shel stood at the bar. He waited a couple moments, waved off a serving girl, and caught Flynn's eye.

Flynn looked like he smelled trouble at once. He crossed over to the bar in front of Shel. "Somethin' I can do for you, boy?"

"Vivian Layton," Shel said, producing his ID. "I want to know about her. I want to know where I can find her."

Shaking his shaggy head, Flynn said, "Shove off. You aren't gettin' anything here."

"Look," Shel said, "we can do this easy or we can do this hard."

Honest amusement lighted Flynn's broad face. "Oh, so it's a choice I have, is it?"

"I look around and notice that you depend a lot on the GIs who come here."

Flynn said nothing. A scowl bit into his face.

"If I don't get some information about Vivian Layton—also called Sunset—in two minutes, I'm going to call the base commander and declare this place off-limits to military personnel. I'll have MPs posted out front to make certain it stays that way."

"You can't do that."

"I can," Shel said in a quiet voice. "I will." He left his ID lying faceup between them.

Flynn gazed contemplatively at Shel for a moment, then dug into his back pocket and removed a tattered notebook. He consulted it, then reached for a cocktail napkin and took a pen from his shirt pocket. "I've got an address. I don't know if it's recent or not. Viv's been through here now and again, but we don't chat the way we used to." He scribbled an address and slid the cocktail napkin across the bar.

Shel trapped the napkin. "What about her phone number?"

Shaking his head, Flynn said, "I don't have it."

"Make sure you don't have it after I leave," Shel said. "If I find out you called her and let her know I was coming, I'll be back." He tucked the napkin into his jacket pocket and left.

33

>> CHINHAE, REPUBLIC OF KOREA
>> THE HAPPY PAGODA
>> 2138 HOURS

Maggie flanked Will as they walked into the Happy Pagoda. The hard-eyed crew filling the bar turned to face them as the news of their arrival spread throughout the patrons.

"Maybe we should have brought backup," Will said. Despite the tension of the moment, his voice remained calm and a touch ironic. "I don't get the feeling that we're exactly welcome here."

"We're not," Maggie assured him.

Will came to a stop in the middle of the club. Women inside the hanging cages continued to dance in wild abandon to the throbbing music hammering the walls. Maybe the Happy Pagoda wasn't exactly happy, but it was definitely rocking.

Sunghee Han sat at the back in the same spot he had last time. He still wore the red-lensed sunglasses.

When Will and Maggie approached, the women seated on either side of him got up immediately, fleeing like birds before a cat. Five men stood shoulder to shoulder in front of Han's table, blocking their way.

Maggie fixed Sunghee Han with her gaze. "We need to talk," she stated clearly as the gang members came closer and closer.

Han stared back at her, his face impassive. "I have nothing to say to you. You have disrespected me by showing up again. I told you last time we were finished."

The gang members closed in. Will and Maggie were out of time.

"Want to know something?" Maggie asked. Her hands flashed and filled with the Berettas she wore under her jacket. She flicked the safeties off with her thumbs and aimed them at the nearest gang members.

Maggie felt Will's surprise. But he didn't move, leaving the encounter in her hands.

The gang members stopped moving and looked nervously at their leader.

Han stood and pulled his own weapon. He aimed at Maggie's head. A ruby laser light kissed her forehead. In a fluid motion, Will took out his XD-40 and aimed at Han.

"Put the pistol away," Han ordered.

"You first," Will said in a calm, controlled voice.

Other gang members drew their weapons.

Maggie knew they were one wrong twitch away from a bloodbath. It was time to play her hand. "Sureshot," she said over her headset, "do you read?"

"Five by five," a confident Marine voice answered. "That's one prickly situation you have down there."

"That's why we brought you along," Maggie said. She didn't allow her fear to reach her voice. "Go live."

"Going live," the Marine replied.

Without warning, every television and closed-circuit broadcast monitor and computer screen in the Happy Pagoda went black, then came on in neon-bright colors. The screens were filled with hot yellow and red images on a purple background. The bright spots clearly resembled the outlines of human figures. Black crosshairs stretched across the images, focusing on one of the bright outlines.

"The bright colors," Maggie said conversationally, "are images of the people in this bar viewed through a thermographic sight mounted on a .50-caliber sniper rifle in the hands of an expert Marine sharpshooter in a helicopter over our heads. The one in the crosshairs is you."

Han glared at the monitor screens and erupted in a torrent of Korean invectives.

Maggie waited for a moment, then interrupted. "Five," she counted backward, "four . . . three . . ." She counted in Korean.

Han looked at her. "What are you doing?"

"When I hit zero, that Marine is going to shoot you," Maggie stated calmly, again in Korean. She knew Will wouldn't understand, so she repeated what she said in English. "Then he's going to pick as many targets as he can."

"This is a lie!" Han exploded.

"Sureshot." Maggie spoke in Korean because she knew the Marine sergeant spoke the language as well. "Have the pilot bring you in. I want them to hear the rotorwash."

"Affirmative."

Han looked up at the ceiling. His image, trapped on the televisions, monitors, and screens, looked up as well. The crosshairs never moved.

"The Barrett .50-caliber rifle in the hands of this Marine," Maggie said, "will have no problem firing through the rooftop and striking you. Death will probably come instantaneously."

The throbbing beat of the helicopter rotors drowned out some of the rock-and-roll music.

"Two," Maggie continued calmly, "one . . ."

"Guns down!" Han squalled. "Now! *Now!*" He led the way, putting his own pistol on the table in front of him. Then he held his hands up as if he were being robbed.

Maybe he is, Maggie couldn't help thinking. She was taking his dignity again.

The gang members put their weapons down and stepped back.

"What do you want?" Han demanded.

Maggie sheathed her pistols and stepped forward, staying clear of Will's field of fire. She pushed Han's pistol across the table back to him. At least she could give him that much respect.

Han picked up the pistol and put it away under his jacket.

"What we want," Will said, putting his sidearm away, "is simple."

Han shifted his attention to Will. "What?"

"You told Special Agent Foley that Lance Corporal Hester was moving cocaine through the base," Will said. "We want some of it."

Interest flickered in Han's eyes. "Why?"

"Because we do," Will replied.

"I don't have any."

"But you know who does. Find it. Call me when you have it." Will laid a card on the table.

The party atmosphere had definitely left the building. The rotorwash continued to beat down. The thermographic images of Sungee Han continued to play over the screens.

"I want it by tomorrow morning."

Han stared at him as though he'd come from another planet.

"The NCIS officer who was killed," Will said, "was my friend. I don't have a lot of those in this world, and he was one of the best. Whoever killed him, I'm going to find him. Or them. They are not safe from me. Do you understand?"

Han nodded.

"Help me," Will said, "or I'm going to go through you to see this finished." He tapped the card on the table. "Tomorrow morning. Don't make me come looking for you." Without another word, he did an about-face and walked toward the door.

"Sureshot," Maggie said.

"Reading you five by five. I've got your six."

Maggie nodded to Han.

"Another time," Han threatened. "Perhaps when your friends aren't around."

"We're the military," Maggie said. "We don't stand alone." She leaned across the table, careful not to blur the helicopter sniper's shot. "And don't try it. The things I'm afraid of in this life? They're a lot bigger than you'll ever be."

Han broke eye contact and looked away.

Maggie left, walking slowly and confidently. She ignored the invective that followed in her wake.

S ⊛ **CRIME SCENE** ⊛ **NCIS** ⊛ **CR**
NAVAL CRIMINAL INVESTIGATIVE SERVICE
E SERVICE

SCENE ⊗ NCIS ⊗ CRIME SCEN
NAVAL CRIMINAL INVESTIGATIVE SERVICE

>> OKINAWA, JAPAN
>> 2250 HOURS

Shel stood on the landing below Vivian Layton's apartment.
Max sat at his side. The Labrador kept pricking his ears at the
sirens and sharp voices that pierced the night. The city stayed
active around them, but the thick shadows made Shel feel iso-
lated and adrift in the darkness.

For the last thirty-seven minutes, Shel had kept watch over
the apartment. The building had no obvious security system. It
was a long way from first class, but even so, it wasn't cheap. This
was not an apartment Vivian Layton should have been able to
afford on a dancer's income. At least, not while performing at a
club as far down the food chain as the Jade Flower.

So where does the money come from?

Nine more long minutes crawled by.

A sleek, bright metallic green Toyota Camry pulled off the

street and slid through the alley to the private parking in the rear. The license plate matched the one Estrella had pulled from the Okinawan motor vehicle records. The car, like the apartment, should have been above Vivian's means.

Shel watched the woman step from her car. She was highlighted briefly by the vehicle's interior lights. She was of medium height. Short-cropped hair dyed bright orange framed a lean, delicate face. Black, sharply arched brows were stamped over cold eyes.

When Vivian noticed Shel, she studied him for a moment, evidently waiting to see if he would try to approach her. A couple minutes passed as she took packages from the car's rear seat. Carrying the packages, she walked up to him. Her key ring glinted in her hand, carried as a potential weapon.

Shel waited. Max rose and shook himself. "Watch," Shel commanded in a whisper.

Vivian stopped a short distance from Shel. "I don't know you." Her accent was British.

"No." Shel tapped his jacket pocket. "I've got ID."

"You a cop?" she asked.

"United States Naval Criminal Investigative Service," Shel said. "You're Vivian Layton."

The fact that he knew her name didn't totally surprise her. "You're looking for me?"

"I need to ask you some questions about Lance Corporal Virgil Hester."

She hesitated and her brows knitted together. "What about him? That was a long time ago."

Shel let the silence grow heavy between them. There were a couple different ways he could pursue the conversation. He decided to jump in with both feet and see what happened. That was more his style anyway.

"Hester's dead," Shel said.

Vivian took an involuntary step back, obviously feeling

somewhat threatened. To her credit—or maybe because Shel offered no outward threat—she recovered quickly. "I see. What does that have to do with me?"

"As it turns out," Shel said, "the guy who was wearing Hester's name and face in Chinhae wasn't Hester. The way my team has got it figured, when Hester lost his place in the chow line, he was here. I want to know what happened to him."

The woman looked down. "I don't know what you're talking about."

Shel showed her a cold grin. "Yeah, you do."

Vivian struggled to take control of the situation. "I think I want my lawyer."

"You've got me confused with a regular cop. I'm U.S. military. Your ex-fiancé's little identity theft in the Marines hits the national-security nerve. You'll get an attorney. Eventually. The Marines will even make sure you have a good one. But you'll be in custody until that time."

"I'm a British citizen."

"Who's wanted there for a number of criminal charges," Shel said. "You fled London a step ahead of Scotland Yard. I'm betting that after we're done with you, they'll be ready to prosecute you themselves. And if they want to lock you away first, we'll be here waiting."

A trapped look filled Vivian's face.

Shel didn't enjoy playing the heavy, but it was a good role for him. And he knew the team definitely needed whatever information Vivian Layton had. "What's it going to be?" he asked. "You can come with me, or I can take you down." He took handcuffs from his pocket and let them hang. "Your call."

Movement drew Shel's attention to his right. But even as he recognized it, Max was barking, braced down and ready.

Four shadowy figures stepped from the darkness of the alley. All of them carried guns. None of them offered any words of warning as they took deliberate aim.

Shel dropped the handcuffs and immediately ripped the .45 from under his right arm with his left hand. He grabbed the woman's elbow, yanking her into motion toward the steps leading to the apartment building's front door. Packages flew in all directions.

Bullets hammered the wall and alley where the woman had been standing. Somewhere in the apartments above, a woman started screaming and men started yelling. The shooters adjusted their aim, and additional rounds chopped into the lower steps, climbing quickly.

Twisting, Shel shoved his .45 forward and triggered three rounds at the nearest shooter. The detonations thundered in the alley. The bullets smashed against the man's chest, driving him back in short, choppy steps.

"Max," Shel called. "Follow."

The Labrador sprinted after Shel, growling and snapping, obviously more inclined to go on the attack.

At the top of the steps, still pulling the woman along, Shel dropped his shoulder and ran at the double doors. Wood split and glass broke as the doors parted. Inside the foyer, he stuck a foot in front of the woman, tripping her and shoving her to the floor ahead of him just as bullets flew overhead like an angry swarm of bees.

Shel quickly turned over and drew his other gun. The first attacker through the door carried an Uzi machine pistol in both hands. He obviously expected his targets to be standing across the room. His brief burst hammered the wall on the other side of the foyer and shattered a vase containing artificial cherry blossoms. The delicate petals rained down like drops of blood.

Shel fired from less than ten feet, aiming by instinct as much as training and experience under fire. The bullets caught the man and threw him backward.

Vivian lay on the floor amid the shattered wood and broken

glass. She held her hands over her head and cringed but wasn't hysterical.

Another gunman stepped over the body of the first.

Regaining his feet, Shel emptied his left-hand pistol into the man's upper body. Immediate dark splotches of blood told Shel the gunman wasn't wearing body armor. Assuming the first man hadn't been either, he'd already accounted for three of them.

"Get up," he growled to Vivian.

The woman shook her head.

"Now," Shel ordered, "or I'm going to leave you lying here. They're after you, not me." He ejected the spent magazine from his empty pistol and slipped another clip from his jacket pocket into the butt. He pressed the slide release and chambered the first round.

Reluctantly, hands still around her head, Vivian got to her feet. Then her hands came forward quickly. Shel glimpsed the small container rolled in her fingers an instant before she depressed the Mace plunger.

Harsh, acrid liquid rushed from the container toward Shel's face. He turned, dragging an arm up in defense. The spray sloshed over his arm and splashed against his cheek and forehead. Thankfully, none of it hit his eyes. Still, the immediate burn of the Mace against his skin and in his lungs choked him. He couldn't catch his breath, and he felt like someone was holding a blowtorch to his face.

Shel raked his arm across his face as gently as he could, sweeping the burning liquid from his forehead and cheek with his jacket sleeve. Tears poured down his cheeks and blurred his vision, but he saw the woman running for a hallway at the back of the building.

"Max," Shel gasped, "takedown."

Quivering with nervous energy, Max rocketed forward like an arrow propelled by a bowstring, his claws clacking against the stone floor.

Shel lumbered in pursuit. The pepper spray wasn't going to kill him or completely incapacitate him, but it made life just short of unbearable.

In seconds, Max overtook the woman and threw himself against her legs as he'd been trained to do. Vivian toppled into a loose-limbed sprawl and skidded along the floor. She tried to push herself up, but Max clamped hold of one wrist and yanked her hand from beneath her, sending her to the floor again. Most of the time in such circumstances, Max would never even break the skin.

Gagging on the pepper spray, Shel stared at the door at the end of the hallway. It was locked, but a panic bar gleamed across it, promising a quick exit in times of emergency.

This, Shel knew, was an emergency.

Swinging at Max, trying to fight him off, Vivian looked up at Shel. Fear widened her eyes as she made herself stop struggling with the dog. "Make him stop."

"At ease," Shel said. Tears continued seeping from his burning eyes, but he could see well enough to navigate.

Instantly obedient, Max backed away. His ears pricked sharply as he glanced both ways down the hallway.

"That was stupid," Shel said. "Blinding me could have gotten us both killed." He didn't mention that he was almost blind now.

The fourth man stepped through the front door with an Uzi in his fists.

Shel sent him into retreat mode with two quick shots. "Swapping lead with these guys isn't going to make our lives easier. And when the JNP arrive, we're going to get locked down. If somebody sent these guys here, now, you've got to wonder who can be bought inside lockup."

The Japanese National Police were a combination police force and military unit. When it came to their jobs, they acted first and sorted out the details later. Shel knew he and Vivian Layton would be incarcerated immediately. They would also be at the mercy of whoever had been sent after this woman.

"We can get out through the back," Vivian said.

"Let's go." Shel stayed behind her as she raced for the rear of the building. He got her to hold up at the door, then went through first with both pistols at the ready.

No one moved in the parking area.

"Your car," Shel growled. "Go."

Vivian started running.

Shel followed with Max at his side.

Vivian used the remote to open the locks of her car. Shel ran around to the passenger side. He tried the door and found it was still locked. Inside the Camry, the woman shoved her key into the ignition. Knowing that she would leave him behind if she could, Shel drew back a pistol and slammed the butt against the window.

It fragmented into thousands of chunks of safety glass. He reached through the broken window and popped the lock while Vivian stared at him in disbelieving silence. He opened the door and urged Max inside. The dog bounded into the rear seat.

Shel slid into the passenger seat just as bullets blazed across the hood and threw out a shower of sparks. "Drive."

Vivian put the car in gear and floored the accelerator. Rubber shrieked as the tires grabbed hold. Shel prayed that none of the bullets would find the woman or himself, and that the tires would remain intact.

Frantic, Vivian kept her foot on the accelerator. The car screamed through the alley, then screeched out onto the street amid belligerent traffic. They crossed bumpers, but Vivian kept the Camry moving.

A few blocks later, with no sign of pursuit behind them, Shel started to relax. "Who were those guys?"

"Yakuza gang members," Vivian answered.

Shel thought for a minute. The presence of the Yakuza changed his plans a little. "Any idea why they'd want you dead?"

"No," she said, averting her eyes. She was hiding something, Shel thought.

"Well, they apparently aren't crazy about the idea of you talking to me."

"Where are we going?" Vivian asked.

"Camp Butler," Shel replied. It was the only safe place he could think of. Plus he needed more information from Vivian. He needed to know how the Yakuza were involved in this. He'd let Vivian sweat a little in an interview room until she was ready to tell him what she knew.

Given the fact that one imposter had gotten inside the U.S. military structure and that others had killed Frank Billings to protect that fact, Shel wasn't certain if they'd be safe there or not.

CRIME SCENE ✳ NCIS ✳ CR

NAVAL CRIMINAL INVESTIGATIVE SERVICE

E SCENE ✶ **NCIS** ✶ CRIME SCEN

NAVAL CRIMINAL INVESTIGATIVE SERVICE

>> CHINHAE, REPUBLIC OF KOREA
>> AMERICAN NAVAL BASE NCIS HEADQUARTERS
>> 2337 HOURS

Tracking the communications back through the base intranet systems proved difficult.

Challenged and fatigued by the arduous task, Estrella leaned back in the office chair and longed for the custom-built chair she had back at the NCIS offices in Camp Lejeune. A good chair was everything to someone who spent most of her days in one.

She'd been staring at lines of code for hours, feeling jet-lagged and tense, and she needed a break. Stubbornly, she made herself stay. She'd already sent Remy off to get something for them to eat. Now, feeling stymied, Estrella wished she'd gone with the SEAL. Maybe a short diversion would have helped.

Time to get out the bag of tricks, chica, she told herself. For the past few hours, she had known that course of action was what she was going to have to do. But she'd put the decision off, not wanting to endanger the admissibility of any evidence she might find with the questionable methods she was going to use to obtain them. She leaned forward over the keyboard again and set to work.

Normally when she handled trace-backs through a computer network, Estrella tried hard to remain within the NCIS-approved guidelines for retrieval of electronic documents and trace evidence. But before she'd joined the Navy, back when Julian was still alive and Nicky was just a dream they had for someday, she'd worked deep into the Internet. Several of the software tools she and Julian had used to ferret out information to sell to corporations weren't legitimate. Or nice. She'd written them herself, designing and coding them to be barbed and deadly and unstoppable.

She and Julian had tested corporate Internet security and designed firewalls to deflect potential spies and saboteurs. They'd created honey pots to trap and identify others. They'd lived in a small apartment in Chicago, and Julian had dreamed big of creating his own game-design studio.

They'd almost had it. In the end, losing that dream when it seemed almost within reach had been too much for Julian. And Estrella hadn't seen it coming. Ever since, she had not been able to convince herself that it was really all her fault that Julian was dead.

Don't go there, Estrella told herself. She'd caught herself looping into that old memory, just moments away from seeing Julian dead again. Unshed tears burned her eyes. *Stay away from that. You don't need that.*

She closed her eyes, took a deep breath, and opened a new application on one of the other monitors while the other programs ran. She went off-site, stealthily sliding through the base's firewall like a quick-footed fox playing in shadows.

Every good cracker—gifted cyberhounds like Estrella called themselves crackers instead of hackers—kept software hidden on a Web page, already bundled for a quick crash through someone else's cyberscape. And Estrella was a good cracker.

After uploading a packet-sniffer utility, Estrella keystroked the program with the operating parameters of the concealed communications data streams she was certain were hidden within the base's network. Once the upgrade had been completed, she set the sniffer free. The program ran through the base computer systems like a gale-force hurricane.

On still another screen, data compiled in neat columns.

Her search parameters were complex but elegant. She accessed all of Virgil Hester's e-mail, then the e-mail of everyone who had contacted him. There were more than a few.

When the list was complete, she shifted the paradigm, searching for any of the imposter's contacts that had gotten e-mail immediately following the shooting in the alley. It was possible that the person who had killed Frank had operated independently, but she doubted it. Whatever they were following up on was too well organized.

The process dragged out for several minutes.

Her quick eyes took in the packet-sniffer's progress. She felt a smile twist her lips, one of her truest ones that came from the old days of too much Starbucks coffee and the unfettered freedom that was the Internet.

One name surfaced

That's a hit, she told herself triumphantly. *I've got you now.* The cursor froze and winked. *Now that I have you, let's see where you've been.* Miraculously, the way it always happened when success came along, the pain and fatigue dropped away.

She stroked the keyboard, layering in search commands and tracking the outside message that had come in through Virgil Hester's e-mail, looking for the invasive program that had disrupted the navy base's communications and security systems. Despite the cracker's attempts to hide three off-site accounts, she found them.

"You left a ripple when you invaded the system, *cholo*," she said aloud to the unknown cyberinvader. "You weren't as good as you thought you were." She tasked the system to identify the name on the accounts. "Or maybe I'm just better than anyone you've ever been up against."

The monitor lit up immediately as the query returned a name: *Achmed, Seaman First Class Ahmed.*

Estrella called up the sailor's field-service record from the databases she'd been cleared to use. The FSR started downloading to her computer at once. She tapped a key and brought up Seaman First Class Achmed's photo.

Achmed had dark brown eyes, black hair, and the dark skin of a Middle Easterner. He was twenty-six years old but looked much younger, hardly more than a teenager. In the jacket photo, he wore a neutral expression, but the brown eyes were dead, like frozen marbles completely devoid of life.

A slight shiver passed through Estrella as she looked at the man's photo. A superficial glance through his file showed that his MOS was as a surgical tech assigned to Chinhae.

A surgical tech could have easily sabotaged the system that allowed the imposter's body to be taken away. Achmed would have known where the cameras were and where the corpse was kept.

And killing Frank like that? Estrella wondered. *Had that come to him so easily too?*

Due to privacy laws, the military was forbidden to obtain information about recruits' religious affinities, so Achmed's file had no information about that. But looking at the photo, Estrella had to wonder. Was there a possible religious connection here?

In the next instant, everything went black.

A chill ghosted through Estrella. The lights shouldn't go off without the backup system coming into play. She suddenly felt very alone in the dark. Breaking free of the paralysis that held her, she tried linking over the headset.

Nothing. The unit was dead.

She walked toward the door. In the darkness, she felt some-one watching her. She tried to convince herself it was only her imagination. But despite her best efforts, she didn't believe that.

She felt a rush of movement behind her and tried to turn, but it was already too late. A strong arm seized her around the mid-dle. A hand clapped over her mouth hard enough to split her lips against her teeth. She tried to fight back, but her arms were pinned to her sides. There was nothing she could do.

>> **DOWNTOWN CHINHAE**
>> **2352 HOURS**

Remy Gautreau stood waiting for his and Estrella's order at the combination restaurant and tavern not far from the naval base.

The small business all but overflowed with patrons. Most of the food was served to go because of the limited seating. Smoke danced in the air in front of the big-screen television across the crowded room.

"Hey, bro, you got a light?"

Turning toward the speaker, Remy said, "Sure." He reached into the pocket for his Zippo. He didn't smoke, but fire was a tool used by every Special Ops warrior.

The speaker was a black sailor about Remy's height. His accent carried the musical lilt of the Caribbean. The man was younger and lighter than Remy. He had soft brown eyes, but the whites held glints of orange fire, mute testimony that he was under the influence of something.

Remy flicked the lighter and allowed the man to light his cigarette.

"Thanks." The sailor waved a hand through the cloud of smoke that roiled up from the cigarette.

"No prob," Remy replied.

"You new around here?" the sailor asked.

Remy looked at the man, grateful for the distraction and knowing he was about to get hustled in some way. Growing up around New Orleans and Iberia Parish, Remy had learned all about the ways grifters baited their marks.

"My first day," Remy agreed.

"Well, welcome to Chinhae, sailor." The man held up his beer bottle to toast Remy.

Remy lifted his own bottled orange soda and toasted the man back. "*Bonne chance*," he said.

"Spanish?" the sailor asked.

"French," Remy replied. "Or to be more precise, Creole."

"Creole? From Louisiana?"

Remy nodded and smiled.

The sailor smiled. "I been through New Orleans back before the flood took it." He tried to get the authentic sound, saying *Nawlins,* but like most outsiders, he couldn't pull it off. "Now that there, bro, that was a party town."

"Yes," Remy agreed. As he talked about it, a thousand memories shot through his mind. He'd grown up in small towns outside New Orleans, but his teenage years and early twenties had been spent in the city. All of those memories were gone now, washed away by Hurricane Katrina.

"Mardi Gras. I been through there during Mardi Gras. The streets came alive, didn't they, bro?"

Remy nodded.

"You need anything . . . special?"

Knowing the guy was talking about illegal substances, Remy started to pull out his NCIS identification and wave the guy off, but he didn't. If the guy was tied into illegals, he probably also knew about the black market. "What do you got, sailor?"

The sailor smiled. "Call me DJ Phreak." He opened his jacket to reveal pockets filled with small plastic bags. "Got some stuff that'll make you think somebody done screwed off the top of your head, poured straight happy in, then clamped your head back together and shook it."

"You got blow?" If DJ Phreak peddled cocaine, maybe he knew Hester.

"I got blow." Phreak smiled. "Best blow you're gonna find on base, bro."

"I think I want a taste of that," Remy said. "How about small arms? I think I'd like a little something to carry. This place, it don't look exactly safe."

The sailor nodded. "I got some Smith & Wesson merch. Three fifty-sevens. Nine mil stock. What's your flava?"

"I prefer nine mil. Maybe we can get together on a price."

Phreak shrugged. "We can try."

"A man I talked to said I should try to hook up with a guy named Hester when I got here," Remy said. "Said Hester was the man to get to know."

The sailor hesitated. "Hester got himself killed."

Nodding, Remy said, "That's what I was told. But they said Hester had good stuff."

"I dealt with him. My stuff's as good as his." DJ Phreak patted his jacket. "How much do you want?"

Phreak had just incriminated himself, Remy knew. It was time to make the bust and get this guy back to HQ for questioning. Remy did his best to appear nonchalant as he moved his hand slowly toward his jacket pocket.

The light in Phreak's eyes turned steely. He'd picked up on the movement and knew exactly what it meant. He threw his beer bottle at Remy's head and shoved away from the bar. He streaked for the door, shoving people out of his way.

Remy's adrenaline spiked. Excitement surged within him. Chasing and being chased, that was what he lived for. With life or death balanced on the line, there wasn't time for worrying about past guilts or future hells.

DJ Phreak made good time, but Remy made better. He was Phreak's shadow as the man ran through the door. Their footsteps drummed against the pavement as the sailor caught hold of the doorframe and made a rapid turn. He ran out onto the street.

Remy threw himself into the man from behind, hitting him squarely in the shoulders. They flew through the air for a second, then hit the hood of a car moving slowing along the street. The car's forward momentum caused them to wash up on the windshield hard enough to knock the wind from Remy's lungs.

Then they were over the vehicle, spilling onto the street. Remy pushed himself up, focusing on his opponent. He barely heard the blaring horns all around him as traffic braked to a stop.

DJ Phreak came up with a knife in his fist. He lunged, obviously intending to put a quick end to the fight.

The knife flashed toward Remy's right eye. He caught his opponent's wrist with his left hand and stepped to the side, shoving the blade past him so it missed by inches. Remy caught the man's elbow and twisted viciously. The joint came apart with a brutal pop.

Phreak screamed shrilly as the knife fell from his hand.

Whirling in a wrestling takedown move, Remy wrapped his right arm around his opponent's neck, then yanked him across his hip and threw him to the street. Abruptly he dropped a knee into the small of Phreak's back and pulled both his arms behind him and up, forcing him in an arched position that was anything but comfortable.

In less than a minute, ROK security surrounded them. One of the men shined a flashlight in Remy's face.

"I'm United States Navy Chief Petty Officer Remy Gautreau," Remy said. "This man is my prisoner."

E SCENE ⊛ **NCIS** ⊛ CRIME SCEN

NAVAL CRIMINAL INVESTIGATIVE SERVICE

>> CHINHAE, REPUBLIC OF KOREA
>> AMERICAN NAVAL BASE NCIS HEADQUARTERS
>> 0017 HOURS

Will stared into the inky blackness that filled the stairwell leading to the underground headquarters the NCIS team had been
given to work out of in Chinhae. The darkness remained unbro-
ken below where lights should have been.

Without a word, he reached for his pistol and glanced over at
Maggie. She'd drawn her own Berettas and held them loose and
ready at her sides.

At the bottom of the steps, Will paused and opened the headset channel he and his team used. "Estrella," he called softly.
"Gautreau."

"Gautreau here," Remy responded.

Will thought the SEAL sounded out of breath. "Why are the
lights out down there?"

"I couldn't say," Remy answered. "I'm off-site, Commander."

"Where are you?"

"Getting dinner."

"Is Estrella with you?"

"No."

Anxiety filled Will's mind. He kept remembering how Frank had looked after he'd been killed. *God, let her be okay.*

"Commander?" Remy asked.

"Stay online," Will instructed. He glanced back up the stairwell, finding Maggie behind him.

"There's another way out," she whispered.

Will knew that. A duplicate set of stairs at the other end of the short corridor made a *U* through this section of the basement.

"I'll cover that." She started to move.

"No," Will whispered. "We'll be too spread out. We stay together."

"Call for backup?"

"No." Will slipped a Mini Maglite from his jacket. He held the flash facing down from his palm, his wrists crossed as he pointed the XD-40 and went forward. The yellow cone of bright light illuminated the hallway before him.

Whoever was in the hallway would know he was coming, but that couldn't be helped. He had to assume that since they'd chosen the darkness to cloak their movements, they had a way of seeing through it anyway.

At that moment, Will spotted a flurry of movement near the door leading to the borrowed lab and swung his flashlight in that direction. A man dressed in black brought up a pistol. Thick-lensed night-vision goggles masked his upper face and lent him an insectlike appearance.

Will threw himself to the floor just as the man fired. The muzzle flash split the darkness. Maggie returned fire from behind and to his right. Will tried to draw a bead on the man in the near darkness, but before he could fire, the man was up the stairs at the far end of the hallway and gone.

Security Klaxons screamed to life. Evidently the gunplay hadn't gone unnoticed.

Holding the flashlight in front of him, Will went into the lab. "Estrella."

"Here," she called in a choked voice.

Will swung the flash in the direction of her voice and caught sight of Estrella as she forced herself to her feet.

"Are you okay?" Will asked.

"Fine," Estrella croaked. She massaged her neck. Will's flash revealed the bruising already taking place. "I'm fine."

"Commander," Remy called over Will's headset.

"We've got her," Will said. "She's safe."

"I'm on my way," Remy said. "I've got a prisoner. He knew Hester."

"Bring him in," Will instructed.

Noise sounded out in the hallway. A man's voice barked orders.

"Base security just arrived," Maggie said.

Will turned his attention to that problem, changing frequencies on the headset to inform the base provost marshal's office that they had survived the incident without casualties, but the enemy had escaped.

>> OKINAWA, JAPAN
>> CAMP SMEDLEY D. BUTLER
>> 0134 HOURS

The young Marine standing guard over the door to the interview room nodded at Shel, then opened the door. Shel walked in and approached the center of the room where Vivian Layton sat in a metal chair screwed into the floor.

Nearby, stretched out against the wall, Max looked up at Shel. The Labrador stretched and yawned, then laid his big head back down.

With the choice of three other chairs around the table, Shel took the one opposite the woman. Earlier he'd sat beside her, but that was when he'd been using the proximity to build trust and the illusion that they were on the same side. Sitting opposite her now would point out that he was free to come and go while she had to remain in the room and be escorted even to the bathroom.

Shel placed two large containers of coffee on the table. A carton contained a dozen fresh-baked donuts. The doughy aroma filled the room.

Vivian glanced up at Shel with a reproachful look in her bloodshot eyes. Mascara hollowed her eyes, and the left side of her face showed abrasions where he'd shoved her to the floor back at the apartment building.

"I was beginning to think you weren't coming back," she told him.

Shel tore the tab from the top of his coffee cup. "I didn't know if I was coming back. Got tied up in something else." He'd been letting her sweat, letting her wonder how important she was to his investigation. He took a chocolate-covered donut from the assortment.

That didn't sit well with Vivian. "I thought you said talking to me was important."

"It could be," Shel said. He tore the donut in half and put one of the halves into his mouth.

"It *is* important," she said. "I *know* things."

Unconcernedly, Shel ate the other half of the donut. He'd always had good luck interviewing women. Estrella had assured him it was because he possessed some of the most naturally annoying qualities she'd ever seen in a man.

"The man who became Virgil Hester wasn't the only one who was replaced in the military," she declared.

"Start talking," Shel said. "But if you miss anything, I'm going to get suspicious of what you're telling me. Understand?"

"Yes," Vivian answered. "A few months ago I was approached by a Yakuza member. He wanted to hire me."

"To do what?"

"To hang out with Virgil. Occupy his attention."

"You were hired to seduce him?"

Vivian took a breath. "Yes."

"Why?" Shel asked.

"At first I thought the Yakuza just wanted to blackmail Hester. But that didn't make sense to me because the position he had didn't seem all that important."

"So if they weren't after blackmail, what did they want?"

"Virgil handled cargo. Makes sense they wanted somebody to help move contraband through the U.S. Navy. Right?"

Shel considered. It did make sense. It also meant that whoever was supplying the drugs and weapons that Hester's imposter was selling in Chinhae had the means to hire or bribe the Japanese Yakuza. This was getting bigger and bigger. To Vivian, he said, "And you went along with it."

Moisture clouded Vivian's eyes, and she took a ragged breath. "They didn't give me a choice. If I hadn't gone along with it they would have killed me. I was actually surprised they didn't kill me after Virgil was replaced."

Guess they changed their minds on that one, Shel thought. Aloud, he said, "When did you know they planned to replace Hester?"

Vivian looked away. Tears fell then. "Not until that stranger came home wearing Virgil's face."

"You could tell he'd had plastic surgery?"

"No. But I knew right away it wasn't Virgil." She took a short breath. "Virgil was nice. The new person wasn't." She wrapped her arms around herself.

"What can you tell me about the new Virgil?"

"Nothing. I have no idea who he was. He just showed up that day bragging about how easy it was to take over someone's identity. He said there were others like him too. Then he said he'd be leaving in a few days and we had to stage a breakup so people wouldn't ask questions."

Shel waited as Vivian's tears slowed, then finally stopped.

"He was a thief," Vivian said finally. "A real klepto. Couldn't keep his hands to himself. Everywhere we went while he was mixing in with Virgil's friends, setting up the fights so we could 'break up' and he would have an excuse to leave Okinawa, he stole things. He'd come back to my place with his pockets stuffed with all sorts of things. Lighters. Watches. Pens. Just OPP."

"OPP?"

"Other people's property."

"So he was a petty thief."

"Yes. But he was also a dip." Vivian looked up and noticed the blank look on Shel's face. "You don't know what a dip is?"

"Tell me."

"A dip is a pickpocket. Whoever this guy was, he had skills, you know. I've been around that kind of guy before, but this man was really good. I nearly got busted at a club before I figured out what was going on. Bloke that lost his wallet thought I'd snatched it. Wasn't till we got back home that I figured out what really happened."

Shel considered the information. If the imposter was a habitual criminal, he might have left a trail. Of course they'd have to be able to identify him before they could investigate that. He filed the thought away.

"Do you know what happened to the real Virgil Hester?" he asked.

Tears spilled down Vivian's face again. "No," she answered in a hoarse voice. "He just disappeared. I never saw him again."

SCENE ⊛ **NCIS** ⊛ CRIME SCEN
NAVAL CRIMINAL INVESTIGATIVE SERVICE

>> CHINHAE, REPUBLIC OF KOREA
>> AMERICAN NAVAL BASE NCIS HEADQUARTERS
>> 0214 HOURS

"So who's our guy?" Will peered at the monitor that showed the interview room where Maggie sat with the prisoner that Remy Gautreau had brought in.

"Seaman Second Class Darius Greendale." Estrella sat at the workstation. The bruising around her neck had darkened but she seemed to have recovered from the scare she'd had. It wasn't the first time she'd been in a tense situation.

"Have you confirmed that?"

They'd had the man in custody for over two hours now. Maggie had initiated a brief Q & A session; then they'd let the man sweat. They had him cold for possession and intent to distribute.

"I have confirmed his identity," Estrella said. "His dental records match his hometown dentist's records."

"Any chance of tampering there?"

"There's always a chance. But I also compared his finger-prints to the local police department's files. I made a call and had them ship me Greendale's prints."

"They had them?"

Estrella smiled at Will. "Believe it or not, Commander, Greendale hasn't been a model citizen. Before he joined the Navy, he was investigated regarding a string of burglaries. After Shel's report of his interview concerning Lance Corporal Hester's imposter and the fact that the man probably had a criminal record, I decided to check there."

"Those could have been tampered with as well."

Estrella nodded. "Of course. That's why I had the PD pull the original ten-card to scan."

The ten-card contained the physical impressions of a person's fingerprints.

"He's Greendale," Estrella said.

"Good job," Will told her. He started to leave the room to deal with the interview, then turned back. "You doing okay?"

Estrella looked back at him. "Yeah, I'm all right." She paused, her dark eyes searching his face. "What about you?"

"Me?"

"I know about your family problems. I know how stressful that can be."

"Yeah. Well . . ." Will looked away.

"I know it's not easy for you, being here instead of with your family," Estrella said. "It's not easy for me either." She paused. Then she said, "This job means a lot to me. It means a lot to my son. Without it, I don't know if I could take care of Nicky." She glanced down for a moment, then asked, "Do you know how my husband died?"

Will shook his head.

"Julian and I were crackers. Do you know what that is?"

"You developed and dismantled security systems involving computers." Will knew that from the cases NCIS handled.

"That's part of the job. Julian and I, we were good at it. Two of the best. We were making a good living, making a few dreams come true. But Julian had this one dream—of becoming a major video-game designer. Not so much for the money but for the opportunity and self-satisfaction of creating something a lot of people would stand up and take notice of."

Will listened quietly.

"Julian invested everything he had into the company he was building—everything *we* had. And he borrowed even more money. All for this dream." Estrella had to stop for a moment. "I was pregnant with our son, but Julian didn't even seem to notice. We talked about it sometimes, but he was consumed by the game. He started using drugs to stay awake, to put more hours in the day. I had a lot of sickness and trouble with the pregnancy. For a while I didn't know if I was going to be able to carry Nicky to term. Then, everything seemed to catch up to Julian. He got stuck on the game design, ran into problems that he couldn't solve, started blowing contract deadlines for security work that I was too sick to help with." She took a deep, shaky breath. "I watched him destroy himself. And I couldn't do anything about it."

"I'm sorry," Will said, hating the weakness of those two words.

"I came home from the doctor's office one afternoon," Estrella whispered. "Julian never told me how bad things were getting. But I knew he was worried all the time and he wasn't sleeping. While I was gone, he'd put a pistol to his head and shot himself."

Will stood silent, not knowing what to say.

"I thought I was going to die today. When that man grabbed me, I thought I was never going to see my baby again. When something like that happens, it makes you think about a lot of things." She paused again. "I wanted you to know that what happened to Julian is not going to happen to me. I'm going to stay on the case and give it my best. I guess I need to know that you're going to do the same."

"I am, Estrella."

"I'm glad, sir."

"Maggie."

Will's voice echoed inside Maggie's head through the headset. She sat across a small table from Seaman Darius Greendale. Greendale was clad in an orange jumpsuit, cuffed hand and foot. He wasn't happy about the accommodations.

"I'll be back," Maggie said to Greendale. She stood and crossed the room to the door.

"Hey," Greendale called. He lifted his cuffed hands. "These are too tight."

Maggie looked at him. "No, they're not."

Grumbling and cursing to himself, Greendale dropped his manacled hands back into his lap.

Maggie let herself out and found Will in the hallway. Nearby, the two Marine guards stood at attention and watched over the interview room.

"We have Greendale by the short hairs," Will said. "He's going down. He should be willing to talk."

"He is. He'll talk all day. Ask him a question, he'll give you an answer." Maggie sighed. "The problem is, he doesn't know anything."

"Shel's report says there are more imposters than just Hester's, but Greendale isn't one of them. Estrella confirmed his ID by contacting his hometown dentist and police department.

Whatever Hester's imposter was doing here, Greendale wasn't in on it. His only link to the imposter was the cocaine."

"The lab is processing the cocaine Greendale had on him," Maggie said. "As a precaution, I sent part of the cocaine on a flight back to Camp Lejeune so our lab guys can look at it. Then we can compare the results. At least then we'll know where the imposter's cocaine came from."

"But we only have Greendale's word that the cocaine came from Hester's replacement."

"When Han delivers—"

"If," Will interjected softly.

"He will," Maggie said. "When Han delivers your cocaine, we'll have two independent batches. We can use them to validate each other. The chemical signatures should be the same."

One of the surprising things Maggie had learned since signing on with NCIS was that illegal chemicals—like the cocaine the imposter sold—was as identifiable as a fingerprint. Even when working from the same chemical recipes, batches ended up unique because of the ingredients used or because of the "cooks" that made them.

"It will be interesting to see where the drugs came from," Will said. "Does Greendale know how much cocaine and how many weapons the imposter was moving?"

"No, except that he thinks it was a lot."

"Why?"

"Because the imposter always had cocaine to sell."

"And that was only a small fraction of what was coming here."

Maggie nodded. "Like Shel's report says, the imposter was a thief. He couldn't pass up the opportunity to take some of the drugs and guns and sell them on the side. But the cocaine wasn't intended for South Korea. There was no increase in the cocaine activity in the area. It was only passing through Chinhae."

"We need to know where it was going," Will said.

❀ ❀ ❀

>> AMERICAN NAVAL BASE, NCIS LAB
>> 0518 HOURS

Will's monitor flashed, indicating an incoming call. The caller ID showed that it was the base security calling.

Will closed the picture Wren had drawn in crayon and scanned into an e-mail before answering the call. "Coburn," he said, hearing his voice thick and phlegmy in his throat.

"Commander," a young Marine said from the monitor's speakers. "Were you expecting a visitor, sir?"

Curious, Will lifted an eyebrow. "A visitor?"

"Yes, sir. I'll show you." The Marine patched in a digital image of a black car in front of the base security gates. "We captured images of their faces."

Digital photos of three men slid into place at the bottom of the monitor. All of them looked Korean and young.

Will didn't recognize any of them. "They asked for me by name?"

"Yes, sir. Said they had a package for you."

Understanding, Will said, "I'll be right there."

"Want me to come along?" Maggie asked from her workstation.

"No. Keep working on the jacket Estrella pulled up on Achmed. If he killed Frank, I want to know about it."

Will crossed the room to Remy, who lay on a cot in a relaxed posture with his eyes closed and his hands laced behind his head. "Are you awake?" Will asked.

"Since the phone rang." Remy opened his eyes. Without training in forensics and computers, he didn't have much to do right now.

"Roll with me," Will said.

"Are we expecting trouble?" Remy rolled effortlessly out of

the cot. He checked the H&K P9S semiautomatic on his right hip and the Smith & Wesson .357 revolver under his left arm. The 9 mm held nine rounds, but the .357 was there for sheer knock-down power.

"Better to be prepared for it," Will said as he headed for the door.

38

>> CHINHAE, REPUBLIC OF KOREA
>> CHINHAE AMERICAN NAVAL BASE
>> PERIMETER GATEHOUSE
>> 0526 HOURS

Remy stopped the jeep at the security gates. The Marine guards came out and signed both Will and Remy out even though they'd be back in minutes. It was standard operating procedure and the Marine security stood by it to the letter.

Beyond the heavy gates, the black sedan sat idling. The three men inside didn't move.

After the gates were open, Remy drove through slowly. "How do you want to handle this?"

"Stay back with the jeep. Keep me covered." Will put on a Kevlar-lined helmet. He wore a bulletproof vest under his jacket.

"I could go get whatever they're delivering."

"No. I'll handle this."

Remy pulled the jeep to a halt a few feet short of the sedan. He took the machine pistol from between the seats and got out on his side of the jeep as Will stepped out. The SEAL fell into position beside the military vehicle.

Will walked to the car.

"Coburn," one of the passengers said.

"That's me," Will said. He stopped just out of arm's reach and stayed out of Remy's field of fire. "I was told you had a package."

The passenger held up a small cloth pouch. "From Mr. Han."

"Throw it over here."

When the man in the passenger seat tossed the pouch over, Will caught it. He loosened the drawstring and peered inside. Small glassine envelopes containing white powder filled the bag.

"Mr. Han also said to tell you that you are not welcome at any of his establishments," the man in the passenger seat said. "He said to tell you that he can't be responsible for any unpleasantness that might befall you."

Will took a deep breath. Anger ignited inside him and he couldn't hold it back. His life had been out of control for a long time, even before all the events in Chinhae had transpired. He was sick of it, tired of running and doubting and being afraid. He drew his sidearm and pointed it at the man.

"Get out of the car," Will ordered.

The gang member started to move.

"Your hands," Remy said in a loud voice. "If they come up any way but empty, you're a dead man."

The ruby-colored aiming laser from the machine pistol centered on the man's face. In the next second, more ruby lights from the Marine guards' rifles touched the men inside the car. Reluctantly, all three got out of the car.

"Over there," Will ordered, motioning them to the side of the road.

The three gang members walked where they were told.

Without a word, Will walked to the jeep, tossed the pouch into the passenger seat, and took a fuel can from the back. He looked at the Marine. "Get a fire unit here."

The Marine grinned. "Yes, sir."

Returning to the sedan, Will opened the fuel can and dumped the gasoline over the vehicle, taking time to slosh some of the contents inside.

The three men began yelling in Korean. One of them finally managed, "What are you doing?"

Will reached into the car and found a book of matches that bore the Happy Pagoda logo. He took out one match, lit it, then used it to set the other matches aflame. When the matchbook was burning brightly, he tossed it into the car.

The gasoline ignited instantly, gurgling a liquid *whoosh!* The flames quickly engulfed the car.

Will moved toward the three men, watching the way the fire-light played over their shocked faces. "Tell Mr. Han I'm not big on threats. Tell him that so far I haven't threatened him; threats are not my style. Tell him that he doesn't want to bother me or my team or I'm going to roll over him." He paused. "Are we clear here?"

"Yes," one gang member said. Reflections of the twisting flames burned in his eyes.

"Good. You better get started. It's a long walk back." Will turned from them and walked away. Tiredly, he dropped into the jeep's passenger seat.

A siren screamed back on base.

Will stared at the fire-gutted car. Flames stretched from inside, wrapping around the vehicle, bubbling the paint. The front-left tire sagged as the air rushed out of it; then the car crumpled forward like a horse going down on its belly.

Remy backed the jeep away from the pyre just as the base fire truck arrived. Firemen spilled from it and dragged hoses toward the fire. Jets of water sluiced over the flames, muting them a little.

As Remy pulled back through the gate, the Marines on duty at the post smiled and saluted Will.

"You know," Remy said, "you are a very unpredictable man."

"I know," Will said. He picked up the pouch and looked at the glassine envelopes. Somewhere in all that, he hoped there was a clue, a shred of evidence that would point them in the right direction.

⊛ ⊛ ⊛

>> CHINHAE AMERICAN NAVAL BASE NCIS LAB
>> 0559 HOURS

Will spread the last of the glassine envelopes on the workstation, then reached for the fingerprinting kit. He swabbed the duster over the packets, spreading the gray powder over the surfaces.

No fingerprints showed up.

He flipped the packets over and repeated the process. All of the packets were devoid of fingerprints.

"Anything?"

Looking up, Will saw Maggie standing there. "No. They're clean. Like they'd been made on a factory line and untouched by human hands. I understand the packets you took from Greendale had prints all over them."

Maggie nodded. "Unfortunately, all the prints we were able to lift belonged to Greendale."

"Did you get the report on the cocaine?"

Maggie leaned in and used the keyboard to activate the monitor, then brought up the electronic report. "The cocaine was identified as being of Colombian origins. The isotope ratio analysis also matched the cocaine Han's men delivered to most of what Greendale had to sell."

"So they're all from the same batch." Will was familiar with the analysis. Carbon atoms of different weights occurred regularly in nature. Plants, like the coca leaves harvested in South America, broke down into unique chemical signatures according to region and even to the individual batches they were cooked in. Batches could be identified by such unique qualities as soil type, carbon-dioxide concentration, and humidity.

"Yes." Maggie tapped the keyboard again. "This particular batch came out of Cali, Colombia. That city's history is rife with narcobarons. This batch was made by Ernesto Gacha Luis. As usual with Spanish-American names, the middle name is his paternal one."

An image of a grim-faced man appeared on the monitor. Will figured Gacha was in his fifties. He wore a thin mustache and goatee. The man looked sullen and dangerous, like he'd never known a kind day in his whole life.

"Does Gacha have a history of dealing inside the United States military?"

"No. He's never even been around U.S. bases. He steers clear of American soil. The cocaine business is different than it used to be. It's more compartmentalized. In the old days, a group grew and harvested the coca leaves, transported them to a jungle lab, rendered them into paste, shipped it again, and turned the paste into powder. Then they sold it on the streets through dealers they owned."

"But it's not like that now?"

"Now," Maggie said, "each one of those steps is managed by a different crime family. One family plants and harvests. Another transports. And so on."

"Gacha handles the mixing?"

"Yes. He's known for the jungle labs he operates. He's a hard, sadistic man, Will. Peasants are recruited and pressed into service. Anyone who steals from him—man, woman, or child— is killed on the spot."

Will knew the cocaine wars in South America had gotten even more violent than they had been back in the 1980s. The

Drug Enforcement Administration had fought a nasty series of wars with the narcobarons, and good DEA men had died as well as Colombian policemen. With the investigations the NCIS did, Will came face-to-face with some of the drug cartels' handiwork on occasion.

"So Gacha's people made the cocaine Hester's imposter was distributing here," he concluded.

Maggie nodded. "The imposter stole it from the cargo that he was helping push through here."

"Do we have any information yet about where Gacha's product is going?" The DEA kept tabs on the transportation of controlled substances as well as on the chemicals used to manufacture them.

"That's where this thing gets really twisted," Maggie said.

39

NAVAL CRIMINAL INVESTIGATIVE SERVICE

>> CHINHAE, REPUBLIC OF KOREA
>> AMERICAN NAVAL BASE NCIS HEADQUARTERS
>> 0819 HOURS

"This is Russia we're talking about, Will," Director Larkin said over the video hookup. "With the way things currently stand between South Korea and North Korea, and China ready to jump in and pick a side just one step ahead of us—all of which might drop a huge conflagration into the laps of the Russians—we're not exactly welcome there."

Will paced, feeling the nervous energy spike within him. "I know that, sir. I'm trying to connect the dots with what's going on here. According to the information Maggie got from the DEA, Gacha's cocaine has turned up in Moscow. Colombian cocaine doesn't often show up in Russia. There are a lot of home-grown suppliers, but not many supplying Colombian drugs. To move the amount that's on the streets there, based on the seizures the Ministry of Interior has reported, someone has had a pipeline to a big source."

Larkin leaned back in his chair. "Did you time-frame the arrival of the Colombian cocaine there?"

"The cocaine started hitting Moscow just days after Hester's replacement arrived here. We're guessing that the cocaine hit Chinhae, then was disbursed through local traffickers who pushed the Colombian product into Moscow. But if cocaine is going in, something was coming out. I need to know what. That's why I want to talk to the Moscow police. If I know who was getting the cocaine in Russia, maybe I can figure out what was being bought."

"Why does anything have to be bought?" Larkin asked. "How do you know this isn't simply about profits?"

"Because it doesn't *feel* that way," Will answered. "I can't give you any more than that. Not without knowing more."

Larkin was quiet, thoughtful. Finally he said, "Someone's using the United States military to move cocaine around. We're not going to be able to contain this for long. Someone somewhere is going to leak the news to the media." He blew out an angry breath. "By the time I start getting asked questions, I want to know the answers. If there's any way possible, I'll get you your interview with someone from the Moscow police department."

"Thank you, sir," Will said.

>> **CHINHAE AMERICAN NAVAL BASE NCIS HEADQUARTERS**
>> **1902 HOURS**

Inspector Ivan Rushaylo of the UBNON, the Directorate for Combating Drug Trafficking in Moscow, looked like a cop in any language—even on the monitor. He was in his early fifties, gray-haired and a little heavy, brusque, and hard around the edges. Thankfully Rushaylo's English was good.

"Thank you for talking to me," Will said. "I know it's a bit irregular."

Rushaylo pushed up rounded shoulders that looked like they bore the weight of the world. "Not so irregular." He riffled through a pile of paperwork. "No tactic can be ignored in our struggle against the baser elements of society. At times, it even seems we are making progress, thank God."

The quiet acknowledgment to God startled Will a little because Russia was generally thought of as an atheist country. Of course, that didn't explain all the beautiful small churches and icons that clergy had made over the years. And there had been a definite shift since the Berlin Wall had come down in 1989.

Rushaylo laced his fingers. "I was told you know something of the cocaine that has deluged my city."

"I do. We're in the process of dismantling the supply route."

"On behalf of my country, I thank you for that."

Will figured that the thanks would be short-lived once it became common knowledge that the U.S. military had been ferrying the drugs to their destination through one or more of its own supply routes. "I need some information from you that might help me with what I'm doing."

"Of course."

"Who was handling the cocaine in Moscow?"

The Moscow inspector pulled his keyboard over to him. He hunted and pecked with two fingers. "Forgive my ineptness, Commander Coburn. I am not so accomplished in the computer as some of my junior associates."

"It's no problem."

A moment later, an image opened in the lower left quadrant of Will's monitor. Will moved the transmission to another monitor at the workstation and kept the phone link to Rushaylo.

The image showed a man with long blond hair and a beard. He didn't look any older than his thirties. Flat gray eyes held only anger. A bruise darkened one of his cheekbones. Will figured the picture had been taken following an arrest.

"His name is Isidor Kuzlow," Rushaylo stated. "He is very well-known to us. He has killed his way to the top of a *Mafiya* group here in Moscow but maintains several interests in Eastern Europe."

"Kuzlow is moving the cocaine inside Moscow?"

"*Da*. He and his crime syndicate. In greater volume than we have ever seen. On top of this, we can't find him in his usual haunts. I was hoping you might offer a clue as to where I might look for him."

"I've no idea."

Reaching into a desk drawer, Rushaylo took out a pipe and a small bag of tobacco. He grinned sheepishly. "My one vice. I simply can't afford any others." He filled his pipe. When he asked his next question, it seemed vague and innocuous, merely a passing thought. "Tell me, Commander, have you heard of a man named Vladimir Gronsky?"

"No. Who is he?"

Rushaylo lit his pipe, waved the smoke away, and shook his head. "Just someone that Kuzlow knows. Will I be correct in telling my superiors that you have the cocaine problem well in hand at your end?"

"Yes," Will responded.

"Good." Rushaylo smiled through a cloud of smoke. "The Ministry of Interior is always and forever sticking its nose into my work. Wanting to know when and why and who, and what I'm going to do about all of it. I'm sure you have the same stories to tell."

"It's the nature of the business," Will agreed.

"I'm curious," the Moscow cop said. "How is it that I'm talking to someone from the United States Navy rather than your country's Drug Enforcement Administration regarding this interest?"

"I'm with Naval Criminal Investigative Services. We'll be resourcing the DEA soon. Primarily, I police military bases and personnel."

"And ships? You police those as well, yes?"

"Aye," Will replied.

"Interesting work, I'm sure." Rushaylo smiled again, but the humor never lighted his pale blue eyes. "Perhaps we'll talk again, Commander."

"Perhaps," Will said, understanding that neither of them had told everything they knew or suspected.

>> **2317 HOURS**

Maggie stared at endless streams of data on her monitor. She still felt a little groggy from getting up from bed a short time ago. Glancing over her shoulder, she saw that Estrella was still at her workstation, and couldn't remember if the woman had managed any sleep at all.

Will was out, crashed gangly-legged in a chair, looking like he'd fought sleep with every ounce of resistance in his body.

At the back of the room near the door, Remy sat cross-legged on a cot. A handheld game system sat to one side of him and a pile of magazines on the other. He wore his pistols. Sometimes he slept in that position. At least, Maggie thought the SEAL slept. Remy didn't know enough about the kind of work they did to help with the research load.

The phone rang and she brought it up on-screen with the click of a button. "NCIS. Special Agent Foley," she answered.

The man at the other end of the connection was intense. He had dark hair and dark eyes and a definite predatory look to him. He was sleek and shiny, almost sharklike. The smile that curved his lips never touched his eyes.

"Special Agent Foley," he stated in a quiet, flat Midwestern tone. "I'm Assistant Director Clyde Burcell of the Central Intelligence Agency."

Maggie brought up the connection confirmation and verified the veracity of his claim. "What can I do for you, sir?" she asked politely.

"Actually," Burcell said, "I was hoping I might be able to do something for you."

Maggie waited. *Sorry, Charlie, I don't buy that. I've dealt with the CIA enough to know that you people don't call someone and offer to help them out without planning on getting more in return.*

"It appears the NCIS has been in contact with someone in Russia's Ministry of Interior," Burcell went on. "Might I ask why?"

"I'm afraid that's classified."

A little irritation showed through the CIA director's aplomb. He scratched the tip of his nose and forced a laugh. "That's funny. You have to admit, that's funny. You telling a CIA director that something is classified. I thought maybe we could share information."

"I'd be happy to," Maggie said.

"Why did you contact the Ministry of Interior?"

Without hesitation, Maggie asked, "Why do you want to know?"

Burcell lost some of the pleasant look. "I thought we were sharing information."

"So did I."

Burcell picked up a pencil and tapped it against the desktop. "We've been in contact with Inspector Rushaylo regarding a certain matter."

Maggie let that pass.

Estrella had gotten interested enough in the exchange that she'd left her workstation and come over to listen.

"Maybe we're working on the same matter," Burcell suggested.

"Wouldn't the inspector have mentioned that?" she asked.

"I didn't speak with him."

"Then how do you know we talked to Rushaylo?" Maggie asked.

"One of his associates confirmed your conversation."

"You're spying on the inspector?"

"No."

"Then his associate is spying on him for the CIA?" Maggie noticed that Estrella was smiling to herself.

"No." Burcell cleared his throat and started over. "I was talking to the associate regarding an unrelated matter. He mentioned that Commander Coburn had contacted the police inspector."

"An unrelated matter?" Maggie repeated. "Then why would you be interested in what the commander spoke to Rushaylo about if you know the matter is unrelated?"

"Miss Foley—"

"Special Agent Foley," Maggie interrupted without a trace of rancor. "Or Maggie."

Burcell nodded and adjusted his tie. "Of course." He addressed her as neither. "I was interested in what prompted you to make contact with Russia's Ministry of Interior."

"An unrelated issue," Maggie said sweetly.

Burcell looked like he might go apoplectic.

"We're tracing cocaine we believe was transported through the Chinhae Naval Base in South Korea," Maggie said. "According to the DEA's tracking database, a lot of that cocaine showed up in Moscow."

"So what? No doubt a lot of that cocaine showed up in California and other United States areas as well."

"Yes," Maggie said, "but I bet those drugs weren't shipped through South Korea to get there."

"No," Burcell said weakly.

"I've told you my unrelated story," Maggie pointed out. "What are you working on?"

From his brief hesitation and the way he leaned back slightly, Maggie knew she wasn't going to get the full story. "An ex-Russian military officer has gone missing."

"Vladimir Gronsky?" Maggie asked. She remembered Gronsky's name from Will's conversation with Rushaylo. Estrella had searched for background and received hits almost immediately. Gronsky's wife had reported him missing days ago.

"Yes. How do you know the name?"

"Rushaylo asked the commander if he'd heard of him," Maggie replied. "Why is the CIA interested in a missing Russian colonel?"

"The Russian State Department asked us to look into it, Maggie." Burcell smiled. "Personally, I'm thinking the guy is retired and fed up with puttering around the house all day. He probably just stepped off his wife's radar and she hit the panic button. But, in light of everything that's going on in the Koreas now, the State Department thought this might be a show of goodwill."

Maggie knew she wasn't going to get anything further from the man. "Will there be anything else?"

"No."

"Then I have a question. What do you know about a Colombian cartel member named Ernesto Gacha Luis?"

Burcell spread his hands. "Other than the fact that he's a criminal, nothing."

"Have you heard of Isidor Kuzlow?"

Smiling, Burcell shook his head. "Not until this very minute. Sorry, Miss Foley. I'm just a cog in the wheel. Today I'm looking for a retired Russian army colonel. I've got to get back to it. You have a good day."

"You too," Maggie said. The screen closed, leaving her staring at the psych evals again.

"He's lying about something," Estrella said.

"You think?" Maggie asked sarcastically, though it wasn't

directed at the other woman. "Personally, I think he was lying about everything."

"I could maybe take a peek at his files," Estrella said.

In the past, Estrella had used her computer skills to get the NCIS team through firewalls and security measures of dozens of international businesses. When it came to national security, no stone was left unturned and restraints got shoved out the window.

"I think it's a good idea, if you can," Maggie said.

A confident gleam showed in Estrella's eye. "I can."

"It'll be Will's call."

"Do it," Will said in a sleep-fogged voice.

Looking over her shoulder, Maggie saw that Will was awake in the chair. "How long have you been awake?"

"I heard most of the discussion between you and Burcell." Will sat up. "We need to know whatever they know. Without them knowing we know it."

"I'll get on it right away," Estrella said. "But first I have something you should see. I've been researching Gacha's background, and I turned up something interesting."

S ✴ **CRIME SCENE** ✴ **NCIS** ✴ **CR**
NAVAL CRIMINAL INVESTIGATIVE SERVICE

40

SCENE ⊛ **NCIS** ⊛ CRIME SCEN
NAVAL CRIMINAL INVESTIGATIVE SERVICE

>> CHINHAE, REPUBLIC OF KOREA
>> AMERICAN NAVAL BASE NCIS HEADQUARTERS
>> 2323 HOURS

"His name is Ricardo Toledo Munoz," Estrella said.

Will studied the sullen-faced young man on the computer monitor. Toledo had fair skin for a Hispanic but possessed the dark hair and eyes. His eyebrows were thick and almost grew together, and his folded-arm attitude was a definite challenge. Will thought there was something familiar about the way he held himself.

"Who is he?" Will asked.

"The nephew of Ernesto Gacha Luis," Estrella said. "He grew up in Colombia but moved to the U.S. when he was fifteen. Since then he's been in trouble with the law almost constantly. He's been arrested three times for possession with the intent to distribute, four times for assault and battery, nine times for petty theft including shoplifting, once for grand theft auto, and twice for attempted rape."

"Nice kid," Remy said.

"Toledo only spent two and a half years in a county jail in Texas on four separate charges," Estrella went on. "He was a juvenile for most of the charges, and the district attorneys' offices involved never could get him arraigned as an adult."

"Why is Toledo interesting?" Will asked.

"He's missing." Estrella tapped the keyboard in rapid syncopation. "DEA wiretaps have recorded Gacha having conversations with men he's sent to South Korea to look for his nephew."

"South Korea?" Will asked.

"Not just to South Korea," Estrella said. "To Chinhae."

"Why would Toledo be here?" Will flipped the possibilities around in his head.

"Watching over his uncle's property," Remy suggested. "The cocaine came from Gacha's labs in Colombia. Means it has his brand on it. If the drugs get stepped on too hard, they won't be worth much."

By "stepped on," Will knew Remy meant the cocaine would get cut, mixed with cornstarch, crushed or powdered vitamins, flour, or sugar to increase the amount the second seller had to market. "So Toledo could be at this end verifying shipments?"

Remy shrugged. "When you make your product your business, you gotta keep a good name. Otherwise, the people who are buying from you go someplace else."

"But Gacha has a lock on the transportation through military cargoes," Will said, going with it. "No other cocaine is hitting Moscow."

"And there's only one dealer at that end," Remy said. "Isidor Kuzlow. Looks like everybody involved has a pretty sweet racket."

"Looks that way," Will agreed. He looked at Estrella. "Are you digging into the CIA records?"

She nodded. "I should have something soon."

"Let me know as soon as you do." He stood up. "Remy, let's go."

"Where are we going?"

Will shrugged. "If there are Colombian cartel members in town, I don't think they'll be hard to spot."

"But you don't speak the language, *amigo*," a deep voice said.

Turning, Will saw Shel McHenry standing in the doorway. The big Marine had a duffel over one shoulder, was outfitted in camo pants and an OD green T-shirt under a camo jacket. The baseball cap needlessly advertised USMC. Max stood at his side.

"When did you get back?" Will asked.

"Little while ago." Shel nodded to Estrella and Maggie, then his eyes cut toward Remy. "This the newbie?"

Will made the introductions, and the men shook hands.

"If you're rounding up a posse," Shel said, "I'll saddle up and go with you." He rolled his neck. "Spent too many hours on a plane these past couple days. Be good to get out and stretch my legs."

"All right," Will said.

>> DOWNTOWN CHINHAE
>> 0118 HOURS

Finding the Colombians was ridiculously easy. Will decided that if they hadn't been concentrating their efforts on Han and the imposter, they doubtless would have tripped over the drug-cartel members before now.

Will, Remy, and Shel asked around in a couple of bars. It didn't take long to find a bartender who had seen them. A few bars later, they found the Colombians themselves.

There were four of them. All of the men were heavily scarred, men who had spent every waking moment since childhood immersed in violence. Will talked to the bartender, who said the men had been looking for Lance Corporal Hester.

Will walked to the back table in the small bar with Remy and Shel flanking him.

The four Colombians glanced up warily. Their hands slid beneath their jackets.

"Good evening, gentlemen," Will said. The clock on the wall showed that it was 1:19 a.m.

A bearded man with thick jowls stared at Will as if he were a minor annoyance. "We would like to be left alone," he said.

"You're looking for Lance Corporal Hester," Will said. "I want to know why."

The man shook his shaggy head. "I know no one by that name."

"You've been showing his picture around town," Will said.

"It is our business."

"And I'm making it mine."

One of the other men spoke in rapid-fire Spanish.

The first man waved him away. "We do not wish to be bothered."

"I want answers," Will said. "We have a standoff."

"No," the second man said in broken English. "No standoff. You leave."

"We can have this conversation here," Will said, reaching into his jacket and producing his NCIS badge, "or we can have it on base. Either way, I'm getting answers to my questions."

"*Policia,*" the second man said. He pushed up from the table and dragged a pistol from his shoulder holster.

Shel moved at once, seizing the man's gun wrist in one huge hand and the back of the man's head in the other. He wrenched the man's wrist and caused the pistol to fall free, then caught the weapon in midair even as he slammed the man's face into the table. The Colombian relaxed, obviously unconscious.

One of the other men rose suddenly. Remy's foot blurred into motion as he kicked the man's wrist. Bone broke with a crack that shut down the bar noise and made some of the clientele start bailing for the doors. Remy's next kick caught the man full in the face and sprawled him out over his companion.

By that time, Will had his pistol in hand and was aiming it at the Colombian leader. "Your choice," he said in a calm, cold voice, "whether you walk out or we carry you out."

>> AMERICAN NAVAL BASE NCIS HEADQUARTERS
>> 0641 HOURS

Will left the interview room, leaving the Colombian to Shel, who had more dogged determination than anyone Will knew. His eyes felt like their lids were coated with sandpaper.

The interviews had lasted over four hours so far.

In the hallway, Maggie greeted him with a cup of coffee. "Anything?" she asked.

Will shook his head. He stared at the monitor on the workstation just outside the interview room. "We keep getting the same story. Gacha sent him here to look for Toledo. Ruiz, the man in there, was told that Lance Corporal Hester would know where they could find Toledo."

"So Toledo was in business with Hester's imposter?"

"That's what it looks like."

"They didn't know Hester was dead?"

"No." Will wasn't surprised. News differed from country to country, the coverage as well as the slant. "Running a drug lab in the jungle probably doesn't leave much time for keeping current on world events. And Hester's death was a blip on the screen for the attention of most people."

"Then where's Toledo?"

Will sighed and watched as Shel continued asking the same questions of Ruiz they had been asking for hours. The investigation constantly kept taking on new kinks, new twists and turns he hadn't seen coming. "I don't know."

"How were they supposed to get in touch with Toledo?"

"Through Hester. That's all Gacha told them." The whole thing was getting frustrating. Will knew they were close to having answers. But they didn't quite have all the pieces. "Has Estrella found anything out?"

"That's why I was coming to get you," Maggie said. "She got through the CIA's firewall unscathed and grabbed Director Burcell's files. Retired Colonel Vladimir Gronsky had a lot more going on than the CIA, or Inspector Rushaylo, told us about."

>> **AMERICAN NAVAL BASE NCIS HEADQUARTERS**
>> **0703 HOURS**

"Nine months ago," Estrella said, flicking through images on the computer monitor, "Colonel Vladimir Gronsky headed up an arms raid near the Black Sea. Supposedly, he was protecting the Caspian Sea oil refineries and the Caspian Pipeline Consortium that transports the crude to the tankers waiting at a port of Novorossiysk in the Black Sea. It's a believeable cover story since the area is a hot spot with the rising oil needs around the world."

"That's not what he was really doing there?" Will asked.

"The CIA found out that Colonel Gronsky was tracking some of the nuclear weapons that went missing after Communism fell in Russia. Somehow during the transfer of the weapons, a few of them disappeared."

Dozens of nuclear weapons had disappeared after the Berlin Wall fell, Will remembered. Some of the weapons had been sold outright to international buyers to fund Communist leaders who wanted new lives in other countries or a comfortable life in the confusion that was left in Russia. Others had arranged to be "stolen" while under security.

"According to the stories the CIA got," Estrella went on, "some of the missiles were mocked up to look like American weapons."

"Why?" Maggie asked.

Estrella shook her head. "The CIA doesn't have any documentation, but the speculation is that the missiles were going to be 'found' in Turkey, giving evidence of American support. From the CIA reports, they believe Gronsky arranged for the missiles to get stolen by a local mafia."

"Isidor Kuzlow?" Will asked, remembering the name.

Estrella searched the file for Kuzlow's name. "There's no mention of him here."

"Does Burcell have a file on Kuzlow?"

After a brief search, Estrella nodded. "He does."

Will leaned back, pondering what it all meant. There were far too many links to be coincidental. Sorting things through in his mind, he knew that a lot was at stake. The cocaine. The imposters. The missing nuclear weapons. Any one of those things threatened his team, the Navy and the Marines, and his country.

>> 0710 HOURS

"Let's take it by the numbers," Will said as he surveyed the room and his team. "Lance Corporal Hester was replaced by an imposter whose body was later stolen by a serviceman working within the base in Chinhae."

"Whom I've identified through e-mail archives," Estrella said. "Ahmed Achmed."

"Right," Will said darkly. "The man who murdered Frank. Who may also be the same man who killed Hester's replacement."

"He could also be the same person who attacked Estrella," Maggie pointed out.

"And he's still at large." Will paused, marshaling his thoughts. "We know there was a lot of cocaine flowing through whatever cargo ships the imposter was helping with. We've got a tie to the cocaine in Moscow through physical evidence as well as the Colombians we picked up. That couldn't have happened through military supply routes without some serious inside help. We know there are other imposters involved as well."

"You're talking about a huge expense, laid out ahead of time," Shel said.

"What expense?"

"Plastic surgery for the imposters," Estrella said. "Paying off the people like Vivian Layton who helped set up the original men who were replaced. Paying off mercenaries like the Japanese Yakuza and Sungee Han's inside man. Replacing federal files and tampering with surrounding documentation so those imposters wouldn't get caught."

Will sat on the corner of his desk. "We know the cocaine was passing through Chinhae. We know Hester's imposter had access to it. But the stakes had to be higher than that."

"We also have documentation from the CIA claiming that nuclear weapons went missing near the Caspian Sea," Estrella said.

"Right," Shel said. "The CIA thinks Colonel Gronsky allowed those weapons to be stolen by a mafia crime family."

"Then he went missing," Remy added.

"It's an easy jump to assume the cocaine traffic and the missing weapons are related," Maggie said.

"Hold on," Will said. "We don't know for sure that the *Mafiya* group selling the cocaine in Moscow is the same group that stole the missiles."

Shel shrugged. "Plenty of organized crime over there. It could be two separate groups."

"On the other hand, circumstantial evidence suggests it might be the same group," Estrella pointed out. Inspector Rushaylo told me that Isidor Kuzlow is responsible for the cocaine distribution in Moscow, and he asked me about Gronsky. The CIA is investigating Gronsky in connection with the missing nukes, and they have a file on Kuzlow too. I think Rushaylo thinks the two are connected, and so does the CIA."

"But what's the connection?" Maggie asked. "Is Kuzlow involved with the weapons, or is Gronsky somehow involved in the cocaine shipments?"

"Gronsky has disappeared," Shel reminded. "Russian ex-colonels don't disappear over cocaine distribution. However, disappearing after nuclear weapons have gone missing is a totally different matter."

"Check through the CIA files," Will said to Estrella. "See if you can find an explicit link between Gronsky and Kuzlow." He paced while Estrella worked.

"Affirmative," Estrella said. "Apparently the CIA raided Gronsky's electronic files from Military Intelligence. Gronsky was investigating Kuzlow regarding drug distribution to refinery works in the Caspian Sea."

"That's a police matter," Will said.

"Yes, but with oil being as important as it is to Russia these days, the protection of those areas has been placed under the military."

"Did Gronsky ever make his case or bring up supporting evidence?"

Estrella continued scanning the file. "No."

"Well now—" Shel smiled broadly and crossed his arms over his chest—"I'd say that gave Gronsky and Kuzlow a chance to get to know each other. Wouldn't you?"

"It's still circumstantial evidence," Will said.

"Men have been convicted, sent to prison for life, and even

given the death sentence with circumstantial evidence," Maggie said.

"For now, it's what we have to work with," Will said, getting into the flow of his reasoning now. "What are the three elements of a crime?"

"Motive, means, and opportunity," Maggie answered immediately.

"Right," Will said. "Let's give everybody connected to this thing means and opportunity, and maybe we'll start to see the motive. Start with Hester's imposter. We still haven't identified him, but we know he was involved in the drug and weapon shipments that passed through Chinhae."

"How were they shipped?" Maggie asked, playing the devil's advocate.

"I don't know. Cargo manifests. Something like that."

"That's a big jump."

"There are men in the Navy and the Marines who are imposters," Will continued. "Why are they there?"

"To help with the cargo shipments," Shel answered. "The Hester imposter helped with warehouse security. I'm willing to bet that if Estrella took that mainframe apart she'd find back doors into the programming architecture. Some way for Hester's replacement and whoever else was working there to change manifests."

"We're assuming Hester's imposter was working in a pretty big organization," Will said. "Why would he risk taking cocaine and weapons to sell through the black market on his own?"

"Because he couldn't help himself," Shel said. "Vivian Layton indicated that this guy was a thief, probably with klepto-maniac tendencies. No matter who he was responsible to, he couldn't help stealing for himself."

"All right," Maggie agreed. "The imposter's motive was personal greed. I'll buy that. But why was he killed?"

"Because he had drawn our attention," Will said. "Whoever's in charge knew that if we pressed hard enough, we'd find the link to Moscow. He had to be taken out. Unfortunately for them, we found the link anyway."

"We know we can link the cocaine shipments to Kuzlow in Moscow," Maggie said. "His mafia group is selling the Colombian cocaine Gacha made."

"Kuzlow's motive is profit," Estrella agreed. "I can see that. He has a mainline source for Colombian cocaine."

"Gacha's motive is simple too," Will added. "He's making money from the drugs he's selling."

"That doesn't explain Gronsky or the missiles," Maggie said. "What's Gronsky's connection?"

"I think he allowed Kuzlow to steal the missiles."

"You can't prove that."

"For now I'm going to assume it's true and work to disprove it."

"What is Gronsky getting out of the arrangement?"

"Money. He brokered the deal, made it happen, then got out of Dodge," Will said.

"Who paid him?"

"Whoever wanted the nuclear weapons."

"Who wanted the weapons?"

"I don't know," Will answered, frustrated.

"Who paid Gacha for the cocaine?" Shel asked.

"What are you talking about?"

Shel shrugged. "Do you think Gacha would just give his cocaine to a guy in Russia he might never see again?"

Will concentrated on that for a moment. "Kuzlow could have put the money up front first."

"We're talking millions of dollars," Shel said. "Would Kuzlow have put up millions of dollars to a guy in Colombia who might not come through?"

"No. You're right," Will said. "The only way that deal could have happened is through a middleman."

"Gronsky?" Maggie suggested.

"How would Gronsky get to know a Colombian cocaine baron?" Will's mind unlimbered as he spun out the twists and turns. "Gacha was in no position to bury imposters within the U.S. military. Neither was Gronsky or Kuzlow."

"Someone other than those three, then."

Will nodded and kept pacing. "Someone who has connections that can touch all those worlds, and who has—or can hire—the computer experts necessary to purge files on the federal and military level. Someone who can afford to put agents under a plastic surgeon's knife so they can become someone else." The more he thought about it, the more certain he was that he was correct.

"What does this mysterious person get out of the deal?" Maggie asked. "Money?"

Will shook his head. "Something bigger. The drug profits are one thing, but this guy has already fronted the money for that to Gacha."

"Could he be taking a piece of Kuzlow's action?"

"Why take the risk?"

"It's profit."

"Spread out over half a world away," Will said. "I wouldn't like those odds. This is for something more. Gacha and Kuzlow are a straight line. Let's take another look at Gronsky."

"We're not even sure he's involved."

"Allow it for the time being. The CIA and the Russian Ministry of Interior see a correlation." Will worked through it. "The CIA believes there's a tie between Gronsky, Kuzlow, and the missing missiles. What if the missiles are our middleman's payoff? Suppose, in exchange for the cocaine business they were getting and the introduction to Gacha, Kuzlow's mafia group had to steal those missiles. With Gronsky's approval."

"You're reaching."

"Maybe so. But there're means and opportunity there."

"So what about motive?" Maggie asked. "Why does the middleman want the missiles?"

"Could be profit again," Shel said. "There's big bucks out there for stolen nuclear weapons."

"I don't think so," Will said. "Remember, the middleman has money. According to this scenario, he fronted the cash for the cocaine deal."

"Ahmed Achmed killed Frank and stole the imposter's body," Estrella said. "So if he's also the one who killed the imposter, it stands to reason he's working for the middleman. And he's Middle Eastern. There could be a religious motive here."

Will looked at Estrella. "If the person behind the cocaine deal is the same person getting the nukes, and if the motive for obtaining the nukes is religious, we have a big problem on our hands. We need to find the middleman."

"But we don't even know for sure if there *is* a middleman," Maggie said. "Our only lead is Gronsky's connection to Kuzlow, which may or may not exist. And Gronsky is gone. We're looking at a dead end."

God, Will prayed silently, *what we truly need right now is a break. Just something. Show me the next step.*

The phone on Maggie's desk rang. She answered it, spoke swiftly, then turned to Will as she took her pistols from her desk drawers and shoved them into her shoulder holsters. "Fishermen out in the harbor just brought in a body. From the description I just received from Captain Pak, it looks like it might belong to the man who impersonated Virgil Hester."

SCENE ⊛ NCIS ⊛ CRIME SCEN
NAVAL CRIMINAL INVESTIGATIVE SERVICE

>> CHINHAE HARBOR, REPUBLIC OF KOREA
>> 1058 HOURS

Shel drove the jeep to the harbor. Will rode shotgun decked out
in a bulletproof vest under his jacket, a Kevlar helmet, and with
an M4A1 at his side. Remy and Maggie rode in back. Max lay on
the rear deck but kept his ears pricked and his head moving.

A combination of Republic of Korea forces and U.S. Marines
occupied the dock where the fishing boat was tied up. Captain
Pak was prominent among his soldiers, but he gave the Marines
room to secure the area.

Will smelled the salt of the sea and the stink of the fish that
pervaded the timbers and concrete docks. Waves lapped at the
pilings. The fishing boat and its grisly catch had drawn a crowd
at least two hundred strong.

Shel edged the jeep through the crowd. The ROK soldiers
and Marines helped clear the way.

Captain Pak wasn't happy to see Will. "Ah, Commander Coburn, I've not had an opportunity to speak with you since your return."

"It's been busy." Will dismounted from the jeep, his eyes focused on the fishing boat. The craft was old; all its truly good years were behind it. Still, it was neatly trimmed, and the coaming and patched sails showed care. Tires tied to the sides of the boat added cushioning against the pier.

A narrow plank spanned five feet of dirty brown water from the dock to the fishing boat. The vessel bobbed on the wake from the Navy boats—South Korean as well as American—in the harbor.

A twin-rotored CH-46E Sea Knight floated overhead. Will felt the downdraft as the whirlybird passed.

"Marine air support," Shel said as he stepped onto the plank. He smiled. "Doesn't get any better than that."

"Maybe," Remy said. "I'd rather have SEAL snipers aboard a helo. Marines tend to spray an' pray."

"Don't know who you been talking to," Shel growled, "but they sure got it wrong."

"A bit much, don't you think?" Will asked, squinting through his sunglasses at the hovering helicopter.

"We're advertising," Maggie said. "By the time we got here, everyone on the docks knew. Whoever we're looking for knows too." She nodded toward the shore. "Look."

Following her line of sight, Will spotted two media groups along the docks. Reporters were already filing stories, and their cameramen were busy capturing images.

"Not much we can do about that," Will said, and turned his attention to the catch.

Five South Korean fishermen, three in their sixties and two little more than boys hardly older than Wren, stood in the prow. The nets hung from the boom arm. Fish flopped inside the coarse hemp, but a human arm thrust through one of the holes.

The smell of the decomposing body mixed with the stench of fish was overpowering. Will breathed through his mouth as he stepped forward and studied the corpse. Most of the head was gone, from the bullet that had killed him as well as the creatures that had fed on him. A visual identification would be impossible.

Whoever he had been, the sea had not been kind to him.

Maggie pulled on a pair of surgical gloves. "Look at this." She reached through the net and moved fish around.

Stepping behind her, Will saw torn flesh around the naked man's ankles.

"These elliptical impressions indicate they wrapped a chain around his ankles," Maggie said. "Then threw him overboard."

"If he was weighted down, how could he come back up?" Remy asked.

"After a body starts to decompose," Will said, taking a closer look at the corpse, "the flesh starts to slip. It turns loose and sloughs off. That's how the chains loosened. Gases inside the body cause it to rise. As long as the body stayed whole, it would have found its way up and to the nearest coastline." Will turned to the boat crew. "Where did you find the body?"

The old men and the boys looked at each other. Then the oldest boy said, "No English. No English."

Maggie spoke quickly in Korean, getting an immediate exchange. "They brought the body up this morning," she said a moment later. "It was out in the Korea Strait. They snared it in the net just as they were about to head home."

Will felt Captain Pak stiffen beside him.

"Impossible," the captain muttered.

Will looked at him quizzically.

"Have you been out in the Korea Strait, Commander?" Pak asked quietly.

"No."

"The Korea Strait has a natural current that takes things *out* into the open ocean. This body should be gone. For it to be here, now . . . it's nothing short of a miracle."

Unable to help himself, Will stared at the ROK captain. "A miracle?"

"Yes." Pak nodded.

"God will give you what you need, Will. He always does. Most people just don't realize that." Frank's voice came to Will clear and clean.

"You think you're gonna be able to identify the body?" Remy asked.

"We're going to try," Will said. In truth, though, the task looked all but impossible. What the bullet going through the man's features hadn't destroyed, the long time at sea among hungry sea creatures had. He tapped his headset transmitter, activating a connection with the base. "Estrella," he called.

"Aye, Commander."

"Call Nita. Tell her we need her here."

>> JACKSONVILLE, NORTH CAROLINA
>> 0032 HOURS

The Navy pilot, dark hair and big blue eyes, maybe in his midtwenties, was cute. Nita Tomlinson gave the guy that. However, he knew he was cute and that took away a lot of the overall appeal.

She knew she shouldn't be in the bar. But with the rest of the team in South Korea again, she had a lot more free time on her hands than she normally did. *"If you were any kind of wife and mother at all,"* her mother's voice criticized in the back of her head, *"you'd be home with your husband and daughter."*

Nita sipped her drink and drowned her mother's voice. That had been her mother's view on life, not hers. She hadn't asked to end up married, hadn't asked to end up a mom. Life had simply thrown a monkey wrench into her own plans. Being a mom had never been part of the overall picture.

"A pretty lady like you shouldn't be sitting in the dark and drinking alone," the Navy pilot said.

Nita smiled at him, knowing her response was only going to challenge him more. She'd seen him talking to his two buddies before he'd crossed the floor to her table.

"I'm serious," he went on, as seriously as he could.

"So what should I be doing?" Nita asked.

"Dancing."

"Now wouldn't I look silly dancing by myself?"

The pilot smiled like the answer should have been obvious. "Dance with me."

Nita swirled her drink and waited, knowing he wouldn't go away. She was pretty and he had to save face in front of his friends. He was hooked.

"C'mon," he said in a low voice. "Dance with me."

Nita sipped her drink again and thought about it. She'd been thinking about it for months, just wanting out of marriage and motherhood because she knew she wasn't going to measure up in the end. Her mother hadn't. And her mother's blood was in her.

She was a scientist and a medical doctor. She knew she couldn't escape her DNA.

Her cell phone buzzed for attention. "Just a minute," she told the pilot, then answered the call. "Tomlinson."

"Nita," Estrella said, "we need you here."

"In Chinhae?" Nita couldn't believe it. "Why?"

"I can't go into it now. Will wants everything kept low-key until we find out how good our communications security is."

The pilot continued to look hopeful.

"Ship the body back to me," Nita instructed. If they were calling for her, a body had to be involved. She didn't want to go to

South Korea. She didn't like to travel and she didn't like being in foreign countries. "It would be faster and I've got my lab here."

"Will wants you here. This may get more involved. I've already made your travel arrangements. I've e-mailed your itinerary to you. We'll see you in fourteen hours."

The cell phone went dead.

"Body?" the pilot repeated. His eyes were slightly glassy, and she knew he was more than a little intoxicated.

"I'm a medical examiner," Nita said, thinking about everything she was going to have to do to make the trip. She grew angry and thought about calling back and demanding to talk to Will directly. Except that she knew Estrella was managing communications for the team and wouldn't put her through. Even if Estrella did, Will didn't issue orders lightly.

"A medical examiner," the pilot repeated. "Cool."

"I'm glad you think so." Nita finished her drink and stood.

That caught the pilot off guard. "Where are you going?"

"I got called in," Nita told him. "That's the not-so-cool part of the job." She started to walk away.

"Hey," he said, "maybe we'll catch up with each other again."

Nita smiled at him, just enough to twist the knife a little. "You never know, flyboy. Maybe." Then she was across the floor, out the door, and into the night.

>> 0111 HOURS

At the small home off Marine Boulevard that her husband's great-grandfather had built seventy-nine years ago, Nita pulled into the covered driveway and sat for a moment.

Coming home.

It got harder to do every day. The house no longer felt like a home to her. It was a cage, a trap, a reminder of everything she would never be.

After Joe had inherited the two-bedroom home, he'd added another bedroom and an office area, a sunroom at the back of the house, and a covered veranda that ran along the front and side of the house. He'd added the extra bedroom because he wanted a lot of kids, and the office because he thought his wife would need a place of her own for business or crafts. He'd worked hard, and the house looked beautiful.

It was nothing like the rental houses and apartments Nita had grown up in while being dragged all over the Southern states by her mom.

This was a home. It was a beautiful place for Celia to grow up. The tree house in the backyard wasn't very high off the ground, but it was big enough and stable enough that Joe could crawl up in there while he and Celia eluded pirates or were magically transported to foreign places filled with colorful unicorns and singing dragons.

Joe's muddy Blazer 4x4 sat under the carport. Nita guessed that her husband and daughter had gone fishing again. If he finished early at the boat slip or was waiting on parts, Joe sometimes spent the day on New River with Celia. Nita knew her daughter would be filled with stories that she would recite for hours, and she'd beg her mom to come fishing and camping with them again.

Snarling a curse, she pushed out of her Ford Mustang and went into the house. She walked through the neat living room filled with handcrafted furniture that would probably last forever and to the hallway closet.

She took out the big suitcase, the small travel bag she kept stocked with cosmetics, and a carry-on she always packed for emergencies because luggage didn't always end up where she did. She put them on the couch.

When she returned to the closet, Joe stood in the bedroom doorway. His work on boats, construction, and repairing, kept his tall frame lean and hard. His hazel eyes held a child's inno-

cence but he was nobody's fool. He wore cutoff jeans and was
bare-chested and barefooted.

"Leaving?" Joe asked in that deep baritone that used to
vibrate through her in a way she'd never before known.

Nita kept moving, taking clothes out of the closet. "Will
called me in to Chinhae."

"South Korea? Where Frank Billings was killed?"

"Yes."

Concern touched Joe's eyes. "Going there doesn't sound very
safe."

"I don't have a *safe* job," she said.

Pain showed in Joe's eyes.

Nita hated the way she felt responsible for that. Before her,
Joe had seemed so . . . complete. He'd been a rock, totally happy
with building boats, hunting and fishing, the company of his
family and friends.

He doesn't deserve this, Nita realized. No matter how hard
she tried to hide that fact from herself, she knew that the fallout
of her own emotions and fears weren't Joe's to bear. *But he's the
one who insists he be part of everything that goes on in my life. If
he'd leave me alone—just simply leave me alone—he wouldn't
have to deal with this.*

"Right," Joe said softly. "Do you know when you'll be coming back?"

Nita picked out jeans and pants. "I got called out in the middle of the night. I didn't expect that. How should I know when
I'll be back?"

Joe nodded. "Anything I can help you with?"

Nita forced her hands to stop trembling as she listened to her
husband's calm words. Any man her mother had ever had would
have been throwing a temper tantrum if he hadn't been throwing
punches.

But not Joe Tomlinson. No, he just affected that Christian
calm and stance and let her know he was better than she was.

"I've got it," Nita told him. But she was thinking, *If you had any real guts, you'd leave him now before you hurt him more. Once you're gone, he'll stop trying to save you and be able to concentrate on himself and Celia.*

Nita knew she'd get something out of it too. She'd be able to stay out, party, meet new people, and not get too attached to anyone. She could go back to the life she understood instead of trying to hang on to the one she grew more scared of every day.

"Mommy?" Celia stood in the hallway dressed in pajamas printed with fairies and unicorns. Her long blonde hair, the exact color of her father's, hung down to her waist. Nita hadn't wanted to deal with the long hair because it was difficult to maintain, but Joe had volunteered to do their daughter's grooming. Celia was brown as a nut from summer and had her father's eyes.

Looking at her in the blunted moonlight coming through the blinds, Nita couldn't help feeling that little of her had even contributed to her daughter's makeup. She'd merely housed Joe's daughter till she was born.

Celia ran into the room, her arms outflung. Her blonde tresses swung wildly. "I missed you, Mommy."

Nita caught her daughter in self-defense so she wouldn't be bowled over. As she lifted the little girl, Celia's arms slid around Nita's neck.

"I'm glad you're home, Mommy," Celia said. "Daddy missed you too."

Unable to speak past the lump in her throat, and because she didn't trust herself not to scream in frustration, Nita held her daughter. Celia's hair smelled like green apples and was soft and cool against Nita's cheek. Celia held her fiercely.

Conflicted, trapped between wanting to leave immediately and wanting to hold her daughter, Nita stood motionless for a moment. She felt Celia's tiny heart fluttering against her breast.

Without a word, Joe continued packing for her.

"I can do that," Nita said.

"I know," Joe told her. "I just wanted to help. Figured you're on some kind of deadline."

"I am."

"Sit down. Tell me what you need."

Not knowing what else to do, Nita sat and held Celia, who mumbled softly about wanting to go on a picnic soon.

In a few minutes, Joe had finished packing and had carried the suitcases and carry-on to Nita's car before coming back inside. Celia slept in Nita's arms.

"She missed you today," Joe said.

His words shoved knives into Nita's heart. She hardened herself against the pain. "I have to work," she said. "I've got a career."

"I can support us, Nita. You don't have to—"

"Have a career?" Nita interrupted. "Be independent? Have a life of my own that isn't swallowed up in being a wife and a mother?"

Joe took a breath, folded his arms over his chest, and remained silent.

Nita stood, slowly and carefully so she wouldn't jostle Celia into wakefulness again. "We've talked about this before, Joe. I got an education for a reason. I don't want to be like my mother. Needy and dependent."

"It doesn't have to be like that," Joe said.

"Please take her."

Joe tenderly took their daughter.

Not wanting to endure another moment of the tension, Nita kissed her sleeping daughter and left the room.

"Nita," Joe called.

She froze at the front door but didn't look back.

"Be careful," Joe said. "I love you."

"I know," Nita whispered. And for some reason unknown even to herself, she said, "I love you too. Take care of Celia." Then she was gone, fleeing into the night.

E SCENE **NCIS** CRIME SCEN

NAVAL CRIMINAL INVESTIGATIVE SERVICE

>> PROVIDENIYA, CHUKOTKA, EAST RUSSIA
>> 1420 HOURS

The journey from South Korea to the northwestern tip of Russia had been a long and arduous one, but Qadir Yaseen was at last about to take possession of his long-awaited nuclear weapons. According to Isidor Kuzlow, the missiles had arrived yesterday and were now awaiting him aboard the *Arctic Hauler,* an ocean-going freighter docked at the Port of Provideniya.

The Russian *Mafiya* had transported the missiles from the Caspian Sea, where they had been taken with Colonel Gronsky's blessings before that man's untimely demise. Once Gronsky had been taken care of, Kuzlow's organization had transported the missiles overland to the northern coast. From there, two separate ships had sailed along the coast to Provideniya across the Bering Sea from Alaska.

Yaseen owned *Arctic Hauler,* though the paper trail to show that ownership could never be traced. Officially, the ship specialized in bringing fish catches out of the Bering Sea to processing plants in Europe. But over the last seven months, once Yaseen had other facets of his plan in action, the freighter had taken on a specialized crew that had refitted her at sea. Now she would carry a much different cargo to the South China Sea, where Yaseen's plans would finally be accomplished.

Yaseen walked up the gangway, hunching his shoulders against the arctic wind blasting across the ship's deck.

Captain Aabid Usayd stood ramrod straight in a full-length coat and captain's hat. He was in his early fifties and had given his entire life to the sea. For the last four years, he had given his allegiance to Yaseen.

"Welcome aboard, honored one," Usayd said in Arabic.

"Thank you," Yaseen replied in the same language. "Has everything arrived?"

"Of course." Usayd led the way across the deck to the cargo hold. The wind whistled across the deck.

Excitement flared within Yaseen. Several years' planning had gone into the effort that was about to culminate in the South China Sea. At Usayd's wave, Yaseen climbed into the hold on a metal ladder that quivered beneath his weight.

Dim lights illuminated the metal corridor leading through the freighter's bowels. The ocean slapped against the outer hull with sonorous booms.

As always, Yaseen felt the tiniest bit of fear inside the vessel as he descended yet another series of steps. He was well below the surface of the freezing sea now. The thought coiled at the back of his mind and bit with sharp fangs. He'd always enjoyed the sea when he was in his yacht or on the deck of a sailboat, but he hated the heavy steel ships that traversed the oceans of the world. He'd always thought that he would hate to die trapped in the hulk of a ship drowning beneath the waves.

A crewman opened a bulkhead door and allowed Yaseen to pass.

Inside the next room, Yaseen saw that the conversion was nearly completed. Men worked with welding torches and air-powered riveting guns to hang the steel framework necessary to create the two missile launch tubes. The stink of burning metal filled the hold, and smoke rolled against the ceiling high overhead. Smiling, Yaseen leaned against the railing and watched the work.

"You have everything?" he asked as Usayd joined him.

"Yes."

"The missiles?"

"They arrived yesterday."

"Show me."

The missiles were kept securely locked down in the next container.

At last. The sight of the weapons sent a tingle of anticipation through Yaseen's body.

"As you can see," Usayd said, "we are prepared."

"Yes," Yaseen said. Excitement coursed through him. Only a matter of days remained before *Arctic Hauler* would be in position to deliver its vicious payload. "Perhaps we could look at the command center," Yaseen said.

Usayd took the lead, guiding them farther astern. The next compartment held a cutting-edge control room. Computers filled all the available space, broken up by four separate workstations.

"We have been busy since you told us to proceed with this phase of the project." The captain's voice held a hint of pride.

Yaseen walked into the room, liking the feel of it at once. He dropped into one of the seats and brought up the operating system.

The cursor blinked.

He typed in a password.

Instantly, the cursor flickered and the system came online. Computer screens around the command center came to life.

Yaseen typed again, linking the system with the communications satellite that he owned and had set aside to handle the mission *Arctic Hauler* was assigned to. So far, everything was in place. Within a matter of days, deep in the South China Sea poised between North and South Korea and Russia and China, he would set in motion the events he had planned for years.

The Americans would learn the price of their interference in the Middle East.

>> CHINHAE, REPUBLIC OF KOREA
>> AMERICAN NAVAL BASE NCIS MEDICAL LAB
>> 0530 HOURS

Will stood outside the OR for a moment and watched Nita Tomlinson working on the corpse they'd recovered from the South Korean fishing boat nearly three days ago. She moved with deliberation, at a steady pace and with a thoroughness that Will had learned to respect over the years they'd worked together.

He knocked on the door and waited.

After a moment, Nita swept off the wireless microphone she wore and waved him in.

Will entered. "How's it going?"

Dressed in pale green scrubs, Nita put both gloved hands on her hips and arched her back. "It's going. The reconstruction program is running now."

Glancing at the computer screen on one of the workstations, Will saw the imposter's head turning slowly on the screen. "You're ahead of schedule."

"Only by a few hours." Nita walked to the coffeemaker in the corner. She rinsed her cup in the sink and filled it with coffee. The coffee scent barely touched the chemical odors and the stink of the body on the table.

Will stepped to the table. Despite the years of looking at corpses subjected to all manner of violent death, he still had a momentary pause when he saw what Nita's examination had done to the dead man.

The body lay nude on the table. The time the body had spent in the water had resulted in a number of postmortem wounds from fish and crustaceans feeding on it. Some—according to Nita's prelim reports—had even needed to be evicted from the corpse.

Half of the dead man's head had been shot away in the alley. Nita had stripped his remaining face from his skull, leaving tendons and muscle beneath the fatty layer of flesh. His remaining eye stared sightlessly at the ceiling.

"His eyes were brown?" Will asked.

Nita joined him at the table. "Yes."

"I thought they were blue."

"He wore contacts," Nita said. She picked up a small container, opened it, and shook the contents until a blue-tinted contact lens plopped into her palm.

Will thought about that. "No one mentioned that he wore contacts."

"Part of the disguise." Nita handed over a folder filled with printout sheets. "Lance Corporal Hester's eyes were blue, so the imposter needed his eye color to match. You can't change eye color with plastic surgery."

"What about the fractures?" Will asked.

"The fractures all match Hester's field-service record. They just don't match Hester's parents' accounts of his childhood accidents."

"What about the hospital records?"

"The ones that still had them had all been changed. However, closer examination of this body's fractures has proven interesting."

"How so?"

Nita stepped to the body and picked up forceps. Without

pause, she pushed open the flesh over the body's right knee where she'd made an incision. "He had a knee replacement, remember?"

"I remember," Will said.

Nita tapped the knee replacement. "This is old work."

"How old?"

"Judging from the calcification around the repairs, probably twenty or twenty-five years."

"Have you been able to find out how old this man was?"

"Again, I'm going by the calcification of bone around the joints. I'm throwing out the bad knee, of course, but judging what I've seen of the wrists, skull partial, and the spine, I'd guess that he's thirty-five or forty."

Will thought about that. "Older than Hester."

"Yes. The facial reconstruction and bleaching and peeling the skin also contributed to a younger look."

"Peeling?"

"Probably trichloroacetic acid. The peel had to be a deep effort. I found evidence of acne."

"The peel could account for the skin lightening, couldn't it?"

"Some of it. But this guy was bleached too. Really aggressive procedure."

"What about the facial reconstruction?"

"I'm working on that now," Nita said. She gazed at the slowly turning monitor image. "If I'd had his whole head in one piece, deconstructing what was done would be easier. I had to remove what was left of his face to find all the collagen injections and implants." She tapped the corpse's chin with the forceps. "He also had his chinbone shaved to alter its shape. If I hadn't removed his face, I might not have caught that."

Will returned his attention to the dead man's leg. "What about the knee?"

Nita tapped the metal kneecap. "Titanium reconstruction."

Will looked at her. "Okay . . ."

"Nobody in the United States does titanium reconstruction

these days," Nita said. "The medium is too limiting. Especially on somebody this young. What I should have found was a cobalt-chrome femoral and tibial tray with a polyethylene tibial liner in a mobile-bearing joint." She shrugged. "The normal knee has about fifteen degrees of rotation. You only get eight degrees out of the mobile-bearing joint, but it beats the two degrees you get out of the older fixed-bearing device that used to be used." She tapped the knee again. "The type that was used here."

"So you think the work was done outside the United States?" Will asked.

"I'd bet my last dollar on it."

"Where then? Europe?"

"Europe started implementing the mobile-bearing joints before we did. American doctors didn't want to learn how to perform the new surgeries until they had to. Something else I learned." Nita opened the knee again and reached for a magnifying device. She switched the light on. "See the groove along the femur here?"

Peering closely, Will studied the indention. "Looks like someone drilled a channel along there. Just barely caught the surface."

"What you're looking at is a tool mark."

"A tool mark?" Will looked at the woman.

"Yep. And that was a .45-caliber tool." Nita flipped the flesh surrounding the knee so the exterior showed. She pointed to a slight, puckered indention. "That's what remains of the bullet-entry wound." She turned the knee over, showing a larger scar on the other side. "That was the exit wound. He was just a kid when his knee was shot out. There are other bullet wounds, too."

Will straightened. "How many other times was this man shot?"

"Five times that I can document. At least two different incidents, based on the calcification of the bones that were struck." Nita touched the corpse's shoulder. "Remember the dislocated shoulder that showed up in the X-ray?"

"I do."

"That was caused by a bullet injury. Cosmetic surgery took away most of the external scarring, but I found evidence of it inside. That was a heavier caliber bullet. Maybe a 7.62 mm or a .30-30. I found two more scars in his abdomen. Small-caliber bullets. I don't know if they were at the same time."

Will looked at the body. "So where can you grow up that allows you to get shot on a regular basis?"

"A war zone."

Nodding, Will said, "Yeah. The problem is, we have our pick of war zones."

"Not for guys who have access to the medical treatment he received," Nita said. "The titanium knee reconstruction isn't the best, but even so, it's not cheap. There's something else too." Nita opened the chest cavity and revealed the lungs. "His lungs are enlarged. When I noticed that, I took a sample and ran a tox screen on the tissue." She pointed to a computer monitor. "I found latent traces of glyphosate. It's a herbicide and defoliant. Frequent exposure to glyphosate can trigger gastrointestinal problems, vomiting, the destruction of red corpuscles in mucus membranes. And enlargement of the lungs."

"He was exposed to glyphosate?"

"I found traces of it in the tox screen. It's been years, but the residual is there. I'm betting that's what caused the lung enlargement."

"The DEA shipped tons of glyphosate into Colombia as a deterrent to coca farming," Will said. "And we've already got a Colombian angle on this. I'm going to take that and run with it. See where it leads."

SCENE ✪ NCIS ✪ CRIME SCEN
NAVAL CRIMINAL INVESTIGATIVE SERVICE

>> CHINHAE, REPUBLIC OF KOREA
>> AMERICAN NAVAL BASE NCIS HEADQUARTERS
>> 2314 HOURS

Will sat at the workstation in his borrowed office looking at the latest picture Wren had sent him. It was a crayon drawing of the new puppy Jesse Harlan had bought Barbara. The vocal message Wren had embedded into the e-mail sounded excited.

"His name is Rascal, Daddy," his daughter said. Her exuberance made the loneliness of the office even more pervasive, reminding him of how many thousands of miles separated him from his children. "He's a chocolate Lab. That's short for Labrador. But you knew that. You guys have Max. I bet Max and Rascal will be great friends. Call or write me back as soon as you can. I love you. Bye."

Leaning back in his chair, Will laced his fingers behind his head and stared at the picture of the yawning brown-furred puppy. The animal's pink tongue lolled out. Wren wasn't a talented artist, but she had gotten her point across. The picture would have been comical, Will thought, if it hadn't been of a pet that he felt certain his wife's—*ex-wife's*—boyfriend had given her in order to win over their daughter.

Barbara doesn't care that much for dogs, Will thought. She was the one who had always said they didn't have enough room in the backyard. But there was small solace in that. Jesse Harlan evidently knew exactly what he was doing. Golf with Steven. A puppy for Wren.

And what for Barbara?

The potential answers both hurt and angered Will. There had been so much that he hadn't given Barbara at the end, so much pain that he had brought to her doorstep.

A shadow filled the doorway.

Looking up, Will saw Maggie standing there. She carried two cups of coffee.

"Now that's an intent look," she said.

"More a disguised look of frustration."

"Maybe I can help with that." Maggie handed him a cup, slid into a seat next to Will, and started tapping the keyboard. "I looked through old news stories in Colombia," she said. "I concentrated on Bogotá, since it's the capital city."

Most of the drug business took place in the city even though the shipments didn't. Will sipped his coffee and gazed over her shoulder.

"Nita said the imposter's knee injury happened twenty or twenty-five years ago, right? So I started looking for stories twenty-five years ago. I concentrated on shootings. You wouldn't believe how much violence goes on there."

"Yes, I would, unfortunately," Will said. "This isn't the first investigation I've had that's led back to the cocaine traffic out of Colombia."

The country remained in a constant life-and-death struggle between the government and the narcobarons. Judges had been assassinated by the cartels, and the cartel members had been deliberately caught in deadly cross fires generated by the Colombian military with the DEA assisting.

"The hard part was knowing that I was looking for a child," Maggie said hollowly. "So many kids get caught up in what goes on over there. It took me almost sixteen hours, but I found something. This was shot by an ABC News cameraman twenty-two years ago. During Operation Hard Target."

"I remember when the DEA was helping the Colombian military identify the narcobarons," Will said.

Maggie nodded. "Unfortunately, there were drawbacks. Other drug cartels started following the DEA and Colombian military that were following rival drug cartels. Several assassinations were attempted; many were successful."

The monitor screen showed a video of a group of men dressed in suits coming out of a restaurant. Three young boys walked with them. The man in the forefront looked familiar.

"Who is that?" Will asked.

Maggie tapped a button and froze the image. "Ernesto Gacha Luis." She opened another window, pulling up front and profile views of the drug baron.

"The man whose cocaine Isidor Kuzlow is selling in the streets of Moscow," Will said.

"Yes. And look at this." Maggie moved the cursor over one of the boys accompanying the men. "This is Ricardo Toledo Munoz." An enhanced image of the boy popped up on the screen.

"Gacha's missing nephew."

"Actually, I don't think he's missing anymore. Watch." Maggie tapped the keyboard. Toledo's image disappeared and the digital video was in motion again.

On-screen, a long black sedan swept around a corner. Will's stomach tightened in sick anticipation as he realized the three boys were about the same age as Steven. Gunfire erupted from the sedan. All three boys, along with several of the men, went down immediately. Other men threw themselves on top of Gacha and drew their weapons. A moment later, the sedan went out of control and smashed against a building a short distance from the camera operator. Gacha's bodyguards crossed the street, pulling out Uzi machine pistols.

Maggie paused the video again. "Gacha's men executed everyone in the sedan, but not before Gacha's son was killed."

"And Toledo?"

"A .45-caliber bullet from a MAC-10 destroyed his knee. The replacement was performed almost ten months later by a Colombian orthopedic surgeon using a titanium fixed-bearing device. He was fifteen."

"So Ricardo Toledo Munoz isn't missing."

"I think Toledo is lying on Nita's table."

>> **0541 HOURS**

Thirty hours later, while Will was working his way through more information on Gacha's cartel and picking at a ham-and-Swiss sandwich he was calling dinner, the phone rang. The caller ID ran below the image, identifying the caller as the United States Sheriff's Office in Webb County, Texas. Will lifted the receiver and said hello.

"Commander Coburn," a man said.

"I am," Will said.

"Deputy Sheriff Mynor Trujillo of the Webb County Sheriff's Office, sir. I'm responding to your request for DNA samples from old cases we worked here."

"That's right." Will chafed at the delay. He'd had to forward the request through Director Larkin's office and through the proper channels.

Trujillo sounded uneasy. "You do realize that juvenile records are supposed to be sealed."

"I do. You were told that this was a matter of national security, Deputy?"

"Yes, sir."

"I've been waiting almost twenty-four hours since I made the request to my director."

"Yes, sir. I appreciate that, but we still had to get a judge to sign off on this."

"I just need the DNA for a possible match, Deputy."

"My dad worked both the cases you're reviewing," Trujillo said. "For my money, Toledo is a bad dude and needs to be put down like a rabid dog. He was on trial for two rapes, and both the girls involved in those rapes were scared off at the trials. Without their testimonies, the district attorney couldn't put the cases together."

"But you kept the DNA from the crime scenes," Will said.

"Yes, sir, you bet we did. In cases of aggravated assault when biological matter is collected and subjected to forensic DNA testing and the testing results show that the matter does not match the victim or any other person whose identity is readily ascertained, there is no limitation on the crime. If we could get those women to testify against Toledo today, he could go down for it."

"Send me the DNA," Will said.

>> **AMERICAN NAVAL BASE NCIS HEADQUARTERS**
>> **0612 HOURS**

Arms folded, Will watched as Nita compared the DNA result he'd gotten from the Webb County Sheriff's Office. She pulled both pieces of paper from the printer and laid them side by side.

She only took a moment, then looked up. "We're conclusive." She nodded at the body lying on the table. "That's Ricardo Toledo Munoz."

"So how did he become Lance Corporal Hester?"

Nita moved to the computer and tapped the keyboard, bringing up the original three-dimensional image of the dead man's head. The gaping wound looked oddly aseptic.

"First, I'll rebuild him as Hester's imposter," Nita said.

Quickly, the missing part of the brain and skull filled in. In seconds, Will was looking at the face he'd seen in Hester's field-service record; the face he'd thought belonged to Hester.

"Now I'll take away the cosmetic surgery I detected during my examination." Nita tapped more keys.

Toledo's face changed subtly and his chin lengthened.

"It helped that Toledo looked a lot like Hester to begin with," Nita said. "Of course, the bleaching of the pigmentation is a dead giveaway."

On the monitor, the head's skin and hair darkened immediately.

"And the blue contacts, of course."

The eyes shifted from blue to dark brown.

Will approached the body. The musculature and bones of the face lay bare under the bright lights. Nita hadn't returned the dead man's face. "Can you put a face back on him?"

"You mean the one I pulled off? I thought we'd keep that as evidence."

"We will. I meant his original face."

"I can do a close approximation in clay." Nita sounded interested. "We can render it in PhotoShop to pull it together enough to fool anyone who looks at it. Why?"

"Ricardo Toledo Munoz's face," Will answered. "I think it's time Ernesto Gacha Luis learned what happened to his nephew."

Selling Director Larkin on the idea proved more difficult. Will paced the floor in front of the computer that encrypted the communication between Chinhae and Washington, D. C.

"Let me get this straight," Larkin said. "You want to contact Ernesto Gacha Luis and let him know that his nephew was killed there in Chinhae," Larkin said. "For what reason?"

"To reveal the third leg of the triangle," Will answered. "We know that the cocaine shipments benefitted Gacha and Kuzlow. But I'm fairly certain there was a third party involved. Someone who fronted the money for the initial exchange."

"Why?"

"Because I think Kuzlow and Gronsky are linked. If they are, that means the disappearance of the nuclear weapons Gronsky was supposed to take into custody is tied into this."

"And you believe Kuzlow took the weapons?"

"If he's connected to Gronsky, it makes sense. But I need to know who the third party is. We have a possible Middle Eastern connection. Someone got those nukes; we need to know who."

Sighing, Larkin nodded. "What do you hope to get out of contacting Gacha?"

"I'm hoping he'll burn his contact. The DEA has taps on all his phones. I want access to those. I want to know who he calls once he finds out his nephew was killed."

"Let me see how fast I can make this come together. Having Toledo's positive identification and the other probabilities factored in should grease the rails. I'll be in touch as soon as I know something."

S ✪ **CRIME SCENE** ✪ **NCIS** ✪ **CRI**

SERVICE

E SCENE ⊛ NCIS ⊛ CRIME SCEN

NAVAL CRIMINAL INVESTIGATIVE SERVICE

```
>> CHINHAE, REPUBLIC OF KOREA
>> AMERICAN NAVAL BASE NCIS HEADQUARTERS
>> 0642 HOURS
```

"How did my nephew die, Commander Coburn?" Ernesto Gacha Luis asked. Despite his current standing as one of Colombia's most feared cocaine barons, his tone was soft and polite, perhaps even a little sad.

The two men were connected via a video feed as well as by phone, and Will saw anger mixed with regret in the narcobaron's face. "He was shot, Senor Gacha," Will said.

"You're sure this is my nephew?"

Will pressed a button and picked up the camera view from down in Nita's autopsy room. Nita had done a good job with the clay remodeling.

"DNA confirms it, Senor Gacha," Will said. "That is Ricardo. Your nephew." He blanked the camera feed.

"Who shot him?"

"We're trying to find that out. I was hoping you could help me with that."

Gacha shook his head. "I have many enemies, Commander. It is the nature of my . . . business."

"I understand that, sir." Will shifted slightly. "I also have four of your men in custody here. They said they were here to find your nephew."

"I sent them."

Will brought up the picture of Toledo as Hester so Gacha would see it on his monitor. "They were under the impression that your nephew would look . . . different. Do you know anything about that?"

Gacha hesitated. "No. When I last saw my nephew, he was healthy."

"What was your nephew doing here in South Korea?" Will asked.

"I have no idea."

Will glanced down as if he were going over notes he had written on the legal pad in front of him. "When your nephew was found, he was in possession of cocaine."

"Not surprising," Gacha said. "Ricardo had a passing acquaintance with the drug."

"I see."

"He was not an addict, Commander. More like an enthusiast in recreation."

Nita's toxicology had confirmed that. Toledo hadn't been a hard-core user.

"Commander," Gacha said, "if you'll excuse me, there is a matter I must attend to. Now that you have told me what has happened to my nephew, I must tell my sister. She has been frantic with worry. If you need to contact me again, please feel free."

The monitor blanked abruptly.

"I'm betting he's not calling his sister," Shel said. He sat across the room, out of sight of the camera attached to the monitor that had broadcast Will's image to the narcobaron. "Any takers?" He grinned broadly.

"I'm not gonna throw my money away," Remy said. He sat beside Max, stroking the dog's head.

"You had Toledo fixed up so he looked like himself," Maggie said from her chair in front of the desk.

"Because our commander has a sinister, sadistic, and twisted streak," Nita said, flashing them a cold, mirthless grin. "I'm beginning to see him in a whole new and interesting light. He had me make up our corpse with his original face to make Gacha paranoid. Am I right?"

Will nodded. "There's a chance Gacha never saw Toledo as Hester. It wouldn't have done for the DEA agents and Colombian military people keeping tabs on him to have pictures of Hester in Colombia when he was supposed to be in Okinawa."

Remy matched Nita's grin. "Now Gacha's wondering if he's been played. Or set up. He's sitting there in his ranchero wondering how much weight is gonna fall on him."

"The last thing Gacha expected to see was Toledo looking like Toledo," Maggie said, understanding.

"Exactly," Will said.

"Now, if Gacha's paranoid button has been well and truly pressed," Shel said, "he's trying to get in contact with whoever masterminded this deal."

"That's the plan," Will agreed.

>> SOUTH CHINA SEA
>> ARCTIC HAULER
>> 0717 HOURS

Qadir Yaseen sat at the communications area belowdecks in the *Arctic Hauler*. The ship had traveled from the Bering Sea to the

South China Sea without incident. Now she sailed for the deadly rendezvous from which he intended to springboard his war against the American Satans.

Everything was in place.

His secure cell phone vibrated, and Yaseen activated the connection.

"Senor Yaseen," a calm, cultured voice said. A hint of anger and savagery lingered in the words.

Yaseen recognized Ernesto Gacha Luis's voice immediately, and in the same split second knew that something was very wrong.

"Why are you calling me?" Yaseen demanded. "You have been paid for your product. I made it clear you were never to contact me directly."

"My nephew is dead," Gacha said shortly. "I want to know why."

This was a problem Yaseen did not need. "An unfortunate accident."

"An accident? He was shot in the head," Gacha accused.

"His death was unavoidable. His foolishness attracted the attention of the wrong people. He died while wearing the other name. He cannot be traced back to you."

"You're wrong," Gacha said. "You told me that his face had been changed for your masquerade. Yet, when I saw my dead nephew, he was wearing his own face."

Yaseen shot from his chair in surprise. "Impossible!" No one should have known the two men were the same. "When did you see your nephew?"

"Tonight. He—"

"Who told you about him?"

"A Navy commander. A man named Coburn. He is there in Chinhae."

Yaseen thought quickly. The NCIS team was more resourceful than he had given them credit for.

"What is going on?" Gacha demanded. "I have a right to know."

Taking the phone from his ear, Yaseen broke the connection. There was no further need of communication. Gacha's indignation was of no significance. NCIS's discovery of the imposter's identity was unfortunate but unimportant. His plan was too far along to be stopped now.

He settled back into his chair and activated the ship's state-of-the-art surveillance system. A dedicated satellite uplink tracked *Arctic Hauler* and an Ohio-class submarine, *Michigan*, in the South China Sea. The blue triangle that represented *Michigan* and the orange dot that represented *Arctic Hauler* were on a collision course. They would never see him coming. His ship's sensors were sharper than those onboard the United States submarine. Yaseen was certain of that.

Everything still looked on course. He would intercept *Michigan* within the next fourteen hours. The local time in the Koreas would be nine o'clock when he launched his missiles. The destruction visited upon Pyongyang would be spectacular. With the tensions between the United States, China, the Koreas, and Russia, Yaseen had every reason to believe that a large-scale war—in fact, even a world war—would follow.

That was his goal.

Yaseen turned his attention briefly back to Gacha. The man had become a liability. And Yaseen would not tolerate liabilities.

SCENE **NCIS** CRIME SCEN

NAVAL CRIMINAL INVESTIGATIVE SERVICE

>> CHINHAE, REPUBLIC OF KOREA
>> AMERICAN NAVAL BASE NCIS HEADQUARTERS
>> 0737 HOURS

"The CIA was tracking Gacha's call too," Estrella said. "They've got a tap on his phone, so they probably have audio, but it doesn't look like they were able to trace the call's destination.

Will looked at her and waited.

Unable to hold it back, Estrella smiled. "But I was."

"So where did he call?" Will asked.

A confused look filled her face. "That's what's strange. The signal was bounced around to a lot of places, obviously prearranged, and it was encrypted so I couldn't snoop. But it was sent to a ship out in the South China Sea. I'm still trying to find out information about the ship."

Elation sailed through Will, pushing away the fatigue he felt from the brief catnaps he'd managed throughout the night. "Did you ID the man Gacha called?"

Turning back to her computer briefly, Estrella nodded. "The call was placed to a cellular account owned by someone named Qadir Yaseen."

"Who is he?"

"I have no idea."

"The name sounds Middle Eastern," Will said. "This could be our guy." He stood. "Maggie," he called.

"Yes."

"See what you can find out through naval intelligence regarding a Qadir Yaseen."

Maggie went to her own workstation.

Will's monitor indicated an incoming call, which he answered immediately. "Coburn."

Assistant Director Clyde Burcell of the CIA appeared on the monitor. He wore an angry look as he unleashed a steady stream of invectives. "What did you just do, Coburn?"

Will regarded the man in silence. "I don't know what you're talking about."

"You just had a conversation with Gacha," Burcell accused.

"I did," Will admitted. "We identified his missing nephew."

"Where?"

"Here in Chinhae."

"What was Ricardo doing in Chinhae?"

Was, Will thought. *If Burcell knows Toledo is dead, he must have been listening in on the call.*

"Were you eavesdroping on my conversation with Gacha?"

"I heard what you told Gacha," Burcell snapped. "We have his phones tapped. I want to know what Ricardo was really doing there."

"You know," Will said, "for a man who claimed to know nothing at all about Gacha except that he was a criminal, you seem to know a lot now."

"I took an interest."

"That was all," Will said. "I told Gacha we had found his nephew. He sent a crew over here to find him."

"I know about those guys."

"Then you know as much as I do."

Burcell shook his head. "I don't think so."

"Why did you call me?" Will countered.

After a brief hesitation, Burcell said, "Because whatever you talked to Gacha about just got him killed."

Will took that in and didn't say anything.

"Gacha left his house to make a phone call at a nearby pay phone."

"But you had it tapped as well," Will said. Estrella had piggybacked off the line.

"It's something we do," Burcell said. "Gacha had a conversation with the man we believe helped him set up the cocaine delivery to the Russian *Mafiya,* though we haven't figured out the logistics of the shipments yet. He talked to this guy, wanted to know why his nephew was dead and why he was wearing his own face." The assistant CIA director gave Will a hard look. "I don't suppose you know anything about that."

Will ignored the gibe. "You said Gacha was killed?"

"Yeah. Before Gacha arrived back at his *casa,* one of his lieutenants pulled out a gun and blew him up. The Gacha cartel just experienced a hostile takeover."

>> AMERICAN NAVAL BASE NCIS HEADQUARTERS
>> 1143 HOURS

Will played the copy of the phone call between Gacha and Yaseen over again, listening to the tight intonations between the two men. Burcell had sent over an electronic copy of the audio file immediately, showing good faith on his part. In exchange, Will had instructed Estrella to forward the coordinates of the call's destination.

From across the room, Maggie said, "I may have found something."

Will crossed to her workstation. "Show me."

On her monitor Maggie had a file called *Yaseen, Qadir.*

She opened the photograph, revealing a Middle Eastern face that showed strength and contempt. His hooded eyes were harsh and black.

"I found this in the terrorist data files," Maggie said. "I'd say he has the connections and financial means to be our middleman. I wanted to be sure I had the right Qadir Yaseen, so I compared a sample of his voice from Burcell's recording of the phone conversation to a voice sample I found online. The audio forensics match."

"Where did you get the sample?" Will asked.

"FOX News," Maggie replied. "Yaseen hasn't been in front of the camera much, but he has been quoted a few times."

A video opened on the second monitor. Yaseen stood on a war-torn battlefield. A slug line at the bottom of the screen read *Near Baghdad, Iraq, April 5, 2003.*

"The American president will not stop until he has consumed all of the Middle East," Yaseen declared. He waved a hand toward the burning buildings in the background. "This atrocity must not be allowed to continue. The United States is not here hunting weapons of mass destruction; they are here to secure a beachhead in the oil-producing nations. These soldiers are here representing their country's need for what the Middle East has. If given the chance, they will take it from us and give it to the Israelis." He paused. "If you find an American soldier, kill him. Send a message home to his country. We will tolerate no boot upon our necks. We will fear no one." He drew a pistol and held it. "I have pledged my life to the destruction of Israel. I will die to see that finished. I will teach the Israelis and the American Satans to fear me."

The video ended, leaving a frozen picture of Yaseen on-screen.

"The voiceprints match?" Will asked.

"Yes."

"Why have I never heard of this guy?" Will asked.

"He's been low-key," Maggie answered. "He's been on the radar screen for a lot of different intelligence agencies, but never anyone's primary focus. Our military files indicate that he's been linked, in a support capacity, to the Palestinian Islamic Jihad, Hamas, Abu Nidal Organization, and the Popular Front for the Liberation of Palestine."

"In what way has he supported them?" Will asked.

"Financially and by providing manpower he recruited," Maggie answered.

"Where does the money come from?"

"Yaseen has several business interests." Maggie opened another file and displayed the contents. "I've only been able to put together a partial list at this point, but I expect I'll find more."

"He owns all these businesses?" Will asked in surprise.

"Yaseen is charismatic by all accounts," Maggie said. "He has several followers who have pledged everything to his cause. It also doesn't hurt that the man borders on suicidal." She frowned. "He's been wounded and nearly killed on several occasions. The man has been incredibly lucky, but there's no discounting skill and experience. He's an accomplished killer, and he doesn't mind getting blood on his hands."

Will's mind raced.

Maggie continued, "Yaseen does things that other anti-American Middle Eastern interests would not dream of risking. When it comes to jihad, Yaseen pulls no punches."

A montage of pictures scrolled across the two monitors, featuring Yaseen at different ages. In all of them the aura of evil seemed to hover around him like a diaphanous cloak.

He was a man, Will knew, who would never give up as long as a breath remained within him.

"He's lobbied long and hard in the Middle East for the destruction of Israel," Maggie said, "but lately—since the second war on Iraq—he's turned his attentions to the United States. He's suspected of funding sniper teams to go inside Iraq to shoot American soldiers and of helping to capture several hostages who were later tortured and murdered."

Maggie continued scanning the file, reporting information as she found it. "Yaseen was born a month after Israel was made a nation after the end of World War II. He lost his parents, two brothers, and three sisters in the Six-Day War. He was a protégé of Yassir Arafat, but more violent."

"Arafat was capable of violence," Will pointed out. "The man didn't get to be head of the PLO by being a pushover."

"No," Maggie said. "I concur. However, Yaseen has had an almost *insane* bloodlust fueling his efforts."

"Losing your family to war would be an enticement," Will admitted.

"He actually lost *two* families," Maggie said. She tapped one of the pictures. "He got married in the late 1970s. He fathered two sons. Both of them died in Operation Wooden Leg."

"The Israeli attack in 1985."

Maggie nodded. "After the Oslo Accord that Arafat signed with the Israelis, Yaseen stepped away from his mentor. Since that time, his involvement in attacks against American, European, and Israeli people and holdings has increased. He wants payback for what was done to him, but he also wants to split the U.S. and Israel."

Will studied the harsh face on the computer monitor. "So you believe this is the face of the enemy?"

"This," Maggie said, "is the man who spoke with Gacha."

Will thought about it. *God have mercy.* "If what we're think-ing is true, if Yaseen somehow brokered a deal for cocaine that he used to buy mocked-up nuclear weapons from Russia, then he can only have one objective."

"To strike America or Israel," Maggie agreed.

"Either of those places would be hard," Will pointed out. "Our security levels are at an all-time high. Getting through defenses would be difficult."

"But not impossible," Maggie said.

Restless unease filled Will. Something wasn't right. "It has to be another target. Striking Israel or America would be bloody, but not to the degree that I think he wants. He's planned this thing out too well. He's after something bigger."

"Bigger than whole cities destroyed?" Maggie sounded as though she couldn't believe it.

"A trigger," Will said, turning over the implications in his mind. "Think about a snowball. You throw a single snowball, you aren't going to have much effect."

"There's a lot of difference between a snowball and a nuclear warhead," Maggie stated.

"But if you toss a snowball at the top of a mountain, and it gathers mass and momentum, it becomes an avalanche," Will said. "I think that's what Yaseen wants: an avalanche. But how would he trigger one?"

Silence filled the room.

Then Estrella, who had been listening to the whole conversa-tion, said, "I think I know."

Will turned to her, hearing the cold fear in her voice.

"I told you the CIA lost Yaseen's signal," Estrella said.

"You also said you kept track of it."

Estrella nodded. "I did. He's on a boat in the South China Sea. I just brought up a satellite scan of that region. There's a U.S. nuclear submarine in that same area, and Yaseen's ship is head-ing right for it. Why would he be trying to intercept a U.S. sub?"

Will waited.

"Think about it. What better way for Yaseen to trigger a global conflict than if the world thinks the U.S. just launched nuclear missiles into a hostile region? If Yaseen has nuclear weapons, I don't think he's going to target the U.S. I think he's going to target North Korea. And it's going to look like the missiles came from our submarine."

Will stared at her, stunned.

"I've been backtracking all the cutouts and relays. I just picked up a call Yaseen made to Chinhae."

"Here?"

"Yes, sir."

"Maybe he's trying to get in touch with Ahmed Achmed," Maggie suggested.

"No," Estrella said. "The call was routed to a Navy ensign aboard SSN *Michigan*." She looked up. "*Michigan* is the submarine Yaseen is trying to intercept."

"There's only one reason Yaseen would contact that ship," Will said. "There's another imposter aboard that boat."

>> **AMERICAN NAVAL BASE NCIS HEADQUARTERS**
>> **1201 HOURS**

"*Michigan* is an Ohio-class nuclear submarine," Estrella said, staring at the large monitor she'd chosen for the display. "She's currently in the South China Sea on patrol."

The NCIS team sat at a conference table, listening intently.

"How long has she been there?" Will asked.

"Six weeks. Before Ricardo Toledo Munoz was killed here."

"But Yaseen made contact with someone on that boat?"

Estrella nodded. "With Seaman Second Class Edward Dill."

On the monitor a personnel file opened to reveal a smiling young ensign in his dress whites. He had dark hair and eyes.

"How long has Dill been in the Navy?" Will asked.

"Almost two years."

"What do we know about him?"

"Not much," Estrella answered. "Yet. I'm still pulling information together. I'm waiting on medical records from his hometown; if his Navy records don't match his childhood medical history, we'll know he's another imposter."

"Has he always been a submariner?"

Estrella flipped through Dill's FSR. "No. He changed MOS a year ago. He was on a carrier till then. It took him four months to get reassigned to the *Michigan*."

"Did you trace the incoming call from Yaseen?" Will asked.

"From the triangulation I was able to employ, I'm certain it originated somewhere in the South China Sea," Estrella said. "I couldn't pinpoint that either, but I know it's within a hundred miles of the *Michigan*. That's a lot of water out there."

"What about satellite recon?" Shel asked.

"I'm working on it," Estrella said. "With all the tension going on in this part of the world, we've got sat recon, but we just don't have the fine-tuning I need to search the ocean. I'll find that point of origin for the call, but I can't tell you how soon. This is harder than tracking a cell phone without a GPS locater through cell-phone towers."

"But we know where the *Michigan* is?" Will asked.

"Yes."

"Then we'll go there and talk to Seaman Second Class Edward Dill," Will said.

S ✷ CRIME SCENE ✷ NCIS ✷ CRI
SERVICE
NAVAL CRIMINAL INVESTIGATIVE SERVICE

46

>> SOUTH CHINA SEA
>> *ARCTIC HAULER*
>> 1431 HOURS

Aboard *Arctic Hauler*, Ahmed Achmed moved with an economy of motion. He crossed the freighter's pitching deck like he'd been born to it. Rime-laden wind whipped at his clothes and peppered his exposed skin. He noticed none of it.

He wore a peacoat over jeans and a flannel shirt but went bareheaded except for orange wraparound sunglasses. A cut-down shotgun hung from a whip-it sling on his right shoulder. Two 9 mm pistols in paddle holsters hung from his belt at his back. Two long combat knives rode in his boots.

He'd arrived by boat the night before, making the rendezvous with the freighter through GPS coordinates Yaseen had given him. He'd brought ten additional men with him. Three were military personnel, but the rest were men embedded in various support agencies within the United States base. Getting men into those areas hadn't been as hard as replacing or recruiting military personnel. All of them were trained killers loyal to the cause.

His walkie-talkie chirped for attention. He answered it.

"There has been a development," Yaseen told him calmly. "The NCIS team has departed Chinhae in a plane. There exists the possibility that they somehow found out about our connection onboard the submarine."

"What can I do, master?" Achmed asked.

"Make certain the work is finished before we rendezvous with the submarine," Yaseen answered. "I want to be ready for them. As long as we are prepared, there is nothing they can do to stop us. We have come too far."

"It will be done." Achmed turned and shouted orders to the crew, urging them to greater speed.

Work crews bolted 7.62 mm machine guns and three deck-mounted Mk32 surface vessel torpedo tubes into place. The SVTTs had been left over from upgrades to World War II corvettes. They launched the MK-46 lightweight torpedoes, but they would be enough to sink an Ohio-class submarine. There were also depth-charge launchers set up on port and starboard. Yaseen had arranged for all the weaponry. The fittings had been prepared a long time ago, and the armament slid smoothly into place.

When the American Satans from Chinhae arrived, they were in for a deadly surprise.

>> SOUTH CHINA SEA
>> 1735 HOURS

"Two minutes to target, Steadfast Leader."

"Roger that," Will responded. He stood in the tail section of the C-130 Hercules cargo and troop transport plane. The vibrations caused by the four turboprops echoed through his wet suit. A belt around his waist supported several pouches containing a medical kit, a dive knife, and his pistol. Parachute packs covered his chest and back.

SSN *Michigan* floated on the green water below them. Larkin had been hard-pressed to make the meet happen, but he had come through using the documentation Estrella had put together. Ensign Dill was due for an interview. And a pedigree check.

Shel and Remy carried the crime-scene gear. Maggie, like the others, was outfitted in a wet suit and parachute as well. Sixteen other men, all of them Marines and SEALs borrowed from Chinhae, were similarly clad. All of the men were young and restive, laughing and joking, but never breaking their concentration.

"Stand ready, Steadfast Leader." The jumpmaster opened the cargo plane's tail section. The blue sky met the dark water of the South China Sea at the horizon. There was no sign of land. "Thirty seconds."

Will approached the ramp. He'd jumped several times before, but it had been a long time since he'd jumped from a C-130. His stomach rolled at the prospect of slamming into the tail section by accident. Maggie stepped into position behind him, with Remy and Shel after her.

Changing channels on his headset, Will said, "Steadfast Five, do you read?"

"Loud and clear, Leader," Estrella replied. She was staying with the cargo plane.

Will quickly went through the rest of the team.

Shel was designated Steadfast Three. Maggie was Steadfast Four. Remy was Steadfast Six. No one was taking Steadfast Two; that had been Frank's call sign on their ops.

"All right," the jumpmaster bawled. "Go! Go!"

Will ran forward, hit the end of the ramp, and fell into the sky. His breath froze in his throat as the weightlessness hit him for a moment. Then gravity took over again and he plummeted toward the ocean. The long, cylindrical shape of the submarine lay almost directly below. Three groups of men with collapsible boats pushed off the submarine and spread out in the water.

"Five, can you patch me through to Starfish Leader?" Will asked. The wind whipped by him as he glanced up. He spotted Maggie, Shel, and Remy falling through the sky above him. Satisfied everything was all right, he pulled his parachute-release cord and watched as the white canopy blotted out his teammates and the sky above.

"Patching, Leader," Estrella responded.

The C-130 kept flying westward, away from Korea. Will wasn't certain what was going on inside the submarine or who might be watching, but he knew he was probably facing the largest threat he ever had.

God, he prayed, *I know I'm here by your hand. Please guide me and show me the way. Keep me strong. And please keep my team in your sight.*

"Steadfast Leader," a calm male voice said. "This is Starfish Leader."

"Affirmative," Will replied. "Just making sure you have us on your radar."

"We do," the submarine captain said. "Still have no clue what this is about."

"We'll talk once I'm aboard."

"Aye," the captain said with an edge. "We will. I don't like surfacing in open water unless there is a real need. We're safest when we run silent and run deep."

Knowing that was true, Will ended the connection. He adjusted his canopy and angled his descent toward the submarine. A moment later, he touched down on the sub's steel hide.

Shel, Remy, and Maggie made the same touchdown, avoiding the water through skill and a little bit of luck. The landings were impressive, but all it would have taken to spoil any of them was a brief gust of wind.

"Commander Coburn," a stocky black man said.

"Me," Will said, stepping out of his parachute harness. Two of the seamen stepped forward and started collapsing the canopy, fighting against the wind, then against the drag of the sub as it cruised slowly through the ocean.

"Commander Deon Henderson. I'm Captain Jacoby's XO." Will shook the executive officer's hand.

"Welcome aboard, Commander." Henderson waved Will toward the conning tower.

After taking a last look around, seeing nothing but the open sea, Will clambered down into the submarine.

>> SSN *MICHIGAN*
>> 1801 HOURS

Captain David Jacoby was old school Navy. Everything that took place aboard his submarine was supposed to be under his purview. The presence of Will and the rest of the NCIS team flew in the face of that.

Will met with Jacoby in the captain's quarters midboat. The 154 vertical launch tubes that held the Tomahawk nuclear missiles in readiness occupied the center of the submarine with the crews' berths spread out around them. Will wondered how the sailors slept in their racks knowing they were only a few feet from weapons designed to destroy cities.

Jacoby sat behind a small desk built into the bulkhead. "I'm not happy about your team being here, Commander." The captain sat relaxed and in control. Gray touched his brown hair at the temples and lines showed in his weathered face.

He was in his early fifties, filling out his final years before retirement. But he had an important job and he knew it. Captain-cies of nuclear-bearing submarines weren't just passed around. Jacoby had proven himself both resourceful and resilient over the years.

"Aye, sir," Will replied. "We won't be here any longer than we have to be."

Breathing in through his nose, Jacoby nodded. "Proceed."

Will was aware of the vibrations that remained constant within a submarine. The propellers cut through the ocean, and the boat dove into deep waters where she was safest.

"Do you know Seaman Second Class Edward Dill?" Will asked.

"I know every man who serves on this boat," Jacoby said. "Whatever Dill stands accused of by the NCIS, I can assure you—"

"Treason," Will interrupted softly. "We believe he's a threat to national security."

"Ridiculous. I don't know what brought you out here, but you'll have to prove to me that—"

Will placed a Tablet PC on the desk and brought Dill's files up with a touch of his finger. "We don't believe he is Edward Dill." Quickly, Will went over the events that had led them to the discovery of Hester's imposter.

Grudging wariness showed on Jacoby's face.

Then Will brought up the information they had on Dill, including the medical chart Dill's childhood physician had for-warded to Estrella. "Whoever's placing these men in the military is good. The files don't show any signs of tampering. It's like magic. The best my computer forensics person has ever seen. But the childhoods of these men can't be taken away." He flicked through pictures of Edward Dill as a young boy. "Dill fractured his left orbital arch when he was nine. His left eye had a tendency to wander after that, but it wasn't enough to keep him out of the service. That injury doesn't show in the X-rays your seaman had three months ago when he suffered a concussion during a car accident off base."

Jacoby was still studying the X-rays displayed side by side on the PC monitor as he opened a comm channel. "Chief Walters."

"Aye, Captain."

"Take a security team and round up Seaman Dill. Restrain him and bring him to my quarters. With all due caution, Chief. I want you and your men armed." Jacoby unlocked the desk drawer and brought out a 9 mm pistol that he stood and belted onto his hip.

"Aye, Captain," Walters responded.

Will respected the speed with which the sub captain shifted gears.

"Why are these men being replaced?" Jacoby asked.

"I'm not entirely sure. That's one of the questions I want to ask Dill." Will wasn't ready to divulge everything he suspected about the link between the cocaine, the missing nuclear weapons, and Qadir Yaseen.

"It shouldn't take long," Jacoby said confidently as he settled back into his chair. "Now go through this again, Commander."

>> **SSN** *MICHIGAN*
>> **1804 HOURS**

Abdullah Hassan stood in front of the stainless-steel mirror and gazed at the face he'd worn for little more than a year. The face wasn't his. He wasn't Seaman Second Class Edward Dill. He was one of those whom Qadir Yaseen had raised to be his personal weapons. For as long as he could remember, he'd prided himself on being one of the select few.

But his effectiveness could only exist if the American Satans did not know they suckled a viper to their breast. And that was over now.

He looked in the mirror at Rasool standing behind him. Rasool wore a Western face as well, red hair, and a pale complexion.

"I'm sorry," Rasool said in their native language.

"I know, my brother. Do not miss."

"I won't. I'll see you in heaven, my friend."

Rasool grabbed him by the hair and yanked his head back to bare his throat. The straight razor in Rasool's hard-knuckled fist gleamed once. Then crimson sprayed over the bathroom mirror.

47

SCENE ✹ **NCIS** ✹ **CRIME SCENE**
NAVAL CRIMINAL INVESTIGATIVE SERVICE

>> SOUTH CHINA SEA
>> SSN *MICHIGAN*
>> 1807 HOURS

Shel floated along in the wake of Chief of Boat Liam Walters, holding his own among the security team. The COB was Irish, solid, and no-nonsense. He exuded the bearing of the kind of career guy who lived by spit and polish and never asked for a thing. Shel had respected him immediately.

He also knew that with Will camped out in the captain's company, the COB and the security division would be the first to see action. Remy had gone with them as well, obviously thinking along the same lines.

A group of sailors played cards on a bunk, glancing up as the security contingent moved through.

"Where's Dill?" Walters asked.

"The head," one of the sailors answered, barely looking away from his hand.

Shel knew Dill was probably aware that they were looking for him since right after Walters had checked the duty roster. News traveled fast through a submarine. If Dill was going to make a last stand inside the head, there could be trouble. Shel's stomach tightened.

The COB walked to the head and entered. A moment later, Walters cursed and backed out. Peering over the shorter man's head, Shel saw Dill collapsed against the far wall, pales eyes turned upward in a thousand-yard stare that was immediately recognizable. Blood tracked the walls, the mirror, and the floor.

Hand on one of his pistols, Shel stepped into the head. No one else was there. "I'm taking over now, Chief," he growled. "This has just officially become a crime scene."

Walters glared at him, as if the dead man were somehow Shel's fault.

"Call it in," Shel advised. "Give the captain a heads-up." He tapped the headset behind his ear. "Steadfast Leader, this is Three." He stared at the dead man again as Will answered the call. "We've got trouble."

>> **1815 HOURS**

"Ever worked a murder scene aboard a submarine before?" Maggie asked.

"No," Will said. He wore a coverall from the equipment cases they'd brought. They never went anywhere without being able to field an investigation. He also wore surgical gloves and clear goggles. He stayed outside the perimeter they'd marked off while Maggie finished photographing the area.

"Looks like he got his throat slashed while he was standing at the sink," Maggie said.

Several minutes passed. The camera clicked and purred as the images were saved to the memory card.

When she was finished, Will advanced, scanning the floor for evidence. There were no footprints. Evidently, Dill—or whoever he ultimately was—had bled out after his killer had fled.

However, Dill had fought against his impending death. Crimson marks on the floor showed where he'd pushed his feet against the surface, streaking crimson in all directions.

Will knelt on Dill's left so he could better examine the wounds. "Straight edge. But the weapon is missing."

"So there's an accomplice on board."

"No," Will said softly. "There's a murderer. Let's find him."

>> 1821 HOURS

Will broke the tasks down quickly. Shel went with Chief Walters to get a list of men who normally worked with Dill. Once the list was generated, the information was sent to Estrella aboard the C-130 Hercules. The cargo plane was capable of fourteen hours of sustained flight with its normal fuel load.

Sending and receiving the information, though, required the *Michigan* to rise within sixty feet of the surface so the periscope and communication mast could be raised. Communication under the water at depth was impossible. The buoyant wire antenna that could be used at greater depth wasn't an option because the system couldn't handle the digital imagery transfer that was necessary for the intel exchange.

Will and Maggie worked the crime scene with Remy, teaching the team's newest recruit as much as they could under the conditions.

The sub's medical doctor had officially declared Dill deceased, processed the paperwork, then handed the body over to Will. Under ideal conditions, Will would have had the corpse shipped to Nita Tomlinson or the nearest medical examiner.

"Blood is one of the greatest tools of a crime-scene investigation," Will said. "It tells you a lot about what happened and what didn't happen." He nodded to the corpse. "What do you see?"

"I see a dead man," Remy said, hunkered down next to the body.

"How did he die?"

"Someone cut his throat."

"The first thing to determine is whether someone did it to him or whether he did it himself," Will said.

Remy looked around, then said, "I don't see a knife anywhere, so this can't be suicide."

"Good," Will said. "You could have a future with NCIS after all. Look at his scalp. See where hair has been pulled out and the scalp is bloody?"

Remy peered at the top of the dead man's head. "Yeah, I see it."

Kneeling again, Will pointed along the dead man's arm. Blood spatter was clearly evident along the arm, but halfway between the elbow and the wrist there was a break in the pattern. "Here's an interruption."

"Something was over his arm," Remy said.

Will nodded. "The arm of whoever grabbed Dill's head and slashed his throat."

"There's bruising on Dill's right temple and forehead," Maggie said. She rolled his head over to expose the slight bruising.

Will considered the marks. "Our murderer held Dill's head back while he cut his throat. How tall is Dill?"

Maggie referred to her notes on her iPAQ. "FSR says he was six feet two inches tall."

Pointing to the brutal slash across the dead man's throat, Will asked Remy, "Does that cut look lateral to you?"

"Yeah."

Will looked at Remy. Teaching was one of the things Will most enjoyed about his job. Even though the business of death was a horrible thing, there was a lot that had to be learned. "What does the cut tell you?"

"That it killed Dill."

"True," Will said. "Stand up and turn around."

When Remy did so, Will walked up behind him. "Even with a sharp knife, it takes a strong man to cut through someone's throat all the way back to his spine."

Remy nodded.

"That means you have to pull hard, use your weight to get the job done."

"I know," Remy said. "I've done it before."

That stopped Will. In all his years in the Navy, on the aircraft carrier and as part of NCIS, he'd never killed a man like that. Getting in that close, using that kind of violence, was foreign to him.

"I'm trained as a SEAL," Remy said quietly. "I've seen a lot of action. Shel, he probably knows about cuttin' throats too."

Will had never thought about that before. "You're right. He probably does." He moved in and drew a finger across Remy's throat. "You're taller than me."

"Six-three," Remy said.

"I stand six feet one inch tall," Will said. "If I cut your throat and really work at it, I'm going to have a tendency to cut *down*." He drew his finger along the side of Remy's neck, angling down. "If I'm taller than you, I'm going to have a tendency to cut *up*." He released Remy and stepped back. "Understand?"

Remy looked at the dead man again. "The man who did this had to be the same height."

"Right," Will said. "Already we know we're looking for a right-handed sailor who's six feet two inches tall. That will narrow down the list. The fact that he may well still have blood on

his left arm narrows it even more." He looked at the corpse.
"Now we see if we get really lucky."

"What do you mean?"

"The killer touched Dill's face. He may have left prints we
can recover."

>> *ARCTIC HAULER*
>> **1912 HOURS**

In the communications station in *Arctic Hauler*'s midships,
Yaseen watched the computer monitor with keen interest. The
view was brought to him through a communications satellite
owned by an international company that was sympathetic to
Middle Eastern causes.

The murky green expanse of the South China Sea stretched
in all directions. *Arctic Hauler* was converging on a bright red
blip that represented SSN *Michigan*. The satellite search had followed the C-130 that had carried the NCIS team to the submarine, then stayed locked on the known route the *Michigan* had
been assigned to. When the submarine had surfaced nearly an
hour ago to report the murder and communicate with the Hercules circling overhead, computers onboard *Arctic Hauler* had
picked up the new coordinates instantly.

Glowing red numbers in the upper-right corner of the screen
showed the time remaining till the interception: thirty-two minutes and seventeen seconds. Night would fall on the ocean only
minutes after that. Yaseen was counting on darkness to help
mask what happened afterward.

All was ready aboard the freighter. As long as the *Michigan*
remained at communication depth, the depth charges and torpedo launchers aboard *Arctic Hauler* should be able to cripple or
destroy the submarine.

Even though he had men aboard the submarine, Yaseen couldn't trigger the launch from there. That would have taken a call to the Pentagon to learn the launch codes, and it would require the captain and XO to be working with him. He hadn't managed to get those men. Replacing sailors was much simpler than replacing officers.

But once the sub was under attack, Yaseen would begin the launch sequence aboard the *Arctic Hauler*. The nuclear missiles would leap from the hidden blast tubes and streak toward Pyongyang, North Korea. Even if American interceptors in South Korea scrambled to blast the missiles from the sky, it would be too late. North Korea would launch an offensive at once, a retaliatory strike to take out their opponents.

The targets would include American, Russian, and Chinese cities. North Korea had so many enemies—and no time to effectively figure out who was behind the launch—that they would strike without hesitation. The North Korean generals would assume they were at war with the world.

Afterward, even if the Koreas were utterly decimated in the nuclear strikes, Russia, China, and the United States would be at each other's throats. Either China or Russia would figure out soon enough that a U.S. nuclear submarine had been stationed in the exact area from which the first nukes had been launched. The United States would look guilty. More wars would break out, and the battle places would take form across the globe.

Yaseen smiled in anticipation. As a result, the Middle East would be in an even stronger position. The United States would be so busy covering itself and trying to rebuild their broken cities that they wouldn't be able to effectively maintain police action to protect Israel. The American people would become even more against involvement in Middle Eastern affairs and want to keep their soldiers safe and handling security along their own shores.

Twenty-eight minutes and fifty-three seconds remained.

✸ ✸ ✸

>> **SSN** *MICHIGAN*

>> **1914 HOURS**

"This," Will said, removing the device from the field kit, "is a Sirchie iodine fuming gun." He broke the seals and put the pipette to his lips as he leaned over Dill's head. He breathed out and a small cloud of orange vapor pulsed out over the dead man's skin.

Maggie manned the digital 35 mm Canon SLR. The single-lens-reflex camera was outfitted with a one-to-one system that offered eight megapixel shots that uploaded onto the gigabyte-sized flash card. With the ratio resolution, the Canon could reproduce images that were actual size. She'd put the camera in a snap-together metal frame over the dead man's head.

Will shook the fuming gun. It was a slim plastic tube not much bigger than his finger. "Disposable. The crystals inside are iodine. When I breathe through the gun, the heat of my breath sets off a physiochemical reaction that reduces some of the iodine into vapor."

The orange cloud hugged the dead man's flesh for a moment.

"Fingerprints—more properly called friction ridges—are made up of oils from the skin," Will continued. "Patent friction ridges can be seen unaided by the naked eye. Latent friction ridges need a little help. Usually we help with chemical stimulation or special lighting."

Will and Remy watched as friction ridges slowly took shape on the dead man's flesh.

"You can use powders to acquire friction ridges off skin," Will said as they waited for the chemical reaction to process, "but you have to get to it within fifteen minutes or so. The oil left by fingers deteriorates quickly on most surfaces. The iodine can work up to four hours later as long as the cadaver's temperature doesn't drop below 70 to 75 degrees Fahrenheit."

When the friction ridges had totally developed, Maggie started taking pictures.

"If we get a good print," Will said, "then we get our killer."

"Because every man on this boat," Remy replied, "has his fingerprints on file."

"That's right."

Maggie took the camera from the frame.

"Go see if we have a match," Will said. "I'll clean up here."

"All right," she said, and left.

The friction ridges on Dill's face faded.

"Are they supposed to do that?" Remy asked.

"That's why we took pictures." Will rummaged in the kit. "We're going to try to lift the ridges, but if we can't, we have the pictures." He handed the fuming gun to Remy and took a black plastic rectangle from the kit. "In the old days, CSIs used silver plates and actinic lighting to transfer and lift the ridges. This is RC photo paper that's been developed." Removing a hair dryer from the kit, he plugged it in and warmed the plastic rectangle.

"Why heat it?" Remy asked.

"Makes the surface more friendly to the fatty and waxy contaminants left behind by the oils in the friction ridges," Will explained. He pressed the rectangle against the dead man's head. "Hold it for fifteen or twenty seconds. Then put it in a protective envelope." He tucked the rectangle into an envelope and stored that inside the kit. "Later we'll fume it with superglue and see if we can't recover the print to support the digital images Maggie took."

"I got a lot to learn," Remy said.

"You will. Let's bag his hands." Will took paper bags and duct tape from the kit. "We use paper bags because he has blood on him."

"Paper will let the blood dry."

"Exactly. Not all of the blood may be his. We need to be able to take samples." Will set to work, bagging one hand while

Remy did the other. "Besides the blood, we'll check under his fingernails for DNA."

"This stuff is pretty interesting."

"It is," Will agreed. "When I first made the jump to NCIS, I didn't know if I'd like it. I do. There's something about the hunt, about wondering if you're smart enough to use observation, reasoning, and science to find out what happened at a crime scene."

Remy looked uncomfortable. "I got to be honest, Commander. I'll learn what you got to show me. But don't get too used to seeing me around. This isn't what I signed on for. Soon as my CO gets through being mad at me, I'm going back to my team."

"All right," Will said.

"It's not personal."

Will nodded, wondering why Remy Gautreau had ended up as part of his team. And why Remy's CO had seemed so certain the SEAL was having problems.

>> *ARCTIC HAULER*
>> 1937 HOURS

Aboard *Arctic Hauler,* Achmed stood in the prow and gazed down at the periscope and communications mast that stuck up through the ocean. They slid slowly by less than three hundred yards away.

"I see the sub," Achmed said.

"Excellent," Yaseen replied, standing beside him. "It is time."

Achmed took up the M4A1 assault rifle at his feet. Belts containing extra magazines for the rifle and pistol he carried hung around his hips. Kevlar armor covered his upper body.

"Depth charges," Yaseen bawled out to the crew standing on the deck.

All the warriors had been handpicked by Yaseen. Like him, they had been waiting for this moment. In seconds the men had swept the rime-coated gray tarps from the weapons they'd installed on the freighter's deck.

"Fire!" Yaseen roared.

Immediately, the depth-charge launchers shot the drumlike explosives into the air with loud *whumps!* that echoed over the choppy ocean surface. They flew true, though a little wobbly, and landed less than thirty yards from their target.

"Adjust," Yaseen ordered. "Fire again!"

Before his words faded, geysers shot up from the ocean. The flat, basso explosions followed, rolling hollowly over the freighter.

Standing beside his master, Achmed waited expectantly for only a heartbeat before the depth-charge launchers slammed into full speed. The sky filled with hurtling drums. Lying only sixty feet under the surface of the murky water, virtually at rest to maintain satellite contact, the *Michigan* was a sitting duck.

Achmed grinned in expectant triumph.

S ✳ **CRIME SCENE** ✳ **NCIS** ✳ **CR**
NAVAL CRIMINAL INVESTIGATIVE SERVICE
E SERVICE

48

>> SOUTH CHINA SEA
>> SSN *MICHIGAN*
>> 1937 HOURS

Maggie stared at both monitor screens in the room where Captain Jacoby had let the NCIS team set up communications. The monitor on her left held the image of friction ridges Will had brought to life on the dead man's temple. The monitor on the right cycled through the friction ridges of the fifteen officers and one hundred and forty crew aboard the *Michigan*. Maggie had already identified twelve points of reference on the captured image.

"It's a good image," Estrella transmitted over the headset. She was still maintaining vigilance from above in the C-130 plane.

"Thanks," Maggie said. She pushed up from the chair and stretched. Being inside the cramped submarine was beginning to make her feel slightly claustrophobic.

"We'll get a match," Estrella said.

"I hope so."

"You sound stressed."

Maggie watched as the monitor on the right continued to flip through friction ridges. "Ever been on a sub this size?"

"A few times."

"I haven't."

"It takes some getting used to."

"I feel really closed in," Maggie said.

"The fact that one of those crewmen murdered Dill to cover up his secret doesn't have any bearing on that, right?"

"That may be adding to it."

The monitor on the right stopped cycling.

"We've got a match," Estrella said.

"Who?" Maggie leaned in to the computer.

"Give me a second."

"Hey," a male voice called from the doorway.

Looking up, Maggie saw a crewman in an enlisted uniform and cap. The man was a couple inches over six feet. He looked like he was in his midtwenties. His hair was red, cut close, and his hazel eyes held a hint of feral intensity.

"Can I help you?" Maggie asked.

"Actually," the crewman said, "I thought maybe I could help you. I think I know who killed Dill."

Suspicion darkened Maggie's thoughts instantly. "Why didn't you go to the captain?"

Taking the continued conversation as permission to enter the cabin, the crewman stepped through the door. He talked in a quiet whisper and glanced over his shoulder. "Because I think maybe the captain ordered Dill murdered. There's something . . . strange going on around here. I've been noticing it for weeks. I didn't know who I could trust. I'm kind of putting my life in your hands."

His story was believable enough. Outside of her team, there

wasn't anyone aboard whom Maggie was ready to rule out as a suspect.

"Why would you think the captain was involved?" Maggie asked.

The crewman shrugged. "He knew you people were coming. He wanted to protect himself."

"Protect himself from what?"

Shrugging again, the crewman said, "From whatever you're investigating."

Maggie's hackles went up. The crewman was too relaxed for someone who was bucking the chain of command aboard ship. And for someone who thought they had information about a cold-blooded murder. "What's your name, sailor?" she asked.

"Maggie," Estrella said over the headset. "I've got him. His name is Seaman First Class Anthony Gillespie."

"Tony," the sailor said almost at the same time. "Tony Gillespie. Seaman First Class."

The second monitor filled with the image of the man whose fingerprints matched the ridges on the cadaver Will and Remy were still working. Those features also matched the face of the seaman standing across the desk from her.

Sensing movement, Maggie looked up, her right hand reaching for the Beretta tucked under her left arm. But before she could free her weapon, Gillespie jumped across the desk and smashed into her. The monitors slid off the desk and crashed to the floor.

Maggie tried to remain on her feet but the bed against the wall caught her behind her knees and tripped her. She fell onto the bed, and Gillespie came down on top of her, pinning her arms to her sides with his thighs. He pulled a lock-back knife from his pocket and flicked it open in a practiced maneuver.

"Time to die," he whispered hoarsely with a cold grin, as he clapped a hand over her mouth so she couldn't call out for help. He moved the knife, preparing to draw it across her throat.

"Shel, Will," Estrella called over the headset. "Dill's killer is with Maggie. Maggie! Maggie, can you hear me?"

With Gillespie's hand over her mouth, Maggie couldn't respond. But she wasn't prepared to die either. Gillespie had made the mistake of getting too high on her body in his attempt to restrain her arms. She bucked her hips upward, using his awkward position to her advantage to help throw him off balance.

Gillespie was caught off guard by her strength and her sudden movement. He rocked forward. His face slammed into the bulkhead with a sickening thud. His hand came away from her mouth.

Maggie didn't waste time calling out for help. Estrella had already done that for her. She bucked again, this time shoving her arm down rather than trying to free it. She got just enough clearance to bend her elbow. Closing her fist in the material of Gillespie's shirt, she rolled, trying to put her attacker's face into the bulkhead again.

Instinctively, not wanting a repeat of the battering, Gillespie jerked back. Blood leaked from his nose and mouth. One eye was already turning puffy.

Maggie pulled on the fistful of shirt with all her strength and felt Gillespie roll off her. She quickly kicked up her leg and planted a foot against the underside of the man's jaw. She used the added leverage to push him backward, slamming him back against the desk.

Gillespie recovered before Maggie could pull her pistol free. The knife whistled for her face as he cursed her. Maggie shifted, caught the man's elbow, and pushed herself to her feet. Trapping his wrist with her other hand, she twisted violently and snapped Gillespie's elbow.

Yelling in pain, Gillespie dropped the knife.

Maintaining her hold on the man, Maggie pulled him around and stuck a foot out to trip him. He went face-first into the bulkhead beside the desk. Before he could get to his feet, she was on him, holding him down while she fished her handcuffs out. Expertly, she cuffed his hands behind his back.

Maggie stood and drew in a deep breath.

"Maggie," Estrella called again over the headset.

"I'm fine," Maggie responded. Then she repeated herself so everyone on the team could hear. "I'm fine. The situation is under control. Gillespie's down."

Gillespie continued cursing.

"You get one warning," Maggie told him. "Quiet down or I'll take your socks off and gag you with them."

The sailor stopped cursing. He managed to flop over on his back and glare up at her. The pain in his eyes and the blood on his face took away a lot of the threat. "You haven't won."

"Feels pretty good from where I'm standing," Maggie said.

He scowled.

Shel was the first to reach her. He had his SOCOM .45s in both hands and a fierce look on his face. "You okay?" he asked.

"I'm fine," Maggie answered. "Caught me by surprise."

Shel nodded. He put his weapons away and took a roll of duct tape from the crime-scene kit on the desk. He knelt and quickly taped Gillespie's ankles together. "Looks like maybe you surprised him right back."

Will and Remy showed up next, both of them armed as well.

Remy glanced at the downed sailor. "You do good work, *chéri.*"

The submarine heeled over suddenly. The sound of explosions followed immediately.

"What was that?" Maggie asked, bracing against the bulkhead.

Will glanced up, listening intently. "That sounded like depth charges."

Klaxons sprang to shrill life throughout the submarine. Red

lights flared to fill the hallways. Sailors rushed by the open door.

"All hands to battle stations," Captain Jacoby called over the PA with tense authority. "We're under attack. Prepare to dive."

"Under attack by who?" Shel growled.

⊛ ⊛ ⊛

>> OVER THE SOUTH CHINA SEA
>> 1941 HOURS

Estrella tried to access a friendly satellite with her computer aboard the circling C-130. Unfortunately, none of the ones in the area appeared to be near enough to get a close-up view of the action taking place down below.

"Steadfast Five," Will called over the headset.

"Here," Estrella said. She abandoned the computer workstation and ran to the cockpit.

"We're under fire. What's going on up there?"

"I don't know. I'm looking." Estrella peered through the window. She addressed the pilot. "Find that submarine for me."

The pilot banked the plane and came around. They had been flying in a big circle, maintaining a loose proximity to secure the satellite communications between the *Michigan* and the plane. The SEAL team aboard maintained vigilance, ready to provide backup. It looked like they were going to get the chance.

Borrowing a pair of binoculars, Estrella peered at the ocean as the plane lost altitude. She spotted the freighter first and only picked up the sub's position because of the towering spumes of water exploding around it.

"There's one surface vessel, Steadfast Leader," Estrella said. Fear coiled through her like a broken-backed snake. During her time aboard ship, she'd never had an actual encounter with an enemy ship. She'd faced death as an NCIS special agent, but that was on a more personal level. What she watched below her was frightening. Especially knowing that her team was in the middle of the battle.

"Copy," Will replied. "One vessel."

"They're armed with depth charges, torpedo tubes, and heavy machine guns." Estrella ran the binoculars the length of the ship. Just then, she saw the freighter crew working hard to remove two circular sections from amidships. "There's something in the middle of the ship. They're uncovering two areas." She looked at the pilot. "Can you take us across that ship? Low enough that I can take a look at what's going on there."

The pilot guided the plane into a steeper dive, heading for the freighter. Then, for just a glimpse, she saw the distinctive shapes inside the freighter's hold.

"Steadfast Leader," Estrella said as calmly as she could. *Nuclear missiles!* her mind screamed. *Those are nuclear weapons!*

Now she knew where Gronsky's stolen missiles had gone.

She raised her voice. "Steadfast Leader."

There was no response.

Estrella tried again. "Steadfast Leader, do you copy? Steadfast team?"

Only white noise filled her headset. Evidently the communication mast had been damaged in the onslaught.

The pilot looked up at her. "We just lost the satellite relay."

"Did you get an update to Central Command?"

"They knew something's gone sour out here, but that's all. There wasn't time for specifics."

Even if a message had gone through, it would be at least an hour before other planes with the range to reach them could be in place. Switching over to the local communication band used by the SEALs, Estella said, "Captain Fenwick."

"Aye, sir," the SEAL captain answered immediately.

"Ready your men. We're going down." Estrella looked at the pilot. "Get us an approach path. We need to deploy the SEALs."

"I've got weapons with this bird," the pilot responded confidently. "I can put that freighter to the bottom of the ocean."

"And if you accidentally set off one of those nuclear weapons aboard that freighter?"

"What nuclear weapons?"

"Missiles," Estrella said. "They've got nuclear weapons aboard that ship. Get your tail section open and get us to a jump site."

"Affirmative." The pilot banked the plane again.

Grabbing the doorframe, Estrella heaved herself from the cockpit and made her way toward the back. "Captain Fenwick."

The SEAL officer stepped away from his team. He was in his late thirties, lean, hard, blond and blue-eyed. His body was covered with weapons.

"We've got to get down there." Estrella stopped at her workstation and snatched her SIG-Sauer P-226 9 mm, settling the shoulder rig over her shirt.

"We?" Fenwick asked as the tail section yawned open.

"We," Estrella confirmed. "My team is down there, Captain. I'm going with you."

Fenwick didn't argue. He turned to two of his men and jerked a thumb over his shoulder at Estrella. "Suit her up."

Swiftly and expertly, the two SEALs put Estrella in Kevlar body armor and strapped a parachute on her.

"Jump point fifteen seconds," the pilot called.

"Simmons," Fenwick barked.

"Sir," a young SEAL responded.

"Take care of Petty Officer Montoya."

"Aye, sir."

Simmons was compact and black. He stepped in front of Estrella. "You ever jump before?"

"Jump!" the pilot called.

The SEAL captain went first, leaving his second to get the rest of the team through the hatch. The men carried camo-colored Zodiac RIB inflatable boats equipped with dual high-powered outboard engines.

"I've jumped enough to qualify," Estrella said.

Simmons grinned and gave her a thumbs-up. Then he fitted a helmet with a built-in radio over her head. "Outstanding. You're gonna be fine. This will be just like a field jump."

Except we're landing in the ocean and there are explosions everywhere, Estrella thought. Still, she was going. Every man mattered. Even with twenty SEALs, she guessed they were going to be outnumbered by the freighter crew. And once they were in the ocean, there was no returning to the relative safety of the C-130.

"Just remember," Simmons yelled over the roar of the wind, "you gotta cut loose from the parachute harness before you hit the water. If you don't, you could get tangled up in the shroud lines and drown."

Estrella nodded to let him know she'd heard him. Her stomach flipped and flopped. She thought about Nicky, wondering if she'd hugged him tight enough when she'd last seen him, wondering if she had said everything she'd meant to say to him in case she . . . in case they didn't get to talk again.

She pressed her fingertips against the St. Christopher medallion under her Kevlar jacket and shirt. Then Simmons pulled her into motion, and they were rushing for the tail section.

She didn't jump when she reached the end of the ramp. She just kept running till her feet had carried her into the open air. Pulling her arms in close to her sides, she dropped quickly, emulating the SEALs' descent. When their parachutes started opening, Estrella pulled her own ripcord.

Once her parachute deployed, Estrella adjusted her descent and stayed with the SEAL team. Simmons locked in beside her with expert skill.

"You're doing fine," Simmons said over the radio.

The ocean came up fast, rolling and pitching. The sounds of the explosions rolled over her. Without warning, her parachute jerked. She looked up, amazed to see fist-sized holes punched in the material.

"They've seen us," Fenwick said over the radio.

Glancing at the freighter less than a hundred yards away and still several hundred yards below, Estrella saw machine gunners standing at the railing. Flames burst brightly from the muzzles of their weapons.

A few of the SEALs returned fire. Their machine pistols stuttered in short bursts. One of the men aboard the freighter went down.

"Lucky," someone commented through Estrella's headset.

"I'll take it," someone else said.

"Get those Zodiacs deployed soon as we're down," Fenwick ordered. "We need to be moving. Otherwise we're sitting ducks."

What about the sub? Estrella wanted to ask. The submarine had gone below, but the freighter's depth charges hadn't stopped chugging out drum-sized death.

"Lose the parachute, Petty Officer Montoya," Simmons said. "Now."

Estrella fumbled with the parachute release and finally managed it. She threw her arms up to clear the harness. Free of her weight, the parachute pulled up away from her and she dropped like a rock.

She folded her arms over her chest and crossed her feet just before she hit the water. For a moment the pain in her ankles made her think she'd broken one or both. Then she was submerged several feet below the ocean's surface.

Once she achieved natural buoyancy and her descent was stalled, she struck out for the surface. She experienced a brief moment of terror when she thought that her gear was too heavy, was making her too slow to reach the surface before her lungs sucked in seawater.

All around her, other SEALs were swimming upward as well. Bullets sliced through the water, leaving streamers in their wake.

One of the SEALs was hit. A cloud of blood boiled out, turning the water dark around him for a moment, then dissipating. The SEAL's movements stopped at once and he started to sink. Another SEAL grabbed his harness and swam upward with him.

Estrella came up, took a deep, grateful breath, and swam for the nearest Zodiac.

Simmons was already there, smiling broadly when he saw her. He offered his hand and pulled her aboard. "You made it," he said.

Before Estrella could reply, four of the other SEALs opened fire on the freighter as the dual outboard engines came alive with thunderous roars.

Simmons pushed her down. "Stay low," he advised. "Let us do our jobs."

The three Zodiac boats sped toward the freighter, the fiberglass prows smashing through the waves. Spray fell back over the Special Forces warriors.

Machine-gun fire from the freighter pocked the sea's surface and filled the air with additional noise between the explosions of the depth charges.

Looking around, Estrella noticed the tension on the faces of the SEALs. They knew the risks they were undertaking. It wasn't like they believed they were invincible. They were men out to do a necessary and hazardous job. The body of the wounded man on the floor of the Zodiac was a grim reminder of that.

Simmons reached down and picked up the SEAL's MP5. He offered it to Estrella. "Do you know how to use this?" he asked.

"Yes," she said.

Simmons pressed the machine pistol into her hands.

Estrella checked the weapon to make certain it was charged. There was blood on it, and when some of it came off on her hands, she wiped it on her pants. She took the bandolier of extra magazines Simmons offered.

The small boat was close enough to the ship now that the

freighter filled her vision. She still didn't know what kind of shape the submarine was in or whether her team was intact.

She tightened her grip on the MP5, then knelt and added her fire to that of the SEALs. The machine gunners aboard the freighter were forced back from their positions. Some of them dropped as they were hit by the SEALs' rounds.

"Prepare boarders," Fenwick yelled.

The boat's pilot slewed the craft around at the last moment. The Zodiac spun and slammed its stern against the freighter. Two SEALs fired grappling hooks over the ship's side, then braced the ropes as the others swarmed up them.

Estrella slung the machine pistol over her shoulder and gripped the rope. The image of the nuclear weapons sitting in the ship's cargo hold wouldn't leave her mind. She pulled herself up, walking along the freighter's rust-covered hull.

# 49

E SCENE ✷ **NCIS** ✷ **CRIME SCEN**
NAVAL CRIMINAL INVESTIGATIVE SERVICE

>> SOUTH CHINA SEA
>> SSN *MICHIGAN*
>> 1941 HOURS

Will raced through the submarine, dodging through the hatches and trying to stay out of the way of the sailors. Everything happened too fast, making the unfamiliar environment even more disturbing. The screaming Klaxons and red glow of battle stations changed things even further. No Navy man who'd ever gone to sea hadn't spent some time thinking about going down with a ship. Still, the fact that the sailors all appeared to know what they were doing inspired confidence.

Shel, Remy, and Maggie pounded along after him.

Once he was through the next hatch, he was in the navigation center. A fresh wave of explosions rocked the sub, throwing Will against the bulkhead.

Commander Deon Henderson, the sub's XO, stood in the

navigation section talking over a headset. "No, Captain, we've lost all satellite communications. The depth charges could have knocked out the communication mast. We've still got onboard contact in most areas. We lost engineering. I'm checking on that now."

A sailor ran through the hatch Will had just entered through. "Commander."

Henderson looked at the man.

"We've got flooding in the engine room, sir," the sailor said. "We're taking on water like a sieve. The chief said to tell you the outer and inner hulls have been breached. We're trying to seal them off, sir, but it's hard going. We need help."

Another series of explosions hammered the stricken sub.

"Take as many men as you need," Henderson responded. He quickly informed the captain of the situation.

Not wanting to bother Henderson, Will turned to one of the security men guarding the XO. It was standard operating procedure during a battle situation. "What's going on?" Will asked.

"We're under attack."

Another salvo of depth charges shook the sub from stem to stern.

"Do we have communications in place?" Will asked.

The sailor shook his head.

"Where's the captain?"

"Command and Control." The sailor pointed.

Will rushed forward, riding out the sub's sudden heaving by holding on to one of the chairs bolted to the deck.

In the next room, Captain Jacoby held on to the periscope, turning it around as he tracked something. Bright green light from the instrumentation panels lit the captain's stern face.

"Steady as you go, helmsman," Jacoby said as calmly as if he faced battle like this every day.

"She's sluggish, Captain," the helmsman replied.

Will knew that a submarine's best defense was diving. However, with the hull integrity breached, the increased pressure of the lower depths also presented a threat to the boat.

"Torpedo!" someone yelled.

"Brace yourselves," Jacoby called.

When the torpedo hit, it felt like the world had suddenly stopped. For a moment Will thought the submarine had buckled and broken open like an egg.

"We're lucky," Jacoby said. "They're packing MK-46s. If they'd had bigger warheads we'd have been hurting."

"Captain," Henderson called over the shipboard radio, "we've got new leaks in crews' quarters."

"Helm, can you bring us around?" Jacoby asked.

"Trying, sir. That freighter's circling us. She's got a tighter axis than we do."

Jacoby glanced at Will. "It appears the C-130 knows that we've been attacked. I don't know if they're in a position to lend a hand."

"I brought a contingent of SEALs with me," Will said.

"We've got a SEAL team onboard as well," Jacoby said. "Maybe we can expect some relief at some point. For right now, we're little more than a sitting duck. Their first strike damaged our steering and propulsion, and we're taking on water in several areas. Diving to get clear of the situation isn't an option."

"Did you identify the ship that's attacking us?" Will asked.

"Comm made an inquiry. She's *Arctic Hauler*."

"Where was her last port of call?"

"According to the ship's manifests, she came out of Russia."

In an instant everything came together in Will's mind. Gronsky had arranged for nuclear weapons to be stolen. Kuzlow had stolen and delivered the weapons in exchange for cocaine supplied by Gacha. The only missing link had been the middle-man. Yaseen had fit the bill, but his involvement had been a stretch. Now Will was sure that Yaseen's part was more than mere conjecture. It all fit. He had supplied the money for the cocaine deal in return for the nuclear weapons. And Will was pretty sure Yaseen was on board the attacking ship. Were the nukes there too?

"While we're waiting on your SEALs," Jacoby said, "we're going to try to manufacture some of our own rescue."

"My team can help," Will said.

"Lieutenant Parker," Jacoby called.

A man clad in a wet suit and strapped with weapons stepped forward. "Aye, sir."

"Get your men together and get down to the DDS, Lieutenant," Jacoby instructed. "When you're in position, we're going to break out of this circle and run straight. With the speed we're able to manage now, we're not going to be able to outrun that freighter. Take the ASDS and see if you can get a clear shot at that vessel before it sinks us."

"Aye, sir."

"God keep you, Lieutenant."

"Thank you, sir."

Will looked at Jacoby. "We're going with the SEALs."

The captain shook his head. "You'll only be in the way. They're trained to work together."

"This is my investigation," Will said.

"You can investigate that ship after they sink it."

"There may be nuclear weapons aboard," Will said, deciding to lay his cards on the table. "If there are, I need to know that."

Jacoby stared at Will. "That information would have been useful to know at the outset."

"It's a guess," Will said. "Maybe even an incorrect one. This investigation was complicated from the outset." He paused. "I need your permission to join that SEAL team, sir."

Jacoby hesitated just a moment, then nodded. "I'll have them wait."

"Thank you, sir." Will took off at once to notify the others.

✳ ✳ ✳

>> *ARCTIC HAULER*
>> **1951 HOURS**

Yaseen paced in front of the computer monitors and listened to the sounds of battle above. He wanted to be there, but he needed to be here to control the missile attacks.

Three monitors offered different satellite views of the area. One of them tracked the C-130, which had regained altitude after deploying the parachutists only moments ago. The other two tracked the submarine. Other monitors displayed views from the ship's security system.

"Achmed," Yaseen said over the ship radio connection.

"Here," Achmed answered. Gunfire sounded in the background.

"The submarine has started running south, southeast of our position."

"I know. We have it in sight."

Yaseen felt *Arctic Hauler* come about. Evidently the submarine captain had timed his attempted escape well, catching the freighter pointed almost 180-degrees in the wrong direction. Still, given the sluggish way the submarine was handling, Yaseen knew the vessel had been badly damaged.

"That submarine can't be allowed to escape," Yaseen said. It would be hard to claim that the submarine had fired two of its nuclear missiles if it limped back to a port with all of its deadly payload intact.

"It won't," Achmed replied. "We will catch it and sink it."

Noticing movement on the freighter's starboard, Yaseen leaned in and tapped the keyboard, increasing the magnification. Black-suited figures clambered up the ship's side, clinging to ropes as they fired at the ship's crew trying to hold them back. Three small boats paced the freighter like hounds harrying a bear.

"We're about to be boarded," Yaseen warned. "The men from the American plane are climbing our sides."

"No," Achmed said, "they won't be successful."

Yaseen watched the screen intently. Nothing could go wrong. He'd planned this event down to the last minute detail, including computer-generated video of the *Michigan* opening her tubes on the surface and firing two of the Tomahawk missiles she carried. That would be anonymously released to news outlets as soon as the missiles fired, giving additional testimony of how the *Michigan* had attacked Pyongyang, North Korea.

Yaseen had researched the captains carefully before making his decision which boat to put his men on. Captain Jacoby had a history of espousing that something more direct should be done to bring the North Korean generals to heel. His oldest son, a Marine, had died while serving on a border detail less than three years ago. That incident alone offered a lot of motivation.

The freighter came about smartly for her size, then began the pursuit of the submarine. It was immediately apparent that the damaged sub wouldn't get far.

Yaseen smiled, readying himself for the coming triumph and the destruction that would be triggered. He watched as the freighter bore down on the red marker that showed the submarine's position. The chase wouldn't take long. *Arctic Hauler* was already overtaking the submarine.

Estrella clung tightly to the rope as the freighter rolled over the waves, caught broadside. Her body slammed against the rough, rust-covered hull, barking skin from her knuckles and left cheekbone. Her hands slipped, allowing her to fall several inches, but she clamped on again and stopped her fall.

Simmons looked down at her. "Climb!"

Shoulders aching with the strain, Estrella found her footing again and started up once more.

Another rapid burst of gunfire sounded directly over her head. A SEAL stumbled back, hit the cable ringing the ship's deck, and slid through. Sick helplessness coiled in Estrella's stomach as she watched the young warrior plummet past her. His face was a bloody mask. Then he disappeared into the murky water as *Arctic Hauler* surged forward.

"Special Agent Montoya," Simmons called down. *"Climb!"*

Focusing, thinking of Nicky—*Oh, queriedo, I hope that you never know how your mother risked never seeing you again*—Estrella pulled herself up the rope.

She was shaking by the time she reached the deck's edge. Simmons grabbed the back of her Kevlar vest and yanked her aboard. Heavy machine-gun fire slammed against the steel containers where the SEAL team had taken cover. Estrella pulled the MP5 into her hands and looked around.

Fenwick had men moving through the maze of containers situated across the deck. The containers had helped mask the presence of the weapons. Now their placement gave the SEALs a small edge that was immediately offset by the sheer number of men on the vessel.

Estrella did a quick head count and found that they were down to thirteen, counting her.

"We're outnumbered," Estrella shouted to Simmons.

"Don't think of it as being outnumbered," the SEAL replied. "Think of it as a target-rich environment."

Gathering her courage, aware that she had never been this deep into an operation this dangerous before, Estrella peered around the container toward the middle of the ship. The holes she'd spotted from the air were clear now. The missiles could be launched any time.

"Incoming!" one of the SEALs screamed.

Turning toward the voice, Estrella saw one of the ship's crew bringing a rocket launcher to his shoulder. A puff of smoke jetted from the rear of the weapon as the 40 mm warhead jumped forward.

In the next instant, the rocket detonated against the container where Estrella had taken cover. Shrapnel filled the air, carving holes in the containers that weren't hit and leaving a huge gaping hole in the one that was. Inside the container, electronic goods caught fire and filled the immediate vicinity with an acrid, choking smoke.

One of the SEALs clipped the rocket-launcher operator with a short burst that spun the man around and left him sprawled on the deck.

Before the SEAL got back to cover, another man with a rocket launcher fired from the top of a stack of containers. The warhead landed at the SEAL's feet and blew him backward into the container behind him. He crumpled to the deck.

Estrella lowered the MP5 in her hands, took aim, let out half a breath, and started low when she squeezed the trigger. The machine pistol only rose a little. The bullets slammed into the edge of the container, then bit into the man. He disappeared at once, flopping back out of sight.

"Good shooting," Simmons congratulated tensely from behind her.

Estrella nodded, but she took no satisfaction in her actions. She'd killed a man, and they weren't in a better position. If something didn't happen, they were all going to die or be forced off the ship back into the ocean.

And no one would be able to stop whatever the men planned to do with the nuclear weapons.

Will followed the SEAL lieutenant into the navigation room, then to the back wall where a SEAL Dry Dock Shelter was attached to the sub's exterior just behind the con.

Two of the missile tubes had been replaced with diver lock-in/out chambers as well as mounts for the Dry Dock Shelter. The DDS consisted of three spheres, which allowed the SEALs to exit the sub while it was submerged. The spheres lay in a line beneath a shaped shell that reduced drag.

Entry from the submarine led to the second sphere. Lieutenant Parker switched on lights as he went, moving confidently. He immediately headed for the rear sphere, the hangar that contained the Advanced SEAL Delivery System.

The ASDS was a sixty-five-foot bullet shape that looked—and acted—like a miniature submarine. It had independent air and power, and was capable of 125-mile trips underwater on the lithium-ion polymer batteries.

"Carter," Parker ordered, "you're the pilot."

Carter went forward at once and Parker named a navigator. The ASDS and DDS shivered with the impact of a torpedo striking the *Michigan*.

Will, Maggie, Shel, and Remy took seats. Parker called eleven other men into the ASDS, filling the little craft to the max. He ordered the other SEALs to gear up and stand ready to deploy the inflatable Zodiac boats kept in the hangar.

Remy worked to help the others secure their gear. "Get this on," he said calmly. "Normally, we stay dry down here. But that's for long hauls. This trip is gonna be short and quick. Better to have your gear in place."

Will nodded and realized how much of an addition

Remy was going to make to the team. For however long he stayed.

Parker gave the order and the pilot released the ASDS. They floated free in the water for a moment as depth charges exploded around them. Then the pilot switched on the electric propeller and shoved the small craft forward.

There were no windows. Only the pilot and navigator knew where they were.

Will forced himself to relax.

"Captain," Parker called over the ship-to-ship communications.

"Reading you five by five," Jacoby responded.

"*Minnow* is away."

"Affirmative. Good hunting."

Without a word, the SEALS—including Remy and Shel—checked over their gear. Shel had a combat shotgun as his lead weapon.

"The crew aboard *Arctic Hauler* appears to be occupied," Jacoby said over the radio. "The SEALs from Commander Coburn's contingent evidently landed aboard the freighter."

"Boo-yeah!" one of the SEALs yelled. He reached up and knocked on the domed roof. "Let's rock and roll. We got guys up there depending on us."

Will felt the chill of the ocean eating into him through the ASDS's steel walls. Maybe they stayed dry inside the vehicle, but they definitely weren't warm. He looked at Maggie beside him, seeing how tense she was. Then he remembered that she didn't like closed-in spaces. The ASDS had to be rough on her.

She noticed his gaze and smiled. "I'm okay."

Another depth charge went off close by. *Minnow* jumped and rolled with the blast.

"We'll be coming up on the port side," Parker said. "Back toward stern. From what the captain says, the other SEAL group is forward and starboard. We'll pincer the hostiles and break them down. We don't have time to play nice, gentlemen. When you put down a target, make sure that target stays down. We can't fight this battle on two fronts. We're going to fight forward, not backward."

Will knew that the lieutenant had just passed a death sentence on to everyone the SEALs encountered. He couldn't argue the logic. Not if the nuclear weapons were aboard the freighter.

The ASDS flew through the water, streaking for the freighter. The ship had to lose serious speed before it could come around to attack the submarine. They had a narrow margin of making the counterattack work. If they failed, Will was certain whoever was manning the freighter would kill them all.

✷ **CRIME SCENE** ✷  ✷ **CRI**

>> SOUTH CHINA SEA
>> 1959 HOURS

Minnow surfaced port stern of *Arctic Hauler*. The pilot flung open the ASDS's forward hatch, and the navigator shot a grappling line from his M4A1 assault rifle using an M195 blank cartridge to propel the grappling hook. The hook sailed over the freighter's stern and caught.

Swiftly, the SEAL clambered up the rope, followed by another warrior. Once they were in place, unnoticed, they kept watch while another SEAL fired a second line.

Will spotted the thick black smoke that roiled from the freighter's deck in several places. Something was on fire. Actually, several somethings looked like they were on fire.

God, if Estrella is up there, please watch over her.

Two of the SEALs grabbed the rope lines and hauled a fishing net up out of the ASDS. When the net reached the freighter's deck, the two warriors on the ship tied the lines off, suspending the net. In quick order, the rest of the SEALs, except for the pilot, climbed the net, followed immediately by the NCIS team.

The coarse rope bit into Will's hands as he climbed the net and thudded against the freighter's hull. The M4A1 he carried banged against his back.

"Zodiac teams," Parker said, "we're onboard. Make your ascents."

Glancing to the wake of the freighter, Will saw the three Zodiac boats filled with the SEALs who hadn't accompanied them on the submersible pop up like ducks surfacing in a pond. The men quickly shucked out of their scuba gear as the boats powered forward, leaping across the waves.

"Flank the ship for now," Parker ordered. "Let them see you and give us a chance to get into position."

The Zodiacs raced forward, drawing enemy fire from the heavy machine guns. One of the torpedo-launcher operators unleashed a salvo. The three MK-46s shot into the sea and cut across the surface like metal sharks.

Thankfully, the spotters aboard the Zodiacs saw the torpedoes and got the pilots to speed up. MK-46 torpedoes operated with acoustic homing and could move at 28 knots. The closest distance they could operate at, though, was twenty yards.

The Zodiac pilots pulled within the twenty-yard radius and stayed behind the torpedoes rather than in front of them. All the torpedoes missed and shot out to open sea. Only one of them exploded where Will could witness it, probably impacting against debris in the sea thrown off the freighter or left behind by the submarine.

Will held the assault rifle in his hands as he moved forward in a crouch.

Parker waved two of the SEALs toward the door to the wheelhouse. One of them tried the door but it didn't budge. The man stepped back and placed a shaped charge on the door, counted down with his fingers, and pressed the electronic detonator.

The explosion tore the door open. The SEALs moved in at once, holding their MP5s to their shoulders and blasting the three men inside the wheelhouse.

"Estrella," Will called over the headset.

"Will?" Estrella sounded surprised to hear from him. And weak.

"We're here," Will said. "In the stern aboard the freighter. We're coming."

"I'm . . . I'm hit, Will. I'm bleeding pretty badly." Will heard panic in Estrella's voice.

Will went forward, hugging the containers, keeping close to cover but staying in motion. The smoke from burning containers stung his eyes and burned his throat.

Shel moved at Will's right, clutching the shotgun in both hands. "I've never heard her like that before, Will." His voice was strained.

"We'll get her," Will said.

Fighting covered the deck around them. Fortunately for the *Michigan,* most of the crew aboard *Arctic Hauler* had become aware of the two groups on her deck and had turned away from the depth-charge launchers. Most of the organized effort among the freighter crew had disappeared.

At the next container, Will peered around the corner and barely dodged out of the way of a machete a man waiting there swung at his head. The metal edge bit into the container with a resounding clang.

Shel leaned toward Will and squeezed the shotgun's trigger. The double-aught buckshot blast blew the man backward.

"Thanks," Will said.

"You can't hesitate here, Will," Shel growled. "You hesitate now, you're going to cost somebody's life."

"I know." The world was madness around Will. He moved

between the containers and spotted a man shouldering a rocket launcher, preparing to send the round into a group of Parker's SEALs.

Will centered the M4A1's iron sights over the man's head and shot him just before the man pulled the rocket launcher's trigger.

As the man fell, the rocket launcher fired into the deck. The roiling blast picked the man up and launched him into the air and over the side, into the sea.

Will kept moving, following the starboard line.

"I'm going up," Remy said.

Turning, Will saw the SEAL clamber up a stack of containers using finger- and toeholds. He was barefooted, his shoes hanging around his neck by their laces.

"Sniping position," Shel said.

Only a short distance farther, Will spotted Estrella lying on the deck behind a burning container. Two SEALs lay sprawled near her. One of them would never rise again in this life.

Three of the freighter's crew closed in.

"Pick her up," a burly man ordered.

"We do not have to pick her up to kill her," another man said.

"We will use her for a hostage."

Blood covered Estrella's left leg. She looked like she was barely conscious. Desperate, she tried to drag herself away from the men. One of the men turned and caught sight of Will by the container.

"Will," Remy said softly over the headset, "drop down. Now!"

Dropping into a squat with his assault rifle across his knees, Will watched as the man who had spotted him suddenly jerked backward. The second man spun to his left as Remy put a round through his heart. By that time Will had his rifle to his shoulder. He fired three times, driving the remaining man away from Estrella.

Maggie and Shel took up positions in a defensive perimeter while Will went to Estrella. Remy stepped off the containers and dropped to the deck.

"The nuclear missiles are here," Estrella said. "I saw them. They've built launch tubes."

A chill ghosted through Will even though he'd been expecting the nuclear weapons to be aboard the freighter. Gently, haunted by the memory of losing Frank, Will turned Estrella over. A metal shard stuck out of her thigh.

"I guess you were right about Yaseen," Estrella said. "You've got to find him and stop him, Will."

Will surveyed the piece of metal in Estrella's leg. Everything in him screamed to pull it out, but he knew he shouldn't. The shard was helping keep down the blood loss by blocking the wound.

Estrella reached for the shard.

"Don't touch that," Remy said as he crossed over to her. "That shard looks like it's really close to the femoral artery. You move it wrong and you might cut through the artery. If you do that, you're gonna bleed out in less than a minute, and I can't do anything to save you."

Will was grimly aware that they didn't even know if the submarine or the freighter was going to stay afloat long enough for a rescue effort to reach them.

"For now," Remy said, taking Estrella's hands gently in his, "we're gonna immobilize that leg and wrap it with that shard still in it."

"Go, Will," Estrella said, grimacing in pain. "Find Yaseen."

Will looked at Remy. "Can you take care of her?"

"Yeah, man. I'll take good care of her."

Switching his gaze to Shel, Will said, "I need you to stay here."

Shel looked like he was going to protest.

"If Remy's watching over Estrella, he needs somebody watching his back. I don't have time to argue about this."

Reluctantly, Shel nodded. "If you need me—"

"I'll let you know. Right now I need you here."

"I'm coming with you," Maggie insisted.

"Right. I've got point." Will took off at once, heading for the nearest cargo hold. Now that he was looking for them, he could see the circular openings in the deck.

The freighter rolled sickeningly on the waves, evidently locked on autopilot with no human hand at the wheel.

Two men stood at the cargo hold, obviously intending to descend and get away from the SEAL sharpshooters who had found posts among the high crates. A burning container sent twisting spirals of black smoke into the blue sky.

Lifting his M4A1 into position, Will fired a series of short bursts that sent the men spinning away. Enemy fire drummed the desk and one of the rounds bounced off Will's Kevlar vest, hitting hard enough to cause him to stutter-step. He kept going, though, throwing himself down beside the opening so he could peer into the hold.

Movement shifted twenty feet below.

Will pulled his head back just before bullets cut the air where it had been.

Maggie slid into position beside him, rising quickly with the assault rifle in her hands. Two men ran along the line of containers, bearing down on her position. Calmly and coolly, never rising above a crouch, Maggie shot both of them. She looked at Will, then at the cargo hold. "Going below?" she asked.

"More of them down there," Will said. "They're covering the entrance."

"Any SEALs down there?" Maggie asked.

"I don't know." Will adjusted the mouthpiece on his helmet. "Quicksilver Leader, this is Steadfast Leader."

"Go, Steadfast Leader," Fenwick responded at once. "Quicksilver reads you."

"Do you have anyone belowdecks?"

"Negative. We're shutting down the firepower topside first."

"Have your men stand clear of the launch tubes at the center of the deck."

"Repeat that, Steadfast Leader."

"Our target has live missiles below. He may try to launch."

"Do you need help?"

"When you can. We're going on ahead."

"We'll catch up when we can. We're taking heavy fire at the moment."

Will took off his helmet and waved it over the cargo hold. A bullet knocked it to one side and left a gray smear. The guards below weren't backing off.

Maggie grabbed the foot of one of the men she'd shot and pulled him over to her. She fisted a pair of grenades from the man's combat harness, pulled the pins, then dropped them into the hold. She looked at Will as he gathered himself. "Those won't blow out the hull, will they?"

Before Will could answer, two explosions reverberated, sounding huge in the trapped enclosure of the hold. Then Maggie was in motion, dropping the assault rifle and leaping through the cargo hold.

Startled, Will was a half second behind her. He dropped into the darkness, noting three crewmen blown from the epicenters of the grenade explosions. All of them were dead.

Maggie stood stock-still, staring at the carnage she had wrought. Her face was pale and frozen.

She didn't expect this, Will thought. *The grenades were supposed to be a diversion.* Instead, they were fragmentation grenades, designed for antipersonnel. The nearby crates were studded with rips and impact points.

"You didn't have a choice," Will said. His mouth was dry and he felt a little sick at everything he'd seen. The team had never gotten this bloody before.

But the stakes have never been this high.

"You didn't have a choice," Will repeated. "Now move." He put a hand on her and shoved her into motion.

Staggering just a moment, Maggie lifted her eyes from the dead men and peered into the darkness.

Will took the lead. He held the M4A1 in both hands and stayed low, using the crates for cover every chance he could.

The hold was packed with cargo, but it all ringed the two missile-launch tubes that thrust up through both decks like smokestacks.

Movement caught Will's attention to his left. He went to the ground, shouting a warning to Maggie. Bullets drummed the bulkhead where he'd been standing, throwing sparks in all directions. Two of them slammed into the back of his Kevlar vest, but the rounds were nearly spent and carried little force.

Maggie brought up both her Berettas and fired at the men. One of them staggered back immediately and went down. The other man fired his assault rifle with deliberation, chasing Maggie into cover.

Rising, staying within the protective shadows and pulling the assault rifle into his shoulder, Will sighted in on the other man's muzzle flash. He squeezed the trigger, aiming two inches above the muzzle flash.

A dark shadow whirled and fell away.

"You okay?" Will asked.

"I'm good," Maggie said. She kicked the empty magazines from her weapons and reloaded in seconds, holding one pistol then the other under her arms. "Let's go."

Will went, knowing they were racing a deadly clock against doomsday.

A chill slid greasily along Will's spine as he went forward. The gunfire and continued explosions taking place on the top deck rolled through the hold.

Arctic Hauler rocked beneath the onslaught.

>> SOUTH CHINA SEA
>> *ARCTIC HAULER*
>> 2011 HOURS

Yaseen watched the computer monitors in disgust and bright anger. The distant gunfire and explosions coming from the deck above echoed inside the hold. The two SEAL teams were making serious inroads against the freighter's crew. Even though the American Special Forces teams had been outnumbered, their skills and determination were carrying the battle.

Cursing, Yaseen tried to quell the helpless frustration that batted against his rib cage. The *Michigan* still glided through the South China Sea under her own power when she should have been on her way to the bottom of the ocean. Yaseen had no doubt that the submarine had suffered extensive damage, but she wasn't done yet.

The freighter had overtaken the sub, but with no one at the

helm and half the depth-charge launchers and torpedo launchers wreathed in flames, Yaseen knew he could no longer hope to sink the submarine.

And that meant his planning—his years of careful preparations—had failed. Worldwide destruction was out of the question. The *Michigan*'s survival ensured that the world would know that *Arctic Hauler* had initiated the contact. Retribution—if any—would be focused on the Middle East, not the United States.

Blind rage filled Yaseen's heart. How was it possible that he had been bested by that imbecile NCIS team? Had Allah abandoned him?

And then he knew.

The freighter had already taken a lot of damage. Several inches of water swirled at Yaseen's feet, but the launch system was protected. He could still launch.

The missiles were capable of intercontinental flight. He could send them anywhere in the world. His initial target had become impossible, but he could still strike the enemy. He reached for the keyboard and tapped a series of commands. The launch system responded immediately. Yaseen watched as the monitor reflected his target changes. The missiles were no longer aimed at North Korea. In moments he would strike the Great Satan at its own evil heart. As soon as the launch system had reached full readiness, the nuclear missiles would be on their way to Washington, D.C.

He still had to enter the launch codes into the separate system in the control room. He radioed Achmed to join him, then stood, prepared to meet his destiny.

>> 2012 HOURS

Will ran down the second flight of metal stairs and dropped the last few feet into water nearly up to his knees. Light from the electric torches mounted on the walls and hanging from the ceiling revealed that the freighter's lowest deck was filled with sluggish water.

"Steadfast Leader," Captain Parker called over the headset.

"Go, Quicksilver Leader. Steadfast reads you." Will wheeled around a stack of crates and fired the M4A1 at two men standing guard in an aisle. He hit one of them.

"We're on our way. What's your twenty?" Parker asked.

"Second hold," Will said, taking up a new position as the survivor of his burst ran for cover.

Maggie caught the man with four rounds, knocking him off his feet and up against the crate behind him. The water floated the man Will had shot, lifting him from the deck and scooting him toward the stern as *Arctic Hauler* climbed a wave.

"The ship's taking on water," Will said over the headset. "It's nearly up to my knees." He waded forward, holding the assault rifle against his shoulder with the muzzle angled down so he could bring it up quickly. "How is the *Michigan*?"

"She's holding her own. For now. If we hadn't silenced the freighter's deck guns, she wouldn't have made it."

"There," Maggie said.

Following her pointing arm, Will spotted the control systems near the base of the Tomahawk launch tubes. As he watched, two Arabic-featured men stepped inside the small room that contained the system.

The smaller man spotted Will and yelled to his companion.

Cloaked in the shadows of the hold, the other man spun and brought up a pair of pistols. Muzzle flashes strobed the darkness and bullets filled the air. In that faint light, Will recognized Ahmed Achmed.

Will went to ground, going facedown in the swirling water and taking shelter behind cargo. Bullets crashed into the crates and barrels in front of him. Oil bled out into the water, creating twisting rainbows in the flickering fluorescent light. "Maggie!"

"I'm fine."

Glancing up, Will rose into a kneeling position and brought the assault rifle to his shoulder. He fired the clip dry, pursuing both men. Achmed brought up the rear, dropping his pistols and drawing another pair. He emptied his clips as well, chasing Will and Maggie back to cover.

Will charged through the water as Achmed and his companion disappeared behind a steel door. The electric torches caught the splashes made by his boots and turned them silver. At the door Will tried the handle and found it locked. He stepped back and aimed his assault rifle at the electronic lock. "Watch yourself," he told Maggie.

She moved behind him, covering his back, both pistols thrust before her.

Will pulled the trigger and blasted the lock. Sparks showered as the unit went to pieces and shorted out. When he tried the door again, it slid open.

Sudden gunfire cut loose behind him, pocking the walls of the hold and throwing more sparks. Will turned, intending to help Maggie return fire, but the ship shifted and the rising water hammered him into the room. The door slammed shut behind him.

He slipped and fell beneath the water that had pooled in the room. The ship rolled again, giving up against the savage strength of the sea. Water smashed against Will, lifting and moving him.

A shadow moved to his right. He reacted a split second later as a muzzle flash bloomed in the firelit room and reflected from the drenched floor.

Surging up from the water, Will swept the M4A1 around in a tight arc, knocking the pistol from Achmed's hand.

In the next instant, the terrorist shifted and backhanded Will in the mouth, whipping his head around. His senses whirled. Before Will could recover, the man tore the M4A1 free of his grasp.

Lying on his back, his face covered by the roiling water, Will

kicked upward, knocking the assault rifle away before his opponent could use it. Outside the door, gunfire drummed and Will
thought about Maggie out there by herself. She was good in a
firefight, but how many crewmen were after her?

Will pushed himself up, losing the Kevlar helmet. He
bunched his left fist and drove it into Achmed's face, knocking
him back. Out of his peripheral vision, he saw the other man sitting at the computer console. Light flickered over the man's
strong features, and in that instant Will recognized him.

Qadir Yaseen.

And he was about to launch the missiles.

Struggling, Will got to his feet and reached for the pistol holstered at his hip.

Screaming incoherently, Achmed launched himself at Will.
They slammed against the wall. Will hit hard enough to drive the
air from his lungs. Then Achmed roared in triumph and locked
his hands around Will's throat and bore him to the floor again,
plunging him back into the water.

"I will kill you!" the man roared almost incoherently.

Will grabbed the man's wrists and tried to pull them from his
throat. He tasted the brackish salt water. Pain pounded at his
temples and behind his eyes.

"Die," Achmed snarled. His eyes looked black, soulless, in
the dim light.

Will's head slipped beneath the water.

"Have you ever seen true Evil, Will?" As he fought against his
opponent's incredible strength, Will remembered Frank's words.

"I'm talking about true Evil," Frank had said. *"The kind of
Evil that wants only to oppose God and his work in the world.
The kind that desires nothing more than the simple pursuit of
Evil for its own sake. I've seen it. Not everywhere, and not often,
but I've seen it enough times to know what it is."*

Looking up at the water-blurred face of the man drowning
him, Will felt certain he knew what Evil looked like.

"Most people," Frank had said, *"don't think muh about evil. Sure, they think about sin. About the effects and repercussions sin will demand on their lives. But they get so busy looking for the bad things in themselves when they get lost that they forget that true Evil is out there waiting for them. True Evil is hungry, Will. I've seen it. I've run for my life when I've encountered it."*

Achmed's grip was unbreakable. Will's lungs cried out for air. He thought about Steven and Wren and Barbara, about how he wasn't going to see them again.

God, Will prayed desperately, *help me because I can't help myself. I don't want to die. There's too much I've left unfinished. But if it is your wish, then please look after my family.*

Will's vision started to grow black. Then, somewhere in that darkness with Achmed yelling, a calm touched Will. Despite his desperate situation, he felt whole, at peace.

It wasn't his time to die. Not yet. There were still things he had to do, people he was supposed to meet and witness to. He felt that.

Will put his hands together on his chest, then drove them up together between his attacker's arms, breaking the choke hold the man had on him. He wrapped his left arm around the back of Achmed's head. Holding Achmed against him, Will bent his right leg and forced his body over, reversing their positions till he was on top. He hit his opponent four times in the face, watching Achmed's face turn bloody in the flickering light.

Still, the terrorist's reserves were incredible, almost super-human. He pushed himself up, shoving Will back. The man slipped a combat knife from his boot and threw himself at Will.

Ducking the blade twice, backing into the wall behind him, Will sidestepped his opponent's next thrust, caught the man's right elbow in his left hand, and wrapped his right hand over Achmed's.

The knife came around and whipped into Achmed's throat. Surprise rounded the man's eyes.

Will controlled his opponent's arm, not daring to let go. He was all in, hardly anything left. The fight ended now. It had to. Then Achmed's eyes glazed over as awareness left them. His knees buckled and he fell.

Will turned, breath rasping in his throat, and saw Yaseen still tapping the keyboard, working through the launch sequence. Metal gleamed in the rolling water in front of Will and he recognized his pistol. He lunged forward and scooped the weapon up, not knowing how much—if any—time was left.

"Qadir Yaseen!" Will called.

Yaseen ignored him.

Will fired, but the ship rolled and threw his aim off. The bullet crashed through the monitor. He took aim again, this time at the tower mounted on a bracket on the wall. Sparks flared, showering out over the room.

Yaseen moved from the chair with incredible speed. He whirled, dragging a pistol from his robe and shoving it toward Will.

Gazing at the terrorist leader over the barrel of the pistol, Will never flinched.

Yaseen squeezed the trigger over and over. Somewhere in there, a bullet—perhaps two—struck Will in the chest. But they were deflected by the Kevlar.

Will's own rounds hammered Yaseen against the bulkhead. The pistol trickled from Yaseen's nerveless fingers and disappeared into the water. He opened his mouth, his black eyes dark with hate, and blood flowed over his lips. Then he went slack and dropped.

Will approached the body carefully, weapon still pointed. Everything outside the door had gone quiet. He keyed the headset. "Maggie?"

"I'm here."

Thank God. Will felt the terrible ball of dread unwind in his stomach. "The missiles?"

"They didn't launch, Will. They're still in the hold."

The monitor shut down completely, leaving only the occasional sparks of the failing electrical systems.

Wearily, Will bent down to make certain that Yaseen was dead. Then he picked up his M4A1 from under the water and staggered to the door. When the door slid open, he found Maggie standing there. Behind her, coming from the other end of the ship, Parker and the SEAL teams slogged through the water.

"You okay?" she asked.

"I am. I'm fine." Quickly, Will contacted the rest of his team, finally relaxing enough to put his sidearm away.

They'd made it. All of them had made it.

Thank God.

And there in the rumbling echoes filling the belly of the drowning ship, Will Coburn leaned against the bulkhead and gave thanks. In the days to come there would be reports to file and explanations to make. The world would demand a reason for how close it had come to disaster. His divorce waited for him back home as well.

But for now it was enough to know that his team was okay, that God had watched over them. *Thank you, Lord,* he prayed again. And then he stumbled back toward the stairs, back toward the light and the open air and the sea.

GO MILITARY.

Best-selling author **MEL ODOM** explores the Tribulation through the lives of the men and women serving in the U.S. military.

APOCALYPSE DAWN

The battle for the earth's last days begins . . .

APOCALYPSE CRUCIBLE

The Tribulation has begun, but the darkest days may lie ahead.

APOCALYPSE BURNING

With lives—*souls*—on the line, the fires of the apocalypse burn ever higher.